# ONLY GIRLS BLEED

Elaine Lawless

The Book Social, 51 Gower Street, London, WC1E 6HJ
info@legendtimesgroup.co.uk | www.thebooksocial.co.uk

 British Library Cataloguing in Publication Data available.

Print ISBN 978-1-91505-400-5
Ebook ISBN 978-1-91505-401-2
Set in Times.
Cover design by Ditte Løkkegaard

All characters, other than those clearly in the public domain, and place names, other than those well-established such as towns and cities, are fictitious and any resemblance is purely coincidental.

Dr. Elaine Lawless has devoted her career to ethnographic research in the fields of folklore, religion, and women's and gender studies. She is the author of ten academic books and numerous articles. Her work has included studies of Pentecostalism; women's literature; human rights, social justice and violence against women. She has also co-produced two documentary films: *Joy Unspeakable* and *Taking Pinhook*. In 2003, she co-founded and produced the Troubling Violence Performance Project, with Professor Heather Carver of the University of Missouri Theatre Department.

For more information, see her website: elainelawless.com

For all the girls, everywhere—

# Prologue

*At night, when I dare, I sneak my notebook and pen out from under the mattress and wait until the guards go back through the double doors for the last time. In the uneasy quiet, I breathe in the darkness that settles on the cavernous room where I live with seventy-five other caged women. When the shuffling and whimpers cease, I slide off the bottom bunk and sit cross-legged, wedged into the corner, my giant sweatshirt pulled over my arms and legs, the hood over my head—invisible. My nifty plastic pen is poised above the paper, a tiny circle of light at the end waiting for me to write what happened to Molly and me. When that doesn't happen, I decide to start where I am, but my pen still doesn't move.*

*Turns out, it's not that easy. You ever try to write in the dark? It's like those games where you have to draw something with your eyes closed. At night in this crumbling pile of bricks, far from any place I've ever known, there is no light when the moon hides its face and the windows high on the concrete walls disappear. I try to conserve the little light in my pen, but I'm never sure I'm writing in straight lines, or if my words are crossing over each other.*

*I know there's a chance if I'm caught writing after lights out, I'll be punished. Like Brer Rabbit, they'll take away the only joy I have in this place—dusting books in the prison library and reading a few pages when I can. For years, I could never find time to read, with Wilson gone and me raising Molly by myself, all the shit that happened, and then us on the run. Now, I finger books like they are magic, like they have answers, like maybe they can teach me how to live, or how to die.*

*The irony of that song, "You've Got Time" from the TV series,* Orange is the New Black, *is not lost on me, or anyone else in here, for that matter. We "got time" and now we have too much time to think about our story. Funny thing—when you're living your life, it's not a story, like that joke about why fish don't feel wet. Only now can I look back and see what happened as a story, maybe a story worth telling. In many ways, it's a common tale of women, our blood, and how laws written by men end up wrecking our lives. My furtive scratching on paper makes me think of that scene in* The Handmaid's Tale, *the one where June carves her name near the baseboards of the closet to say she'd been there. I saw the movie in the common room when I first got locked up, and I still think about it.*

*Boiled down, a version of my story was splashed across the state of Missouri without my permission, not that long ago. I hated seeing the headlines everywhere, each one a variation on a theme of betrayal, violence, and blood. Those headlines convicted me before the courts did. I never had a chance. Of course, like most stories, mine is more complicated than such salacious headlines might suggest. The problem is how to sift through the stuff that isn't important in order to find what is, so you'll understand why I did what I did. I certainly didn't plan any of it. Mostly, I was flying by the seat of my pants, hoping above all to protect Molly. It wasn't easy, but I'm proud to say, so far, I've managed to do that—protect her. I have given my daughter the gift of life, twice. I do have regrets, lots of them, but not about that. Some things are worth shedding blood over, depends on what's at stake.*

*One more thing it's important for you to know—this journey changed us. For years, I thought of myself as an insignificant woman intimidated by life and the unpredictable challenges of being a young wife and mother, just trying to carve out a life in a crappy region of the country that no one knows about or cares. And Molly? Molly was just a confused little girl who didn't deserve what happened to her. Neither of us did, for that matter. We've been abandoned, betrayed, and violated, but we both survived, and we're stronger for it. That's not to say anybody else should have to go through this, just because you might be born female. The saving grace in all this was the embrace of my mother's sister and her friends who took us under their wings and spirited us across the border. Now, Molly has a chance at a normal life as a young girl on the mend, cared for and protected.*

*It wasn't their fault I landed in prison. I did that all by myself.*

# Chapter 1

## Molly Stops Walking

The first hint that my life was fucked was when my little girl stopped walking. Well, to be truthful, that wasn't the first hint, that was maybe the third or fourth or, whatever. Who am I kidding? There were lots of things that made it clear that my life was getting more and more difficult, and there was no relief in sight. What I didn't realize at first was that this was only the tip of the iceberg, and that things would get much worse before I had a clue what was going on. I felt like I was the last to know, in fact, and since those days I could not see beyond the tip of my pudgy nose, it all hit me pretty hard in the end.

The truth is, when Molly was six, or seven, somewhere around there, she just stopped walking. It's hard to nail down when exactly, because it came on slow, for no apparent reason, at least not one I could figure out. She didn't one day just hesitate on the sidewalk, or fall down, or injure her leg. It wasn't like that. I mean, *over time*, she got to where she couldn't walk—her once-sturdy legs would just give way, and I had to be there to hold her up, make sure she didn't fall, help her get from one place to another. It was exhausting. We were connected at the hip, her leaning on me to go anywhere, me holding up her weight as we coordinated our steps. It pained me to see her forehead slick with sweat, putting all she had into the most routine motions to cross a room or go through the door. Occasionally, we'd both land on the sofa laughing hysterically at our graceless tricks. More often, we would collapse in tears. I quit my job at Wendy's, ordered the state homeschool curriculum and taught her myself, something I was not at all prepared to do. It didn't help, either, that a pandemic had hit the country, although folks where we live refused to wear masks and the kids stayed in school. As it was, our absence from the world didn't really make a dent.

Molly had walked just fine as a toddler, early even. In those days, her absent dad, Wilson, was around a lot more, and we delighted in the joy our little girl brought to our lackluster lives in southern Missouri. Our Molly was bright and lively and healthy and learned to cruise around the living room before she was one. At three, she could run dizzy circles with the other children at the neighbor's backyard preschool, and she literally danced into kindergarten at the local elementary. She was such fun to watch, although by this time Wilson was losing interest. Molly would skip and jump and twirl and act crazy and laugh all the time she was moving, which was pretty much every minute she was awake. She became the only bright spot in my life.

I can see now that when Molly stopped walking and dancing and skipping and twirling, she also stopped laughing. It was as though a spell came over her, as though she'd been cursed, as though we'd both been cursed, and we had no idea why, or who, had decided to ruin our lives. By then, of course, it was just the two of us. Wilson had decided he'd rather work far from home and left us to deal with things by ourselves. Some days I'd think it would be nice to just disappear, too, but I didn't have that option. I was determined to find out why Molly's legs had stopped working. Spending all day, every day with her, I watched her too closely. I felt like I was missing something, but I didn't have a clue what that might be. I'd never read a parenting manual in my life, and my poor, deaf mother had little to share with me about the tribulations of raising a girl.

What I did do, week after week, was drive Molly from one specialist's office to another, trying to get a diagnosis for what was happening to her legs. Early in the mornings, I'd help her settle into the backseat of the car, gas it up, and hit the highways. We both became weary of traveling to her appointments, seeing doctors who really didn't have a clue what was wrong with her. Sometimes I'd turn the radio up, and we would sing to golden oldies she didn't know before these trips. After months of driving around the region, Molly could belt out all the words to Willie Nelson's "Red-headed Stranger" and Chris Stapleton's "Tennessee Whiskey" along with me. That seemed to take our minds off the fact that none of these trips were paying off.

From our home in southeast Missouri, we have driven to Louisville and Memphis once, Nashville twice, and St. Louis too many times to count. Chicago is next on the list, and the Mayo Clinic is a new possibility. "The specialists are in the cities," the local doctors tell me. But months later, and learning not much new, Molly and I are both exhausted and frustrated. I know there are better places to live than here, places where it might be easier to find the help Molly needs, but the truth is I've never lived anywhere else, so I wouldn't really know where that might be, or how to get there. I just keep driving wherever they insist we go, one city after another, hoping someone can tell us what's going on with her. None of them will ever come anywhere close, but I didn't know that yet. I decided no one gave a good god-damn about us, and that wore on me like a bad blister.

* * *

Late one Friday afternoon, a sultry July day, I pull into my driveway, cut the engine, and pause in the pink light that filters through the car. My ears are ringing and my body hums with the vibration of old tires on asphalt, rotation after rotation, covering the two hundred miles from our place to St. Louis and back in one day.

Sitting in the silent car as the soft light fades, I try to stop thinking about the shitty day we just had and risk a cigarette. I tap one out of the pack and place it between my lips, not expecting to taste the sharp tinge of blood on my tongue. My teeth have torn my bottom lip to a messy pulp, a nervous habit when I am anxious, which seems like all the time these days. Against my better judgment, I suck and swallow, shuddering at the notion that this is exactly how vampires begin their unsavory careers, but I can't help it. I've come to cherish both the pain of the tearing and the distraction of the blood, anything to disrupt the thoughts that spill through my brain, leapfrogging over each other to get my attention.

I know I should get out of the car and help Molly into the house, but her dozing form framed by the rearview mirror convinces me to sit a bit longer and enjoy the peace. At nine, Molly has developed an edge that is only getting worse. I know this is probably true of most kids, but I remember her as a cheerful little kid, quick with kisses and hugs, a softness she seems to have misplaced. Now, no matter what I do or say, she pushes back, rolls her eyes, treats me like an idiot. She seems angry with me all the time, but I have no idea what I've done to cause this, or what I can do to make it better. It doesn't help that she adores her Uncle Robert, my brother, who lives next door and always greets him with big smiles and an eagerness I envy.

Sitting in the car, I'm not in any hurry to enter the house that sits dark and empty. I know the air inside will be stale, the smell from the garbage sharp and rancid. It hurts that no one is in there eagerly awaiting our arrival, no one to come to the door and greet us, ask how our day went. Molly's father works several hours away on large corporate farms up near the Iowa border and hasn't come home for months, but I try not to think about that right now. I put the cigarette back in my mouth and quietly roll down all the windows. I know it's a bad habit, but having survived the trip, I need the relief the cigarette promises, breathing the smoke deep into my lungs, justified in my vice.

I would love to remind someone how much I hate to drive on the highways. I would welcome the chance to say that I am not, never have been, a good driver, mostly because before this, I'd never driven very far from home in my whole life. It might help to describe to someone how I clench my jaw, chew my lip, and stare straight ahead without blinking when I drive in heavy traffic. How I clutch the steering wheel too tight as the speeding lanes of cars and trucks and vans and motorcycles rush in both directions, two, four, six, then eight lanes into and out of the city, the center lines approaching, then receding too fast when I miss poorly marked exits. How scary it is when I panic and pull onto the grassy divide, praying the trucks won't smash us flat, the robot voice of the GPS parroting "recalculating, recalculating," while my heart races in my chest and the skin on my scalp retracts, something I recognize as pure fear.

When I return home from these trips, I hate to admit how insanely relieved I am to see the highway signs for our dusty town, following the Walmart trucks chugging past the strip mall signs flashing "BEER, LIQUOR, and SMOKES," even in broad daylight. I smile in spite of myself every time I see the ten-foot tall, yellowed angel hovering over the door of the Dream Queen Laundro-Mat, there to bless your laundry. I am also comforted by the smaller "Thank you, Jesus" signs that mark my neighbors' lawns. Jesus mingles comfortably in this southern region known as the "Bootheel" of the state, a parcel of land that slides down the Mississippi River on the east side and dips down into Arkansas to the south. Folks here have taken to calling themselves "Rednecks" with pride and look forward to the upcoming Pig Fest, the Turkey Raffle, and the famous Sikeston Rodeo, complete with drag racing in the streets. Most days, I find all this irritating, but the familiar works its magic when I get near my own street. I can feel my clenched body begin to release, my arms shift from my moist armpits, my stiff fingers wiggle from the wheel. I'd love to tell someone just how difficult these trips are, but I know no one wants to hear all that, and besides, who would I tell?

"Then why go?"

I am drawn into an imaginary conversation with a thoughtful listener who sounds a lot like my only friend, Barb, someone who might be willing to listen to me vent, and who might ask the right questions.

"Why would you put yourself through that?" she might ask, thoughtful as she is.

"Because no one in this crappy town has any idea what's wrong with Molly and they have nothing to offer except instructions to 'travel to the city and find a specialist,' like that's no big deal. And, while I'm at it, I'll admit it isn't easy with Wilson off God knows where. It's all up to me, and I'm getting sick of it."

"Well, then," the conversation in my head continues, "was it worth it? What did you learn?"

I ponder the question.

"Well, I have to admit that nothing makes any more sense now than when I helped Molly into the backseat and strapped her in at 5:30 this morning. I hate to complain, but I began the day with a dull headache that still hurts fourteen hours later, mostly from asking so many questions about why my little girl can't walk, getting no reasonable answers and barely surviving the driving that nearly wrecks me every time. I'm afraid I'm going to kill us both."

My imaginary friend disappears, but my mind keeps going on its own, unable to stop the reel of our day. How I explained again to an orthopedic doctor, actually two of them, that Molly had walked fine when she was younger, but they kept badgering me with their questions.

"When did you notice she was having trouble walking?"

"Has it been a month?"

"Six months?"

"Longer than a year?"

"Do you have any test records?"

I have a three-inch stack of "inconclusive" test records that I pull out of my purse every time we go to a new doctor, but nailing down the dates is getting harder. I got annoyed when the one doctor just wouldn't let up with the questions.

"Well, I don't know *exactly*." I told him. "It's not like I marked it on the calendar, *Today Molly stopped walking*. I could tell he didn't like my tone, and I tried to be nicer, but how many times do I have to explain to these guys that I can't remember exactly when it started. Like I said, it was *gradual*."

I had explained, "She was about six, maybe a bit older, when she told me and my brother, Robert, one night at dinner, she'd felt 'a little dizzy' during recess at school. And then there was that day, a few months later, when she said her legs 'weren't working right.'" She asked us both what we thought was going on. I remember her eyes bright with tears as she looked at me first, then Robert, holding her stare for a beat too long.

I remember that night distinctly, because Robert left almost immediately after she said that. He must have had something that needed his immediate attention. I wasn't sure what made him bolt, but I wasn't surprised. Robert could be like that, make him uncomfortable and he'll split every time. I stacked up the dishes, helped Molly with her bath, and got her into bed. I didn't ask her any questions or talk with her about it that night, instead I just watched her to see how she was acting. Robert and I didn't talk about it, either. I didn't think he'd be much help anyway, because he's never been very good at sensitive stuff.

For months, Molly hasn't been sleeping well. She calls out for me at night, crying that she's had a nightmare, and she wets the bed, something she hasn't done since she was two or three. I don't know what to make of all this. She can never describe the nightmares or tell me what her fears are, but I can tell they are very real. She'll just lie there in her single bed and shake like a little rabbit, until I crawl under the covers and hold her as she falls asleep. These long nights make me wish my husband stayed home more, but I know that isn't likely to happen. For one thing, Wilson apparently doesn't actually like me very much. He told me last time he was home that I "was a pain in the ass" to live with, and I know he agrees with his mother, Gail, that I am, by and large, "a difficult woman."

Who wouldn't be difficult, what with him taking off for farms unknown, doing this "important" job he is so bloody proud of and leaving Molly and me to fend for ourselves? In fact, before he left the last time to manage a big farm that actually stretches beyond the state line, he casually admitted he "wasn't too keen on being married, and all," which pissed me off, because here we were, for sure, "married, *and all*," with a house, and a kid—now a kid who can't walk. *What was he thinking*? Seems like he prefers to hang out with the farm hands and the other managers doing whatever unattached men do in their spare time, than be home with us. I admit I gave him what for as he walked out the door, gave him a piece of my mind, which wasn't pretty and probably didn't help much.

I'm certainly not happy being left to care for the house and Molly by myself, but since he is still depositing a good bit of his paycheck into our bank account and the insurance is in his name, I figure I better hold my tongue best I can, at least as long as I keep racking up all these doctor bills. My biggest concern has to be Molly, and I don't think Wilson's disappearance has much to do with her wetting the bed or not walking. But who knows what goes through a little kid's head? She doesn't seem to miss him much, or not that I can see. At least I want to find out what is going on with her before I decide what to do about him. Anyway, at this point, it is mostly Robert and me taking care of Molly. We have to help her get around, or carry her, something that hasn't been easy for me as she gets older and heavier, although Robert doesn't seem to mind carrying her around at all, his brown arms solid and muscular. She loves it when he picks her up and carries her off to his truck, like her own private knight in shining armor.

My brother's comfort around Molly these days causes me to recall how he first responded to her when we brought her home from the hospital. Such a tiny creature, she completely baffled him and made him extremely nervous. He couldn't hold her, certainly, and would rarely even touch her without recoiling in fear that he might soil or harm her in some way. As she grew, her lithe, naked little body was a terror to him. If he happened to arrive when she was running around the house or yard without clothing, his mouth clammed up and he seemed to hyperventilate as though he were allergic. Those days I watched these antics of his nervousness with amusement, smiling to see him so discomfited by my small child. Once Wilson stopped coming home regularly, and I needed someone to stay at my house and watch over Molly so I could do the shopping or go to work, Robert would agree to do so only if she was asleep. If she might be awake, he implored me to call Wilson's mother or a babysitter, who could stay for those hours and play with Molly while I was away.

So it was that Molly was rarely even aware of Robert sitting in her room watching over her. She was asleep when he arrived and, if all went well, she was still asleep when I returned. This continued to be our routine even as Molly turned three, then four, when she only took a short afternoon nap. My excursions to the store or to see my friend, Barb, were cut shorter and shorter. I never knew exactly what happened when I was gone from home. I assumed Robert sat by her bed and watched over her like a hawk, terrified she might wake up and somehow engage with him, force him to acknowledge her or interact in a way that would make him uncomfortable.

When Molly turned five, she decided she wanted to be naked all the time. She ran around the house completely nude and insisted she needed no clothes or blankets when nap time arrived. I found it humorous to see how this affected my brother. On the days she took naps, he would arrive to sit with her when I needed to leave, avert his eyes from her naked little body, and, apparently, look out the window until I returned. I sometimes asked him if I should call Gail, Wilson's mother, for the afternoon, but he always insisted he would be okay as long as she kept sleeping. Of course, as she grew, this became impossible to predict, and it wasn't long before Robert decided it was time for him to retire as my babysitter. Although I hated to see him stop coming to help when I needed him, I agreed to find someone else.

Not long after, Molly stopped napping altogether, and I was forced to take her with me or call Gail, who huffed and puffed that she really didn't have the time, but then glowed when she arrived, happy to be with Molly, as I knew she would be. Talk about the pot calling the kettle black. "Pain in the ass," I muttered to myself, every time I left her in my home with Molly. But I knew where my bread was buttered and saved my most gracious smiles for her upon her arrival, and, again, when she left several hours later. The least she could do, I thought, given that *her son* was derelict in his duties as helpmeet and father, after all.

Remembering how reluctant Robert was to be with Molly when she was younger makes me all the more thankful that he is right beside me these days helping to care for her. Although he doesn't drive to the doctors with me, he is always around to help in any other way that he can. When Molly turned four, then five, and no longer needed to sleep in the afternoons, I often asked him to get her out of the house for a bit. These days, with Wilson gone months at a time working, my personal life is pretty non-existent, and Robert knows that. When I ask him to help with Molly, he laughs with delight, picks her up in his arms and carries her to his truck. She is delighted that he can carry her around so easily. Certainly, she has few memories of her father doing this, so her time with her uncle has become very special. He props her in the seat next to him and holds her a little tighter than is necessary as he changes the gears between their legs, taking her across the road toward his own house and barn for an afternoon of greasy chips and documentaries about sharks and dolphins.

I shake my head to stop thinking about Robert and Molly and remember how flustered I was today at the clinic. I got angry with the doctors when I realized I haven't kept good enough records about Molly's problems and that embarrassed me. I try to recall all the strange names of the many conditions that Molly has been tested for, like myositis, Guillain Barre, muscular sclerosis, cerebral palsy, even dystonia, all of which went nowhere. The doctors we've seen are convinced she has none of them. Most days, I don't think they know what they are doing, or I'm convinced their tests are wrong. Why is this so hard? It frustrates me and makes me want to lash out. I'd like to hit something, or someone, or cry on someone's shoulder. But none of that is likely tonight, I know.

Going over and over the long day doesn't help. My head throbs as I stare into the heat mirage that shimmers beyond my house, where the dark fields threaten to take over the unmarked blacktop streets. My thoughts have distracted me from the glow of the receding sunset filtered through the dense humid evening. I remind myself to notice the hint of color in the sky, to breathe in the cooling air, and appreciate the evening smells, hoping all this will help me calm down. I take a few deep breaths and wait for it.

It doesn't arrive before I hear Molly shifting in the backseat and know I must leave the sanctuary of the car. I sigh quietly and roll up the windows, step out to crush my cigarette, then help her out of her seatbelt. Supporting her weight, I walk awkwardly alongside her into the house, over the door frame, and down the hall to her bedroom, my free hand flipping on one or two lights as we go through the rooms.

"You ready for bed, Molly?" I ask, gently. "Or do you want to sit up for a bit?"

"What a choice," Molly grumbles. "It's not that late, and that overhead light is too bright. Why can't you turn on the lamp?"

"Sure," I agree, wondering why she doesn't turn it on herself. I had been careful to put it where she could reach the switch from her chair, but I say nothing.

"And open the window," she orders. "I hate the smell in this room, and I'm really hungry. Hand me that book. I'll read until dinner is ready."

She looks at me hard, a bold suggestion that I get going back into the kitchen to fix food. I'm also hungry, but the way Molly speaks to me makes me want to slap her or run away. Of course, I do neither. Instead, I try something a bit lighter, while I open her window.

"You know, I just heard that whip-poor-will again, the one we've been hearing in the field this week. Why don't you see if you can hear her mate call back and let me know, okay?"

Molly doesn't answer. She's flipping through her book, looking for the page where she left off.

I keep trying.

"Hey, did I ever tell you that bird is a member of the nightjar family? What strange names—'whip-poor-will,' 'nightjar.' I love saying those words, don't you? We should find out where those names came from. I'd like to know, wouldn't you? That would be a fun research project, don't you think?"

I repeat the bird names to myself as I turn to leave the room, feeling like the dolt Molly thinks I am. From somewhere, I seem to remember that the call of the whip-poor-will portends someone's death. I don't mention this to Molly, but I wonder if it's true.

I'm almost to the door to escape when she speaks in a flat, irritated voice. I turn to listen.

"Well, today was a total bust. We didn't learn a thing. Why don't the doctors know what's going on with me, with my legs? They are supposed to be the experts, but I think they are idiots, all of them. And the way they talk to me, like I'm *four*, or something! I don't want to go to any more doctors. Ever! And that's final!"

I stop and walk back toward Molly's chair. I'm not surprised to see her eyes fill with tears, shining in the poor light. I start to speak, but she's still talking.

"It's all bullshit," spouting a word I didn't know she knew or had ever spoken.

"Just bullshit!" she repeats. She's on a roll.

"Today didn't help at all. Why did we go there? Do you admit all this is a waste of time? Well, do you, Mom? Do you agree it's just a waste of time?

"Besides, you hate to drive, don't you? You are not a good driver, even I know that. And you're so tense and mean when you drive. You never talk to me, and I'm so bored back there by myself. You're never, ever any fun. Never."

I take a deep breath and force my voice to stay neutral, resisting the impulse to remind her of our singing fests.

"Well, you got at least one thing right, Molly. I do hate to drive on the highways. This is true. But you must know, all of this is for you. I'll just keep driving until we figure this out, okay? That's what Moms do. It's my job, and we'll keep traveling until we get some answers. Besides, have you noticed I'm getting better at it?"

I try to smile through my lie.

"Well, maybe," Molly agrees, but she doesn't seem convinced. Suddenly done with this conversation, she remembers she's hungry.

"Are you going to fix dinner now?"

Dismissed, I tell her, "Of course, that's a great idea. I'll check it out."

In the kitchen, I turn on my mother's old radio and find a station playing the kind of classic rock my brother loves, thinking this could pull me out of my tired slump. I take a few spins around the small kitchen, bopping between the stove and the refrigerator to Tina Turner belting through "Proud Mary." I don't know why I don't listen to music more often. I should fill the house with it all the time, but I don't. I guess I let life get in the way. If I'm not happy, music cannot instantly make it better. But sometimes it can help, so I think to get some cheap headphones for Molly for our car trips. She might like that. I make a mental note and add it to the long list of things to do.

Quietly, I open more windows to let in fresh air and push out the screen door in the back near my garden. I wonder if all my plants are wilted from the heat, but I can't tell in the gray dusk. I sit on the step and steal another minute, knowing I'm asking for trouble. Through my pants, I can feel my butt bones on the still warm concrete. When I think about it, I miss the more ample ass I used to have, the one the boys in high school admired, the one my husband once told me was "so fine." Now, I think, life has worn me down to this, a bony white woman not yet 40 with a bad haircut, stuck in this Podunk town built with cheap bricks carved out of the sand, sitting alone smack in the middle of miles and miles of crops marching all the way down to the Delta. It wears on me, this flat landscape that reminds me of all the years I've lived here, never going anywhere else. Robert and I used to dare each other to find a way out before we got sucked into staying. You can see how well that went as Robert's barn sits just around the corner of my back yard, even today. Next door neighbors, me and Robert, who would have thought?

Lingering on the steps, the mental image of my daughter inside the house pains me. I feel a swell in my throat like I'm about to cry, but I stamp it down, knowing I need to feed us both and get some sleep. It wears on me, though, the thought that my daughter has become disabled. I wonder if there's something else going on, something I can't figure out on my own. The chatter in my head is a running litany of a life with a troubled daughter and no husband around to help or talk to.

Sitting there, alone in my backyard, I allow myself to wonder again if Wilson has any plans to come home again. I can't stop myself.

Then, I think with a chuckle, *will I ever come again?*

Left on its own, my mind flits about trying to cover my bases, keep up, not drop the ball, not let the other shoe drop—from my daughter, to the heat, to my garden, to money, to food, to Wilson, to sex. Briefly, my mind goes on another tangent, remembering how Robert and I smirked and giggled that time Mom walked around the house singing one of her favorite songs, "Oh, come, come, come, come, come to the church in the wild wood," when we had just heard a neighbor boy that very day explain what "cum" meant to a small group of eager ears sitting in the back of the school bus on the way home. These days, I think that's a very good question, *when will I ever come again*? There aren't many chances for that to happen with Wilson working so far away and absolutely no chance for me to "step out," as my mother would have said. My reverie is broken when I hear a noise behind me, twigs breaking in the dark, a scurry, but I hardly bother to peer out at the bushes. My worst fears are inside, not out here.

My second cigarette, down to ash, burns my fingers. *Damn it!* Only one left, but I know better than to ask my brother to pick up a pack for me. He disapproves of my smoking, although he smokes himself. Probably a "guy thing" about women not smoking, or drinking, like our dad, but in most things we're still on the same page, Robert and me. The saving grace of my life right now is my brother. What would I do without him, I wonder, not for the first time.

Before I leave the back step, my mind pictures an ice-cold beer I know is not in the refrigerator. I salivate, imagining I can taste it, cold and crisp on my tongue, sliding down the back of my throat. What's in there, I know, are off-brand colas that are for shit. On sale, six for $3.00, bought yesterday at the local station when I filled up with gas. That was the best I could do, no beer left on the shelves. Not worth the money, for sure. Now they sit in the fridge just to taunt me. With my foot, I push the last of the cigarette off the step into the sand below and pull myself up to go inside. My eyes blur, either from the smoke or from what waits for me on the other side of the screen door, or both. The fabric on my legs peels off as I stand, but I know it's probably cooler out here than in the house. I blow the limp hair off my face and take one final breath in the evening air.

# Chapter 2

## Alice and Molly

When I reach for the door, I hear Molly yelling from down the hall.

"Mom! Where are you? Mom? I need to pee. Come here! Help me to the bathroom. MOM!"

I pull gently on the door handle that lost one of its screws last week and is hanging by one corner, and I rush inside. I head down the hallway that is now dark for some reason, sensing the narrow walls with my body, shoving stuff out of the way with my foot, hoping I don't step on the cat that has sneaked in the door with me. I realize that Wilson needs to work on the ceiling light, too. The house is like a cave, the lights flickering when they work at all, things falling off their hinges.

"Oh, Molly, I'm so sorry," I murmur to the girl in the corner. "I was outside and didn't hear you."

She glares at me as I move toward her in the darkened room. I stub my toe on the crude wheelchair Robert put together for her from pieces he'd found in an abandoned shed on the property next door, the chair that doesn't move, and I scream in pain.

"Shit, shit!!" My cry pierces the air, and I hop around a bit, cussing a blue streak at the same time. Even with the pain, I try to make a joke of my awkward dancing to get Molly to laugh, but she is a tough customer and refuses to smile for my efforts.

"Sorry, I'm not angry with you," I croon as I reach over to touch her head.

"Don't pat me on the head! I'm not a dog," she growls, jerking her body away from me as far as she can.

"Why were you outside? Why aren't you fixing dinner? I'm starving. I thought you were cooking. Get me out," she insists, raising her arms for me to pull her upright.

"I'm so sorry, Molly," I say again. "I wasn't thinking. Silly me. Here we go."

I gently pull Molly out of her chair as she puts her right arm around my neck and shoulders, gripping my neck tighter than she needs to, her fingernails digging into my skin. I circle her waist with one arm. We do our little tripod walk down the hall and into the small bathroom, clumsy, but it works. Both our arms have become stronger for it, and sometimes we manage to laugh a bit at how awkward we are. Not tonight. Molly is not in the mood. Once through the door, she expertly spins around to use the toilet and pushes me away.

My nose quivers when she urinates into the porcelain bowl. Her pee is strong and steady. I feel rotten knowing she has probably been miserable for a while now, trying so hard to hold it in. We both grimace when the pungent odor fills the small bathroom. Then, to make her laugh, I utter an elongated "PEE-U" into the air.

"Girl, you've got some serious pee going on there!" I tease. "What have you been eating? Too many of those green peas, or was it the okra we cooked last night? Whatever it is, it sure is potent." I don't seem to learn from my mistakes.

No response. I should have known not to try. I suspect some of the pee has already trickled down Molly's leg and onto her foot, but I don't check to see.

"I hate that smell," she says instead. "I want a bath tonight."

I hate to disappoint her, but I remind her the water heater hasn't been working. This is definitely something I can't tackle, and I know Wilson would not be happy if I call someone to repair it. I am careful what I say, trying not to blame her daddy.

"You know, your dad had to leave in a hurry last time he was here and just didn't get around to fixing it. I'm sorry. I would love to have a bath, too. I'll have to see if Robert can help with that. Okay?"

What I want to say is, "Your shit for a dad didn't bother to look at the water heater when it quit working. He'd rather get in his truck and take off for parts unknown and leave it to me to fix. Well, I fucking don't know anything about water heaters, and I guess I'll have to get Robert to fix it, just like everything else your father doesn't want to take care of."

But I don't, of course.

Molly stares hard at my face and cuts her eyes away, disgusted with me. It would be unlike her to say anything negative about her dad, and I am careful not to model that for her. I turn and pretend I'm preoccupied with something else.

What I notice in that moment are the changes in my daughter's body, the slight patch of pubic hair that was hardly there before. I know Molly has noticed the changes as well. Alone in her chair, or on the sofa, I have seen her secretly examine the new knobs on her chest with her fingers and sniff her new smells. We don't talk about it much, but Molly did say recently that her armpits stink. I'm wondering, too, if she has noticed her "down there" is producing an odor she doesn't recognize as well.

My ridiculous approach to all this is to think if I don't talk to her about her body's changes, maybe they will go away. Molly is far too young to develop the way she is, especially since she's mostly immobile, unable to run and play like a "normal" girl. I know I am being totally irrational, and I own that my behavior is not likely to work for much longer. I suspect Molly might not want to talk about it either, because to talk about the changes in her body would be to acknowledge her body is changing without her permission, and it's doing too much of that already with her legs refusing to work. So, neither of us brings it up, beyond a comment or two here and there.

I don't actually know what Molly knows about her body and what all the changes mean. She reads about ninth grade level in fourth grade and devours books from the library and the Bookmobile, but I'm not sure what they reveal to her. I keep meaning to get some anatomy books, so I don't have to tell her what this means. I'm so sorry she is missing the sex education courses at her school, since she's staying at home doing her lessons with me. I want to kick myself for not being a better, braver mother, but where would I start? I haven't a clue.

Not wanting to look too closely at her body, I remember to step just outside the door to give her some privacy. Leaning against the wall, my mind goes back to earlier in the week, when Barb and I did some research on wheelchairs on the internet. She has an old home computer that works, and since Wilson has taken our laptop with him, I go over to use hers. I keep hoping to hear from the social worker who promised to help us get a wheelchair that works, but there have been no signs of that happening. Barb and I found one online for about $250, but I am reluctant to go ahead and buy it, thinking that might put a stop to the agency's willingness to help us by providing one, such as it is. Besides, I know absolutely nothing about wheelchairs and this cheap, foldable model did not look particularly sturdy. I'm at a loss what to do about getting Molly set up with a chair that actually moves. And the truth is, I do not have an extra $250 right now to spend. I'd like to have a conversation about this with Wilson, but I know that's not likely to happen, either.

When Molly finishes her business, I help her up and hold on to her as she adjusts her clothing. We hobble together into the kitchen, where I deposit her onto a kitchen chair. The house has become darker than I had imagined, so I have to shuffle across the linoleum floor and flip the switch over the sink, a single bulb that blinds me for a hot minute. My anger flares with the light. I can hear my husband's voice telling me he "could fix that easy," but obviously that hasn't happened. I would have done it myself, if it didn't need more than a new bulb. *Damn you, Wilson. Where are you when I need you?* I blink away the spots and open the refrigerator door, still hoping for a miracle. But the cold, white mouth of the fridge chides me for expecting anything different.

"I hate that music," Molly grumbles.

Scolded, I reach over and turn off the radio.

"Where is he, anyway?" She asks out of nowhere.

I flinch, thinking she can for certain read my mind. Scary thought. She doesn't often ask questions about her dad, and I keep my answers vague. I make it sound like I am answering truthfully by responding in a light voice.

"Oh, you know, Molly, your dad is the manager of a big farm up by the Iowa border. You know where Iowa is, right, the state just north of Missouri? Well, it's about five or six hours from here, so he has to stay there on the farm and take care of everything, like the equipment and all the men who work there. It's a big job, and he really helps us by sending money every month so we can buy groceries and everything we need."

Molly's next words shock me. I'd never heard her like this.

"Well, I don't think he's ever coming home," Molly states flatly. "I think he's gone for good. He doesn't want to be here. He doesn't like us anymore. I hate him. He's not ever here when we need him. Besides, I like Uncle Robert more. At least he lives here, and he helps us. I like it when he comes to get me and takes me to his house. I like the way he fixes fun things to eat, like fries, and we watch cartoons together, or sometimes documentaries. I like those, too, and Robert loves the one about the ocean and sea creatures. Why don't we ever watch shows like that, Mom? Robert makes popcorn. You never make popcorn. And Robert can still carry me. Dad never carries me anywhere. I like the food Robert brings us. Has he been here today? What did he bring? I told you I'm starving."

I hear the impatience in Molly's voice as she chatters at clip speed, jumping from one thing to another without taking a breath. I nod in agreement when I think I need to, trying not to respond to her negativity about Wilson. I admit freely that Robert is a big help. He is.

My brother is a good soul, a steady man who takes care of us as he is able. He's never been super ambitious, but he seems to have a soft spot for broken things. At all hours of the day, and night, folks will drive out to Robert's place to ask for help with vehicles they can't fix on their own. He never cheats them or overcharges them for his work, so he keeps busy with the older sedans that litter his front yard, or the odd pickup truck used only for local jobs. Folks in the Bootheel never poke too much in other people's business if it can be avoided, and Robert is no exception. He'll nod to folks on the road and mutter 'Morning' in passing when he can't avoid it, but mostly he keeps to himself and helps everybody out. He worries about me, because he knows I am basically at the end of my rope with my husband gone and Molly not walking. It's a lot, he gets that.

Sometimes I confide in my brother, but he's not an eager listener to my problems, mostly because he doesn't know how to help me. He has no real suggestions for me, although occasionally he does tell me I should "kick that jerk of a husband to the curb like the dog he is and move on." But since he has no idea how I might do that, he mostly keeps his thoughts to himself.

I turn away from the empty refrigerator and rummage around the cabinets for cans of food.

"Actually, Molly. I don't think your uncle has been here, sorry, but I can heat up this can of beans, and I have some hot dogs in the crisper that should be okay. I can hear my stomach growling now, or is that yours?"

"Crap." Molly's not happy, but then she has an idea and perks up. "I'm thirsty. Do we have anything good to drink? Can I have a soda?" Molly slants her eyes toward the refrigerator and makes a silly face, mischievous for once, knowing I am likely to say no. But when I peer into the fridge again, I am surprised that some of the new cans are orange, so I try to make peace by letting her have one tonight before dinner, hoping it won't keep her awake later or cause her to wet the bed.

As I try to get excited about dogs and beans, I glance back at Molly, who is drinking her orange soda with her eyes closed, enjoying every sip. Her hair is a lovely mess, and her eyelashes are long and dark, curled naturally against her olive skin. Looking at my daughter sitting there, I am reminded of what our neighbor Mrs. Gibbons says every time she stops by to deliver a copy of the church bulletin, which I have never asked her to bring. Invariably, looking at Molly, she will say, "So young, but she is already a big girl. Such a big girl. Too bad, too bad." Without another word, the nosy woman keeps "tsk, tsking," as she edges out the front door and waddles back to her car.

I know exactly why the neighbor lady thinks it is "too bad" that Molly is "such a big girl." It's not *only* that Molly is larger than a typical girl her age, it's also because she is maturing way too fast. She looks like a young woman. None of the neighbor girls look like Molly at age nine, Mrs. Gibbons knows. Their tender bodies run around nearly naked in the backyards, screaming through the sprinkler system Robert installed on the hose at the back of his house, an invitation for the children to play in the cool spray of water in the hot afternoons. The woman's nasty comments only remind me that Molly is growing too fast, even as she sits still in her room, trying so hard to stay small.

I prod myself back to the cabinets, and *bam!*, I hear a loud noise and think, *speak of the devil*. I am relieved to hear Robert slam the screen door against the wall as he barges into the kitchen with a box of vegetables picked from his garden and some extras he has likely 'borrowed' from the neighbor's patch. I know he will kick the door back in place with his left foot as he always does, careful not to let in the flies. He's thoughtful like that. In a little dance between the door and the table, surprisingly light on his feet, he heaves the box onto the counter and smiles at his "girls," as he calls us.

"Well, you're a sight for sore eyes, Robert," I greet him with all the warmth I can muster.

"I am here to please," he answers with a small bow to me, then Molly, at the table.

"Uncle Robert!" Molly blurts out, rising from the table before she remembers her legs won't be strong enough to support her. She puts her hands on the table to brace herself as Robert sweeps an arm around to hug her tight. I want a hug, too, but I can see he has only enough awkward affection for Molly.

"Glad to see you made it home in one piece," he says to me, gently helping Molly sit back down.

"I been watching when you might get back, so I could run this box over. Figured you'd need something to eat."

"We do, thanks. We had a long day that wasn't that great. We really didn't find out anything that was of any help. I'll tell you all about it, sometime when you've got time to hear me complain."

"Can't wait," Robert says, without conviction. He's heard it all before.

"Got a man in the yard waiting for me right now. The lights aren't working on his pickup, and he needs help to drive home. Gotta' go, girls. Enjoy!"

I wave at his back, and Molly yells, "Bye, see you tomorrow?"

"Maybe," he answers lightly through the screen door on his way to his truck.

At the sink, I begin to clean the dirt off the carrots and take a bowl of peas over to Molly, asking her to hull them as quickly as she can, so I can boil them. As I sweep back and forth, I see that Robert has laid three small eggs on the dishtowel for us.

"Look at this, Molly! Where did Uncle Robert get these eggs? They're green, of all things. Usually, they are brown when he gets them from Mrs. Davis up the road, but I haven't seen green ones in years."

As Molly reaches out a hand to hold one, I'm pleased to see she seems interested in the eggs, and I think to tell her a story about my mother.

"I bet you didn't know, but my mom used to have one hen that would lay green eggs, and she swore they were no different from white or brown ones. She used to laugh when folks from town would drive all the way to our house to buy her brown eggs, because they thought they were healthier than the white ones in the store. Mom thought that was such a hoot. None of it was true, she'd say, just town folks' ignorance. 'White, brown, green, don't matter. They're all the same, just different hens lay different colored eggs,' she'd tell us. I think she'd charge them more for the brown eggs, and they'd pay it, you know, because they didn't know any better. I can't remember if they liked her green eggs or not. My guess they were too weird for the town folks who came to our place to buy eggs."

I am surprised to hear the happy lilt in Molly's voice as she coos, "I think they're adorable. I can't wait to eat them. I wonder if they really do taste the same. Let's make an omelet, okay, Mom, and see?"

"Absolutely! What a great idea. Here, you break them into this blue bowl. It was your Grandma Angie's bowl, you know, how appropriate. Put those green eggs into this bowl and whisk them frothy. I'll see what we can find to put into our omelet. So glad Robert stopped by even when he's super busy. We're lucky to have him around."

"You know, Mom, I don't think I could love him any more than I already do." Molly's eyes fill up to the brim as she vigorously whisks the eggs. I wonder at her tears, but I don't ask. I'm surprised to hear her next question.

"Mom, don't baby chicks come from eggs?"

"Yes, why?"

"Well, why don't these eggs have baby chicks in them?"

"Wow, very good question. That's another thing my mom taught me. I don't think most people know the answer to that question! Or, they think they do, but they actually don't."

"So?" She really wants to know, and I'm happy to grab this "teaching moment" while she's curious.

"Well, to get chicks, you have to have a hen, the female, and you need a rooster, that's the male chicken. My mom always had quite a few hens, even ten to fifteen females, all different colors and breeds. I remember her calling the black and white speckled ones 'Domineckers,' but I'm not sure that was their actual name. Mom made up her own names for things, so I can't be sure. She also had red hens, a few black ones, and I remember one white one she didn't like very much, because that hen would get so dirty, rolling around in the dirt, and that bothered my mom.

"Your grandmother loved to go into the chicken house and lift the hens off their nests to gather the eggs, and they would let her do that. Then, she'd shoo them out into the yard, where she'd throw feed on the ground so they could peck at it.

"She only needed a couple of roosters, but she was so proud of them. I'm not sure if she bought them special or saved them from a batch of chicks, but she thought their bright, flashing colors were really special. They'd strut around the chicken yard and crow like they were proud of their feathers, too. Then, they'd jump one of the hens and hold her down. Mom would watch to make sure they weren't too rough with her and push them aside if she thought they needed to back off. She loved her precious hens.

"I don't know if you remember, but she kept that old chicken house until it nearly collapsed from age and storms. She still had chickens when she died."

Molly nods.

"When I was little, I remember going to the chicken yard with her and into the little chicken house, but I was too scared to reach into the nests and grab the eggs. I'd wait until she got the hens out before I'd collect the eggs. I thought that was so much fun. The eggs were still warm, and I'd put them into a little pail she kept for me to gather them in."

"But, Mom, why did the roosters jump the hens like that? Were they trying to hurt them?"

"No, no, not at all. In the chicken yard, the fancy rooster would strut around and show off for all the hens, to get their attention. It was like he was 'courting them,' you know what that means? To get their attention, like a boy might act to get a girl's attention, or a girl might do something to get a boy's attention. Then he would pounce on a hen and grab the back of her neck with his beak, kind of like a bite. Yeah, think of it as a love bite."

Molly looks at me like she's about to get more information than she bargained for, but I plunge forward, seizing the moment. Her eyes are wide.

"Real quick, while he's up there, he deposits his sperm in her private area and that will fertilize the eggs that are inside her. Are you with me? You following all this?"

"Yeah, I guess so." Molly doesn't look convinced.

"Well, after that love bite, so to speak, somehow the hens know their eggs have been fertilized by the rooster, and they start sitting on their nest for days at a time. That's called 'brooding.' My mom would notice if a hen wasn't getting up from her nest, didn't want to be disturbed, and she would let that hen sit there as long as she wanted and not gather her eggs. She knew those eggs would hatch as baby chicks, because they had been fertilized by the rooster."

"Why does she have to sit on them?" Molly asks.

"Well, they need to be kept warm while the chicks form in the eggs. That's called incubation. It's kind of like when a baby is in a mother's womb and is kept safe and warm in there until it's fully formed and ready to be born. Make sense?"

"Humm, I guess. So, then what happens?"

"That's the cool part. When they are ready, the chicks start pecking their way out of the shells themselves and move around a little in the nest. In a few days, their mother uses her wings to help them jump down and run around the chicken yard, careful not to go too far from their mother."

"I wish I could see that!" Molly's eyes sparkle.

"You know, Molly, we could get some chickens and a rooster, then you could watch the whole process yourself. It wouldn't be hard to do. There's a feed store down the road from Robert's, and I think they have baby chicks in the spring. We could get a dozen of them and see what happens. Some folks say they can tell male chicks from female chicks, but I always thought that was baloney.

"My mom would buy a 'straight-run,' which means you get twelve chicks and 'you get what you get.' She always thought it was fun to see how many males and how many females she got. She would also wait to buy them a bit older when they've been 'sexed,' hoping she would get mostly hens, because you need more hens than roosters. But even then, it's often a crap shoot, pardon my French. My mom loved to tell how once she got a straight run of twelve two-day-old chicks and got seven roosters and five hens. Not what she wanted. The next time she paid for pullets, which means they were all supposed to be females, but she got four roosters in that batch, too. Moral of this story? Sexing chickens is really difficult!"

Both of us are laughing now, and I love watching how Molly's face wrinkles when she laughs, a rare thing these days.

"You want to get some chickens?" I speak too quickly.

"Yes!" she agrees without hesitation. "Maybe Uncle Robert would let us use one of his pens at the barn. It would be so fun to get a straight run and find out how many roosters and hens we get. He still has lots of hay up in the hayloft. I've seen it. We could use that to make nests for the hens."

"That could work, and I'm sure Robert wouldn't mind at all. That way, we would have fresh eggs every day, and we could share with him. I think he'd like that."

"And we'd get one or two roosters, right? Then, we could let some of them hatch. I would love to watch them peck their way out of the shells!"

Molly hands me the bowl with the eggs, and I add the other things I've chopped up, putting the mix into a skillet to make our omelet. The bowl feels smooth and round in my hands, a comfort from my mother.

This is the first time in a long time I've seen Molly eager to do anything at all. I'm thinking this is such a simple thing that we could do together. Until I realize how difficult all this would be for Molly right now with her legs not working. I don't spoil our moment by saying anything, but it makes me angry all over again that I haven't been able to find help for her. I plaster a smile on my face, serve the omelet on our most colorful plates, and forget to ask Molly how she knows there is still hay in Robert's hayloft.

That night, lying in bed with her, I pull out my phone and google "Chicken sex." She giggles as I scroll down to a site with colored pictures. The explanations are simplified, but we find lots of information that captivates Molly for a few minutes before I declare it's time for her to sleep.

"Okay, enough of this! Lights out. Goodnight, my dear girl."

Back in the kitchen, my eyes linger at the dark window over the sink, imagining Wilson's truck lights coming down the driveway. I know he feels responsible for everything at the farms, but I just wish he felt more responsible for his own family. Until this year, I have always trusted he will come home at some point. But this time, after more than three months, I have begun to seriously worry that he might never come back. How could he just not come back? Can that even happen? Most weeks he calls me to check in, but this week I haven't yet heard from him. He insists I should not call his room or the farm's central number, that I must wait for him to call me. So, like an idiot, I just wait for the damn phone to ring. I taste blood and realize I'm chewing my lip again. I pull the shade down against the night, erasing the face that haunts the glass.

After cleaning the kitchen, I seek the escape of the back steps again, drawn to the heaviness of the night, noisy now with the screeching of insects, the chirp of tree frogs, an owl hooting on a limb high over my head. My thoughts turn to my good friend again, wishing she could come over and talk with me for a while, but I know it's too late.

Barb knows how bad things are for me right now. When she can get away from her own family, she drives her ancient sky-blue Impala across town to sit and visit. She has very little to offer other than coveted companionship and occasional cigarettes. Unlike Robert, Barb is a thoughtful and generous listener, has been since we met working at Wendy's, which now seems like a lifetime ago. Although none of Barb's children has ever been truly sick, she tells me she cannot imagine the extra burden of a disabled child, one that is not likely to get better, a girl who cannot walk, but she can totally relate to stories of a neglectful husband who has little regard for his faithful wife.

When Barb visits, we sit and smoke together on the front porch, as long as Molly is quiet in the house or is at Robert's. Sometimes we talk about our husbands, sometimes about our kids. Once in a while, we imagine living in a place different from where we are now.

"Why isn't the Bootheel part of Arkansas, anyway?" I asked my friend not long ago, trying to recall facts from my fourth-grade geography lessons.

Barb had to think about it. "Well, I can only remember that Missouri became a state before Arkansas, and some politician wanted to include this region when they drew up the territory that would become the state. When they were done, the shape of the state looked like a boot, you know, like a cowboy boot, and this area down here was the heel of the boot, right?"

"Right." I'm remembering hearing some of this stuff from my dad, who was a history buff.

"How appropriate, we're just the heel of the boot. You know, I grew up thinking folks were saying 'the Boothill,' like 'boots up on the hill,' like in a graveyard. In fact, I don't think most people who live here actually know it's 'Bootheel,' not 'Boothill,' the way they say it so fast and loose like that."

Barb shook her head, agreeing that probably people have no idea. "It beats me why anyone wanted this crappy swamp land, anyway. I wish they had just cut it across the bottom neat and clean and let Arkansas have it. My husband calls it the 'the armpit of the state.'"

"Right," I said. "And Robert calls it the 'butt-hole of the state' when he gets disgusted with life down here. Makes me wonder why he doesn't just up and leave, but that sure doesn't sound like Robert, does it? And what would I do if he did?"

"I don't really know your brother all that well," my friend admitted, "but I know he's lived here all his life, even in the same house, and I don't think he'd leave you and Molly."

Barb sat quietly for a bit, then added, "I can't imagine living anywhere else, can you? Been here my whole life. Wouldn't know how to just up and move."

I found myself not wanting to agree with my friend, but I shook my head like I couldn't imagine such a thing either and touched her shoulder with my own. I took a sip of the beer she had brought me, savoring the taste, wishing I could drink enough beer to feel a little light-headed, a bit tipsy, just for a change, something different. But I knew I couldn't with Molly just inside the house, and Wilson nowhere in sight. As the shadows darkened the porch, we sat quietly for a bit, our weary resignation balanced between us like a bitter fruit we'd been required to eat.

# Chapter 3

## First Blood

My last cigarette finished, my image of Barb vanishes when I can no longer see anything and realize the mosquitos have decided to eat my face and neck, my ankles. I force myself up from the steps with a grunt, knowing I should also put myself to bed. I'd love a bath, too, but tepid water will not soothe my weary bones. We will both have to wait until Robert can look at the water heater to see why it isn't working. I resign myself to frustration, and swear I am not thinking about my husband anymore tonight. I go around the house and make sure the doors are locked and close some of the windows. Wilson always hates it when I leave the windows open while the air conditioning is on, but I can't resist letting in some fresh air, especially at night when the heat lifts. We used to argue about that all the time. Now, I just leave them open. What's he going to do?

I am half asleep when I wander into the bathroom one last time. I can smell the toilet before I get to it. *Oh, crap, we forgot to flush it*. I chuckle at my own silly joke and reach over for the lever, but something stops my hand. Feeling foolish, I stare down into the pool of yellow piss to see shadowy swirls of dark blood.

I am so surprised by what I see in the toilet, I have to sit down on the edge of the tub. I know the blood is not my own. I finished my period the week before. How could this be? It makes no sense.

But then I realize, *of course it makes sense*. I want to slap myself for not realizing where this was going, for being so dense. Even if I don't want to admit it, I know the evidence in that toilet. I can hardly breathe as I reach to flush, turn off the light, and slowly make my way down the hall back to my room. The night sounds follow me through the open window. I lie down flat on my back, staring at the ceiling in the dark, grieving for a daughter who will never have a carefree childhood, who sits by the window watching the world go by without her, a child who has suddenly become a woman without even knowing it.

The next morning, I'm frantic to talk to Barb but, first, I walk Molly to the bathroom and check to see if there's any blood in her panties. I'm relieved to see only a slight pink hue that she doesn't notice. No real discharge yet. I'm trusting there won't be any mess until I can get back, so I call and ask Robert to come get Molly and take her to his house for a bit. He comes over with a big grin on his face, always happy to help. He picks up Molly from the sofa, walks easily through the door with her, and places her safely on the bench seat of his old truck. I hardly take the time to thank him. Quickly, I call Barb and tell her not to leave the house before I get there. I feel like my head will explode if I can't talk to someone about my discovery, and that someone definitely cannot be Robert. I drive too fast across town.

When I arrive at Barb's, I march through the front door without knocking and turn to face my friend, who stands there waiting, her eyebrows high on her face.

"OK," I blurt out, "I cannot cope. This is too much. I need your help. Tell me what to do!"

I know I am being ridiculous, but only with Barb can I act like a banshee, a woman gone berserk, and not regret it later. Barb actually laughs, her graying curls nodding in the bright sunlight as I barge past her into her house.

"Good Lord, Alice, I'm getting whiplash from all the stories you bring over here. You know, I cannot save you! What is it now? It can't get much worse, really, it can't. Tell me you're not pregnant again!!"

I freeze, stare at my friend, close my eyes, and take a deep breath.

"No, but I may as well be. And, yes, it can get worse! And it has. The die is cast. The moon is moving into a darker phase, and it's all out of control."

Barb laughs heartily again at my ridiculous words.

"You crack me up, you silly woman. Slow down and sit down. I'll make tea. You're not making any sense. Go on. Sit!"

Barb takes me by the shoulders and bodily guides me toward a kitchen chair at the end of the table.

"I hate tea," I mumble toward her back.

I watch as she steps back toward the stove and takes a few minutes to make tea, which she believes is an art form, a chance to move slow and brew a fresh cup for restoration. Her own mother had said to her many times, "When you make tea, make tea." She'd taken that as gospel then and still does. Her measured preparations give me time to catch my breath and settle in. Unlike my own hard ones, Barb's chairs are cushioned with soft lovely needlepoint, a relief to my tired behind. With care and deliberation, my friend fills her best Christmas cup with fragrant Chamomile tea with honey and brings it to the table for me, hoping the bright red and green will seem festive and soothe my mind, even in the summer heat.

"Now, drink this slowly and decide how you're going to tell me what has got you so upset."

I am still too frazzled to speak coherently. "The worst. The very worst has happened. I don't know if I can even say it out loud to you. I am that freaked out."

"Well, then try." Barb attempts to hang onto her patience.

Shaking my head, I realize I am being more than a little dramatic, but the truth is, it's difficult to explain how shocked I am about the revelation the night before. I hadn't slept, thinking about what it means. I try to breathe deeply before I speak, but by now Barb is more than a little curious.

"Well, this isn't helping at all. Open your mouth and speak to me, calmly."

"Good God, what am I going to do?" I squeak and gulp air. "Okay. Here goes. My daughter, nine years old, stuck in a chair that doesn't move, can't walk, you know all this. Molly has just started her period! I saw it plain as day in the toilet. Blood in her urine, swirling around like nobody's business. That's what. What am I to do with *that*, I ask you, my friend? What do I do with that? The girl can't walk and now this?"

Barb hardly moves. She sits with my words for a few moments before she speaks.

"Humm, this is somewhat unusual, I agree." As usual, Barb gives the situation her honest consideration, not knowing yet how best to diffuse the moment and calm me down.

"I can see this has you very upset. However, Molly isn't the first girl to bleed at the age of nine, almost ten, nor I'll wager that she will be the last. So, what is driving you so crazy? Your little girl has been blessed with her period. It's your job to tell her what's going on, and she will cope," Barb pauses for effect, "as will you. You hear me?"

I can hardly focus on her words. I don't think I can cope, and I certainly don't know how to tell Molly what is going on. Where would I even start? I give Barb my best deer in the headlights stare. She surely understands how crazy this makes me feel, but she chuckles and stares out the kitchen window, as though she's far away.

"Remember I told you I had three brothers and two sisters? Well, our mother was a very private person, a super prude.

We, by that I mean all of us girls, including her, were not allowed to talk about our 'female problems,' or mention our periods ever, at all, around 'the men.' That was a strict order from Mom. Never, ever, should we speak of 'women's stuff.' The men were not to know anything was going on with us, no pads around or boxes sitting in the cabinets, nothing! We kept them all clueless, even if we had cramps or whatever. I could never complain or mention why I felt like crap. Now that I think about it, that was so dumb. Those boys grew up completely in the dark about all this stuff, as I suspect most men do. Why do women do that, feel like we have to hide it?"

When I don't answer, my friend pauses, then asks another question, "What was it like with your mom?"

Before I can answer her question, Barb throws another at me. "Wow, do you remember all the names for our periods we heard back then?"

I can't help but laugh as we sit there at the table listing all the names we had heard for "that time of the month" from women in our families or from neighbor women, or friends. Breathless, we list what we can remember.

"our monthlies,"

"our 'little friend,'"

"a visit from Aunt Flo,"

"the curse,"

"our period."

We are speaking over each other, laughing.

"How old were you when you started?" I ask Barb.

"Twelve, maybe? You?"

"Probably about the same. It's hard to remember."

We both wince when Barb mentions what her dad and brothers used to say when "the women" were cranky or out of sorts, smirking "she must be on the rag." I had heard that one plenty of times, a favorite of Wilson's, and I always resented it.

Barb is pondering her own comment. "Humm. Where did that come from, I wonder, if they didn't know anything about periods? I guess the husbands knew, because they *would* know, right? Still, it's an ugly thing to say, and, of course, the boys picked up on that, learning women's stuff was disgusting."

I suddenly recall how my mother first told me about my periods.

"I remember how my mother avoided talking to me about it by leaving a weird looking panty with metal clasps in it, a box of pads, and a booklet about menstruation on my bed one day for me to find. I was completely baffled by all that stuff."

Barb shakes her head and responds, laughing.

"I remember sitting on one side of the gym when the teachers talked to the girls about periods and reproduction, and 'how girls get pregnant,' which was, of course, what we all desperately wanted and needed to know. But none of it stuck. We had no idea what the teachers were talking about. Mostly, we giggled and leaned over our knees to watch the boys who were sitting on the opposite side of the gym, apparently learning about reproduction from the male teachers. Even though I didn't understand anything about it, I could never ask Mom any questions."

"Right! Remember those booklets that came with the 'napkins'? Speaking of which, where did that come from, calling pads 'napkins?' I had no idea what the blue liquid was staining the white pad in the brochure. It was years before I discovered my periods were not likely to be blue!"

Barb nods, recalling even the television commercials showed a blue liquid on the enormous pads sold by Kotex. We are both crying from laughing so hard, but we calm down as we chat a bit about our mothers' inability to talk with us about something that is perfectly normal. I try to put into words what I'm feeling about telling Molly.

"They must have been embarrassed trying to talk to us about it. You know, I'm embarrassed, too, and I don't want to admit it, but I feel exactly the same way about talking with Molly about menstruation. I don't even know where, or how, to start with this stuff."

Barb nods her head, but adds, "You know, it's funny. My oldest daughter, Linda, was nearly fourteen when she started her period. She had been upset about starting so late, because all of her girlfriends had started much earlier, at 12 or 13, and she felt left out. She talked about it a lot, although not around her dad and brothers. Her friends were telling her she should feel lucky not to have a period yet, but she wouldn't listen. They hated it, they told her, and referred to their periods as 'Shark Week.'"

"Ugh," I shrug, "That one's got an edge."

We agree that reference won the contest for worst-ever euphemism. By this time, I am calmer, of course, and Barb has done her job well. Deftly, she pivots the conversation back to Molly, telling me, "You know, starting at nine is early, but if it is handled properly, you should be able to help your daughter understand what is happening to her body."

"Okay," I agree, feeling not at all sure how this might go. "I'll tell her, somehow, but I'm going to keep really good records of her cycle. I just pray this is a one-off and not actually the beginning of her regular periods. I have to know for sure."

"Good luck with that," Barb teases. We chat a bit longer and drink our tea, until suddenly I realize how long I've been away from Molly.

"I need to leave and pick her up from Robert's, right now! I sent her over there without telling her anything. I must tell her and show her how to use a pad. Should I also show her a tampon? Too soon?" I'm rambling as I back out the door.

Barb tells me not to worry, assuring me everything will be fine, and Molly will be okay. Her arms envelop me in a big hug as she hands me a half-empty box of feminine napkins from the stash under her bathroom sink.

Back home, my "talk' with Molly falls short of my promises to Barb and myself. I tell her the bare minimum, explaining only why there is blood floating in the toilet and that she'll have to wear a pad while it's happening.

"All women bleed once a month, Molly. It's normal, perfectly normal, when you get older and more mature," I tell her as though this is no big deal.

"First of all, I'm nine years old!" Molly will have none of my pretense.

"Is that older? Am I now more mature? That sounds like an old lady, like you!"

She glares at me, until I have to turn away. She's right, she's way too young for this, but here we are.

"And every month? Like all month?" Now she is in tears.

"Oh, no, sorry, Molly, just once a month, like for several days or a week, not all month!"

She looks like she has been betrayed and cannot bear to hear any more, but I feel required to keep going.

"So, let me try and explain. Just so you know, girls and women who are mature, ovulate every month, that is, we pass an 'egg' through our body, a tiny 'egg' that has *not* been fertilized. Think of it as just a tiny cell that you don't need to keep in your body. It leaves in the blood you pass every month. Does that make sense?"

"I have no idea if that makes sense. I really don't want to hear this or wear this god-awful pad or talk about eggs and that stuff. What does all this have to do with me? I'm nine years old! And I can't walk, and I can't go to school, and I hate you for telling me all this crap. I don't want to hear any more, just stop!"

For a few long minutes, I sit in a chair near her own, and we both stare out the window at the rows of cotton that stretch past Robert's barn toward the horizon.

"I have just one question," Molly's voice is low. I lean my head down to hear what she is saying.

"Do boys go through this, too?" She turns to look straight at me, her eyes black slits of accusation.

I'm caught off guard by her question.

"Well, actually, no. Only girls bleed every month to get rid of an unfertilized egg. Men don't have eggs, so they don't need to get rid of them, or hold them safe and warm when they have been fertilized. They can't get pregnant, and they can't become mothers." I'm now trying to put a positive spin on this terrible news.

"Ok, this is total crap. What is 'fertilized' in a girl, anyway? What does it have to do with being pregnant? And what does any of this have to do with me?" Molly's face is red, her hand is shaking. She starts talking again.

"I need to get out of this chair. I need to walk again. I can't just sit here and let shit like this happen to me. It's because I can't walk, right, Mom? It's because I sit here all day that my eggs are coming through me and coming out all bloody?"

"Oh, no, Molly. No! It's not like that at all. It's only because you've matured a bit faster than most girls do at your age. You know, you've noticed your boobs, that hair on your private parts, your size, these are all signs that you are growing up, maybe a little faster than some girls, but it's all perfectly normal. As you change from a girl to a woman, the hormones in your body cause these tiny eggs inside you to travel. If they are not fertilized, your body gets rid of them, that's menstruating, or 'getting your period,' that is, you bleed. Not because you're hurt, but just to flush out the little egg. It has nothing to do with you not walking."

"Well, I will not do this! This is not fair! How long have you done this? Since you were nine? No, wait, I don't want to know. Go away and leave me alone. I want to read and never think about this again. I don't want to hear any more about it. Close my door when you leave."

My daughter cannot expel me from sight fast enough.

Silently, I creep out of her room, agreeing with everything she says. It is totally not fair. She's right. It's messy and bloody, hurts when it arrives, and it's not fair that only girls have to deal with it. It's even more unfair that Molly can't walk and be normal. I get it, Molly, I get it. For now, I leave it at that, knowing I am not off the hook. I will need to revisit this again, just not right now. I figure I've done enough damage for one day.

During the week, I call Wilson's number at the farm office, even though he's told me not to, and I leave messages for him to call me back. I also call his cell phone, but he never answers any of my calls. Even though Molly is also mad at her father, she still occasionally asks why he doesn't come home more, but I have run out of things to tell her about where her father is. I wish I knew myself.

# Chapter 4

## More Doctors

After the blood incident, Molly and I settle into a life without many interruptions, except for the appointments we make to visit new doctors in every direction. Wilson's visits home become an unpredictable punctuation to our lives, and I wonder how long I can push doing something about my marriage into the future. Right now, I'm happy to see his paycheck arrive at the bank, and I try to appreciate Robert for what he does for us and not feel guilty about relying on him as much as I do. He tells me the best way to pay him back is to feed him once in a while, so that's what I do. We enjoy his quiet company in the evenings, when he walks over to share whatever I can pull together for dinner. Molly usually perks up when he comes, although sometimes she seems distant and confused, even when he sits at our table across from her.

Months pass with no helpful news from the doctors. Blessed Robert fixes the water heater, so we have hot water again, and it's nearly winter but still no sign of Wilson. I can't imagine what he needs to be doing on the farms as they prepare for the snow. I don't allow myself to think too much about this, or I'll go crazy. I tell myself it's easier when I don't have to deal with him, but that's not really true. At night, Molly is quiet as she sits in the bath, letting me wash her like a child. I check her legs as she sits in the sudsy water, and I ask her to tell me what's on her mind. She doesn't have much to say. After her bath, I help her into her pajamas and watch her closely, touch her forehead to make certain she doesn't have a fever. Once she's in bed, I rub her back, until I hear her soft breathing and know she has finally fallen asleep. Lots of nights, she wets her bed and often has bad dreams. When that happens, we spend time changing her sheets before I lie down beside her. I have no idea how else to help my daughter.

None of Molly's strange behavior seems to have anything to do with the fact that her legs still don't work properly. It's hard for me to sort through all the different symptoms and figure out what's going on. Desperate for answers, I make another appointment for Molly with a "holistic" doctor in St. Louis, recommended by one of the orthopedists who found nothing wrong with Molly's legs. I am super skeptical of anything that smacks of "new age" or "holistic" anything, but Dr. Richards actually seems to be listening to me and seems genuinely concerned about Molly.

First, she talks to Molly while I sit in the waiting room by myself. I'm glad she does this, but it also makes me nervous when I can't hear what Molly is saying. After thirty or forty long minutes, the doctor asks me to step into her office alone. Molly is delighted to take the television remote so she can surf while I'm gone.

"Mrs. Campbell," the therapist begins. "I'm concerned that perhaps all of this is some kind of psychological situation with Molly. I'm not at all saying this is all 'in her head,' but since she's seen so many orthopedic specialists without results, it makes me wonder if her problems actually are physical ones. We have to be on the alert for other things that might be going on with her, maybe things in her environment that perhaps frighten her or confuse her into behaving strangely."

"Like what?" I realize my voice is a bit strained,

high-pitched. I feel defensive for some reason and want to protect Molly from where this might be going.

"It's always scary to contemplate something like this," she tells me in a soothing voice I'm not in the mood to hear. "We must explore all the possibilities of what might be going on with Molly that have caused her to regress and stop walking. Do you agree?"

I nod, but I am worried. I'm certain my face is flushed bright, and I look away from her. I decide not to speak, afraid I might blow up and say something I'll regret.

I begin to feel both uncomfortable and guilty. Does this mean I am not a good mother? Is Molly's behavior a symptom of my own unhappiness, some inability to connect with my husband and my child? Is it because we have no friends but Robert and Barb? Is Wilson's neglect having this kind of effect on our daughter? My brain won't stop with the questions. What am I missing, and why can't Molly tell me what's going on in her little head? I notice the doctor is still talking, so I pay attention.

"Frankly," she is saying. "I can tell you that your home situation is a cause of concern. Molly is worried that her father doesn't come more often, that maybe he won't ever live with you and her again. Has she said that to you? She's read about 'divorce' and hopes her parents won't split up for good. This leaves her feeling very unstable about her home life. You can see how all of this is difficult for her and how hard it may be for her to express her feelings about things she doesn't understand or can't control.

"At the same time, I can see that Molly certainly loves her Uncle Robert, and I can see that she has made him a kind of surrogate father. He is affectionate with her, and she sees him on a regular basis. She feels safe and secure in her relationship with him. She recognizes, too, that your relationship with him is solid and will not 'go away.'

"She, and you, are certainly fortunate to have your brother nearby and able to help you as much as he does, but you must not assume that he can provide, or wants, the role of father to your daughter. Should he tire of her or spend less time with her, that would be devastating for Molly. I also wonder how healthy it is for her and him to spend so much time together. I know he's a big help to you, but that may not be in Molly's best interest, either."

"How can you possibly say that," I want to scream at this woman and her "approach," which seems to be digging way deeper into our lives than I'd expected.

"Please, hear me out," she said. "The problem is that if Robert ever does want to move away or not continue to be a kind of stand-in for Molly's father, and your husband, I might add, then think how devastating that would be for her at this point."

This young woman, who seems too young to be a doctor, is actually trying to have a conversation with me, which surprises me no end.

"You know, Alice. May I call you Alice?"

I nod dumbly, like I don't have a brain in my head.

"I'm worried about both of you, to be honest," she continues. "You seem like a bright young woman, and I'm impressed that you have been managing so well on your own. However, it seems like you haven't gotten many breaks in life. Certainly, your husband has not been there for you, even as Molly's health has been a problem. You tell me you have only one good female friend and the help of your brother to keep things going in your life. You have no community to speak of, no social network to rely on, and social services in Sikeston have totally failed to assist you with Molly and with the demands of your lives together. I'm thinking both you and Molly would benefit from seeing someone on a regular basis, perhaps in Cape Girardeau. If you wish, I could do some research and see if there's someone down there who could see you."

My brain is overwhelmed by what this doctor is suggesting. She has said things no other person has even hinted at. She has listened to both Molly and me, but I have little conviction that I can do what she is suggesting. Could I, or we, actually meet with a psychologist in Cape Girardeau who might try to help us deal with the way our lives are right now? Will insurance pay for this? Would I hear more things that terrify me, make me feel as though I've been a bad mother? And if so, how would I handle that?

If this doctor is right that Molly should not be so close to Robert, that their relationship might not be healthy for either of them, then what? I am ashamed to admit I need Robert. I need him in our lives. He is my rock, my only support, the one who helps me, the only one I can trust with Molly, the only one who somehow fills some of Wilson's absence.

I tell her I'll think about it. I can tell she was expecting more from me, but that's all I can tell her at this point. I have no idea what I should do next.

Walking to my car with Molly at my side, I try not to show my frustration with the doctor. She has stirred up so many feelings and left me with more questions than when we arrived. But, for now, I need to get Molly settled in the car for our drive home. Once in the car, I try to make eye contact with her in the rearview mirror, but she's turned away. I wonder what she's thinking, too, and wish we could talk about the visit. Maybe when we get home, I should try then. For now, I keep it light.

"You okay back there? Are you comfortable? Remember there are some water bottles in that bag, if you're thirsty. Could you hand one to me when you get a minute?"

I glance up at the mirror again to see Molly staring out the side window at the fields we are passing. I am not sure what the doctor said to her, or what she told her about her legs or her relationship with Robert, or Wilson, or me, for that matter. She doesn't hand me a water bottle, and I don't remind her. Instead, I turn on the radio to her favorite station. It's the best I can do.

That week, I call Wilson's numbers again three or four times. I leave messages for him to call me back. He never does.

# Chapter 5

## Wilson

When the snow begins to fall, and Wilson no longer has an excuse to stay away, he surprises us and comes home for several weeks. I am so relieved to see him, I nearly forget to be mad at him. Once he's home, it seems too difficult to question our marriage with him there. When I ask him why he never answers my calls, he shrugs and says the office phone messages get deleted by the office person every night before he even hears them. He also tells me his cell phone is overloaded and can't take any more messages, which strikes me as a total lie. Whatever is going on, it's clear that Wilson isn't interested in what I have to say between visits. Maybe he's so busy with his work, he has no time for my concerns and worries, who knows? Out of sight, out of mind, I guess, but it still makes me furious. I try to make a low-key effort to explain this to him, but it only makes him mad, so I drop it.

I am so happy to have him in the house, working together on Molly's needs, I decide not to make a fuss about the phone calls. I consult my notes and tell him about the various doctors we have visited, and we go over all the test results that have offered little information about her condition. I do not tell him about the doctor who has questioned the state of our marriage and how it may be affecting Molly. I'm hoping I can save that for later, before he leaves again.

Wilson's response to the negative test results is to question whether there's anything wrong with Molly's legs. Every day, he tries to get her on her feet, insisting she try harder to stand and walk. I beg him to stop pushing her, when we can both see she is too unstable. She falls constantly. She cries for him to stop, but Wilson is determined.

One day, he goes to the pharmacy and rents some crutches for her, but they make her balance problems worse. They are much too tall, and they make her underarms sore. Wilson is frustrated and tells her she's not trying. Of course, this infuriates Molly, so she sits on the floor in a tangle of legs and crutches and refuses to get up. Wilson leaves the house for a while, and I have to help her untangle and sit down on the sofa, where she continues to sulk and cry quietly. We're both miserable. That afternoon, I have to be the one to return the rented crutches. Wilson is done, he says.

But the next day, we fill out the paperwork to get her an at-home physical therapist, and, for the third time, we request agency help in getting her an adjustable child's wheelchair—one large enough for a little girl who is growing fast. We never hear anything back about our application.

While Wilson is home, a social worker does come to visit. I wonder if it's because Wilson has been calling their office, rather than me. I know how that goes—whiny mother vs. devoted father. Margaret, the social worker, sits at our kitchen table and fills out form after form with us, agreeing that Molly needs all the help she can get. But two days later, she calls to let us know that since she is only "on loan" from a St. Louis-based clinic, she regrets she has been ordered to return to the main office and will not be able to get Molly the help she needs "down here in the Bootheel." I see Wilson's face fall, then settle into anger. He is finally experiencing what

I've been dealing with, and I'm happy to share the frustration with him.

It pays off. A physical therapist from Cape Girardeau calls the house, but no sooner than Wilson answers the phone and puts it on speaker, she informs us she "cannot schedule any visits with Molly until she has a specific diagnosis and a referral from Molly's doctor." She needs that diagnosis first, she insists. Otherwise, her hands are tied. "Once I have this information," she says, "you will still need to contact the Sikeston office to see if there's anyone available for your area."

By now, I have become accustomed to hearing these kinds of excuses, but I can see Wilson's frustration grow as he hears first-hand the lack of resources available to Molly, mostly because of where we live. His temper flares.

"This is bullshit," he says, more than once. "Just bullshit."

When the physical therapist calls again to check in for the information she requested, Wilson is short with her and condescending, which I know probably won't help our efforts.

"You know, I'm not at all impressed with you, *Christine*. What kind of credentials do you have for this work? Are you trained to work with children at all? Do you think we're making all this up about our daughter? Where'd you get your degree? Did you flunk out?"

Wilson hangs up the phone, and I know we won't be hearing from Christine again. I expect him to blow up at me, but what he says is even worse. He turns on me, his eyes dark, his voice low, accusing.

"You know, if I had been here, none of this would have happened. I don't think you're actually watching her, Alice. It makes me wonder, how could she go from a little girl, walking just fine, to a nine-year-old girl who can't?" He pauses to stare at me for a bit.

"It just doesn't make any sense. Are you actually home with her? Where are you most of the time, out with Barb? Someone else? Are you seeing someone, Alice? Are you? I have no idea anymore what goes on around here. Why aren't you watching her?"

I say nothing. To drown out his words, I turn my back and run water over the dirty dishes that wait in the sink. What he's saying is ridiculous. Of course I'm home with Molly, every day, all day. He's delusional if he thinks I'm not doing everything in my power to find help for her, but I don't know how to fight him with words. I have convinced myself that yelling at him won't accomplish anything, because he won't listen, or hear what I'm saying, and I worry that Molly will hear us arguing in the kitchen. I grit my teeth and wait until he leaves the room, before I respond low and deep, careful that he can't hear me.

"Wilson Campbell, you horrible excuse for a husband, go fuck yourself!"

In that moment, I am as angry with myself as I am with him. Why hadn't I challenged him? What does he have over me that keeps me silent? My father had been the same way, and my mother never once denied him the right to treat her like dirt, like his own personal doormat. I want to tell him he's full of shit. I want to tell him not to come home, if he can't control his anger and help us more. I want to tell him I'm done with this marriage; it's not working for me anymore. But in the end, I say none of these things, because I cannot imagine what our life might be like without him as our anchor, without the paychecks he deposits for us to use or the security my marriage to him provides. I realize I don't do or say anything, because it's easier not to do anything, not to rock the boat, or criticize my husband.

Wilson leaves at the end of the month without much of a goodbye, only waving from the doorway to Molly down the hallway on his way out. He leans over and plants a perfunctory kiss on my cheek and tells me he may not be in touch much in the next few weeks. He's headed to a larger farm right on the Iowa border, more than seven hours away from Sikeston, but he will "be in touch." Even though it's now winter, he says he will be working with the farm owners to change out the old equipment and buy new machines for the spring and hiring new workers to do the manual labor. I'm not sure I believe any of what he says, except for the part about him not calling often. That's not new. From the porch, I watch him leave, wishing he'd come more often to help and also wishing he'd never come back.

Watching his truck leave the driveway, I have a lump in my throat that won't go away. I stand on the porch with my conflicted thoughts long after he has gone. I beg my mind to be a blank, but it scrolls out one question after another about what to do next. Mostly, I think about what Wilson has said to me, how he blames me for what has happened with Molly, which makes no sense at all. For a moment, I decide I hate him and wonder where this comes from. Have I ever loved him? I can't remember. What I can remember are the times he made me so angry I wanted to scream.

I let the screen door slam when I go back inside and find myself staring at the wall, imagining a dent in the plaster that isn't here in the kitchen but is still visible in Molly's room, damaged when it was her nursery. Those months waiting for Molly to be born had become almost unbearable. Wilson hated his job at the bank, spent most of his free time at the diner and the bars with his buddies, watching whatever games were on the wide-screen TVs that were on every wall, coming home late, leaving early for breakfast with "the guys" at the diner.

I hadn't realized it then, but today I can see how I had spent so much of my pregnancy angry, biting my lower lip, careful what I did, and what I said to him. Surely there were clues then that I was not happy, but I never once framed it as my unhappiness, only as a worry about his, and how I could make life better for him. I had encouraged him to go out with his friends more, without acknowledging how lonely I had become as I got bigger and bigger and he stayed away more and more.

The only time Wilson seemed to get invested in Molly's

arrival was when the question of gender came up. I told him I wanted to wait, that I enjoyed the mystery of not knowing, wondering if a little baby girl or a boy was floating around in my tummy. I played with names in my head, spelled them out on paper napkins and shared them with Barb when she came to visit. I had no idea Wilson even cared, until one day when I had an ultrasound scheduled, he insisted he would come with me. He'd never gone to any of the other appointments, so I was shocked, and pleased even, that he was taking an interest.

At the clinic, I awkwardly climbed up on the table and waited for the doctor to come in. When he walked into the room, he greeted me with a little pat on my knees and a cursory nod toward Wilson. Standing next to the bed on my left, my husband's eyes were bright as he watched the fuzzy black and white screen of the ultrasound flicker, squeezing my hand as though nervous about what we were about to see. I thought we were both thrilled to see the shape of an actual baby, the doctor pointing out the head, legs, and arms, the umbilical cord floating around in my womb. Every time I saw it, I was so amazed, at a loss for words. Wilson seemed enthralled as well, breaking the quiet in the office as we stared at the screen.

"So, what is it, Doc? We both want to know if it's a boy or a girl. We can't wait, can you tell us? What can you see?"

I was appalled. Had Wilson not heard me say I didn't want to know the gender, that I wanted to wait and be surprised, or did he just decide to ignore what I wanted? I was the one carrying this baby, didn't I have the choice of knowing or not? I wanted to scream at Wilson to stop, but the doctor heard the excitement in my husband's voice and believed that we both wanted to know. So, after some minutes of gliding the wand around the baby's private region, he told us he wasn't sure, but he didn't see any evidence of a penis.

"I can't be certain, you know, because it might not be visible, but I'm thinking at this late date, it might be a pretty good guess that you're having a girl. Don't hold me to that, though, because they can always surprise us."

I was stunned. I had not realized I truly wanted to have a little girl, but in that moment, I was thrilled. I knew it wasn't conclusive, but I could clearly imagine having a girl. I looked up at Wilson to see his face change from a big grin to something I hardly recognized. I could tell he was not happy with the thought that our baby was a girl. He released my hand and walked over to look out at the parking lot. The doctor didn't notice and left the room, reminding me to return in a week, now that I was in my ninth month. I awkwardly got down from the table without any help from Wilson, who was still staring out the window.

"Well, then," he said, in a flat tone I hardly recognized. "Guess I'll have to paint the nursery pink," and with that, we left for home.

That afternoon, Wilson went out and bought the most lurid shade of pink I had ever seen. It wasn't just pink, it was bubble gum pink, and he spent the rest of the day painting the room, without once asking my opinion. Things definitely didn't get any better after that, and I kept quiet, picking my battles, hoping to get past the storm. What did it matter, really? I convinced myself the important thing was that he was painting the room. How bad can it be? It was bad. The ugliest room I'd ever seen. It hurt my eyes every time I went in there and made me wish I could find a way to change the color. I never did, and Molly's room is still pink.

I tried to forget about the paint. I was nine months pregnant, due to deliver any day, struggling through my days with the extra weight. I was anxious about the birth and disgusted with my slow, sluggish body. So much still needed to be done, and I couldn't do a lot of it. Wilson did not seem to share my anxiety, nor my excitement, about the impending birth. We never once sat together on the sofa, or stretched out on our bed, imagining together the arrival of our new baby. I found myself wondering why that might be, but feared looking at it too closely, not wanting to know the answer.

Wilson got angry and resentful when I asked him to do

things that were more and more difficult for me to handle, large as I was, my back aching every minute of the day. After painting the nursery, he ignored my pleas that he put the crib together or hang the mobile, bring down my old cradle from the attic, and put a dimmer on the lights to make them softer for Molly, which was what I had decided to call our baby. Wilson said he didn't care what we named her and left it at that. He kept telling me I was rushing it, that he had plenty of time to do these things after we brought the baby home, that I worried too much. "Chill," he'd say, which always made me angrier than I already was. I literally thought I might explode into a million little pieces all over the nursery.

Thinking these things were important to get done, and Wilson obviously not interested in doing them, I decided to do them myself. One day when Wilson was at the bank, I carefully opened the large box that sat in the nursery and laid out all the pieces on the floor. Feeling proud of myself, I lined up the screws, got a Phillips screwdriver from the garage, and proceeded to put it together myself. I thought I'd done a good job, although in the end, I could tell the corners weren't square, and the crib wobbled a bit, when I touched it with my finger.

*Damn, damn, double damn,* I mumbled to myself, while I waited for Wilson to come back. I left the disaster of the crib in the nursery, shut the door, and took the cardboard out to the recycling bin. Then, I made my way to the kitchen to start cooking dinner, knowing this wasn't going to go well when he got home. Even though I knew he would not be pleased, I was not prepared for the rage that slid over his face when he saw the lop-sided crib standing in the corner of the room.

"What the fuck, Alice. What the fuck have you done? Why can't you leave well enough alone? I told you I would do it, didn't I? I told you I'd do it!"

I was astonished when he turned on me, slapped my face hard, and pushed me against the far wall. I fell backwards and slid down the wall, sitting in a heap on the floor. Wilson did not offer to help me back up. He marched out of the room shaking his head, continuing to berate me as he waved the screwdriver over his head, as though he was going to hit something with it. He threw it against the wall, where it left a dent in the new pink paint and bounced to the floor. I watched him leave the room, relieved he wasn't moving toward me, thankful he threw the screwdriver into the corner and not in my direction. His voice lingered as he stormed out.

"Goddamn woman, bitch, bitch, bitch. Just couldn't wait till I got around to it. I said I was going to do it, but no, you had to go ahead and fuck it up yourself. Now, I'll have to take the whole damn thing apart and start all over."

I heard the back door slam and the sound of Wilson's truck starting up. He left the driveway in a hurry, screeching the tires and scattering the gravel, something I had never heard him do before. I sat on the floor for a few minutes before I began the process of moving my enormous bulk into a position where I could possibly get up. It took a while, but I pulled up on the door handle, hoping it wouldn't break off and managed to pull myself upright. I was breathing heavily and stood there shaking, while my panic subsided. I paused to make sure I wasn't hurt and that everything was all right with the baby. We both seemed okay, but I could still feel the sting of Wilson's slap. My face crumpled and tears ran down my cheeks.

I heard the door open again, hoping maybe Wilson had thought better of his actions and had come back to apologize. Of course, it wasn't him. It was Robert, who had seen the truck leave in a hurry and was worried that maybe I was in labor.

"What's going on, Sis? Is the baby coming?" His concern was genuine. He knew me perhaps better than anyone, and he was always protective of me.

"Was that Wilson? What's his rush? Everything okay?"

I tried to assure him that things were fine. I needed to downplay what had happened. I wiped my eyes and grabbed a tissue to blow my nose.

"I fucked up," I told my brother with a shrug. "He's pissed, but he'll get over it."

"What'd you do? Burn dinner? Why's he so hot-headed these days? It's you got to carry around that extra load, not him."

Instead of explaining, I decided to show him what I had done. I nodded down the hall toward the nursery, where the mangled crib leaned toward the far wall, exactly where Wilson had pushed it in disgust.

"I asked him and asked him to get the crib ready, but he says we got plenty of time, that I worry too much. So, today, while he was at work, I took it out of the box and tried to put it together myself. I was really proud of myself, but, as you can see, I didn't do such a great job. It tilts, and I couldn't get it to straighten out. When he saw it, he lost his mind. I've never seen him so angry. I had no idea he would react that way. And then—"

I stopped. I was not sure I wanted to tell Robert that Wilson had slapped me, had pushed me down against the wall, and left me on the floor. The last thing I wanted was to pit my brother against my husband, so I decided not to say anything more. But Robert had heard the "and then—"

"and then—what?" He demanded.

"—and then—and then, he marched out of the house and left in a big huff, mad as hell, that's what!"

My brother stared at me for a long minute, his eyes scanning my body, my face, my clothing, my hair, until he was satisfied that Wilson had not touched me. I was relieved to think the slap had not left any noticeable marks, although my observant brother had certainly noticed my flushed face and heavy breathing. He didn't say anything, just reached over to grab the screwdriver, walked to the lopsided crib and adjusted the screws until it stood firm and steady. Without another word, he handed me the screwdriver and walked back to the kitchen, leaving through the same door he'd come in thirty minutes earlier. I called out a big "thank you," as I waved to my brother and pulled out the pots and pans to fix dinner.

But Wilson did not come home for dinner. In fact, I was not certain when he got home late that night or in the early hours of the morning. I had not been able to fall asleep when I fell into bed, after I had wrapped up his dinner in foil and left it on the counter, cleaned the pans, and eaten a small mound of mashed potatoes myself. But the day must have caught up with me, and I eventually fell into an uneasy sleep, deep enough not to hear him when he decided to come home. The next morning, Wilson had already left when I got out of bed. We did not talk about the crib that day, or at any time after. I was a bit worried about what Wilson would think or do if he discovered that Robert had fixed my botched job, but I never brought it up, and Wilson seemed to forget the whole thing. I didn't, but I had no idea what to do about it.

I realize my little trip down memory lane isn't going to help my mood one bit, so I try to put Wilson out of my mind and head for the bathroom, silently thanking Robert again for fixing the water heater. Tonight, I decide, we'll have fun. Molly and I will take a bath together. I turn on the faucets and go to get Molly from her room, making a big deal out of how we'll sit in the warm water, creating soap bubbles and dunking our heads to get them wet.

When I help Molly into the tub, it pains me to see how much her legs have atrophied. Her strong, growing legs have become thin and weak. I try not to let her see me looking at her body as I help her sit down. Supporting her as she sits, I slide behind like two kids on a sled, but Molly is not in the mood to play. Obedient, I quietly soap and wash her carefully, shampoo her hair, and dry her off with a soft towel. I help my sleepy girl back into her room and put her gently on the bed, helping her pull on her too-small pajamas. She smiles weakly at me as I lean over with a goodnight kiss and vow to get her new pajamas as soon as I can.

Hoping in some way to connect with Molly better, I sit for a few extra minutes on the edge of the bed and decide to talk with her about our trips and the many doctors we have seen. Even though I know she is tired, I am hoping this might be a good time to talk with her about what is going on. We chat for a while about our "road trips," what was fun and what wasn't, about the motel beds when we stay overnight, some are big and fluffy and other places they are hard and flat. We agree the best things about travel are the swimming pools and the hot tubs—pools for Molly, tubs for me. I casually ask Molly what she thinks is going on with her body.

"Molly, I know this has all been exhausting for both of us. You've been really brave to go with me to all these doctors and hospitals, putting up with all those tests."

She nods her sleepy head in agreement. I move on cautiously, hoping to get her to talk before she falls asleep. It is her body we are talking about, after all, so I take the plunge.

"So, my dear, what do *you* think is going on with your legs? Do you have anything you can add about what's going on with you? Is there anything you need to tell me? Anything you are confused about? Do you know why your legs just quit working?"

I sit still on the bed and wait for her to respond. I feel a bit shaky asking what she thinks, but what if she has some inkling about the changes in her body, something she hasn't told me or the doctors?

She doesn't answer.

"Molly, do you know what depressed means?"

She nods her head, but not in a convincing way. I decide to push it a little more.

"Do you feel depressed, sad, or lonely, Molly?"

I get only a blank stare. Molly seems clueless.

"Is it because Daddy is gone so much? Is it because he doesn't come home very often? Does that make you sad?"

Again, Molly does not make a move, although she has not closed her eyes.

I am desperate. I am thinking fast and speaking faster, no longer calm.

"Has someone hurt you, Molly? Did you fall and I didn't know it, or I didn't realize you were hurt? Were you ashamed to tell me or just forget?"

I watch her face closely for reactions, search her eyes for recognition, for some knowledge I can't fathom, some door that might open to help me understand my daughter. But Molly seems disinterested, unconcerned. She is drifting off to sleep, her cheeks pink from the bath, a tiny smile on her lips. Lying there, she does not seem broken or disabled. She seems content, as though she has not a care in the world. I gaze at her face, her sweet breath growing deeper. I watch her fall asleep, then quietly walk away, flipping off the light but leaving the door open, so I can hear her movements throughout the night.

I wander around the house turning off all the lights and checking the locks on the doors. I straighten the sheets on my own bed and crawl in, reminding myself to throw all the bedding in the wash tomorrow. I place my head on the pillow on my side of the bed, facing the side where my husband should be sleeping soundly next to me. I lie in my bed reminding my body to relax, begging my muscles to let go. I order my mind not to reel in circles, but that only makes my thoughts spin more. I will myself to fall asleep, but that doesn't happen either. I am still awake when Molly cries out. I lie down beside her. I stare at the ceiling in her room, watching the shadows around us shift and fade until the watery light of dawn creeps into her room. Exhausted, I get up, wrap myself in my old robe, made soft with years of washings, shuffle to the kitchen, and make coffee.

I have begun to think more seriously about what that doctor said about my relationship with Wilson. I agree we are definitely in a rut and going nowhere. His last few visits have been painful to endure. I hate it when he blames me for Molly's problems, saying they wouldn't have happened if he'd been home to take care of things. *So, why aren't you home, Wilson?* I want to ask. It's not true that things wouldn't be in such a mess if you were here, but let's test that, okay, why don't you just decide to be here, with us, as a family? What would that look like? Are you even interested in finding out? I decide we need to have that conversation about the future as soon as possible. Tonight, when Molly goes to bed, I will call his number again and beg him to call me.

It's important, I tell his answering machine, but he doesn't call me back.

# Chapter 6

## Wilson Calls

During the day, I know I am watching my daughter too closely, noting her shifting moods, her odd behavior, what she wants to talk about and when. The wheelchair we ordered with the help of the physical therapist has never materialized, so Molly really cannot go back to school yet. At first, I resent this extra labor of teaching Molly, thinking I am not trained to do this. On the other hand, I am encouraged to think we are developing a closer relationship. We are definitely spending more time together. Sometimes we laugh about nothing in particular and talk about things other than the state assignments. I support Molly, big as she is, when we go out into the yard to sit on an old quilt under the trees and listen to the birds. We make lists of the birdcalls we recognize and wonder about those we don't know. I order a bird book, and we learn to document each bird we hear or see, writing down when, where, and what time of day. We learn my phone can help us identify bird calls, and this is fun for Molly. We create our own lesson plans together for history, social studies, and English. I make certain our plans are coordinated with the quarter tests Molly is required to take. She passes them all.

Some days, I get the feeling there is but a thin membrane between Molly's brain and my own. If only I could cross it and understand what is going on in her mind. I have heard nothing from Wilson since his last visit, not even a phone call to check on Molly. My resentment toward him grows and festers, and it begins to influence the way I sometimes interact with Molly. I hate it when I become anxious and snap at her when she won't do her lessons correctly or on time. The least she could do is cooperate, I find myself thinking, given that I have given up everything, my job, my friends, my own life, possibly my husband, to sit and help her almost every minute of every day. But just as quickly, I deeply regret all these thoughts and turn back to care for Molly. At night, I leave messages in the dark for Wilson. "Please call me back. We need to talk. It's important. It's about Molly." Wilson doesn't call.

During the hottest days, when Molly grows weary of her lessons by noon and asks to leave the house and go to Robert's house for a while, I agree. I always feel a bit jealous that she wants to be with Robert, until I realize I need a break, too, and she needs someone else's attention. It won't hurt her a bit to watch some silly cartoons and play card games with Robert for a change. I could use a nap, too, since my nights are always disrupted, or maybe I'll call and see if Barb can come visit for a while. Wandering around my empty house, I think about the fact that none of us—Robert, Molly, or me, has many friends. Even Barb doesn't seem to have friends other than me. Why is that? I don't have a clue.

As usual, we share our light dinner with Robert before he takes an early exit and bids us goodnight. After Molly falls asleep, no doubt dreaming of dolphins swimming in the ocean, I decide I'm not ready to go to bed and watch a television show alone in the dark living room. I don't do this often, but tonight it feels good to lose myself in a drama that isn't my own. I miss the ending, though, when my head leans against the cushions, and I fall into an unusually deep sleep.

Hours later, I realize with a jolt that my phone is ringing. *Thank God, finally*! I raise my head and open my eyes, anxious not to miss what I know is a call from Wilson. I shake my head to clear it and move toward the cell phone charging at the end of the kitchen counter. I see Wilson's name flash across the screen and wonder why it has taken him this long to call. Has he even listened to my many messages? I pick up the phone and note the time: 12:30 am.

"Yes?" My voice is dry. I am tired and have little energy to carry this conversation by myself. I can hear breathing on the line, but he doesn't speak right away.

I repeat myself, "Hello? Who's this?"

But I know. Of course, I know it is Wilson. I wonder what game he thinks he's playing. For God's sake, it's after midnight.

I want to scream into the phone, ask him why the fuck he hasn't returned my calls, tell him how much I've come to hate him for abandoning us, for not asking about Molly. But, instead, I wait to hear what he has to say, before I can question him about our future.

"Hey, Babe," my husband finally speaks.

Long pause. I'm thinking, *what's all this "babe" shit?*

"Guess there's no easy way to say this," he pauses to clear his throat.

I recognize his nervousness, but I won't let him off the hook. He knows I can wait him out, so he begins to talk too fast.

"I'm really sorry to call like this out of the blue with bad news, well, good news for me, I guess. I just got a job offer to go manage some potato farms in Idaho. I met the owner of this new company, and he plans to move some of his operations to the Bootheel, over by Benton, because the sand would be a good place to grow potatoes, they figure. So, he's offering me a contract for five years, three in Idaho and two back in Missouri, as head of operations, which I'm thinking I would like to do, something different, you know?"

Silence. I sit quietly, hardly breathing.

"Babe? You still there?"

"I'm here." My voice is flat, giving nothing away.

"And there's another thing. Up here, near Lancaster, where I've been working for about a year, I've met a good woman who would like to, you know, get married and all. She also works for the company, in the office, billing and stuff. She's a lot of fun, so I'm thinking I'll give it a try."

I can hardly breathe. I milk the silence, mostly because I can't find my voice. A hot flush crawls up my neck and sweat slowly begins to roll down my back. I cannot imagine what he'll say next. He's flustered, now, talking even faster.

"Well, Babe, she knows about you, knows about Molly, sends her regrets about Molly being sick and all. She's a real good woman, Babe, and she would like to go to Idaho with me. 'I'm up for an adventure,' she says. It would be fun, we've decided, to leave Missouri and go somewhere new. Maybe we won't ever come back, who knows."

More silence. I cannot stand up any longer. I creep with the phone over to the table, so I can sit down in a chair. My ears are ringing and bile hits the back of my throat. I'm afraid I will collapse, slide onto the kitchen floor.

"Babe?"

Wilson keeps checking to see if I am still listening. He's not sure I am, but he plunges forward anyway, hoping to get through this phone call with the least amount of trouble.

"So, okay. Maureen's brother, that's her name, Maureen, her brother is a small-town lawyer up in Perryville, and he says he can draw up quick and legal divorce papers for us right away. He says he'll have them delivered directly to your front door. You can sign them while the messenger waits, then you only have to file the papers at the county courthouse in Benton. Can you do that? Of course, I will send money. I'll always send money to help you and Molly along. I want to do right by you both. I really do. I didn't want it to come to this. I didn't see it coming, I really didn't. I guess these things just happen sometimes. One day, there she was, and the rest is history, as they say."

Wilson stops talking.

I continue to wait.

"Babe? You got any questions? You feeling okay? I know this must be such a surprise. I'm sorry about that, but I figure a clean break is just what I need, a clean break. No hard feelings, right? Of course, I'm leaving you the house and all the stuff in it. Only fair. Maureen has put aside some money, and I've saved some, too, here and there, so we'll be okay setting up a place near Boise, near the potato fields."

"Okay, that's basically it. 'Gotta go. Someone from the lawyer should be over soon enough. I'll give him my phone numbers, and he will be able to send you our new address.

"Oh, I nearly forgot. Say hi to Molly for me, and bye, too, I guess for now. I'm sure I'll see her along the way."

Silence. He can't seem to let it go.

"Well, I guess that's about it. See you around. Bye now."

He waits a bit in the silence on the line, but I don't speak. I hear the click as he severs the line on his end, but I cannot let go, my fingers clenched around the phone in my hand. I sit in the dead house and refuse to hang up the phone. My eyes burn as a fire ignites inside of my head. I do not feel sad. I feel angry, deep, searing anger at the man who could do this to us. I'd known for a while our marriage wasn't going anywhere, but I hadn't seen this coming. All the air has been sucked out of the room, leaving me sitting in a blurry vacuum. Finally, I release the phone and place it face down on the counter, stifling a scream. My mind is thinking what I wished I had said to him:

*What an asshole to call me up and lay this on me in a phone call! What a terrible excuse of a husband and father you are to tell me you've met another woman, you want to go off with her, and there is nothing to discuss. You aren't a teenager breaking up with a disposable girlfriend, you are a married man with responsibilities, a house that needs repairs, a mortgage, a disabled child, and bills piling up on the side table.*

*This makes me wonder why you came home last month and actually tried to help with Molly. You knew then what you were going to do, didn't you? You were trying to absolve your guilt for leaving us, for leaving Molly with no help for her legs. You are a snake, an evil, evil snake, not a man at all.*

I blow my nose and wipe my face with a dirty towel. No longer sleepy, I let myself question why I ever married Wilson Campbell. Had he ever been supportive, kind, generous, funny, easy, loving? How many times in our years together has he disappointed me, called me incompetent, told me to "Chill?"

Without warning, I am transported back in time to a different room. I am propped up in a hospital bed, the smells around me rank with blood and antiseptic, machines beep and whir, someone drops a metal bedpan in the hallway, curses. My mind has returned to the day Molly was born, remembering what Wilson said to me that broke my heart and should have convinced me, then, I'd made a big mistake. But what can you do with that on the day your child is born?

My water broke at home exactly on my due date. Wilson was quick to grab the bags I had prepared and left just inside the door. Together we made our way to the car, and he drove me to the hospital, as he had promised. Once I was settled in, though, he left the room, looking for coffee, he said. I knew the next stage might take a long time, so I didn't worry that he'd disappeared. I actually didn't know if Wilson would want to be present during the birth. We'd never talked about it, but now it seemed like he ought to be there with me. After a few hours, I began to worry about where he'd gone. At the very least, I needed him close by.

My contractions were slow and not too strong during

the early evening hours. All very reasonable and expected, the nurses told me, as they documented each one. I spent my time walking down the hall and back with an aide, who seemed to have all the time in the world to spend with me. She was a big girl, plump and friendly, and she was sensitive to what I needed. She let me talk when I needed to talk and respected my silence when the contractions took over.

I learned later that Wilson had gone to a bar after finding coffee and spent a few hours with his friends, drinking too much, until his buddies warned him he needed to get back to the hospital and be with his wife. "You need to get back over there, dude," they'd told him, speaking from experience. "She'll never let you forget it, if you're not there. She'll give you shit forever, man." Wilson finally understood what they were saying to him and left the bar. He actually loved to tell this part of the story. He thought it was funny, his buddies telling him to "get your butt back to the hospital, or you'll regret it."

As it turned out, by the time Wilson had returned to the hospital, Molly had arrived, not as we had expected, but by an emergency C-section, her umbilical cord wrapped around her neck. Instead of Wilson, a nurse had held my hand and reassured me that things were going to be fine. The doctor rolled me over for the spinal block that preceded the surgery, and I watched as he made a tent over the lower half of my body so I couldn't watch what came next. He asked where my husband was, but nobody seemed to know. That was the last thing I remember. When they lifted Molly over the tent and handed her to me, I was so woozy, I could hardly hold her. The nurse took her away, and I fell fast asleep. When I woke up, Wilson was in the room looking down at me in the bed.

I tried to smile as he took in my body, the sheets, the blood, the heavy bandages, my legs wrapped in yards of tape, the IVs, and the beeping monitors. I was self-conscious about how I must look to him and surely he knew this, but my husband did not hold back the very first words that came out of his mouth.

"Well, I should have known you couldn't get this right, Alice. I should have known you'd fuck this up, too."

I was stunned. Big, fat tears rolled from my eyes. My body was one pulsating mound of pain, my mind a haze from the drugs I'd been given, my baby had been taken away, and Wilson was standing over me criticizing me for the poor job I'd done giving birth. I remember wishing I could kill him. I hated him that much. Of course, I couldn't even raise my arm, so instead I turned away and let the tears slide into my ears, muffling the noises in the room and in my head.

My mind returns to the kitchen, startled that I had disappeared into that day of blood and tears. I shake my head like a wet dog to scatter the raw truth of my husband's callous dismissal of his family and decide I must take action. I refuse to accept his judgment that I am a failure, not capable of doing anything right, that any of this is my fault. I remind myself that I've done a pretty good job taking care of our life, the house, Molly's problems, my driving fears that have plagued me for years. If Wilson can dispose of us without a thought, then I can go after whatever is available for Molly and me to survive without him. This chapter is finished, and I want to be the one to slam the door. I will not cry or grovel ever again. I gather my resolve and brace myself for whatever happens next.

My anger fuels my resolve, but my thoughts arrive with a litany of questions. This time, however, my thoughts are not fractured and anxious. With a clear head, I formulate a plan about what I must do, sorting through the questions as they come to me. I write each one down on a 3 x 5 card I had stashed in the bedside table for bookmarks, numbering them in order of importance.

*1. Should I get a lawyer, now, and question Wilson's plans for a quick and dirty divorce?*

*2. Where and how would I find a lawyer? The internet? Who could I call now to get some information?*

*3. How could I pay for a lawyer?*

*4. How can I trust that Wilson will "send money," whatever I need? (What a crock. I absolutely do not believe that. Maybe he'll have to pay for my lawyer, too? Who would know about that?)*

*5. What legal standing do I have? Even though I never made nearly as much as he did, in Missouri don't I get half of what we own and half of his salary going forward? Can a lawyer help me get money from him?*

*6. Can I sue him for abandonment of me and our child?*

Later, after taking Molly to the toilet, I am surprised when I see no blood in the water. It is her time, yet I haven't seen any blood all day. Concerned, I watch closely for the full week following, all the way up to her birthday. I feel super silly watching Molly's urine so closely, but I can't help myself. I have been marking the calendar with a large "X" when I see blood in her urine, and I showed her how she should mark her periods on the calendar herself, to keep track. I tell her this is something she will have to do the rest of her life, because it is always important.

When she does not start her period when I expect, I mark her calendar with a giant "0" to indicate no blood on a day when she should have started. Perhaps my idea that the flow might just stop hadn't been so crazy after all. That would be great. Just slow down and allow my little girl to catch up with her body. She is already dealing with so much. Molly certainly doesn't need to be a "woman" as well. I sigh a breath of relief that perhaps the situation has resolved itself, although I vow to keep watching, just in case.

Friday comes, and Robert and I do the best we can to celebrate Molly's birthday in the ways she has requested. He brings a box of chocolate donuts over for breakfast in the morning after she wakes up. He leaves for a few hours while Molly and I play games and watch a favorite documentary on television, one she has watched with Robert several times. At lunch, we drive to McDonald's in Robert's truck, and Molly orders chicken nuggets with fries and a chocolate shake. The weather is nice, so we sit outside at the red picnic table and enjoy our fast food together. On the way home, Robert plays loud music on the radio with all the windows rolled down, and this time Molly doesn't complain when she hears Creedence Clearwater Revival or The Rolling Stones blasting into the truck and out the windows.

At the Carnival, things are not quite so easy. Robert and I try our best to help her walk around, but on the rough ground of the fields where the rides have been set up, it's pretty slow going trying to support her on each side. What she loves best, though, are the rides. We take turns going on the various rides with her, then we all three climb into the box of the Ferris wheel, twice. After that, she agrees she's ready to go home, a happy girl.

When it's time for bed, I give Molly a dark red satiny nightgown wrapped in silver paper that has no bears or clowns on it. She frowns at the color of the gown, but I quickly explain I couldn't find a purple one. The gown fits her in every way except for the hem. It's much too long, so I tell her I can hem it up tomorrow, and it will be perfect. When she puts it on and looks in the mirror, she seems pleased. As she crawls into bed, we make plans to go to Cape Girardeau the following Monday to look for books she wants to buy. It's hard to believe my little girl is ten. That night she doesn't have any nightmares, and, luckily, she doesn't wet her bed or soil her new gown.

# Chapter 7

## No Blood

Several days go by, then a week, but Molly's period does not return. I keep marking her calendar, thinking any day the flow will make an appearance. It doesn't. Twenty-eight days later, when Molly still does not bleed, I convince myself it was all a mistake. I go to bed, happy to know she's still a little girl, and all this was just a fluke.

In bed, though, the questions start sliding through my mind. Why would her periods just stop? Could this be just one more indication that something else is wrong with Molly? Do any dreadful diseases cause menses to start, then stop? How could this be connected to her legs not working? That doesn't make any sense at all. And, if there's something else going on, what could it be that no medical tests have identified? And there's more—where does her bedwetting and nightmares fit into this equation? Why is Molly regressing to toddler behaviors at the age of nine, now ten?

I cannot find any logical connections between these bizarre facts and trying to makes me realize how weary I am. My brain is fried. I must stop this constant barrage of questions before I go crazy. I lie down in my own bed and will myself to fall asleep.

Suddenly, my eyes open wide in the still darkness. I sit bolt upright in my bed, shove all the covers to the floor, and stand up straight, my entire body shaking.

*What am I thinking? Periods do not just "stop and take a break." Am I delusional?*

My hands reach for my throat and gather there, as if to choke out my own life. I catch myself, releasing my hands to settle on my stomach, clenched as though to protect myself from a blow. Before I can name my fear, I feel the punch of disgust in my stomach. I bend over and feel the blood run to my head. I nearly pass out with the new thoughts that flush through my brain faster than I can decipher them.

This is not that difficult to figure out. Molly's periods had been regular for months. If they suddenly stop, what could that mean? This isn't rocket science, and it isn't connected to anything orthopedic, or even, maybe, psychological. It's biology, pure and simple. Every girl on the planet has to learn the importance of keeping track of her monthly bleeding, once she has "become a woman." If her blood does not arrive on time, if her panties are not pink or red around 28 days of her cycle, she is taught to suspect that she may be pregnant—whether or not she wants to be, no matter if she is married or not, or disabled, no matter her race, or religion, or circumstance, she is taught to always pay attention to what is happening in her body. Her blood is the canary in the mine. She comes to trust that it will come, and it will go, month after month, no matter what, unless she's pregnant. Her periods are the markers of her life as a woman. They become her monthly calendar. She will plan life around them, always tuned to when she should not wear white pants, or go to the pool, or have sex, or go to work with the cramps. She learns to carry a bag, a purse, or a backpack with emergency pads and tampons tucked neatly away in discreet zippered pouches, always, just in case.

And when her blood does not arrive when it should, every

girl's brain is conditioned to wonder or worry. She learns the basic math of when to start counting her days of flow, noticing when it stops, how long it's been since her last period, when it is supposed to start again. Month after month for the rest of her life she is tuned in this way to her body, until she grows old and is no longer able to get pregnant and her periods stop, never to return. All this, because she knows that a missed period can utterly change her life, forever. No matter whether she is young, single, in school, traveling, married without children, married with several children, divorced, wealthy or poor, it doesn't matter. Wondering and worrying will take up most of her brain space for days or weeks if she suspects she might be pregnant. Going to the pharmacy to buy a pregnancy test is a nerve-wracking journey at the best of times, a torture the rest of the time.

Waiting to see if those two pink lines appear can be the longest minute of a girl's life. A pregnancy is monumental. In many cases she knows she will have to deal with the pregnancy by herself, in others she knows her partner will be happy and supportive, in some she will understand her partner will not be happy about it and could be angry with her, or leave, which may or may not be heartbreaking for her. In any case, those two lines will alter her life in ways she can't even imagine, and no matter what her situation is, a pregnancy will have a larger impact on her than on her partner, not only in terms of her daily life going forward, but in terms of being a mother, a caregiver, both physically and emotionally, for the rest of her life. She will have major decisions to make from the moment she sees those two lines. Should she stay pregnant or should she not? For weeks, she may sit with these questions and ponder them long into the night, losing sleep. Yet, the clock is ticking. She knows she has only a narrow window to think about what she wants to do. The laws of the country dictate how long she has to make up her mind. She cannot forget for even a minute what is going on in her body. Her mornings may be filled with nausea and vomiting, while she makes her decision. If she wishes to abort, she must decide whether or not to share her decision with her partner, if she has one. She knows she has limited time to make these decisions, and no matter what, she needs to know about local clinics that can help her, whether they are nearby, or if she will have to travel to get assistance. Week after week her options are changing. She's running out of time.

Now, I'm fully awake. My brain has been working overtime. Suddenly, I have perhaps the first truly political thought I've ever had. THIS is why women protesters carry signs that say: "KEEP YOUR HANDS OFF MY BODY." They know *no man* understands what every woman knows. No man has ever had to worry about how even one night of sex could change his life. No man has ever had to track a monthly flow of blood and worry about whether he is pregnant or not. If he chooses to do so, every man can walk away. A woman can never, ever walk away. She carries the problem within her, literally. It has already become a part of her. "She" and "it" are one and the same, not yet divisible.

I rush to the toilet and throw up everything in my stomach, as though I am pregnant myself, even though I know I'm not.

I vomit because I have failed Molly. I did not explain to her in clear terms what starting her periods actually signaled about the changes in her body. I should have explained what activities are sexual, and how and why these acts could cause her to get pregnant. It was not enough to merely tell her the monthly blood flow meant her body was maturing faster than most girls, that it was perfectly normal, and that the signs of her early maturation included her other bodily changes—her emerging breasts, her pubic hair. All of this is true, of course, but it was my job to explain the rest of it to my daughter, and I did not do that. By my neglect and cowardice, I left my daughter vulnerable.

And all of that is only half of it. I still don't know what has happened to Molly, and who has done things to, or with, her.

When I have recovered slightly and can straighten my

body, I force myself to walk to Molly's room on padded feet. I stand over her for a very long time, silently asking her questions I am afraid she cannot answer. I try to talk to her through my mind—from mine to hers, but my questions are not coherent.

*Could you be pregnant, Molly? Can you tell me why this could even be possible? You must know something has happened to you. Or is that true, would you know what happened, if something did happen to you? Could you speak of the act, even to me? Would you have the words to say it? Could you possibly not know what has happened to you? Of course, that could be true. You might not have any idea what has happened that caused you to be pregnant, but you must know something.*

Finally, I allow my brain to settle on the most horrifying words, the ones no mother can ever imagine thinking.

*Who has touched you, Molly? Who?*

I nearly faint from the pain of those words.

A short list of possible suspects flits through my mind. I discard each one as they come into view. The boy from school who brings her library books and stays to talk a while, sitting next to her wheelchair, looking awkward.

The math teacher who brings her weekly math homework sheets and goes over them with her. He's a creep, but I can't imagine him managing to touch her while they go through the problems she did incorrectly.

The slimy pastor with too much hair gel, who drops by unannounced to invite them, yet again, to come to church. He always makes a point of going into Molly's bedroom and patting her on the shoulder and asking if she wants him to pray for her. She always declines, politely, and I'm always glad to see him go.

I stand over her and watch her sleep peacefully, a quiet smile on her face, wishing she would wake up and talk to me. I am frayed from repeating the questions I cannot ask and my daughter cannot hear. In this moment, she appears happy and content, like a young girl should, as though she can forget that her legs don't work, as though nothing is happening inside her body. I am glad Molly sleeps so peacefully tonight, but I know this cannot last. If she is pregnant, then everything will change. I try to convince myself I am strong enough to do this.

I do not go back to bed. Instead, I sit at the kitchen table all night and watch the light change from blue-black to light purple to orange blush as the sun brightens my kitchen. No part of me is eager for this day to begin, but I am ready now to become the mother I should have been months ago.

At exactly 8:00, I drive to the local pharmacy on the corner of the next street and buy a pregnancy test. Then I go home, make coffee, cook bacon for breakfast, and wake Molly, telling her we need to talk.

"Wow, Mom, what's the special occasion? You made bacon, that's new on a weekday. What's got into you?"

"Well, I got up early and couldn't go back to sleep, so I thought it would be nice to make a good breakfast for both of us. We need to have a serious conversation, and I figure that's always easier on a happy stomach. What do you think?"

"Sure. Works for me. What's the plan? Another trip to another doctor? Ugh. How far away will this one be?"

"Well, yes and no. I think we will be going to another doctor soon, but I'm hoping this visit can be more local. But first, I need to explain why we'll have to go."

Molly starts eating the slices of bacon as though this is just another conversation while I make the eggs. I fill my plate, but I can't eat a thing.

"Molly, we talked about how to mark your calendar on the days when your periods start, right? Lately, you may have noticed that I've put a big zero on the days you don't bleed, when you should have. Right? You've seen me do this. I am sorry, but I didn't explain to you why that is really important. I'm sorry, because it is now obvious that I should be talking to you a lot more about what's going on in your body."

"Okay?" Molly isn't sure where this is going.

"What I failed to explain to you, Molly, is that once a girl starts her period, she technically becomes a woman, at least physically, and what that means is that she will bleed every month for the rest of her normal life, that is, until she's older and doesn't bleed anymore. The reason she keeps track of her periods is because she is now, as a woman, capable of becoming pregnant."

I'm watching her face carefully, hoping she will stay with me and not freak out.

"That little 'egg' I told you about—the one your body creates each month and then gets rid of during your monthly period—*could* be fertilized. That means, if you have any very close touching of your private parts with those of a boy or man, his sperm could enter your body through your vagina and fertilize that little egg, causing you to become pregnant. Do you follow me?"

"Not really, but okay. What's this got to do with me?"

"I know this is unusual stuff to talk about, and I wasn't very smart not to explain more of it to you when you started your periods. Frankly, the fact that you're so young made it hard for me to talk about it or even imagine that it would be possible for you to become pregnant. But now that your periods have stopped, it's clear that I should have told you more then."

"Why? What are you talking about?"

"This is simple biology. I know, and you know, that you are not really a 'woman.' You are still a ten-year-old girl. That hasn't changed. What has changed is that as a girl who has monthly periods, your body is actually mature enough to get pregnant. Our biology, unfortunately, doesn't ask us if we're ready. It just keeps moving on, even if we don't know what's happening or what 'could' happen.

"So, it's possible that, unknown to you or me, some actions by a boy or a man could have resulted in making you pregnant."

Molly's face scrunches up, "What are you talking about?"

"I know, I know. Please just stay with me here."

I take a deep breath and plunge forward.

"You may or may not be pregnant, Molly, but it could be one obvious reason why your periods have stopped. I know it seems like the most unlikely thing you could ever imagine, but, please, hear me out. We have to find out now, rather than later, if you are. We have to know."

Her face relaxes only a bit, but she nods her head.

"While you were still asleep, I made a quick trip to the pharmacy. I bought what's called a pregnancy test. I will show you how to use it, and once we have a result, we will know a lot more. Are you willing to try this with me?"

Molly makes a raspberry noise with her lips and sighs loudly as though she's a bit disgusted but willing to humor me, at least this once.

"Sure," she says. "Whatever. I still don't understand any of this. It doesn't make any sense to me."

"I know, Molly, I know that. You will understand more after you do the test. We need to start with this, while we're still home. You can do it. I know you can. It doesn't hurt, but it's messy."

In the bathroom, I show her the packaged pregnancy test and invite her to read the information on the box. She glances at the instructions, but she doesn't read them, just hands it back to me. I take the plastic test strip out of the box and put it into her hand.

"Now, this will seem gross to you. It is. I can't fix that, but you can wash your hands right after. I want you to sit on the toilet and hold the stick, this side up, and pee on it."

Molly groans and blurts out, "What the fuck, Mom?" I'm thinking, *where does she learn this language?* Then let it pass, thinking that's the least of my worries.

"I know. I know. Gross. I said it was gross, but there's no other way to get a quick answer. You hold it right under where you pee and let the stick get really wet. Can you do that?"

She takes the stick in her right hand and holds it under her body as though it could bite her and grimaces. She's trying to pee, but the situation is so weird, she can't. I look away and try not to watch her so closely, hoping she can get the stick wet enough for the test to work. Finally, I hear a trickle of urine hit the water in the toilet and glance over to make sure she's got the stick where it needs to be. When she finishes, she stiffly holds it out to me, stands awkwardly, and washes her hands with soap and water. I invite her to sit on the edge of the tub with me and watch to see what happens. Her face tells me she's totally freaked out.

"If two pink lines appear in the little window, that's a positive reading, meaning you are likely pregnant. Don't worry. I'll be right here with you."

The air in the small bathroom is stale and close. We sit in silence, shoulder to shoulder, and watch the stick together. I can hardly breathe, and I can feel Molly's body tense in anticipation next to my own.

In a minute or two, two distinct pink lines appear on the stick. I have to fight back the tears in my eyes, because I don't want to distress Molly any more than I already have. She is staring at the stick as though it's about to explode. I swallow and blink, pause until I can speak.

"Okay, Molly. The test indicates that you are pregnant. Last night, thinking about the fact that your periods have stopped, I began to worry that this might be the case. Now we know, that's a good thing."

I look at Molly's face. She shakes her head slowly, back and forth. I'm not sure what she's saying 'no' to, and I don't want to ask. I'm guessing she's shaking her head 'no' to all of it. I understand this is too much for her to absorb right now, and I don't want to push her. I know better than to ask her my other questions right now. Those can wait, this can't.

"Molly, can you hear me? Can you look at me for a second?"

It takes her a long time, but eventually she turns her blank face toward mine and waits for what I have to say.

"I'm going to make some calls, so that we can find out more about what's going on with your body. I want a doctor to examine you and do some tests to make certain you are pregnant and tell us how far along you are. That means they can calculate when you got pregnant and how many weeks you've been pregnant. That's important because the laws are based on how many weeks pregnant you are. Does this make sense to you?"

Molly continues to stare at my face, but her eyes suggest she doesn't have a clue why this makes any sense.

"I hate to move so quickly on this, but I am certain we need a doctor's exam as quickly as possible. I can put the call on speaker, would you like to listen, too?"

Molly nods and motions toward the old sofa in the corner. We move together so that she can prop herself up on the pillows and wait. If she wants to listen, she can, in a place that's a bit removed from the kitchen chair where I will sit to make the call.

I sit down with a cup of cold coffee I know will be bitter and dial the local women's clinic. The woman who answers the phone graciously listens as I explain that my ten-year-old daughter may be pregnant. I tell her Molly's periods were regular for some time, but now they have stopped. She just did a pregnancy test, and it was positive, I say. I want to bring her to the clinic as soon as possible for an examination.

Then, I add, as an afterthought. "My daughter is disabled, and she'll need a wheelchair."

The volunteer does not openly react to my story, but she tells me things I do not want to hear. She tells me that I will need to be patient, because she will need to call some other people, before she can begin a conversation with me about Molly. Calm and considerate, the voice on the phone assures me she will get back to me today or tomorrow, that I should wait to hear back from her. As we hang up the phone, I sit with fear in my throat for my little girl, who has absolutely no idea what is going on. I have a feeling things are only going to get worse, for everyone involved.

# Chapter 8

## The Barn Loft

Days later, with no calls from the clinic, I am concerned that they have not given me any instructions about bringing Molly in for an exam. After we eat lunch, I can't sit still, and it's too hot to go outside and work in my garden. I call Barb, but she doesn't answer her phone. I'm reluctant to bother Robert to come get Molly, remembering the caution of the psychologist about her spending too much time at his house. I think of Gail, but taking Molly to her house seems like such a pain, and I don't really want to invite my mother-in-law to come to my house. God knows what Wilson has, or hasn't, told her about our marriage.

I decide I must get out of the house, even for an hour, so I cave and ask Robert if I can drop Molly off at his place for a bit, telling him I need to make a grocery run and pick up some mail at the post office. I have told him nothing of what has been happening with Molly. I wonder if she will tell him, but I'm guessing not. I doubt she could talk about anything so personal with him, and I'm pretty certain she doesn't understand enough yet to trust herself to talk about it with anyone but me. I'm actually hoping she doesn't talk to him, because I'm pretty sure Robert would go ballistic and ask both of us a lot of invasive questions we can't or don't want to answer yet. I feel a bit guilty not explaining to him what is going on as he's our biggest supporter and because Molly has come to love him so much, but I convince myself I can't possibly tell him until far into the future, when I have sorted it all out—or maybe never, who knows?

Not suspecting anything unusual, my brother agrees, and I deliver Molly at the old shed, where I suggest they watch another documentary so Molly can tell me all about it later. I watch while Robert props her up on the horsehair sofa and listen to them decide to watch the dolphin show until I return. Robert looks content leaning back in our father's old leather chair that looks like it needs to be retired. I always think it's going to flip over one day, and that will be it for the chair, but Robert seems totally content to lean back without any thought of that happening.

I leave the shed and drive to the store to get some groceries and stock the refrigerator. Knowing I'll be needing them, I buy several packs of cigarettes and get some good beer, my favorite this time. I'm not quite sure why I think stocking up the kitchen is important at this crazy moment, but at least it gives me something to do, something else to think about besides the clinic and Molly's pregnancy test. I check my phone to make sure the ringer is on. If the clinic doesn't call today, I'll call them again and insist they find a way to get Molly on their schedule. I'll remind them that she's only ten, and she's already tested positive for pregnancy. What is the problem? If nothing else, I need to know why they are not eager for me to bring her in to see a doctor. I have to know what my next option might be, if they can't examine her.

Too soon, I'm finished with my errands and head back home. In the kitchen, I put all the groceries away, sit on the back step and smoke a cigarette and drink a beer. I appreciate this time alone when I can breathe deeply and think, if only for a few minutes. When I go back inside, my house is profoundly quiet and dark, the way rooms can be mysteriously gloomy even when the sun is shining, remaining cool in the heat. I revel in the peace the house brings me when I need it most. Without thinking it through, I walk over to the sofa and stretch out fully on its welcoming mounds of softness. *I must never, ever get rid of this old sofa* is my last thought before I fall into a deep, exhausted sleep, like death might be, or a sleep that might give me supernatural powers for what is to come.

I wake with a jerk and have no idea how long I've been napping. I glance at the clock and notice the time, thinking I should call my brother to see if he can bring Molly home. Instead, I decide I need the fresh air and want to walk over to his place and pick her up myself. Molly and I can do our tripod walk back to the house, the one we've nearly perfected as she's gotten taller. Happy to get out again, I finish off a half glass of water, take a quick pee with the bathroom door wide open, and slip out the back door.

I realize I haven't walked this path for years. I have driven around to Robert's driveway in front of his house many times, but I can't remember walking the back path since we were kids. Is that possible? Then, the path had been the shortest route we could find between our house and the neighbors, long before there was an actual town, and long before my house had been built a block away. I remember the brambles that have always grown along the fence and take a moment to search out a few of the dewberries hiding in the thicket. I prick my finger and suck the blood, the way we did as children. I pull the berries off the vines and stuff them into my mouth like a child. They are amazing, plump and sweet, larger than blackberries by a mile and better. As children, we would collect buckets of them for our mother, enjoying work that could also be eaten on the spot. My mouth explodes with the sweet and sour mix of the fruit on my tongue, before I realize I have dripped juice on my white shirt. The stain is a deep red, like blood, and I doubt I'll be able to get it out. "*Damn it*," I mutter. I really like this shirt; yet, the berry had been worth it, I decide, screw the shirt.

My brother's house, which I still think of as my family's house, seems strangely quiet as I walk up to the front door. I peer in the windows of the door like a robber, or a pervert. I can tell no one is in the living room, but I can't see into the kitchen. I turn the doorknob, pleased when it opens smoothly, inviting me into his private domain. I rarely come to his house anymore. He usually comes to us, although Molly visits him more than I do. I wander through the downstairs rooms, noting the inconsistency between areas that are neat and clean, and others that are in shambles. I know I should leave the house and check the shed, but I'm suddenly curious. The kitchen counters are spotless, yet the backroom floor is a mess of dirty clothes, computer wires, old tools, and boots, lots of boots. A glance into my parents' former bedroom, dark and formal with heavy walnut furniture I never wanted in my own house, reveals it looks exactly as it did when they were both living. The bedspread is neat with the corners tucked in, but I can see the layer of dust on the bureau and wonder when it had last been cleaned. Not my problem, I remind myself, but it does make me wonder why Robert chooses to sleep upstairs in his childhood bedroom, rather than enjoying the larger room down here with a bigger bed. Again, none of my business. Moving through the clean kitchen, I can see into the garage through the back door, neat rows of tools aligned on the walls, perfectly matched with the chalk lines he's drawn for their shapes, tools that undoubtedly help him fix all the broken things in my house and the damaged cars people bring to him. Robert's an odd mix of precise and careless, something I didn't know about him. Makes me wonder what else I don't know about my brother, at least now that we're both adults.

Without hesitation, I take the stairs up to the next floor, glancing into each of the two bedrooms separated by a tiny room that sports an old commode and a tiny sink hidden behind a thin wooden door made of cheap plywood, now warped. I distinctly remember trying to pee silently in that toilet so Robert couldn't hear and razz me later. One bedroom, which had been mine at one time, is musty and has no linens on the bed, the other has a mussed bed and some rank manly smells that turn my nose a bit. The floor is dotted with dirty underwear and socks, a belt or two, several pairs of dirty jeans, and too many wadded T-shirts to count. I shake my head. This is a bachelor's pad, no doubt about it. It hits me that my brother is not young anymore, but a grown man who lives alone in the same house he had grown up in. For a quick minute, that thought repulses me, but I couldn't have said why.

I walk down the narrow stairwell, go out the back screen door, and head for the shed. I hate to disturb them, wherever they are, but I can hear the sounds of the TV over there and know that's where I'll find them. If the two of them are content watching cartoons or the show about dolphins, maybe I should just leave them be. I know he'll bring her home soon enough.

But then I remember, I need to get Molly home. Tomorrow, and whatever it might bring, is looming larger by the minute. I have to prepare us both for a possible trip to the clinic. What will I tell her? Should I just take her, have her examined, and let the doctor prepare her for what will come next? No, again, I'm shirking my duty. I need to do better than that and tell her more. How to broach the topic of abortion is beyond me. All I know for certain is that my ten-year-old daughter cannot possibly give birth to a child. To even contemplate something that obscene ignores Molly's right to a normal life, whatever that might be, given she already has tremendous challenges ahead of her with her legs not working. There has to be a way to give Molly her childhood back, before it's too late.

The shed is empty when I peer in, the door open and no one about, only the sound of the TV filling the small room. Chuckling to myself, I suddenly know where I should check next, remembering Robert's favorite place in all the years when we were growing up. I stride over to the barn in the bright sunlight and open the enormous wooden doors into the stable. The doors slide apart effortlessly, just as I knew they would, something my brother prides himself on, well-oiled hinges, things that work. His only horse is in his stall and neighs to me in a friendly greeting. I touch his wet nose and take a minute to watch the pink piglets in the next pen suckle their mother's teats. The sow is spread out on the fresh hay, apparently fast asleep as her babies take their lunch. The barn is so quiet and cozy, I wonder why I don't come here more often. It is dark and soothing, like a cave that can hide deep secrets and comfort the soul. I remember how many long hours Robert spent as a teenager lingering in the comfort and familiar smells of this barn or in the hayloft above. Whenever our parents couldn't find him, when his chores were not completed, I knew exactly where to check. Sometimes I would find him here, and we'd conspire to hide as long as possible from the urgent calls of our parents.

Trusting my memory of this place, I look everywhere and glance out at the pen beyond. Not seeing them, I go back into the dark barn, calling, "Molly?" "Robert?"

No answer. I take a turn just where the steps begin, leading up to the loft. They are made of thick and sturdy planks of split logs, undoubtedly built by my father, or even my grandfather, long ago. The tops of the steps are shiny from foot traffic and the slick effects of the hay that filters down from the top, making them shimmer like gold. At last, I know my search has ended. I can hear breathing just beyond the top of the stairs. Has Robert carried Molly all the way up here to show her the loft he loves so much? I know, of course, that he has, probably without a great deal of effort. His arms are strong and his legs even stronger. He would definitely do that for Molly. I nearly trip on Robert's dirty boots near the edge of the steps, left there as though he had just stepped out of them, maybe in a hurry.

I push open the swinging loft door and peer into the musty air that dances before my eyes. Dust motes and bits of hay threaten my mouth and nose. I remember not to breathe in too deeply, or I'll inhale them and choke. It takes a moment to let my eyes adjust in the haze. Blinking quickly, I can see them both lying in the hay, side by side, my brother and my daughter, sound asleep with contented smiles on their faces, breathing deeply in unison.

I squint to distinguish more details of the scene in front of me. I am confused to see Molly's crop top riding high around her neck, and her pink panties lying on the hay next to her body. My brother's arm, heavy with sleep, is slung carelessly across her chest, his underwear wadded at his ankles. Molly's right hand is encased in his much larger one, their side bodies touching, at ease in the hay. I freeze, and I am certain my heart stops. Suddenly, all the little splintered pieces of Molly come together. In this horrifying moment, I know the truth that may destroy us all. I am frozen to the spot where I stand and begin to shake uncontrollably, the only way my body is able to react to what my eyes see and my brain strains to comprehend.

As if from a distance, I hear a strangled animal noise I don't recognize as my own. The growl rises from my belly and crawls into my mouth. I am no longer a person. I am a beast. My body pivots, and my feet move on their own to the corner, where I can see the pitchfork standing at the ready. My hands grasp the pitted handle in both hands and heave the giant fork high in the air, turn, take three giant steps, and thrust it into the body of my traitorous brother. I relish the tug of the rusty tongs as they enter his vile flesh. I am pleased to watch his blood spray over the floor. I feel only relief to see his body recoil in agony, like an injured snake.

Satisfied, I do not stay to watch him struggle but swoop over his writhing body, lift my daughter up and over my right shoulder, grab her clothes in my left hand and leap toward the steps. I take them two at a time, land on the floor of the barn, turn, and run down the path, back to my own house with Molly in my arms. I push the back door open with my shoulder and gently lower my precious girl onto the sofa, my finger to my lips to warn her to be quiet. Her eyes are heavy with sleep, but her mouth is open with questions she cannot ask.

In three minutes or ten, I couldn't have said, I collapse onto the floor next to the sofa where I have placed Molly. For a deranged second, I have the thought that maybe Molly doesn't know what I have done, but I know that is impossible, and I retch my guts onto my living room rug and wait for my body to stop shaking.

At least a half hour later, maybe more, I test my joints to see if I can stand up, but I am still too weak to move. The power of my adrenaline rush has depleted my mind and my body. Hot tears flood down my face and onto my shirt, now stained with two shades of red. My mouth tastes of bile, and my tongue is a slug that will not move for me to swallow. I stare blankly at the sick on the rug, not able to imagine cleaning it up. I cautiously look over at Molly. She still does not speak. Neither do I. There are no words for the empty space that stretches between us.

Seated on the floor, too near the smell on the rug, I blink my eyes to clear them. Flashes of Molly and Robert in the hay, their underwear in disarray, the pitchfork, the blood, and Robert's body pinned to the floor penetrate my brain and scroll past my blurry eyes, reminding me what waits in the barn.

Only one coherent thought arrives.

*I should call someone.*

Shocked by what I have seen and done, I sit with my arms folded tightly around my stomach and rock back and forth. I have left my brother bleeding in the barn with no idea if he is dead or alive. I do not regret stabbing him, but my conscience knows I should call someone to check on him.

*I should call the police.*

*Yes, that's who I should call.*

*But what can I tell them?*

*I cannot tell them what happened.*

*Do I want the police here?*

*No, I absolutely do not want the police here.*

*But I should call them.*

I crawl over to the counter and reach my hand up for my phone. My fingers feel around for the familiar shape, and I grab it. I sit back down on the floor next to Molly's shape on the sofa, holding the lit phone in my left hand. I stare at the screen, unable to press 911.

*What can I say if I call the police?*

*Surely, I cannot say I have stabbed my brother with a pitchfork and left him up in the hayloft to die.*

*How much trouble am I in?*

*I cannot tell them what I did or why I did it, because they cannot know that Molly was in that loft with him.*

Suddenly, I know that's the most critical thing I must remember. With a clarity I do not expect, I realize the single most important thing I must do from this moment on is protect my daughter.

I must protect Molly. She must not ever be asked to tell what happened. What would she say? In time, it may be revealed that Robert molested Molly, maybe for a long time. The thought makes me want to vomit again, I know there is more to this story than I can comprehend.

Above all, I know Molly is a child, and because she is a child, she is innocent, but I can't predict what she might say about being there with her uncle. No matter how she might frame what has happened, Robert is an adult man who has abused her. He has betrayed us both, but I cannot trust what Molly might say. That is why she must never speak.

I watch my little girl as she gently falls asleep on the sofa, and I vow never to get her involved. Even though I saw clearly what Robert had done today, I have no idea what the full story might be. How long has he been touching her? Years? When did he impregnate her? What has he told her?

I do not long for the details, but I know some terrible journey into pain has only just begun, and I know it will not end well. There's not much I can control at this point, but the one thing I can do is protect my daughter, who is pregnant. Time is ticking away, and the light has faded from the room. Robert may be dead, or worse. Maybe he's not dead yet, but he's bleeding out on the hay. If I let him die, I know I'll be in more trouble than if he lives, but I would rather he dies.

I try to moisten my mouth and move my tongue, my finger poised to dial 911.

*I must find a way to speak, but I have no idea what I can say. I will have to make up a story or at least provide a story to get some help for him, but I cannot stay in the house and hide.*

*What could I say?*

*I can tell them I found him stabbed and bleeding in the hayloft, that's what I'll say.*

*I'll tell them to hurry, because I didn't stop to check if he is dead or alive. I ran home to get my phone and called the police.*

*I can act like I'm frightened out of my mind, because I am. That will make sense to them.*

But I still don't dial my phone. I have started thinking about Molly, how she has changed, especially how she has seemed angry with me all the time. I go deep with this and lose myself.

*She was angry with me, because I didn't do anything, I didn't stop it. She was angry, because I didn't see or know the right questions to ask. How could I? Robert was a fixture in our lives—my brother, her uncle, our friend. I had every right to trust him, didn't I? Brothers are close kin, beloved, trusted. Who would have imagined what was going on right here in my house and his?*

*Maybe a better mother would have thought of that. Maybe a better mother would have known or would have been more careful. Maybe a better mother would have suspected her own brother.*

For months, I have been exhausted from all the driving, all the doctors, all the clinics who had no answers. I was angry with them, because they could not solve the mystery of Molly. I realize I am trying to let myself off the hook.

Wilson was right! Oh, how I hate to admit my husband, my *absent* husband, was right. I wasn't watching her closely enough. I was too focused on her legs, and what was wrong with them, to see other reasons that might be causing her physical problems, why she was regressing. Did that last doctor know, or suspect?

That thought lingers in my mind as I try to connect all the threads of Molly's mystery. Was it all related? Her legs? The bedwetting? The regression? Were these all signs of a child not knowing how to deal with something she couldn't control? If so, why didn't any of the doctors pick up on that or mention it to me?

Isn't that their job? Did they make suggestions to me I couldn't hear or contemplate? I understand it would be difficult to bring up. And I, in turn, probably couldn't have heard it.

I bend over my stomach and cry with the pain of not knowing, of not understanding what Molly has been going through. Now, it's too late. She is pregnant, and I know how, but that does me no good. My brain just keeps spiraling, from one angle to another.

Suddenly, my mind explodes with something that is *not* the anger, the rage, the disbelief. This is a feeling I do not recognize—until I do.

*Guilt*. I am flooded with *guilt*—pure, unmitigated, *guilt*—

G*uilt* for not knowing,

*Guilt* for not suspecting,

*Guilt* for depending upon my brother for everything, for trusting him without question.

*Guilt* that I did not protect my daughter.

I am deeply ashamed that I left her with him, placed her into his arms and never asked a single question—*guilt* that I had no questions to ask. In the same moment, I am devastated to realize I should not have trusted my own brother, *my own brother*, whom I have loved all my life. We have always been *good friends*. I could never, ever have thought of Robert as a man who could touch my daughter in unimaginable ways. The depth of his betrayal shakes my very foundation, my trust in humankind, my trust in men.

*Oh God,* I fold into myself and moan, deep and low.

I realize the sun has set. The room is turning a bruised purple, and I haven't noticed. Molly is asleep, or so it seems, and I can smell the stink on the rug getting worse. I know it is long past time to make that call. I activate my phone and touch the numbers for the police. The operator picks up immediately and asks, "What is your emergency?"

I cannot speak coherently, my body and voice wracked by genuine pain, shock, and fear. I barely get out a stream of words the operator strains to decipher, something about my brother and the barn and a stabbing and lots of blood. The woman on the other end of the line is experienced with calls like this. She says she will triangulate my phone location and will send help immediately.

She asks if I am hurt, and I tell her no.

She asks if I am safe, and I tell her yes.

"We are in my house," I say, but I can't remember the address.

When I tell her we are safe, she tells me to wait there until the ambulance and the police officers arrive.

*Where would we go*, I wonder to myself.

I hang up and sit on the floor to wait, staring toward the barn where my brother lies in the hay, the righteous pitchfork standing guard upright in his guilty body.

The doorbell startles me enough for me to finally move from the floor. I struggle to the door to find a uniformed officer on my front porch, standing under the single light bulb that hurts my eyes. I recognize him as someone I went to high school with, but I can't think of his name. He pretends he doesn't know me, which is a good thing. I move aside to let him into my home, but quickly change my mind, gesturing that it would be better if we spoke on the porch. I nod toward Molly, lying in the dark on the sofa, hoping she will never hear the details of what has occurred in the barn.

After writing down my name and my relationship with the stabbed man, the officer asks me a question, his voice low.

"So, what do you know?"

I try to speak, but no words will come out of my mouth. My shaking continues. I am sweating profusely now, but I feel cold as ice. I sob and gulp great wads of snot down my throat and wipe my nose and mouth on the sleeve of my shirt, as though I am a child. The officer must lean toward me to catch my whispered words. The lie comes out of me easily. Molly is not in my story.

"I was supposed to pick up a box of vegetables my brother had picked for me, so I walked over, thinking I could get it from him myself, but I couldn't find him in the house or the barn."

I hiccup loudly. Blink. Close my mouth.

I pause as though I am trying to think and speak as accurately as possible, which I am, but it is more than that. I measure each word carefully, before I share it with the man in the uniform.

"When I got there, he wasn't in the house or the yard," I pause, realizing I've repeated myself.

"I couldn't find him, so I walked around to the shed, where he has a TV, but he wasn't there either, and he didn't answer when I called out."

I stop talking, fear threatening to silence me completely. I swallow. The officer is patient. He doesn't urge me to continue but waits until I am able to speak again. I am breathing deeply now, my chest heaving.

"I opened the barn doors, petted the horse, and watched the piglets for a few minutes, then I went up into the hayloft."

My eyes grow wide and my nostrils flare as though I

might pass out right there on the porch. The officer takes a slight step toward me, afraid I might faint or fall down the steps. I start talking faster, alternating sputtered words and sharp breaths.

"I couldn't believe it. [sharp breath] It was horrible! [sharp breath] I just stood there looking down at my brother with a pitchfork stuck in his body, blood running onto the hay. [sharp breath, wide eyes, tears] There was so much blood, fresh blood, I could tell, but it made me want to throw up. I couldn't look." [lots of shallow breaths in a row]

My voice changes register, rising higher as I describe the horror I found in the barn. The officer involuntarily grimaces, imagining the scene I am describing, empathizing with my terror at finding my brother in such a state. This time, I just run through my story as fast as I can.

"I didn't touch him, I swear, I ran home as fast as I could and called 911. That's as much as I know. I'm sorry I got so flustered and didn't try to help him, but I was just sick to my stomach at the blood and gore of it all. And he's my brother, my only kin in the world. I couldn't deal with it. I panicked."

The fact that most of this is true, and that my horror at the scene is wrecking my body in real time, makes my recollection of what happened in the barn ring true and absolutely reliable.

The officer tells me he empathizes.

"Well, I can understand your reaction, and you did the right thing to call 911. I really can't imagine what it was like to find him there in the loft, stabbed and all."

The officer nods several times as he writes down everything I say, then he makes a sympathetic face and takes a moment to politely ask me how I am doing now.

"I'm still very shaken up," I reply, deadpan and as honest as I can be.

"I vomited on the rug in my house when I got back here. I'm worried that he might be dead. Please let me know what they find up there, will you? Right away?"

I couldn't have said if I wished Robert were dead or alive.

Dead, I suppose, would be my preference. That might make the future a bit easier, unless of course they figure out I did it. Then, it wouldn't be easier at all.

"We'll definitely keep you in the loop," the officer tells me. "I will call you personally when we know more," he adds.

I stand on the porch and watch as some of the vehicles pull around from Robert's driveway, the ambulance leading the way with lights flashing and the sirens screaming. The officer leaves my porch and drives toward Robert's barn in his patrol car to wait for more police to come. Long after it grows quiet, I continue to stand on the porch, my arms wrapped around my body that no longer feels cold, only clammy in the humidity of the early evening air. I am still breathing heavily, but my body has stopped shaking, my sobs subsided to only mild sniffles and a runny nose.

I am surprised that everyone has left without any further questions for me. It seems they have accepted my story as I told it, but I suspect this is only a pause in what is to come. They will be back. In the dark, with spotlights glaring, they are wrapping Robert's house and barn with yellow crime scene tape, sealing all the doors. They will look for fingerprints on the pitchfork, I know. They will note Robert's pants wadded at his ankles, perhaps find semen on his body. The scene will likely confuse them, at least for a while. I keep wondering what I should say, and what I should never say. I wish I had a lawyer or a friend to help me with this, but I know I shouldn't share any of this with anyone yet, not even Barb. *Where is my husband when I need him?* My mind can't resist returning to old habits that do me no good. There is no husband anymore. There is no one to rescue me.

Will it help if I tell them the truth about what Robert has done to Molly? Can my actions be justified in any court of law? Aren't there laws in Missouri about protecting your child from a rapist? I virtually caught him in the act. I saw it with my own eyes. I know now why my ten-year-old daughter is pregnant. The evidence is clear. What more would they need to understand why I stabbed my brother, protecting my daughter from this man, whom I would have defended to my death before today?

I think again it would be better all around if he just dies up there with a pitchfork in his gut. Save them all the trouble of accusations and prosecutions and whatever else might follow when everyone knows Robert is a pedophile, a rapist, the scum of the earth. Can I keep all of that out of the media, away from the police? Should I? Is that my ticket to freedom, or a sentence in prison, or worse? I will need to proceed with caution and secrecy, not knowing any of the legal and political ramifications of where Molly and I stand right now. I know enough to warn Molly not to say a word about what happened. Not a word. She must know nothing, say nothing. She wasn't there.

Despite the blood and the vomit, I square my shoulders and decide to think only about Molly, and what I must do for her before the police return. Molly is a child, and she is pregnant. That must be my top priority, my main concern. I must not get derailed from taking the next steps to finding a solution to what is growing in Molly's belly. That clock is most definitely ticking, and I need to move quickly. I will focus on my pregnant daughter and the trip to the clinic, as planned. I will find help for my violated daughter. I must acknowledge the pain and confusion my daughter has been living, and I must help her understand the devastating truth about what has happened to her and what needs to happen next. Resolved, I turn back into the house, go to the bathroom, wash my face with cold water, and put on a clean shirt, careful to throw the stained one in the burn barrel out back and light a match to it. I need to get Molly ready for bed and clean the rug.

# Chapter 9

## Blessed Mary in Disguise

It has been a week since I talked with the administrator at the clinic, so I call back to make certain they haven't forgotten us. It is early morning, and Molly hasn't awakened yet, which gives me some privacy in the kitchen. Neither of us got much sleep last night. Molly's nightmares must have been more vivid than ever, and I spent long hours in bed with her, consoling her and promising they would go away soon, although I had no idea that might be true. The phone rings too many times when I call the clinic, and the receptionist who finally answers apologizes for the lack of contact. She says she has only a bit of information to share. Things are still not clear. Several people are working on Molly's situation. Her voice is formal, clinical. She is careful with her words. I can tell this isn't going to go well.

"I must tell you," she begins to explain. "We are reluctant to bring Molly into the clinic. We are not really prepared for a client in a wheelchair, and, certainly, wheeling a child in a wheelchair past the protestors or carrying her into the building could cause more of a stir than anyone wants to face. It would likely erupt into chaos, and both of you would be bombarded with questions no one wants to answer on the sidewalk. It would be a media circus. Disabled patients routinely have to be assisted at other clinics that have better equipment and a closer relationship with a women's hospital. We are looking into that possibility.

"But that's not the biggest problem we have," the woman admits, caution in her in voice.

"We do not know yet how to proceed with a case of a ten-year-old pregnant girl. As you might suspect, legal issues of consent for a minor must be addressed. Also, and I'm sure you've thought about this, we are legally mandated to report any case of a minor being pregnant. In every case, this must be investigated as rape and/or incest, or both, and must be reported. The police may need to get involved, if there is a danger of continued abuse, like whether or not the child has been removed from contact with the suspect. That is, if you know the suspect, which may be another major difficulty, which could lead to a criminal trial. This is all going to take time, perhaps more time than you have, given the girl is already pregnant."

She tells me her name is Victoria, and she'll be my main contact at the clinic. She has become flustered, trying to tell me the problems inherent in my daughter's pregnancy and the limits of how she could help. I doubt she has ever been involved in a case like this, and I can sense it deeply disturbs her that so many new laws dictate how she can help women who call for exams. She fears for the organization she works for and has always placed such faith in. I imagine she worries she will not be in a position to help my daughter, even though she's the one stuck with talking with me. Whatever the story is with Molly, she does not see this ending well, and she feels helpless to make it right.

"I wish I had better news for you. I promise I will get back to you as soon as I know anything more."

With that, she mumbles her goodbye. I thank her for her help and sit in the vacuum our conversation leaves.

Her questions about "the suspect" are new to me. I know this will have to be investigated, yet I am surprised that it has become part of the process of helping Molly this early in her case. She needs an examination *now*, regardless of who impregnated her. The more issues get stirred into this mess, the longer it's going to take for her to get the help she needs, and I can see no way to hurry up the process. I feel helpless, thinking how the days on the calendar will accumulate, one twenty-four-hour period after another. One week, two, another week, four, another week, five, then six, and then what? How much time does Molly have?

I drink more coffee, waiting to hear Molly's voice from down the hall, and I groan when a new set of questions start to circulate in my brain, an endless chain of questions I can't answer. When will they begin asking me more questions about finding Robert in the barn, severely injured, about who might have committed the crime of stabbing him? I can claim total innocence to those questions, I tell myself, because I have no idea who my brother's friends or enemies are, if he has any. I do not know the names of the men who bring him broken vehicles to fix, or who he might socialize with. I have no inkling of anyone who might hold a grudge against my brother, or who might have a motive to try and kill him with a pitchfork in his own barn. All of this is totally true. There would be no reason for me to lie. I don't know the answers to these questions. Surely, they will believe me and move on to someone who could give them more answers than I can. I would love to point the finger at someone else, but I know that's crazy thinking. I need to say what Robert did, in order to talk about what I did, and why. It's all connected, and I really can't make any sense of it. Then I realize I'm trying to fabricate a suspect who doesn't exist. I know exactly who stabbed him.

For now, there's no likelihood that the police will have any reason to want to talk to Molly, and that's a good thing. I must somehow prevent her from talking about her time with

like your daughter. I heard them talking about you and Molly yesterday after you called, and I hoped they had found a way to help you. I'm thinking, though, that they will not be able to help you with all the legal stuff tied to this case, so I wanted to reach out and see if I could help. I know the clock is ticking. Are you somewhere you can talk? I hope it's okay that I called."

The relief I feel is visceral. Someone has called *me* to offer help. I grovel for the compassion in the woman's voice and stumble over my words, repeating over and over, "Yes, thank you, thank you so much for calling. Yes, it's okay that you called. Yes, yes. Thank you."

I'm saying too much, but I can't help myself. Tears roll down my cheeks, and snot runs onto my lips and into my mouth. I grab some toilet paper and mop up my face. I'm glad the woman can't see me, embarrassed even that she can hear the desperation in my voice over the phone.

"What can you tell me? Is there anything new? Are you going to be able to help Molly? Can I bring her into the clinic?"

Mary lowers her voice and asks, rather nervously, "I'm sorry, but can I come over tonight, maybe around 8:00 or 9:00? I hate to ask, but I know you are distressed, and I know time is of the essence. I can come now if you give me your address. Maybe I should come after Molly goes to bed."

I don't hesitate, "Yes, of course you can come over. Yes, yes, please do come, please. That would be great."

I give Mary my address and ask her not to ring the doorbell when she arrives, because it will wake Molly up. I am floored that someone is offering to help like this, now, even late at night. Mary must realize how critical all this is for Molly. She must know we need to act fast, not get embroiled in all the rules, protocols, and legal issues. What can she tell me tonight, I wonder as I hang up the phone.

Waiting for Mary in the dark room, with only a small lamp burning on a side table, I am full of hope. Someone who works at the clinic will absolutely know the answers to some of my questions, even if they do not regularly deal with very young clients. These are the things I can talk to Mary about, although I caution myself not to blurt out anything about Robert, or say I know who the perpetrator is. It will be difficult to watch what I say, but I know I must take this opportunity to speak with an expert.

After nearly an hour, there's a quiet knock at the front door. I open it quickly to see Mary on the porch in a blousy dress that reaches her ankles, a huge smile on her face and her long, gray hair pulled into a bun. Before we can get into the living room and close the door, I am being enveloped in her heavy arms and hugged as though we have known each other forever—the way my friend hugs me, the way I desperately need to be hugged right now.

For about an hour, we talk in low tones. Mostly, I talk and ask questions, while Mary listens and answers as best she can. She does not push for information or try to guide me toward any particular solution. There's no judgment from her, either, I realize, for the situation we find ourselves in, no suspicions or judgment. I am relieved that she expresses no opinions about my protection of my daughter (or lack of it), and she asks no questions about who molested Molly. Mostly, she wants to know how she can help me, what things I am most worried about. She is easy to talk to, and I find myself relaxing for the first time in a long time.

It is getting quite late, and I seem to have suddenly run out of steam. I pause to ask Mary if she wants a cup of coffee or tea. I feel like I should at least offer her something, since she's trying so hard to help us, but she politely declines and stands as though she is ready to leave. At the door, she turns to me, her face glowing as though she's on fire.

"I do have an idea how to help you, Alice," as though it has just come to her. "I need to check and see if this might work, before I can explain. If I get permission to help you in this way, please trust me. I will need maybe a day to figure this out, and I'll call you tomorrow. Would that be okay?"

I nod, ready to do anything.

"Good. It might be best if you don't mention my visit or that I have a plan to help you. I hope you understand, I'm doing this without the sanction of the front office. I just can't stand by and see you and Molly suffer, knowing you need some help as quickly as possible. You try to get some sleep, and see that Molly gets some as well. Try not to fret. I will get back to you. One thing, though. You probably need to pack an overnight bag for yourself and Molly, just a few clothes for a day or two. Could you do that? We might need to leave in a hurry, if this works out. Okay?"

"Of course," I agree. "That shouldn't be a problem."

I watch through the door as Mary crosses the dark yard, gets into her car, and drives away. I stare into the night until her rear lights disappear in the distance. I suddenly feel lonelier than I have in a long time. What is going to happen to us? Can this woman actually help us? I will go anywhere with her, as long as she offers a solution to Molly's pregnancy, and I would love nothing more than leaving my house and the scene in the barn as far behind us as possible.

About my own crime, I will have to figure that out later. I allow myself a moment to wonder if my brother is dead and lying cold in the morgue, or if he is alive in a sanitized bed at the hospital up on the highway. It would help if he were dead, I think, again. For one thing, he deserves to die, but how could I wish him dead? I keep going back and forth. It is, after all, Robert I'm thinking about.

Stabbing someone isn't the same as killing him, even I know that. The courts might understand, even forgive, the first, but the second could be my death sentence. Then where would Molly be without me? My life seems to be one long, never-ending string of questions that revolves on a loop, gaining speed as it rolls over and past me, a train I can't stop, or jump from. I dare not think what tomorrow, or even the next hour, will bring, so I can only hang on for dear life.

As soon as Mary is gone, I walk back to Molly's room to

make sure she is sleeping soundly. I think about sliding under the covers and joining her in her already warm bed, but I know I shouldn't risk a good night's sleep for both of us. Not able to take off my clothes, I crash on the sofa and fall asleep. I sleep soundly, which must mean Molly did as well.

The next day, I keep Mary's conversation close and try to think of the possibilities. I remember her guileless face, and I warm to the hope that she has brought to us. I will put my energy toward spending the day with Molly. I fix her pancakes, because I know she loves them. I talk nonstop to her about anything and nothing. She says nothing about Robert, or the police, and I want to keep it that way. We read books to each other, and play numerous games of UNO, most of which I lose on purpose, laughing at my own mistakes in the silly way Molly once found delightful. She doesn't laugh like she did when she was younger, but she also doesn't seem as angry with me or as frustrated. I am careful what I say, what I don't say. Through it all, I listen for the phone to ring, knowing it is too soon for Mary to call, but hoping, nonetheless.

After dinner and a long bath for Molly, I crawl into the tub myself, bitterly recalling the only reason I have hot water is because Robert fixed the pump and installed a new water heater. Remembering this brings fresh tears to my eyes. I try to enjoy the water without the guilt. I ease into the suds, my anger at Robert surging, repeating lines in my head that have become familiar.

*How could you? How could you do this to me, to Molly? I trusted you completely. I've loved you and been your friend all our lives. Maybe you are my brother, but you are an evil, evil man. There's a special place in hell for men like you. Maybe by now you already know that. I hope so.*

When I can no longer lie in the cooling bath water, I get up and get ready for bed. I walk to the front door, but I am not ready to close off the cool night air. Instead of going to bed, I stretch out in the dark living room again, listening to the night sounds through the screen. I must fall asleep in seconds.

# Chapter 10

## Avenging Father

Several hours later, I wake with a start and realize someone is sitting on the edge of the sofa, quietly calling my name and shaking my shoulder. I gasp, sit upright, and stare hard at my husband's dirty face. I cannot imagine what he is doing here.

"How ya' doin', babe?" He asks, as though he hasn't been gone from my house for ages, as though he didn't call me to say he was leaving Molly and me, as though he could just take off with some other woman, leaving us alone to fend for ourselves.

I don't answer. I study his face in the faint light of what must be the moon. It occurs to me to offer him a glass of cold water, but I dismiss that thought as well, thinking I do not want to be kind to him, recalling our last conversation when he blamed me for everything. I want to see what he has to say, find out what has caused him to drive down here straight from his work, hours away.

"Well, I guess you're not doing so good," he says, shaking his head, as though he's gotten a telegram about what was going on with his family.

"Mom called me last night and told me there's been a lot going on over here. She said she doesn't actually know what, but she said it was high time for me to come check on things myself. She says I owe it to my family, and she's worried about Molly."

I'm thinking we are not his family any longer, and I am confused by this sudden visit, sparked by Gail's concern. I wonder if Wilson has even told his mother that he has left us and plans to go off with a woman named Maureen to live in Idaho. I am too sleepy to yell at him, so I sit on the sofa and listen, instead. I let him ramble, saying his mother calls him regularly to report on Molly's problems, telling him how I hadn't been able to get a wheelchair for her, how frustrated and angry Molly seemed when she last saw her. She said enough, apparently, to make him drive all the way to the Bootheel to check on us in the middle of the night. My husband tells me he needs to know everything that has been going on with Molly and me.

*Not on your life*, I'm thinking, *I'm not telling you anything. Why would you even care?*

Fully awake now, I stand up and say, "I'm going to make sure Molly is still asleep and close all the doors." I was fully expecting a loud argument, and I don't want Molly to hear it. For the first time, I feel ready for it. This time, I'll find my voice, but, at this point, I have no idea what I will say.

I look in on Molly, and silently close her door, until it makes a faint click. I walk down the dark hallway, where the lightbulb is still out, and close that door, too. When I return to the living room, I suggest Wilson follow me out to the porch, where we can sit in the light from the kitchen window, far from Molly's room, and talk. I am hesitant to take all these precautions, knowing Molly will be distressed if she calls me and I don't hear her, but I decide that's better than her hearing our conversation. I am not in the mood for small talk, and I do not want to hear about Wilson's new girlfriend. I am also not willing to spend hours haggling with Wilson about what's going on with Molly, so I decide to just tell him. He is, after all, her father and, perhaps, deserves to know. I keep my voice low and flat, no emotion at all. I stand, so I can look down on him.

"Molly is pregnant. No one but me and the staff at the women's clinic knows this yet. I'd like to keep it that way."

Wilson's reaction startles me.

"What?"

He stands abruptly, almost flipping his wooden rocker. His face takes on a look I've only seen a few times before, eyes tight in their sockets, mouth closed and tight, his lips gone. In a cartoon, there would be smoke coming out of his ears.

"My God," he says, his words flooding the night air.

I motion for him to quiet down.

"Why didn't you call and tell me? I deserve to know if *my own daughter* has been tampered with, molested, is pregnant! Oh, my God, this is insane. I knew something like this would happen."

"Wilson, I didn't call you because you never answer, and you do not call me back, ever! What good does it ever do to call you? I gave up on that a long time long ago."

He knows this is true and has no ready answer. I face him down. He is getting more and more agitated, his face too close to mine, his arms shaking me. He's yelling the same words, over and over again.

"How did this happen? How could it happen? Who's been here? Answer me, Alice."

"Quiet! Listen, Molly doesn't even know, not really!" I hiss at him and try to make him understand.

"What do you mean?"

"She doesn't know what happened. How could she? She's just a child. I did have her do a home pregnancy test when her periods stopped, but that's as far as we've gotten. She knows she's pregnant, but she really doesn't understand what that means. I've told her I'll take her to a women's clinic as soon as I can get her an appointment. That's where we are right now, waiting to hear back from them, and I don't want you to fuck this up. Do you hear me? I'm taking care of things. I don't need you here."

"What are you talking about? What do you mean she doesn't know?"

He spits the words back into my face. "OF COURSE SHE KNOWS!"

He keeps raising his voice, but I caution him to quiet down.

"She must know someone did this, did something to her. What are you talking about? How could she not *know* that someone did this to her? You're delusional. She's been raped by someone. Surely, she knows that much! She may not understand she's pregnant, but even at her age she must know something happened! Did you ask her?"

I don't answer him.

He asks again, "Did you ask her? What did she say?" He's in my face, moving closer.

"I'm going to go right in there and ask her myself," Wilson declares, moving toward the door.

"She must be able to tell us who did this to her, when, and where. I must know. I deserve to know the truth. She is not mute or retarded, she just can't walk. And that makes all this worse. What's wrong with you? Why didn't you watch her? I have to know who did this! I knew you couldn't protect my daughter. I should never have left her with you! This is all your fault, Alice, all your fault."

I cringe, listening to his harsh words, but I am resolved not to let him take me down. When he heads for the screen door, I stand and stop him with my arm.

"Sit down, Wilson. I will not allow you to barge in there and talk to Molly. Not now. Sit!"

He continues to breathe acid into my face, and his ridiculous words threaten to puncture me, even as I listen for the sound of Molly's voice. Finally, though, he sits down. He seems cowed by my refusal to tell him anything more.

"Okay, Alice, you must know who did this! Talk to me. You *do* know who did this, don't you? I know you know. What are you hiding from me? Tell me, NOW!"

Wilson has leaned over the chairs and taken me by the shoulders. He is shaking my body back and forth, causing my teeth to rattle in my mouth. His fingers are digging into my skin. I can't wrench away from him. He shakes me again, his spit on my face, then flings me back into my chair and waits for me to respond. I realize I am afraid of him. I know he could hurt me, and no one would know. I force myself to stand straight out of my chair and face him, ready to do battle. He repeats what he's been saying, relentless.

"You must tell me what you know. I am her father. I must know, NOW! Tell me who did this to *my daughter*. I deserve to know what has been going on around here. Why didn't you tell me? What are you hiding? What do you know?"

My shaking body matches his own. I stare into his distorted face, him resolved to get me to talk, me resolved not to tell him what I know. I'm thinking, *there is so much more to this than what you think you want to hear from me. There is so much more, but I cannot tell you. It will break us all.*

I shake my head, "No. I cannot and will not tell you. You deserve nothing. You left us, remember? You hear me, you deserve nothing!"

Wilson stands up and slaps me hard across the face. I surprise myself and try to slap him back, but he easily grabs my hand and wraps his beefy arms around my body, clutching me close in a suffocating embrace.

"You will tell me. I will not take no for an answer. Do you hear me?"

He says it again and again, his voice tight, seething

"You will tell me. I will not let you go until you tell me."

Tears are falling down his face, but I am not persuaded. He wants to break me. He thinks he can fix this. I know he can't.

Desperate, Wilson puts his hands around my throat. He tightens his fingers, and I feel my body go limp. He struggles to hold me up, but I collapse around his feet, unable to withstand his interrogation any longer.

Suddenly, I *want* to tell him. I *need* to tell him. I am aching to tell someone what has happened to Molly, what I discovered in the barn.

Finally, from the porch floor, the words spill out of my mouth. Once released, I cannot pull them back. I can barely hear my own voice, scratchy and pained.

"My brother," I whisper.

"What did you say?" He leans down to hear better.

"It was Robert who's been molesting her. I didn't know. I swear, all this time, I didn't know. I didn't know he was touching her, maybe for years. I didn't know why she wanted to be with him, or why she stopped walking or wetting her bed. I didn't know. I didn't know. When I saw them in the loft, together, asleep, their clothes off, I lost my mind. I tried to kill him. I stabbed Robert."

I close my mouth and put my lips together. I have said more than enough.

I am a heap on the floor. I do not care what happens next, until he says to me, "I knew this had something to do with you, Alice. I knew you couldn't take care of her. You are such a failure. Always a failure. Your own brother. Of course, it was your brother."

Suddenly, I know what I have to do. I pull myself up from the porch floor, walk into the kitchen and grab a large knife with my right hand. Wilson tries to follow me into the house, but I quickly turn and march him back to the door. I hold the knife with one hand and hold the door open with the other. In a steady voice, I order my husband to leave.

"Get the fuck out of my house!" I tell him. "You are scum. You are not a husband and a father. You are nothing to us anymore. Walk out of this door right now, Wilson, or I will use this knife on you. I promise I will hurt you!

"And don't ever come back. We don't want to see you, ever! I will get a lawyer and sue you for every dime you have.

I'll get everything, and you will pay for Molly's doctor bills. I am NOT a failure, Wilson. You'd like me to believe I am, but I'm not. I am strong, I am capable, and I can prove it. I've done everything for Molly. I've done the job of two parents. I am consistent. Do you hear that, Wilson? I am everything you are not. I am a good mother, and none of this is my fault, none of it! You discarded us and never looked back. I am done, Wilson. *We* are done with you. Now, get out of my house!"

My voice is steel. I grip the handle of the knife tighter and raise it in the air. I know Wilson is stronger than me and could probably get the knife out of my hand, but I am suddenly convinced of my own power. If he rushes me, I will plunge the knife into his body, even if he hurts me later.

My husband stares at me as though he doesn't know me. He doesn't know this version of his wife. Something about the way I'm standing before him, knife in the air, convinces him to leave. He walks through the door, strides across the gravel and starts his truck. He spins out of the driveway and speeds away. I have no idea where he is going, and I don't care. I feel only relief that he is gone, hopefully out of my life, out of *our* lives. I go inside, close the door, and lock it behind me.

# Chapter 11

## Hand of Hope

For the next few days, the local police keep a close eye on me, and I try to keep a low profile, not going out unless I need groceries, not willing to cause any suspicion about what actually happened in Robert's barn. Molly reads or watches television, and I wait for the phone to ring, hoping either Victoria or Mary will call back with instructions to get Molly to a clinic as soon as possible. We're both bored and nervous.

Apparently, Wilson left my house that night, found out where Robert was, and attacked him in his bed at the hospital. He nearly strangled him to death before the guard who had been stationed at the door rushed in and pushed him onto the floor. I heard it on the local news and found myself disgusted to hear what he had done. Yet, even as that thought went through my mind, I recognized that his actions were no more reprehensible than my own. He was arrested on the spot and sent to the jail in town.

Thus far, they have no leads on the stabbing in the barn, only my eyewitness account of the aftermath. I can imagine they are waiting for the man in the ICU to wake up, although he has had quite a setback from the strangle-hold on his neck, not to mention the pitchfork they'd found in his gut. Maybe they believe either Wilson, or I, will talk, but so far that hasn't happened.

Come to think of it, I'm surprised Wilson hasn't told anyone why he went to the hospital with the intention of killing Robert. Why wouldn't he tell them the truth, that he came home to check on us, and I convinced him that Robert had raped Molly? On the other hand, it's far better for me if Wilson does not reveal that I told him about Robert, especially because I also told him that I had tried to kill my brother.

If he hasn't told them I stabbed Robert, I'm wondering why. Does he have some idea that talking will get him in more trouble than if he stays quiet? Seems to me his defense of his daughter's virtue would be a good way to gain their respect, but I'm new to all this legal stuff. I don't know what either he or Robert might be thinking, or what they might say to the authorities. It would probably look better if I went to visit my brother in the hospital and my husband in the county jail, but the thought of seeing either of them right now makes my stomach curdle.

I steel myself to stop thinking about what the police know, or want to know, and focus only on the critical business of finding help for Molly. Mary has finally called, and she says her plans are going to work out for us. She reminds me to pack a bag for each of us and wait for her to arrive. I obediently stuff a few shirts and pants, underwear and toothbrushes into two duffle bags, one for me and one for Molly. I include enough clothes in each for a week. I'm not sure why I pack so much, but I do. I hide the bags behind the sofa so no one will notice them, wondering if I should go ahead and put them in the trunk of my car. I realize I'm already thinking like a criminal, or a fugitive. I realize at this point, I am both.

Early in the afternoon, Barb drops by for a visit. She knows Robert was stabbed in his barn, but that's all she knows. She does not yet know about Molly and Robert, although I did finally tell her about Molly's pregnancy. I'm so worried I'll tell her something I shouldn't, I avoid the topic altogether, hoping she won't ask me any direct questions. While Molly watches a TV show in my bedroom, we talk quietly about her situation and if the local clinic will be able to help. Together, we go over the obstacles the clinic related to me, all things Barb had already anticipated, to be fair. When she looks at me with her damp, caring eyes and so much concern in her face, I tell her about Mary's call and her late-night visit. I remind her that I had met Mary a few years ago, when I went to the clinic thinking I was pregnant again.

"Anyway, after I'd called the clinic about Molly being pregnant, and they weren't ready to help us, or couldn't, it surprised me that Mary called me afterward. She still works there. She said I had given her my phone number when I'd been to the clinic myself that one time. Besides, she said, she had access to Molly's file, which included my mobile number.

"When she first called, I was a bit confused," I told Barb. "But she explained she had heard the women in the office discussing Molly's situation, and she felt she should step up and help any way she could. Of course, when she said this, I was so eager for someone to help us, you know? She says she knows a clinic that can provide the help that Molly needs, and she has offered to take us to this clinic herself. I have already packed overnight bags for us, and she's going to pick us up tonight."

I can feel my excitement rise, as I tell Barb how close we are to getting help for Molly. I search her face for the relief I expect to see there, but instead I see concern. I ask her what's bothering her, but she only shakes her head, as though she's trying to remember something she may have heard about the clinic, or about Mary. She repeats the name Mary has given me for the name of the new clinic, "Hand of Hope," and says, "that sounds familiar."

Before Barb can tell me what she's thinking, we both see a police car pull into my driveway. Their timing could not be worse, I think. I don't want to deal with them today, I want to talk to Barb and wait for Mary. I need to leave town as soon as possible. We watch two uniformed men get out of the vehicle and start walking toward my front door. Barb looks at me and whispers something I don't have time to process. "Be careful, Alice. Things are not always what they seem." I don't know if she's referring to Mary, the Hand of Hope clinic, or the approaching policemen. By the time they are all done with Molly and me, it will apply to all three, and more.

The police officers bang on my front door and tell me they need to ask more questions. I am barely civil when I open the door and stand aside to let them come in. I do not invite them to sit down, but I remind myself to introduce them to Barb and tell them she is my close friend. Given this unexpected opportunity, they are suddenly eager to ask her a few questions about "the incident in the barn." Barb is no more friendly to the officers than I am. She tells them she doesn't know anything about what has happened, that she only that knows Robert is my brother and that he's been stabbed in his barn, information she has gathered from the newspaper and rumors in the community. They seem surprised to learn that I have not yet told her that I was the one to find Robert injured in the barn, but it is true. I have not breathed a word of it to her, or anyone else, with the exception of Wilson, but not for the reasons they might think. She does tell them Robert has been a big help to Molly and me.

"My friend often needs help," Barb says, as she nods toward me, "because her no good husband took off with another woman and left his wife and daughter to fend for themselves." I appreciate her critique of Wilson, and her willingness to say this directly to the police. I know it doesn't add much to the narrative they are trying to create about my family, but I'm still glad to hear her paint Wilson as a jerk who has abandoned his family. The policemen nod their heads and say they have met Mr. Campbell at the jail, but he hasn't really told them anything that is helpful. I am relieved to hear that. The less everyone knows, the better.

One of the officers takes this opportunity to ask me questions about my husband, how long he's been gone, why he came back this week, and if I have any idea why he would try to kill my brother. I shake my head and tell him I have no idea why he returned, or why he would go to the hospital to find Robert, which is a blatant lie. I don't look at Barb. I don't want her to read my face. I hold my features still and order my chin not to quiver. I tell them my husband and brother have never had any problems to speak of. If anything, my husband has always seemed to appreciate how much my brother helps out with things around our house when he is gone. I almost add something about how good Robert is with Molly, but I stop myself in time not to say their names together in the same sentence. I give no hint of the story I cannot reveal. Not having anything more to add, Barb moves toward the door, and the police tell her they may have more questions for her later on. She nods and turns to leave, but as soon as I hear the officers' next question, I stop her and ask if she can stay a minute.

The officers are asking me to re-enact my walk to Robert's barn the day I found him stabbed in the loft. Quietly, I ask Barb to please go sit with Molly in her room, while we're out of the house. She agrees, and I take the officers out the back door and lead them down the narrow path past the dewberries. The further I walk, the weaker my legs become. I tell them this is very difficult for me, and they try to be sympathetic, again for the wrong reasons.

I explained to them that I had stopped to eat a few berries that day and stained my shirt. One of them writes this in his notebook. I cannot imagine how that might be important. I take them through the house exactly as I explored it that day when I couldn't find Robert. We enter through the front door, go upstairs, past the messy rooms, the tiny bathroom, downstairs, the spotless kitchen. I make no comment on the state of any of the rooms. I take them past the shed with the TV and the battered horsehair sofa, then I walk them to the barn, swing open the double doors and point out the horse and the piglets. My feet dragging in the fluffy straw, I turn and force myself up the steps into the hayloft. I repeat what I told them before, that I came here looking for Robert, because I remembered he liked to go up to the loft and sleep in the hay as a child. I push the hinged door into the loft as I had done before, and I nearly faint when I see the blood in the hay. The smell fills my nostrils, my eyes, my mouth, and I puke into the soft straw. The officers watch as I clean my face with a tissue. They wait for my eyes to clear, and for me to find my voice.

I look away, trying to locate the pitchfork, but it is gone, not a good sign. My guess is they've taken it for fingerprints. They ask me to describe exactly what I saw when I got to the loft where my brother was lying in the hay, whether he was asleep or awake, if I thought he knew I had come into the loft. I'm thinking this is a trick question. How could he be asleep with a pitchfork deep in his gut? I was caught off guard and wondered if I'd made some huge mistake earlier, when I first told them my story.

They ask a lot of questions about the pitchfork, where it was when I saw it, and where on my brother's body he had been stabbed. I do not lie, exactly, but I do not tell them the whole story. I certainly do not say Robert was lying asleep in the hay. I tell them Robert was lying there with a pitchfork sticking out of his body and blood all over the place. By omitting Molly from the scene, I omit her from my story. I do not mention Robert's pants were around his ankles. I know that is what they found when they got there, but what they make of that is their business. I tell them I have no idea if he saw me come into the loft. I tell them I was terrified when I got up there and thought my brother was probably dead.

What I do not tell the police frightens me far more than what I do. I am constructing a story on the spot, one I must remember, word for word, for all the times I will be asked to tell it over and over again. The fewer words the better. I tell them I ran down the stairs and back to my own house, got my phone, and called the police. Only a small portion of this story is the truth, but as long as neither Robert, nor Molly, nor Wilson, contradict what I have said, I just might buy some more time to get Molly to a clinic that can help her, and for me to get a lawyer. When the officers seem satisfied with my story, I brace myself to breathe normally and not lose my balance as we descend the slippery steps and leave the barn.

Back at the house, I realize they are not finished badgering me with questions, but I'm having trouble focusing. Luckily, my reluctance to speak and tell the gory details seems fitting, given what I tell them I found in the barn. They grant me lots of time to try and remember what happened that day and what I saw. They seem to think it makes perfect sense that I had gone to find him at his place, given that I had not heard from him all afternoon. Robert had meant to bring us some fresh vegetables, I tell them, but he hadn't yet delivered them to my kitchen and that was unusual for my brother, who was always prompt with whatever he promised to do. They do not seem suspicious of my account, and I nod toward the box of vegetables on the counter. Thankfully, they never ask me where Molly was when I walked over to Robert's. Maybe they think she's old enough to leave for a few minutes alone in the house, long enough for me to check on my brother. I am relieved they do not ask to speak to Molly about her uncle. I'm guessing they assume the girl knows nothing about the stabbing, or what might have occurred in Robert's barn. I wish that were true, but I actually do not know what Molly knows or what she saw. I refuse to ask her, and she hasn't seemed eager to talk about it.

When they finally leave, and Barb goes home, Molly asks me about the policemen at our house. Apparently, one officer did walk down the hall while the rest of us were in the barn but didn't speak to her or Barb. At one point, Molly asks me where Robert is. I notice her eyes seem to shift when she asks about him, and I feel bad telling her I'm not sure where he is. Back in her room, she fidgets with her pencils as she gazes out the window at his barn.

I am still wondering if Robert will live and be able to testify against Wilson. If that happens, I realize, he might also be able to testify against me. But right now, I do not have time to think about the police or worry what they might think when they discover Molly and I are gone. Will they issue a warrant for my arrest? Will they come after us and Mary? Every second, I feel more like a criminal, slouching behind the sofa to pull out our bags, packing a few food items and drinks for each of us, making certain I have everything we might need.

Mary calls in the late afternoon to ask if she can come visit again. Overwhelmed with gratitude, I tell her she is welcome to come anytime, although I have begun to wonder a bit about the cloak-and-dagger phone calls and the late-night visits. Such is the life of abortion workers, I think, a sad reality for women in America these days. With the latest news about the Supreme Court rulings, I am learning how the landscape surrounding laws about women's bodies and abortion, in particular, is shifting rapidly. I am reminded, too, of the clinic's warnings about Molly being in a wheelchair and the problem that she is so young. I wonder if these obstacles are severe enough to keep Mary and the staff at Hand of Hope from helping her. At the very least, I am reassured by Mary's determination to go beyond what the local women's clinic can do and personally help us find a solution.

"Of course," I tell Mary. "I've been waiting for you to call and can't wait to hear what you have to tell us about where we are going?"

I sit down with an empty cup to wait. When Mary arrives at 10:15, I make a fresh pot of coffee. We both agree we need it, even at this late hour. Soon, Mary is flushed with the caffeine and seems especially excited with the news she brings.

"First, the bad news, the hard news you're not going to like, but I encourage you to be patient and listen to what I have to say. The bad news is that the clinic here is not in a position to help Molly at this time, just as I had suspected. They regret they cannot help, but with the laws changing with the Supreme Court ruling, their legal standing could be jeopardized and all the health care work they do for women would be called into question. To get embroiled in this case at this time with a disabled girl so young, would call too much attention to the organization and threaten the many ways they can help lots of women, not just Molly. It is also true that they do not have a doctor on staff who has a hospital affiliation, which is a requirement for abortion care. They warned you about this when you first called, right?"

I nod my head, although my eyes have already filled with hot tears I can't control. Mary notices my distress but keeps talking.

"What you may not know, because most people don't, is that there are other agencies helping women who are in the same position as your daughter. Young girls, unmarried women, married women, women who have been raped, who have experienced incest, all women seeking help for their pregnancies. Because Planned Parenthood, especially, has such a large profile in this country, we tend to think they are the only agency offering counseling, medical exams, and solutions to unwanted pregnancies, but that's not the case. In southern Missouri, in fact, there are several smaller, well-funded agencies who stand willing and able to help women through this difficult time. Sometimes their rules and procedures are not as stringent as those of Planned Parenthood, and the services they provide are more accommodating, especially in certain circumstances, such as what you and your daughter face. I'm wondering if you have heard of any of these other agencies here in Missouri?"

"No," I answer, truthfully. "The only one I've known about for ages has been the local women's clinic."

Mary nods with the memory of our first visit.

"Well, you might be surprised to know that these other agencies are eager to help women navigate what have become very rough waters, indeed! Shall I continue?"

For an hour, Mary talks with me about some of the agencies she has researched. She pulls out her laptop and clicks on the links to several "alternative" clinics in Missouri, some further north of us and a few to the south, deeper in the Bootheel. She scrolls through several websites that are especially compelling, professionally designed, full of pictures of smiling women and babies, doctors in white coats, nurses caring for babies in incubators. I make a mental note of the names on the screen: "Your Baby, Your Choice," "Finding Solutions Together," "Hand of Hope," "Preferred Women's Health Center," "Crisis Pregnancy Clinic," the list goes on. Mary notes that most of the clinics offer free exams and assessments of the age of the fetus, free ultrasounds, free medications, free consulting services for adoptions when needed. "I have checked around, and I think 'Hand of Hope' would be your best option for Molly."

"It all sounds too good to be true," I admit to Mary. "But I totally trust you to help me take Molly to a different clinic, where she can get the help she needs."

Agreeing to act quickly, Mary stands to give me a big hug before she moves toward the door, telling me to leave everything up to her. I am happy to be in her good care, thankful someone has stepped up and answered my prayers. I feel so much better. I long to dash into Molly's room and tell her the good news, but I don't tell Molly anything at all. I am in over my head. I need someone else to talk to her first, a professional, someone who counsels pregnant women and girls every day. I am defeated by my cowardice.

The next night, I prepare to leave as soon as Mary returns. I wake Molly from a deep sleep and tell her we need to take a ride, and she can sleep in the car. I am surprised that Mary wants me to drive my car, but without asking any questions,

I sit behind the wheel, after strapping Molly in the backseat and fixing her up with pillows so she can go back to sleep. Mary sits next to me, and we leave my house. She assures me someone will come pick up her car and take it back to the clinic. Only now, she informs me we are going to Kennett, a small town in southern Missouri, where the Bootheel juts down a little further into Arkansas. I remember my earlier thoughts about feeling at a loss, because Molly and I had no one to rely on, but tonight I feel more confident because I have Mary with me. I am most definitely not alone. Mary is a large, capable woman, a loving, kind and compassionate friend who has taken a genuine interest in me and my daughter. I am blessed, and I remember to float a little prayer of thanks that someone is finally paying attention.

Two and a half hours later, we arrive at Hand of Hope and are graciously welcomed by the staff, which has been informed we were on the road. It's nearly midnight, yet some of the workers are there to welcome us. With gentle reassurances, the volunteers thank Mary for delivering Molly. Things seem to be happening quickly, and I am surprised to learn Mary isn't going to stay with us. She has done her part, and now someone else will return her to her regular job at the clinic in Sikeston, while Molly and I will stay here with the staff at Hand of Hope.

"We will take it from here," the director of the clinic says as she joins us in the front foyer to say goodbye to Mary. We whisper our goodbyes and thanks to Mary, who promises to follow up as soon as she hears back from us. She climbs into the passenger seat of the driver's car, and off they go into the dark night. I am a bit flustered with Mary's immediate exit, but I realize this turnover is part of a well-oiled procedure. Mary is just one part of a larger plan to help women, so I try to relax. Within minutes, Molly and I are taken to a bedroom with two single beds and invited to get some sleep. Molly is more than ready to lie down in a nice, soft bed, and I follow her as quickly as I can. Surprisingly, we both sleep soundly.

The next morning around 7:30, a young counselor comes to our door and gestures for us to follow her to a simple breakfast of juice and toast. After we eat, she invites us to go with her to a separate room in the clinic. We sit together in the three chairs in the room, but she speaks primarily to Molly.

"My name is Amanda," she tells us and gives her full attention to Molly. She asks her a few questions about her life, what she likes to read, her friends, simple things Molly can easily answer, although I can see she's reluctant to say she's not in school and doesn't have many friends. Amanda does not ask any questions about Molly's inability to walk or her age. Instead, she goes into the hallway and quietly rolls a wheelchair into the room, inviting Molly to sit in it. Molly is shocked by this generosity and eagerly lets Amanda help her sit in the chair. Once there, she seems to enjoy her new perch and smiles over at me. After a bit of easy conversation, Amanda politely asks me to leave Molly alone with her. This is standard practice, she assures me with a big smile, because it is important to get both of our perspectives of the situation—Molly's and my own. I hesitate, but Molly tells me she will be fine and urges me to wait in the front waiting room.

The wait is long, and I begin to fidget. I do a little meditation breathing to pass the time and calm my nerves. I can't imagine what Amanda and Molly are discussing. I fail at my meditation. Finally, around 11:30, Amanda brings me to Molly's room with the instruction that I let Molly talk to me first about what she is thinking and feeling about her situation.

The counselor leaves the room and closes the door behind her. Before she speaks, I realize Molly has a wadded-up tissue in her hand, and I can see she's been crying. Not knowing exactly what to do, I sit on the edge of the bed and wait for her to speak. I wait several minutes before she seems ready to talk to me, a cautious smile plastered on her face.

"Hi, Mom." Molly's voice squeaks like she's been crying for some time. Although her face is pink, she seems strangely happy. Her face and her tears don't seem to match. I say nothing, just smile like the idiot she used to call me.

"Mom, I don't know how much you know, probably a lot, given that you were the one who brought me here, and I want to thank you for that, for finding help for me. I know this is a big mess, and I'm not quite certain how I got here, but there are so many things I have learned being with Amanda that I want to share with you."

I sit mesmerized by my daughter's voice, which seems to have aged several years in only two days. When she speaks, her words come in a steady stream, as though she has so little time to tell me all she has learned.

"First, I want you to know that I have learned how much God loves me. Even if I have sinned and done things that are wrong in his sight, I know he still loves me. I have been thinking a lot about what I was doing up in the barn loft with Robert. I now know it was wrong and a sin, and it has caused great pain to God. Even so, he still loves me. I am so thankful to know that he loves me. And I know that he will stand by me when I have this baby that is growing in my tummy. He does not blame me for what we did in the barn, because he knows I am only a child and blameless, but now I know God does not want me to kill this baby. He wants me to give it life, which only I have the power to do. I know that because I am pregnant, I am no longer an innocent child, and I know that I must pay for my sins through the pain of childbirth. Then, God will help me decide whether or not I will keep this child and raise it myself, or if I will let Him and Amanda find a family who will care and love it forever. I am so thankful I have come here to learn of God's love for me. Amanda has told me what a great mother you are to bring me here and help me discover what I must do. I'm so happy—"

I am so stunned by Molly's words my heart stops dead in my chest. All the air in the room has been sucked out, leaving only her and me in this nondescript room in an alternate universe. *How did we get here? What am I doing sitting on this bed listening to Molly talk about how God knows she sinned and how he wants her to "keep her baby?"*

With a shiver of horror, my heart begins to thud, fast and furious. I feel the blood fill my face. I rise from my chair too quickly, knocking it to the floor. I don't pick it up. I grab my purse off the bed and reach for the handles of Molly's wheelchair. Without a word, I wheel her around and head for the door. She is upset and cries out for me to stop.

"Mom, what are you doing? What is going on?"

Her voice carries through the rooms and onto the sidewalk outside. I ignore her and push the wheelchair toward the sliding front doors as quickly as I can, hoping no one will try to stop me. I cannot think beyond getting to my car and leaving. I fit the key in the lock with shaking fingers, open the doors, and push Molly into the backseat without buckling her in. I awkwardly fold the wheelchair until it is flat enough to fit into the trunk.

Once I'm in the driver's seat, I lock all the doors. I still do not speak to Molly. My hands are shaking so violently, I fumble with the key in the ignition, then speed away from the clinic, driving down the highway as fast as I can. I do not listen to the sounds of my daughter, who calls out to me again and again, crying, screaming my name over and over. I drive as though a monster is on our heels, a sinister, unknown force, chasing us across the fields of cotton and tobacco that surround the car. In a few furious minutes, I realize I have no idea where we are or where I am going. I glance at the mirror above my head and see that it reads "N." At least I'm heading in the right direction. Beyond that, I cannot think. My brain keeps repeating the same line over and over, no pause, as I race down the highway.

*No, no, no, this cannot be happening,*
*No, no, no, this cannot be happening,*
*No, no, no, this cannot be happening.*

# Chapter 12

## Finding Aunt Ruth

Two hours later, as darkness folds in on us, and Molly is finally quiet, I pull into a service station to buy gas and figure out where we are. I open my car door cautiously, tell her I'll be right back, step out, and lock the doors behind me. I walk into the building to use the bank machine I can see through the window. I take out as much money as I can in one transaction, hoping I can get more later. As far as I know, Wilson and I still have a joint account, and I have access to it. I punch in the numbers, relieved the transaction is going through. I collect the money with greedy hands and tuck the money into three different places in my purse and my pockets, trying to be both calm and rational. I am neither. I buy orange Gatorade, her favorite, and Diet Coke for me. I am going to need the caffeine, but I don't want coffee, thinking it will upset my stomach. I also grab some chips and a couple of granola bars. I type our home address into the GPS, and discover we are an hour and fifty minutes from home, still deep in the Bootheel, moving north away from the Arkansas border. I try to assure myself that Molly and I will be okay down here, although I've heard stories of dangerous rednecks and meth heads all my life, and I know to worry. I pump gas, then turn the icon of the little red car toward home, not knowing what we will find when we get there.

I am thankful Molly has given up crying and screaming at me and has fallen asleep in the back, slumped across the seat. I know it's not safe, but I decide not to wake her, hoping to put as many miles as I can between us and Hand of Hope. At least another hour has passed before I feel I can slow down, knowing a traffic ticket today would not be a good thing for my record. I tell myself no one is likely following us from the clinic. Why would they do that? It doesn't make any sense they would actually chase us down, no matter how assured they are of their own convictions.

As I drive, I try to sort out what has just happened. The voice in my head begins to imagine a plausible narrative, but whatever comes to mind sounds more like a thriller or a bad dream. Mary must be a spy. She works at Planned Parenthood as a regular volunteer, but she bides her time and approaches girls and women who come in seeking abortions, secretly guiding them toward pro-life centers, such as the one we just left, and delivers them to her friends. I feel so stupid. I was the perfect target, so distraught and vulnerable. It never occurred to me that Mary's help was a trick, that it came with a price. I wonder how long she's been doing this, and if she's the only one at the clinic stealing clients away and changing the agenda without their permission? Why has no one reported her?

Instead of focusing on how angry I am that Mary deceived us and how Amanda spoke to Molly in ways I am totally opposed to, I remind myself I should be thinking about what I am going to tell my daughter now. She must be so confused. Because they were kind and generous and thoughtful, she must think Amanda and the other women have guided her to the truth. What can I possibly say to Molly that can help her understand that Amanda has tricked her into believing something that absolutely should not happen to a child of ten?

How can I explain the indoctrination she has been subjected to by people who want to stop all abortions and protect the rights of human fetuses in every situation, even for little girls who have been raped. It may seem like a ridiculous comparison to Molly, but for me, it is *the* critical difference. What words can I find to counter the narrative they have just told her? Is there any way I will be able to offer an alternative story to the one she has just heard by these kind and well-meaning women? Why would she trust my "truth" over theirs?

The voice continues inside my head as I put mile after mile between Hand of Hope and what waits for us up ahead.

*Who can help Molly now?*

*Who can help me?*

*Who do I know that I'm not thinking of?*

My brain is spinning a web of despair and hopelessness. We're out here in the dark of night by ourselves, all alone, Molly and me, and I haven't a clue what to do next. I try to remember any relatives in southern Missouri who might be able help and wonder if I could just call them out of the blue? Surely, of all my aunts, uncles, and cousins all over the Bootheel, there must be someone who would remember me—one of my mom's sisters or my dad's siblings, someone who remembers James and Angie. Struggling with my poor memory of my mother's extended family, I try again to recall all her sisters' names. Most of them lived their whole lives in this area, but I have no recollection of visiting them, except maybe Marjorie, once or twice. I remember my dad liked her husband, that's why we might have visited them. Mom couldn't stand one of her sisters, thought she was a snob, prissy and pernickety, thought she was better than everybody else. And Trudy, I remember Trudy. My mom didn't like her. "Mean as the day is long," Mom used to say.

As I get closer to Sikeston, the hair on the back of my neck rises. What if the police are at my house, waiting for us to come back? Suddenly, I realize with total clarity that I can't let that happen. I press my foot on the gas and hardly blink as I drive past the exit signs for Sikeston, then Benton, then Cape Girardeau, Perryville, and Ste. Geneviève, the little red car on the screen traveling steadily north on I-55. After two more hours, struggling to stay awake, I realize I will soon get close to St. Louis, and I slow down. I don't want to get into city traffic, and we need to find a place to stay the night. I'm exhausted from the day and the anxiety of driving in such a panic. I blink my eyes to clear them, watching the center stripes slip by and pass beneath the car in a blur. I imagine looking down on my car from above, surrounded by darkness, hoping it will swallow Molly and me, leaving not a trace.

When I can no longer think or drive, I pull into a Best Western and park the car. We have no bags, no clothes, nothing, but we do have a wheelchair. I smile to myself as I pull it out of the trunk and knock it into shape, making sure the levers are locked so the chair will not spill Molly onto the asphalt. One more thing to add to my list of crimes, a stolen wheelchair! I gently wake Molly, help her into the chair, and push her toward the front revolving door that cannot accommodate the wheelchair. I pause, not knowing what to do next. It is after ten o'clock, and no one seems to be inside the lobby. I knock loudly on the glass, but no one appears. I try again and wait. Finally, I see a drowsy night attendant come out of a side door, behind the large check-in desk. He comes around and stares at us. He is briefly confused by our dilemma, but with a shake of his head, he finally gestures for us to come to a different door on the left that is wider and has a ramp. I cannot wait to get inside, but I also know there will be no peace with Molly until we talk about what happened, and why I drove us away in such a hurry.

We ride up the too-small elevator in silence. I try not to make eye contact with her but notice she can hardly hold her head up. Maybe our talk can wait. As gently as I can, I put her into bed with a melatonin and tell her to go back to sleep. I promise her we will talk in the morning, but for now she needs to rest. I would love to crawl into that soft bed with her and also fall asleep, but I know I don't have that luxury right now. I need to make a plan.

At first, I decide to use the directory that comes in every hotel room and search for anyone who might be kin to us, someone who could help. But the directory is old and is only for the St. Louis area code. Frustrated, I remind myself I don't even know my mother's sisters' married names and admit this search won't be helpful. I know her only brother died several years ago, so that's no help. I think briefly to search for my father's siblings, but somehow, I feel more comfortable looking for my mother's sisters. I can't say why I feel this way, but I do. It doesn't matter, though, nothing works, and I find no one I can call.

I fall asleep on my folded arms at the desk. When I wake up, three hours later, my arms tingling and stiff, a name appears in the air of the room, just floating there waiting for me to notice it. The memories come in a flush, as though I can hear my dad talking. He is talking about Ruth, one of my mom's sisters, and he is not saying anything nice about her. My dad had a lot of opinions, and many of them had to do with what women should and shouldn't do. I remember him saying that Ruth, who was younger than my mother, had left her husband, a Bootheel man my dad had known growing up, and eventually married a math professor and had moved to Columbia with him. As if that wasn't bad enough, my dad was agitated that Ruth had also gotten an advanced degree and had become a professor herself. How did I remember all of that? And why could I remember my father talking about her, specifically? I can hear him in my head, probably because he was angry with her. I must have tucked that information away years ago, maybe as a note to myself about how he would respond to any woman who "broke the rules."

My father's voice continues in my head. "She never should have done that, left her husband, and her son, too, to run off and marry that other man. He was way too educated for her. He must have enticed her away from her family. And she got all uppity, didn't she? She'd hardly talk to anybody after that. It wasn't right!" I could see him gesture to whomever was listening to him, maybe Mom and me, waiting for us to agree with him. Mom probably nodded, but I remember thinking this Ruth person might be pretty interesting.

Ruth and her new husband were both teaching at the university in Columbia, a big deal for anyone from our family, although my dad would never give her any credit for what she'd done. When I first went to college and said I wanted to be an English teacher, I recall my mom saying, "Maybe you can be like your Aunt Ruth," and my dad saying, "maybe not!"

My head hurts. I am desperate for coffee. I search all around the small microwave, angry the pods for the plastic excuse for a coffee maker are all gone. I drink chalky water from the faucet in the bathroom, wishing for a cold bottle of water. That isn't happening, either. I go back to my phone and type "University of Missouri" into a google search. In the banner at the top, there is a link to the faculty. I click, then click again on "English Department." I don't know Ruth's married name, so I scroll sleepily through the long list, wondering where I could get a cup of coffee at this hour. Might there be a pot of old coffee in the front lounge of the hotel? Could I dare go down there to check? I look over at Molly sleeping soundly and tell myself there's no way I can leave her, even for a minute.

More scrolling, but I do not see anyone with the name "Ruth," until, finally, *I do*. Right there, on the screen, I see "Professor Ruth Gideon." I stare at her color photo, convinced I can see my mother's own face in her features. She is listed as "Professor Emerita," but the website lists two courses she is still teaching on campus. I click on her email address and copy it with her name onto a piece of hotel stationery. I also write down the phone number listed for the English department. Of course, there is no personal number for her, and I know I cannot place any calls tonight, but I open the email account I have rarely ever used and type a short, urgent message.

To: Ruth Gideon
From: Alice Holden Campbell
Re: Help needed from your niece, please respond!

Dear Aunt Ruth, I know this email will come as a complete surprise to you, but I am desperate to find someone to help me. I am your niece, but I cannot remember when, or if, we actually ever met. My mother was Angie Mae Fletcher, until she married my dad, James Holden. I was named Alice Elaine Holden, until I married Wilson Campbell in southern Missouri. My daughter and I live in Sikeston, next door to our old family home. Molly, who is nearly ten and cannot walk, is pregnant. I have been trying to find someone who can help her. Maybe I would have better luck with a women's clinic in Columbia than I have had in the Bootheel. Or maybe we need someone to help us get across the border into Kansas or Illinois. I am desperate and have no one else to turn to. We have stopped at a motel on Interstate 55 near Ste. Genevieve. I will stay here until I hear from you.

Thank you so much,
Alice Campbell, your niece

I add my cell phone number and hit SEND before I have time to change my mind. I've seen enough cop shows on television to know that phone calls can be tracked. That's how they find criminals, but I'm not quite sure how all that works, so I add my phone number, thinking a call from Ruth would be worth the danger of someone tracking my phone. My hands are shaking in tune with my rapid heartbeat. I remind myself to breathe deeply and wing a little prayer across the internet alongside my email. Then, I lie down in the double bed next to Molly and spoon my body around hers, careful not to wake her. I hold on to her gently, hoping together we can do this. I have to believe that we can. We just need a little help from someone who cares. We both sleep till morning and wake up starving. I am ready to face the day and Molly's questions. That's my job, I keep reminding myself. I'm the mother.

The next couple of days pass in a blur of time passing too slowly to track, our minds lulled by the tedium of reruns with laugh tracks, documentaries of penguins in South Africa (who knew?), and fast-food dinners from the place across the street. We share juice and milk, and I drink far too much coffee, sometimes I drink a beer when I can find one. I find an incomplete deck of cards in a bedside table and spend long hours teaching Molly Spades and Gin Rummy, War and Solitaire. I hide the complimentary Bible in a desk drawer, not able to look at it after everything at Hand of Hope, a reminder of what the women told Molly. We take long baths, but neither of us sleeps very well after our fatigue that first night.

Molly's moods are erratic. She hates me most of the time, but other times, she crawls over next to me on the hard hotel sofa and buries her head under my arm, her eyes shaded by my shoulder. If she bothers to answer my questions, she barks her response, or growls, or shrugs, her eyes moldering deep and dark. I grow a thick skin, swearing I will give her all the room and time she needs, but also knowing I will be there when she softens. Even when it's most difficult, I remind myself she is only a confused child.

Molly keeps asking why we don't go home. She has no idea where we are, or why. I tell her we are at a Best Western hotel on I-55, outside of St. Louis, but that's all I know. She acts like I'm stupid not to know more than that, saying "This is pathetic. Why don't you know? I think you're insane, Mom, I really do. What is going on?"

I don't tell Molly not to yell at me, I only ask that she not raise her voice enough to let our neighbors or the hotel staff hear her. I do not want any attention. She has no idea the police are likely looking for me and are undoubtedly watching our house night and day, waiting for me to answer more of their questions or arrest me on the spot. I cringe to think whether Robert or Wilson have talked to the police, which could make my position that much more precarious.

Although I am dying to talk to her and find out what's going on, I don't call Barb, knowing the police can find us by tracing where my phone is being used. I try not to evade Molly's questions about why we're hanging out in a hotel, so I tell her I am waiting for a phone call or an email that might help me decide what we need to do next. She just shakes her head and turns back to the television. She says very little about Hand of Hope, God, sinning with Robert, or the fact that she is pregnant.

Maybe Molly thinks the past few days were just a dream. I wish it were that simple. Sometimes at night, I hold her as she cries against my chest, but she doesn't seem to know why she's crying. I know I have failed her, but I have no idea how to explain the confusion I've brought into her life. The truth is, Molly deserves answers. She has been through so much in the past few years, more than I could have imagined, more than I knew, more than I want to face. The fact that I failed to notice what was going on with her, the fact that I couldn't see her pain and confusion, the fact that I trusted Robert so completely, all that makes me complicit in Molly's betrayal. She is where she is now, a pregnant child, because I did not think about the possibilities, because I could not even imagine them as possibilities. Robert is my brother, and I have loved and trusted him without question my whole life. Doing so blinded me and put my child in danger. I left her on her own to navigate a situation she could not comprehend. She had no skills for what she encountered, so she responded the way a child should respond to love and touch. She was grateful for his attention, happy to feel loved, content with the warmth of his affection. She saw no red flags, because she didn't know what those flags might be, even if they were waving furiously. She felt them ruffling, perhaps, but because she is a child, she mistook them for something else.

I tell myself to stop with the commentary and step up. Feeling guilty isn't going to help Molly now but telling her the truth just may help her recover, eventually. On day three of our hotel stay on the side of the interstate, waiting for someone to rescue us, Molly finally erupts, "So, Mom! Just tell me what happened down there at that clinic? I liked it. I liked the women there, and they really helped me understand what was going on, unlike YOU, who tells me nothing! What the hell happened? Did the baby just go away? And why did you make us leave like that?"

I take a deep breath and hope for the best. The language I'm about to use is new to my mouth. Frankly, I have no idea what I'm doing.

"Molly, at this point, what is in your body isn't actually a baby, yet. You might think about it as the *possibility* of a baby." I'm speaking as calmly as I possibly can to her, trying to make sense of this disaster.

"What do you mean 'the possibility of a baby'? That makes no sense at all.

Mom! Talk to me!"

"Ok, maybe this will help. Last night, when you were sleeping, I found something on the internet that will help me explain it. Want to look at it?"

Like most kids her age, anything digital beats listening to your mother, so Molly sits up straight on the sofa and nods that she'd like to see it. We watch the short video titled "What is pregnancy?" together, twice, then Molly takes the phone and watches it again. She looks at me with a frown that could wither King Kong himself.

"So, Molly, do you have any questions after seeing this?"

"I have no idea," she answers slowly, not meeting my eye. "None of it makes any sense to me. This isn't about me. I'm just a kid, and all this seems like science stuff and not about me." She takes a deep breath and tries again.

"Okay, so what I was doing in the barn with Robert got me pregnant, is that right?"

"Well," I realize I need to tread very carefully here. I take a big breath before I speak.

"I might say that a bit differently. I would say what Robert was doing to you in the barn got you pregnant. I say it this way because it really wasn't *you* doing anything, rather you were responding to what Robert was doing to you, which was as wrong as anything in this world is wrong. That's an important thing to remember. However long your uncle was touching you, however many days or weeks or months—" I pause here because the thought makes me nauseous "—or years, it was wrong for him to do that. Whether you liked it or not doesn't matter one bit. It was wrong for him to touch you. He is a grown man, and, trust me, he knew what he was doing was wrong. You are a child, and you didn't know what was going on. That's why you don't deserve any of this confusion at all. I hope you can hang on to that as we talk about this, okay?"

Molly nods, but her face is full of questions. At least she hasn't shut down or started spitting angry words in my face. I take what grace I can get and continue cautiously.

"So, as the video explains it, sperm is a fluid that comes out of a man's, uh, his penis." I look at Molly's face, pulled tight in a scrunch, as though she absolutely does not want to be talking about men's private parts, and she is not about to tell me whether she's seen Robert's penis or not. That's fine with me. There's just so much of this I can take as well.

"So, as the video explains it, when girls reach a certain age or maturity, every month a tiny egg is released into her womb, which is here, in your tummy," I rub my own stomach, then hers. "It floats around for a few days, making a little nest to sleep in and waits for a partner, that is, she's waiting for sperm to fertilize the egg. If the egg doesn't find a partner, that is, if no sperm connects with it, then the little nest that was getting ready isn't needed, so the tiny egg slips out of your body, along with the little nest she's been building, and that's when you bleed every month."

I know I should have explained this better to Molly before, and maybe some of this could have been avoided, but it's too late. That ship has sailed. There's no going back now. I keep talking.

"Like the video says, if a sperm from a man or boy gets into the space where the egg happens to be floating around, the sperm will try to snuggle with it. If the egg and sperm *do* snuggle in there and connect, that means the sperm has 'fertilized' the egg, like stuck to it. At that point, the egg will get very comfortable in the little nest and stay there. You wouldn't feel a thing. You would have no idea that this has happened inside your body, not for a long time while the little egg grows and develops, which means you're pregnant."

"That is super weird," Molly says, definitely awed by this little story, as she should be.

"Go on," she prods me with her elbow.

"Okay, then," I hope she can sustain this interest before things get more complex.

"Now, this is where it gets tricky. An uncle's love and attention and hugging and being with you and watching TV and playing games are all okay activities, because they are safe and loving. However, if an uncle, for example, starts touching his niece on her private parts, that is never okay. And IF he gets his penis too close to her, or he rubs it around on her private parts, then he is no longer loving her as an uncle should. He is now molesting her, because touching private parts is a big, big mistake, unless you are both adults and you know what you're doing, and you have both agreed to have sex, and you have agreed that you both know this kind of touching could get the girl or woman pregnant."

I realize I'm talking too fast and stop to take a breath. I look directly into my daughter's eyes and hope I'm connecting with her.

"Molly, do you understand that this kind of touching of a child is never, ever okay? Do you get that?"

My face is flushed, my tongue is too large in my mouth. There are images going through my mind of Robert and Molly that I do not want to imagine. Molly's face is also bright red, and she is obviously uncomfortable with this discussion. But I know this might be my best, maybe my only, opportunity to explain to Molly what has happened to her and why.

Molly stares at me as though she is daring me to stop. I plunge on, hoping for the best.

"So, Molly, what you need to know and understand, right now, is that long before there is even a possibility of a baby, when that egg plants itself in the little nest your body has prepared for it, it is still just a little egg, even if it's been fertilized. It is *not* a baby. It is the *possibility* of a baby. It's still just a little egg. It will only become a baby if it grows and develops into one. Does that make sense?"

Molly does not nod. Her eyes have glazed over. She continues to stare me down. I see her swallow.

"The most important thing you need to know right now is this—children do not have children! No matter what! And, Molly, you are a child. Right? A child who needs to figure out what's wrong with your legs, before you can do anything else, right? You need to get back to school and learn how to be a young girl again. Agreed?"

I let Molly sit with that for a few minutes. She does not move. She seems to be thinking hard about something. I wait, hoping she will say something or ask me something, anything at all that will tell me we're on the same page, that she understands what I've been saying.

"Do you have any questions, Molly? Is there something you need us to talk about now? Whatever it is, I can try to explain it to you. I certainly don't have all the answers, but I'm really trying to help you understand what's going on."

I wait.

"No," she answers in a tight voice. "Not right now, go ahead with what you were saying."

"Okay. When you first started your periods, I should have told you more, I know. I'm so, so sorry I didn't explain it all to you then, but I made a big mistake because it was difficult for me to talk about it with you. You are a little girl, a child. It seemed like too much to put on you just as you'd started your periods. But that was weak of me. I should have done a better job. I'm sorry."

Molly doesn't respond.

"Okay, you may have noticed, I started marking your calendar when you were having your periods. I marked the days when you were bleeding. Did you notice that? I may have told you I do the same thing for my periods. It's a good way to keep track of our bodies, what's going on in there. We don't like surprises. We do this so we know what to expect, and every month that we have a period, it is a sign to us that we are *not pregnant*. When we don't bleed on time, then we need to think about it. It could be a sign that we *might possibly* be pregnant. That's our first clue, and after that, we watch very carefully what happens the following month. When you didn't bleed, it caused me to wonder, because you were very regular once you started bleeding. Then, it did occur to me that you might be pregnant, although I couldn't think of any reason why that might be possible."

Molly finally asks a question.

"But a woman would know, wouldn't she? If she's watching and marking the calendar, she ought to know, right?"

"Yes, that's usually right, but sometimes our bodies can trick us, or maybe we're sick or stressed out about something. It doesn't always mean we're pregnant, but it always makes us wonder. It's just part of being a woman, and every woman goes through this every month, wondering if she's pregnant or not, and wondering if she's ready for that, ready to have a child to care for. When you missed your periods, I knew we needed to get a pregnancy test for you, and that's why I had you pee on the stick."

Molly seems to be following now, remembering the day she was disgusted holding the stick.

"After women do that test at home, they need to be sure that the test is correct. That's when we go to a women's clinic to get an examination by a doctor to see if we are truly pregnant and how far along we are—that is, how many weeks pregnant we are. And this is really important to find out for a lot of reasons, mostly because if you need an abortion, you need to get it as soon as possible. When a girl or a woman should not 'keep' a pregnancy long enough for it to turn into a baby, for whatever reason, there are ways for her to remove the pregnancy from her body, long before it becomes an actual baby. That's called an abortion, and we need a doctor to help us with an abortion, otherwise it can be very dangerous to our bodies if it is not done correctly.

"When you tested positive for pregnancy, as your mother, I believed you should have an abortion, not carry the pregnancy to term, which would result in a baby. You are a child, and I do not believe you should have a child yourself. I hope that makes sense.

"I tried and tried, but I could not get help for you at the clinic in Sikeston, not even for the doctor there to examine you. It didn't seem like we could get help in St. Louis, either, because the laws about abortion are changing every day. So, when Mary came to the rescue and told me she knew a clinic that would help you, I trusted her to take us to Hand of Hope, because she told me they would help you get what you needed. But I misunderstood. I didn't realize what kind of help they would offer. I should have asked more questions. That was a mistake, Molly, *my mistake*. The counselors did not want to help you stop the cells in your body from growing into a baby, they wanted something else. They wanted you to let the embryo grow and for you to give birth to a child, even though you never consented to sexual behavior with Robert and even though you are only a child yourself."

Molly is staring at the television, which she has muted. She appears frozen, like the screen. I purse my lips and try not to hyperventilate. Here we are, in the crux of the matter, and I am intensely uncomfortable. I want someone to help me, but there is no one.

Molly sits still for a long time, staring at the blurry television screen. I wait to give her time to formulate her questions.

"It's just that all this is too much," she says. "You can say the words like cell and egg and fertilize, but I still can't see what they have to do with me. It's like everybody is all involved and worried and interested in me, all of a sudden. I just want all of it to stop. But I guess it's not going to stop until something else happens, right? Are you hoping this egg inside of me just decides to slip out? What are we waiting for, here in this hotel room? And why can't we do it at home?"

"You're right, Molly, we can't move on to the next thing, until we get some help. It isn't likely that the cell inside you will just slip out, simply because you're too young for this to happen to you. Unfortunately, sometimes our bodies don't realize what's best for us. And, the truth is, you and I can't do it alone. That's why we're in this hotel room, waiting for help. I have written to one of my mother's sisters, my Aunt Ruth, who lives in Columbia. I am hoping she can help us find the right clinic to help you, one that is not like Hand of Hope, one that will help you get an abortion.

"And, Molly, for the record, I never, ever want you to feel like you 'sinned.' *You* did not sin. Please, if you can believe anything I tell you, please believe this. You did not sin, and God loves you no matter what happens. Can you believe that? As much as you love your Uncle Robert, you must know that *he* sinned. I believe he loves you dearly, and I know you also love him, but *what he did was wrong*, and it could have lasting effects on you as a girl, and later as a woman. And the pisser is, pardon my language, Robert couldn't get pregnant, only you could. Not fair, right? Not fair at all. I'm so sorry to have to tell you all this now. If I had told you all the details before, you would have known. I didn't think you were old enough to hear them, and that was my mistake. If you're old enough to start your periods, you are old enough to know what that means. This was my mistake not to explain it all to you, and I am so, so sorry."

Molly has slumped forward on the sofa, staring at the patterns on the hotel rug. I feel the same fatigue I see in the shape of her body. I lean my head back on the sofa cushions and close my eyes. I reach my arm out for Molly to come closer. She hesitates, then slides over and leans against my body. Deflated, we sit together like that for a few long minutes. I hear her sniffling a bit, then feel her pull away. I look to make sure she's okay. Some of the manic brightness has faded from her eyes, and she seems less panicked, but I know I need to stay close to her and reassure her that I know what I'm doing (which, of course, I certainly do not).

"Can I tell you about Aunt Ruth, and how I found her?"

Molly nods.

"Using my phone, I searched online for her. At first, I had no luck, mostly because I'm not sure where she lives, or her married name. When that didn't work, I went to the website of the University of Missouri in Columbia, where I think she teaches, and I finally found her. Wanna see?"

Molly leans over and stares at the face of a woman who might look like her Grandmother Angie, or even a little like me.

"And?" she asks, not giving an inch.

"Well, that's as far as I got. It only had her university email, so I sent her a message asking her to help us and gave her my phone number. That's why we're still here, waiting for my Aunt Ruth to call."

"Great," Molly grumbles. "So, we're stuck here waiting for a long-lost relative who might, or might not, get in touch. Why do you think she will call you?"

In some ways, Molly's questions are a mirror of my own,

but what she doesn't know is that I told Ruth about her in that email I sent. If anything could compel my aunt to call me, the fact that my daughter is pregnant just might do the trick.

Talked out, we watch one of the first *Black Beauty* movies and settle in for another long day. When my phone rings, Molly and I both jump, perhaps for different reasons. My daughter has no reason to think the police are trying to find me, but she must remember we took a wheelchair that wasn't ours and left the counselor at the Hand of Hope no doubt frustrated and upset. Molly might even wonder if they would try to find us.

My first thought is that the police are calling, trying to find out where we are. My fears about how they can track us through my phone make me feel crazy. I am not really worried that anyone from the clinic would call, but it could happen. But Mary might try to wrangle us toward her point of view, wooing me with her soft voice that disguises her intentions so well. I sit without moving, thinking of all the possibilities that ringing phone might hold. I do not reach over to answer it right away. I want to hear a message first from whomever is on the other end of that line. I want to be smart, but my lack of knowledge about new technologies makes us an easy target. I desperately want it to be my Aunt Ruth, but I dare not assume that it is her, or what it might mean for us even if it is her on the other end of the line.

Molly cannot endure the ringing phone or my refusal to answer it. She juts her arm out to grab it while it's still vibrating on the plastic motel table, but I am faster and grab her hand before it can take the phone.

"Stop!" My voice is harsher than I'd intended, my fear obvious.

"Wait, please," I soften my words and beg her to let me do this.

"*What-ever!*" Molly's rebuke is sarcastic. She has no idea.

We wait, hoping someone, the right someone, is leaving a message. The room is silent, until the air conditioner kicks on with a thud and a gust of cold air floats over our heads. The room is always either stale and too warm or freezing. We'll be cold for a full twenty minutes now, before it decides to kick off and leave us shivering while it heats back up.

Finally, after waiting what feels like an eternity, I reach for the phone and am relieved to see that someone has left a message. If Gail calls with news about Wilson or Robert, if the police call to let me know they know where I am, if Barb calls with the local gossip, it's all information I need, but I can't talk to any of them right now. My nerves are frayed sitting in this ugly room, trying to help my daughter understand what has happened to her, fending off her anger, not knowing one thing about what's going on at home. There's only one person I want to talk to in this moment, and I don't even know what her voice sounds like.

I press the button to retrieve the "one new message" and put the phone to my ear.

"Alice, this is Ruth, your Aunt Ruth, calling. I finally got back to reading my school emails, which I don't do every day since I'm sort of retired. I was delighted to hear from you, but, of course, very concerned to hear about your situation. I hope I haven't missed you. Please call me back and let me know where you are and how I can help. I'll do anything I can for you and Molly."

I turn to my daughter, sulking on the sofa, her arms across her chest, her head bowed, her eyes closed as though she can turn her body inside out and hide from everything that is going on around her.

"Molly, I want you to hear this, too," and I let Ruth's friendly, concerned voice fill the room.

"I need to call her back immediately," I tell Molly, who has straightened her body only slightly. Her eyes are fully open, and she actually nods her head. I step out onto the tiny balcony over the parking lot and speak softly with Ruth, just in case I say something that Molly should not hear. I am careful what I say to Ruth, too. I try not to say anything that might scare her off or make her uncomfortable, until we get a chance to meet her in person. I make no references to rape, or pitchforks, or the police, anything that might color the story I need to tell right now. I have not searched for Ruth for myself, but for Molly, and I want to believe she will know where we should go next and who might help us get there.

That phone call saves us, truly it does. Ruth asks where we are staying, and I tell her we haven't moved since I emailed her. She quickly estimates that we are not more than two and a half hours from Columbia. She suggests we drive to her home and plan to stay with her for as long as it takes to sort out what help might be available for Molly in Columbia. I agree, thank her profusely, and begin to pack the few things we've accumulated in the hotel. We are both excited to get out of that room and hit the road again. In the hall, Molly presses the button for the elevator and expertly wheels herself into the tight space. I am pleased with this show of independence and thankful we have a functional wheelchair, regardless of what it cost us to get it. I try not to think about who might have been listening to my conversation with Ruth, including the information about where she lives in Columbia and my intention to drive there as soon as possible.

In the car, I tell Molly as much about my Aunt Ruth as I can without revealing my father's opinion of her. I tell her that Ruth had left the farm life of southern Missouri, got a good education, and became a university professor. I want Molly to know how strong Ruth had to be to make those choices for her life. Making conversation as we drive north, then west, I tell Molly I am excited to visit my Aunt Ruth in her home and see the university where she works, the largest in the state. Molly does not respond to anything I say, but I can tell by her face and her body in the rearview mirror that she is listening. After a while, I am glad to see her drift off to sleep, just as we turn off the connector highway and cruise toward the middle of the state. Unfortunately, her slumber doesn't last very long, and soon she's hungry. I have to admit I'm hungry, too, so I pull off the highway and grab some fast food, our staple for the trip, and fill up with gas. I try to keep at least half a tank of gas in the car at all times, thinking I may need to get away in a hurry. I'm also keeping my eyes open for ATM machines, withdrawing money we will need in the days to come.

While we are stopped, I type Ruth's address into the GPS, thankful Columbia is not a big city like St. Louis or Nashville. It is a small university town without multiple highways packed with fast-moving vehicles in every direction. I take note of the landscape here, different also from the Bootheel. The houses are further apart, bigger, the farms spread out with black cows munching grass behind well-maintained barns. I notice one farm has built an elaborate corn maze, complete with a vegetable stand painted red along the roadside. It feels more expansive here, with giant irrigation rigs standing in rows and rows of corn and beans, fewer cotton fields and rich black soil between the rows instead of sand.

When we get to Columbia, the streets are clearly marked, and I see a large sign announcing we are on the edge of the university. As much as I'd like to see it, I turn away from the campus and follow the directions to Ruth's house. We find it on a quiet, shady street with lots of mature trees and a collection of older brick homes that have been lovingly cared for. No gaudy McMansions here, no small ranch houses like our own, no manufactured doublewides, such as we see every day in Sikeston, but carefully tended yards and flower gardens, houses with shutters, and smooth sidewalks. Ruth's neighborhood has been around a good while, not recently thrown together next to sandy fields and dusty roads. I glance at Molly and hope she notices the lovely houses and the flowers that are in full bloom. I wish I could wheel her chair down the streets and enjoy the peace and quiet here, then I think I'm getting ahead of myself. We've only just begun this leg of our journey.

# Chapter 13

## It Takes a Village

When we arrive, Ruth greets us at the door with big smiles. She does, in fact, look a lot like my mother. Her house is rather small in comparison with some of the others on the street, but I can see it has a personality of its own, with colorful rugs and unique paintings on the walls. Ruth seems kind, generous, thoughtful, and she smiles a lot at both of us. She is careful to ask if she can give us hugs. I, for one, am starving for a hug, and I can see Molly lean in a bit from her chair to meet Ruth's open arms. She asks if we need the bathroom, a drink of water, some iced tea. She invites us into her living room, making sure Molly has room for her wheelchair and a place to put her drink.

When we finally get settled, Ruth keeps looking at our faces, as if to see her family etched there, to see my mother's face in my own, and in Molly's. She knows, of course, that my mother has died. I have no idea if she was at the funeral, or which of her other sisters were there. I don't remember enough about that day. I felt devastated, empty, thinking I had not talked with my mother enough, or learned things from her I should have, wishing I had known her whole family, all those stair-step sisters, the one odd brother, who was protective of them, always concerned for their safety. Nearly all of them are gone now, I think. I am not certain, but I know it would be rude to ask that question, just as we are meeting Ruth for the first time.

After we've chatted for a while, Ruth puts together a cold dinner for us that is thankfully nothing like the fast food we've eaten for days. She is a magician in the kitchen, throwing together a salad, putting bread that is fresh on a cutting board with deli meat, and good cheese, also a welcome treat. Molly eats well, and somehow seems younger than her years. She grunts and smacks her lips as she eats, which surprises me. Ruth notices her making little noises and gives me an understanding smile. I am a bit embarrassed, but I am reminded just how young Molly is, how vulnerable. I'm just happy to see her enjoying the food so much, and over the moon to be sitting with her in my Aunt Ruth's home.

After dinner, Molly listens while Ruth and I share some memories of my mother and discuss where Ruth and Angie were in the line-up of all those girls. Soon, we can both see that Molly is exhausted. Ruth suggests I draw a bath for her and let her sit in the water for as long as she wishes. Molly agrees. I run the water into the clean tub and notice there is lots of hot water, a blessing. I kneel beside her and help her with her back and legs. I can feel her body relaxing, the steamy air in the room lulling her into sleepiness. It's been a rough week in so many ways, but she does not seem quite as angry with me as she has been. After she towels off, I kiss her on the forehead and ask if she's ready to go to bed. It is still early, but after our time in the car and the days staying in the hotel, I can see she needs to rest.

Molly is delighted and laughs when Ruth brings her one of her old T-shirts to sleep in. It is gold and black, the university colors, and it has a gigantic tiger's head on the front, mouth open in a full roar. I help her into the spare room to sit on a soft bench, while Ruth and I make her bed. As though we've done it hundreds of nights before, we tuck Molly in together, and we both wish her goodnight. Half asleep already, Molly asks us to close the door as we leave, and we do. Ruth insists I should sleep in her room, so I can be close to Molly on the same floor. I am overwhelmed by her generosity to someone she doesn't really know, someone who claims to be her sister's daughter. She swears I look just like Angie, that she would know me anywhere. I'm not so sure about that, but I need to believe we belong here in Columbia with someone I feel we can trust.

Over a welcome glass of wine, I tell my newfound aunt an abbreviated version of our story. I tell her that Molly first developed normally as a young child, but around six she started having trouble walking and, in time, needed a wheelchair. Physically, I explain, even though she cannot be an active child, Molly also developed quickly for her age, starting her period at age nine. I pause to let this soak in.

As though all of this has not been super difficult to share already, I repeat what I had mentioned in my email, that Molly is pregnant. I watch Ruth's face for her reaction. I tell her only that someone took advantage of her. I do not mention incest, the possible long-term molestation and grooming, my brother, my own actions, or my husband's. I talk only about Molly's pregnancy, because that is the most important thing to tell Ruth in this moment. Every week counts, and Molly is running out of time.

Ruth asks about our experiences at the women's clinic in Sikeston, and I tell her all the problems that prevented us from getting help for Molly there. I briefly tell her about Mary and the counselors at Hand of Hope insisting Molly give birth, rather than seek other options, and how confusing all of this has been for her. I am relieved that Ruth is such a good listener. As I talk, she does not interrupt to ask any questions, but her sympathetic face tells me she is following and understands the difficulty of what we've been through. When I finish the only story I feel I can tell at this point, Ruth reaches over to touch my hand. She assures me I am doing the right thing. No question. Not once does she suggest I should have watched Molly more closely or should have known what I didn't know. Although both of those things are true, I am thankful she doesn't voice them. Once I've told her why we're here, Ruth begins to think out loud about who she knows in Columbia who might be able help us.

"Alice, I've heard enough to know we need to move quickly to find out what Molly's options are. Fortunately, I have many good friends and colleagues in this town and at the University, women who are progressive professionals and advocates for women. We've worked on projects together, written grants to fund our projects, done outreach for survivors of domestic violence, date rape, you name it. We are all committed to this kind of work, all of it in service to women's need for justice and access to services and resources. People just like you and Molly."

Ruth laughs at herself and says, "I sound like a commercial for a women's network, don't I? But it is true. We work closely with several clinics and schools, as well as different faith communities in the area, and I'm so proud I don't mind crowing a bit for our efforts. I hope you don't mind," her eyes sparkle. "I truly am glad you found me. I think it must have been preordained."

I am not certain about that "preordained" part, but I am convinced finding Ruth is the answer to my prayers, such as they are. I had no idea what to pray for, yet I know I've found it. In the Bootheel, I felt like I was banging my head against a brick wall all the time. If there were resources, I couldn't find a way to access them. If there were agencies designed to help, I couldn't seem to locate them or get them to assist Molly. If we were promised help, a wheelchair, tutoring, a therapist, a social worker, those promises never really materialized. Mostly, we heard excuses about why we couldn't be helped because of where we live, how funding had diminished, how COVID was still interrupting their work.

Ruth tells me more about her friends and the kinds of work they've done together. She makes a list of the ones she thinks could help Molly. While I wait and listen, she calls and invites several women to come over to her house late afternoon the following day. She does not tell them our story, she just says her great-niece is only ten and is pregnant. She needs help, quickly, she tells each one. Could they come and help brainstorm ideas? I just listen, thinking for sure I'm dreaming.

The next morning, Molly and I spend some quiet time with Ruth, getting to know her and eager to hear about her early life as my mother's sister. She drags out several old albums to show us photos of her parents, my grandparents, of her and her sisters when they were young, pictures of Angie when she was little and on her wedding day. Both Molly and I are entranced and can't get enough of the family photographs. My mother never made photo albums. I just remember several old shoe boxes stuffed to overflowing with curled snapshots without names or dates. I never knew who all those people were, and I can't remember ever sitting with Mom while she identified who was in the photos. It occurs to me that I have not made albums, either, for Molly. Now, I'm fairly certain that's not likely to happen. I feel bad when I think how few pictures we have of her and her dad or his parents, Gail and Stan, or my mother and father. Finding Ruth feels like filling in a gap in my own life as well as new information for Molly's. How odd that we had to leave home to find evidence of our family. I love to see how interested Molly is in Ruth's photos and stories. She seems to be soaking up whatever Ruth can tell her. I'm feeling happy to learn about Ruth's family, but it makes me sad that my own mother did not keep up with her sisters and tell us the stories Ruth has to share. It reminds me of all the cousins I must have all over the Bootheel, people I didn't know—or even know about. What a waste—all those connections severed before they could even begin, the loneliness my mother must have suffered and passed down to me.

Later in the day, both Molly and I are nervous when Ruth's friends come over, some with a bottle of wine to share, others with little cakes and cookies from a favorite bakery, another with a bag of cheesy popcorn. Molly greets them nicely enough, although she doesn't really speak beyond a weak "Hello" and a small smile from her wheelchair in the corner.

I am awed by Ruth's friends. One is a lawyer who teaches at the law school, another is a social worker. Two women, a couple sitting on the floor, are professors in the women's studies department at the university, both involved with Planned Parenthood in Columbia. Next to them on the sofa, we are introduced to the actual Director of Planned Parenthood, who sits with her feet under her, completely comfortable on Ruth's sofa, like she's sat there many times before. Beside her, in a rocking chair, sits a petite woman with short, blonde hair and a small pixie face who introduces herself to us as a minister at a local church and a good friend of Ruth's. She gestures toward the sofa and tells us the name of the woman nearest her, a gynecologist. Next to the doctor is her daughter, who is a pediatric physical therapist and her partner, a large woman in a sari, sitting in a lotus-position on the floor. After all the introductions, a glass of wine, some juice for Molly, and a few shared snacks, I realize quite a bit of time has passed. The woman sitting on the floor nearest Ruth speaks first to the gathered group. I gather that all the women in the room know a bare-bones story about why Molly and I are here in Ruth's home.

"Hi, Alice and Molly, I'm Joanna, and I'm a child psychologist. How can we help you? What do you think should happen for Molly, given her situation?"

Molly and I look around at the women gathered in Ruth's home, women in shorts, jeans, and T-shirts, sandals and capris, flowing dresses, a blue-striped business suit, and cargo pants. The full gamut. I'm thinking fast. How could my aunt possibly know all these women, know them well enough to call them for an emergency meeting concerning her late sister's pregnant granddaughter? I have to work to keep my mouth from flying open and staring at them like I'm from a different planet. Ruth seems to have access to everyone a woman might need if faced with a major life difficulty, like ours. I am not sure how to speak to them, to ask for their help, to imagine why they have agreed to talk with me and Molly. In the long pause that follows the psychologist's question, Ruth notices my hesitation. She seems to understand it will be hard to open up right away. She also knows it might be best if we could talk without Molly in the room, at least for now.

Ruth turns to Molly and asks her if she would rather stay and listen as we talk, or if she would like to read in bed and be alone for a while. Without hesitation, Molly says she'd love to read in bed. I know that is my cue to take her to the guest bedroom and tuck her in for the night. I know she feels awkward to be the center of attention and is as reluctant to speak up in that roomful of strangers as I am. I help her in the bathroom and wait while she slides into the clean sheets of her bed. I pull the string on the lamp above the bed and turn off the overhead light. I notice Ruth has left several paperback books on the table near the bed. They appear to be young adult books, and I wonder how and why she has them in her home. Whatever the reason, I'm delighted to see them here and notice Molly has already stacked three or four of them on the bed. She's good to go. As I leave the room, my grumpy, angry, frustrated, confused child thanks me for coming here. I have to hide my surprise and listen carefully to her small child's voice.

"Thanks for trying to explain all this stuff, Mom. I know this is hard for both of us. I had no idea about where we were and why that matters. And thanks for finding Aunt Ruth. I think maybe she can help."

I want to scream "Yes!" and jump up and down, but I resist. I lean over her in the bed and give her an awkward hug, as I plant a noisy, wet kiss on the top of her head.

"We're going to get through this together, Molly, I promise. There is a better way, and we're going to find it. Read a while, then please try to sleep. I love you so, so much."

When I return, the living room is full of unrestrained talk and laughter. Ruth pours me another glass of wine and asks me to tell her friends what kind of help Molly and I need. I take a sip of my wine, but my mouth is still dry as they all turn toward me to listen. For the first time in weeks, I feel like I'm in the right place with the people I need to help Molly in the best possible way.

"Okay," I start as I look at Ruth.

"I believe Molly has been molested, possibly for years by a close family member. She is an innocent child, and she can't walk. She used to walk just fine, but she just stopped. This man took advantage of her in the most vile ways possible, and I let it happen. It was happening right under my nose, but I did not see the signs or know what to look for."

I pause to look around the room at the faces turned in my direction, then I force myself to continue.

"I have only learned much of this in the past few days. As I learn more, I have to believe that all of Molly's problems stem from her being molested by her uncle, my own brother, Robert—all of it, her sudden inability to walk, her developmental regression, nightmares and wetting her bed, her mood swings, her anger, all of it must have been her response to a situation she did not understand and couldn't control. Of course, to make it worse, she didn't feel she could tell me what was happening, and because I couldn't see it myself, I didn't know how to ask the right questions."

I was fine until I shared this part about Robert, now I'm choked up and can't speak for a minute. Ruth asks if I'm okay. I nod and try to continue with my story.

"Not intentionally, of course, but I did not recognize the signs that she was being abused, and I deeply, deeply regret that. I didn't connect the dots, then. Although now, it seems so obvious. But I couldn't see it. I did not see the danger, until it was too late to intervene. Molly must be about six weeks pregnant, but the Planned Parenthood clinic in the Bootheel couldn't help her, they told me, because of her age and her disability, the new protocols about abortion, the Supreme Court ruling, plus a lot of other things, like their doctor not having hospital privileges, etc., etc. It was endless, the list of reasons why they couldn't help her. I about lost my mind!

"I will also tell you we lost a bit of time when we were diverted by a group of women who misrepresented themselves to me and were able to fill Molly's head with the idea that she has sinned. At 'Hand of Hope,' a place near the Arkansas border, they planted the idea in Molly that God wants her to carry this baby to term, something I am one hundred percent against. I have no idea where you all stand on this, but I do not believe any child should give birth to a child. I am convinced her body is too young to go through a birth, and I believe having a child at the age of ten would destroy Molly's chance for a 'normal' life—whatever that is. Molly is here now and deserves a chance to walk again and be a carefree child, if that's ever possible."

When I stop talking, all the heads in the room turn toward Brenda. As director of Planned Parenthood in Columbia, we all seem to believe she can put Molly's situation into perspective. I notice Brenda seems uncomfortable, and I'm wondering if I am about to hear the same things we heard from the clinic staff in Sikeston. Everyone waits for her to speak. After thinking about it, Brenda finally begins, and I find out the hurdles have followed us.

"Ok, well, this is a tough one, I must admit. We need to get all the cards out on the table right now. It is currently not legal to get an abortion in the state of Missouri, anywhere, even in the case of incest or rape, or due to the age of the pregnant person. Planned Parenthood in Columbia primarily functions now as a useful resource center for women's reproductive health and services. We can prescribe contraception, offer examinations, and on occasion give referrals, when needed, to doctors in other states who still offer abortions. We consider this an important part of our job—to disseminate information to women in need. Therefore, at the outset, I must tell you it is highly unlikely that we can help Molly get an abortion here in Columbia, or at our clinic in St. Louis. However, there is a clinic in East St. Louis, on the Illinois side that does still offer abortions.

"That said, if you and Molly decide abortion is best for her, I think we can steer you away from the highly organized anti-abortion groups in this area. I will tell you they are very well funded and experienced in getting women to make choices other than abortion. I've done research on this myself, just to see.

"For example, if you type 'Abortion in Missouri' into your phone, the very first thing you'll see is a page sponsored by 'Hand'n Hand Pregnancy Center,' a place that will offer you 'options.' The 'Click Here' red button 'guarantees you an appointment with caring health care professionals and free testing and ultrasound.' This is all true, of course, but the hidden agenda is to get your information, and then make certain you do not seek an abortion. It sounds very similar to the experience you just had in the Bootheel, Alice. The second screen you get when you type in 'abortion in Missouri,' is basically the same as the first, except this one is sponsored by the 'Republican Pregnancy Resource Center.' I have no idea what the 'Republican' in the title means, but the Pro-Life message is the same. 'You have options, let us tell you what they are. Click here.'

"Just as you learned in Sikeston, Molly's case is complicated by the fact that she is only ten, and that she is disabled. There are definitely issues of consent that will need to be addressed and anyone who examines Molly is mandated to report her pregnancy to Child and Family Services as abuse. By law, as a child, she cannot consent to sexual relations with an adult, nor can she consent to an abortion. Obviously, Alice, you are a consenting parent, but Molly's father may need to give his consent as well. All of these factors will play into a plan to help her, and all of them will cause difficulties, whether you are in Missouri, or Kansas, or Illinois.

"Certainly, both Kansas and Illinois, the states that directly border Missouri on the east and the west, still offer legal abortions, both surgical and medical, that is, the two pills. In fact, you may have heard that Kansas just surprised the entire nation by passing a voter referendum to protect women's reproductive rights in the state, including abortion, by an overwhelming majority. At this point, I would think that Kansas might offer the best opportunity to get help for Molly, but of course I cannot endorse that as a real possibility. Illinois may also be a good option, but I doubt that can happen in the southern part of the state, which is politically as conservative as southern Missouri. In the end, you might have to go to Chicago to get the help you need, but I don't think that will be necessary."

Brenda stops herself at this point.

"Okay, I'm sorry, I wish I had better news for you. Now, I think we should find out what everyone else knows or might suggest."

The room erupts as several of the women begin speaking at once. Calmly, Ruth suggests they go around the room and see who can speak about some of the legal issues and possible next steps for Molly. Everyone agrees, and for the next hour, the women sitting in Ruth's living room volunteer information about the legal ramifications of an abortion for Molly, as well as voicing concerns about Molly's physical and mental health. I sit in wonder, listening to all the expertise in this room. I try to take notes, but then I give up and just listen. As they go around the room sharing, the lawyer and the psychologist's comments strike me as especially important.

The lawyer, Carol, tells us that there are new "trigger laws" in Missouri that went into effect immediately upon the Supreme Court's ruling in September overturning Roe vs. Wade. She fears these laws will be applied to me if I help get an abortion for Molly. The laws will make it possible for the state to arrest and prosecute me for seeking an abortion for my daughter and for taking her across state lines to get the procedure done, if I choose to go that route. She emphasizes these are new laws that have not yet been tested. If Molly actually gets an abortion, both of us could be arrested, although for what exactly, she isn't sure, yet. Perhaps, even murder. It is unclear.

There is a small gasp in the room, and I feel my body clench tight. That seems so *ridiculous*. Arrested for murder? Is that true, I wonder, but the look on the lawyer's face assures me it is completely possible and should not be discounted. Suddenly, I am struck that I might be arrested for two murders at the same time. My heart sinks.

"Given this, would you proceed anyway?" Carol, the lawyer, asks me, cautious with her question.

"Absolutely! This is about Molly, not about me. What disturbs me even more is that Molly herself could be accused of anything. She's been molested without her permission. Shouldn't that make a difference in how the courts might view her case?"

Carol pauses before she answers. "Yes, these are all things to be considered with Molly, but whether or not the courts will view it that way is yet to be seen."

Brenda tries to deflate the tension and fears she recognizes in the room after Carol's legal comments. She can tell that everyone needs more information, although I'm at a loss how this might help.

"Alice, please, what more are you able to tell us about Molly and what happened?"

I glance at Ruth, who nods and encourages me to talk. Her face does not suggest any discomfort that I am here with my daughter in her house, seeking help for an abortion. My instinct is to be careful what I say, as I was with Barb, but here it seems important to tell them more. I take a deep breath and look around the room at faces I have never seen before and decide to trust them.

"When Molly was younger and couldn't walk, I really struggled to keep it together and care for her. My husband worked as the manager of a large farm operation that sometimes crosses into other states. He was gone from home for weeks, then months at a time. So, I was basically a single parent to Molly for the past few years. I took care of everything with the help of my brother, who lives next door, and my husband's mother Gail. My parents died several years ago, so I have limited help. I used to work at Wendy's, but since I started home schooling Molly, I had to quit. I basically have one good friend, a woman I met working at Wendy's named Barb.

"When Molly started having trouble with her legs, I drove her to big cities I knew nothing about, trying to find doctors who could help her. I'm not a good driver, but I did it. I also filed for PTs, and social workers, therapists, and a wheelchair for Molly, but none of those requests have come through the way I had hoped they would. Some of you may know the Bootheel, in southeast Missouri, where we live. The area offers few resources for women in my situation, and I have no idea how to get help from the few places that should be able to assist us. When my daughter started her period at nine, I was confused and angry that it came so early and with her unable to walk, that somehow made it worse. Then, when her period stopped unexpectedly, I was even more confused. I simply could not think of a single male person who would have the means and opportunity to molest my daughter, a child who sits in a wheelchair that doesn't actually move most of the day. I was beside myself trying to figure it out. Nothing was making sense, but I was pretty sure Molly was pregnant. To be sure, I bought a pregnancy test, and it showed she was, in fact, pregnant.

"One day—" I pause, not knowing how much more to tell these strangers. I decide they may be our only hope and continue.

"One day, I went over to my brother's house to find him and Molly. She often goes over there when I need him to watch her. He loves her, and they have a good time together, watching cartoons and playing cards. But that day, I found him and my daughter in the hayloft, asleep, with most of their clothes off. When I saw them there, I knew exactly what had happened. I had no doubts about that at all!"

I feel tears streaming down my face. Someone hands me a tissue, and I mop up as much as I can, before I continue telling the most horrific story of my life.

"I grabbed my daughter and ran back to my house with her. I did not tell anyone Molly was in that loft with my brother. I have left her out of every story I've told about that day, until now."

I pause to catch my breath. I have said far more than I'd intended, yet I have concealed so much more. Ruth hands me a glass of water. I drink only a little, then I continue to speak. The light leaves the windows, and big shadows fall across our faces. Before I lose my nerve, I lurch back into my story.

"It has been seven weeks since I discovered my daughter was no longer bleeding. That means her time is running out to get a legal abortion. We still need to know what is wrong with her legs, and why she is not walking, but right now she needs that abortion. I hope you can help us."

The room has gotten even darker, with only one or two small lamps offering soft light in the corners. It is so quiet, I begin to worry. I realize what I have done. I have not told anyone else that my brother has molested Molly. I have not told anyone how I found him with Molly in the barn loft. As the women look at me, or look at each other, or at the floor, I feel my face betray my emotions, my anxiety, and my fear. I have told them too much. I squirm in my chair and wish I could take Molly and disappear again. But I know that can't happen, because none of this is going to go away, and I have nowhere else to go. I wait for someone to respond.

I feel, rather than actually see, my Aunt Ruth rise from her chair. I glance as she reaches for a notebook off the desk next to the sofa. She writes first in the notebook, then passes it to the woman to her left. As the notebook makes its way around the room, she asks each person to write her full name in the notebook, what they do, where they work, their email address, phone number, and the best way to contact them. She asks them to please check for messages from her and answer them promptly.

Once the notebook has made it around the room, the psychologist suggests that she would like to have a therapy session with Molly as quickly as possible. She is very concerned about Molly's mental health, wondering if the molestation has been going on for a long time, or if the rape was a one-time occurrence. She also believes Molly is going to need to talk to someone other than me about the Hand of Hope experience. I couldn't agree more. I tell her I have tried, but I've struggled to make my daughter understand. We agree that Joanne will schedule a time with Molly as soon as she can.

Carol, the lawyer, tells me she will try to help me find a local lawyer who can help us navigate the legal problems that are already evident. The social worker hands me a list of resources in Columbia that I can contact for help, for both Molly and me. Brenda asks me to bring Molly to Planned Parenthood the next morning for a physical examination, so they can determine how far along she is and begin to make arrangements for an abortion in Kansas or Illinois, wherever we decide to go. She admits Molly may resist doing this again, but it is necessary to get her medical records in order.

The women take their seats again after the notebook comes full circle. I am so grateful for their pledges of help and support. Feeling foolish, I remind myself I felt exactly the same way when Mary called me and came to visit. My radar to distinguish between those who might deceive me and those who can actually help seems off. I trusted my husband when he was gone from us for months. I trusted my beloved brother even more. I got no danger signals when Robert took Molly to his house to help me out. I trusted Mary both times

I met her. I should have been able to trust them all, but that's not what happened.

When all of Ruth's friends gather at the door to bid us goodnight, I am treated to the embrace of warm arms, over and over again. I am thankful I haven't been judged by these women, and I am hopeful I will now have others to stand with me. I am no longer alone on this journey with Molly. In my life, always on my own, I've never known such a network of women might be possible.

I go to bed offering a general kind of thanks to the universe for guiding me to Ruth's house, but I also manage to give myself an imaginary pat on the back. When I got desperate, I didn't despair, rather I dug as deeply as I could, scouring my memory for family members who might help us. Perhaps my mother was still whispering to me from the beyond. Maybe she suggested Ruth's name to me as I drove the car that night through the dark, or as I slept with Molly on the clean sheets of the hotel near St. Louis. For the first time in my life, I feel safe in a place beyond the Bootheel, far from everything I've ever known.

Early the next morning, my phone rings, and Caller ID tells me it's my mother-in-law. Gail offers no friendly greeting for me, nor does she ask how Molly and I are doing. She seems surprised I answered, but tells me she just felt I should know what was happening "at home." Abruptly, she states, "They are waiting to see if your brother lives or dies. He is still in a coma.

"The charge against you will be much worse, of course, if he dies," she states flatly. She tells me they have retained a criminal lawyer for Wilson, a local who seems content to wait it out. I don't really care what happens to him, I tell myself, but I also realize his welfare and ours may forever be entangled in terms of Molly's welfare. At least at the moment, I know where they both are, my husband and my brother, and neither of them can hurt us. Then I remember that both men may decide to speak to the police and tell a story that could make it much worse for me. What they might say is beyond me, but I know to be afraid.

No sooner than Gail hangs up, it occurs to me that she assumes I hurt Robert. What does she know, and what makes her think it will be "worse for me if he dies"? Has Wilson told her what I said that night when I finally confessed that Robert had molested Molly? Is it general knowledge in Sikeston that I hurt my own brother? Suddenly, my fears multiply and threaten to shake my resolve.

I have no time to dwell on my concerns about Gail, because I immediately get another call, this one from Carol, who reminds me to be aware that all my social media accounts can legally be monitored and used against me, if I am ever suspected of talking to anyone about an abortion for Molly. If we are to speak about "the situation," then we should do it only in person. We can make vague arrangements to meet on the phone, but we must not mention Molly or anything about Molly's health or well-being. Pretty much the code we'll be using will be "the situation." Carol will notify everyone whose information is in the notebook they gave me, but she wanted to warn me first to be careful. Her caution is a reminder to me that I should not talk about Wilson, or Robert, in any detail, to anyone.

In the meantime, I encourage Molly to eat some breakfast, telling her we must go see another doctor who might be able to help her. She makes a face but doesn't argue. She's been through this already. It occurs to me to ask if Joanna could meet us at the clinic, thinking Molly may need her around as we go through the day. I leave a coded message for Joanna, and half an hour later, we are in the car with Ruth, driving to Planned Parenthood. Joanna meets us there and explains that she has an ongoing relationship with the clinic, often meeting patients there who need counseling and extra assistance. Even though I know she could also be arrested for "talking with and/or assisting someone who is seeking an abortion," it seems she is willing to take the risk. This is her job, she tells us, and hopefully the courts will not bother her. We go with

Molly into the clinic, and they wait while she and I meet with Dr. Sandy, whom we have already met at Ruth's house the night before. She is kind and gentle with Molly as she does the examination and tells us mostly what we already know. Molly is seven weeks pregnant, and her body seems to be strong and healthy. She tells us she will do everything she can to help Molly decide what to do next.

That afternoon, both Molly and I take long, luxurious naps in Ruth's sweet-smelling beds. We awaken when Ruth returns home and orders a pizza from a local restaurant. She offers Molly a soft drink and me a beer, a good beer, I'm happy to note. Our evening meal is quiet and comfortable. I begin to discuss our day with Ruth, but I am surprised when Molly interrupts and announces she wants to tell her own story. I am delighted and encouraged to see her willingness to share with Ruth. She seems much better, and I wonder what miracle Joanna has worked in her private session with her earlier in the day.

As we finish eating, Molly surprises us both by asking Ruth if her friends can "come over again tonight to talk about what I should do." I had been under the impression that Molly had been sound asleep the previous evening, but maybe she hadn't been asleep and had heard us talking. Perhaps she had gathered some information from that long discussion and wanted to hear us talk with her in the room this time, especially since she just saw the doctor who confirmed her pregnancy, again.

Ruth is eager to see if this is possible. She calls each of her friends and invites them to come to her house to talk with Molly about her options. Not every woman can come the second night, but Joanna and Sandy agree to drive over and spend some time with us, soon Brenda says she can come for a bit as well. When it is time for them to arrive, Molly gets agitated, eager for the doorbell to ring. She keeps wheeling around the house experimenting where her wheelchair will fit, discovering where the doorways are too tight. She is acting like an anxious little girl, and I am both glad to see her acting her age, yet also reminding myself that tonight she must be at her most mature for the discussion she has requested.

Molly wheels to the door every time someone arrives. She pulls the door open and tries to hold it for each guest. When we all sit down with something to drink, Molly bluntly asks the group what they think she should do, and how we might go about doing it. She looks to Joanna for help in letting everyone know what they discussed in their session today. Joanna is tentative with her explanations, not wanting to take over Molly's story.

"Welcome everybody, and thanks for coming back tonight. I can tell you Molly has had a very eventful and emotional day. We went to the clinic and found out how far along she is in her pregnancy. Then, she and I had a productive session together afterward. Molly has been able to share with me that she loves her uncle very much, and that he also loves her. She wants all of us to know this."

Joanna pauses to check with Molly. Molly nods for her to continue.

"Since Molly was very small, she says, her uncle would touch her in loving and gentle ways. When she took her afternoon naps, even as a toddler, her mother often left her uncle to watch over her while she slept. She would sense his fingers lightly touching her body during those warm afternoons. Sometimes, she would pretend to be sleeping so she could feel his touch on her back and legs. When she would fully awake, her uncle would always be gone."

She pauses again, concerned that she will damage the moment, or cause Molly to be uncomfortable. Molly's face is a blank, so Joanna decides to say more.

I have frozen in my seat. This is the first I've heard about those days when Robert watched over my little girl. I am stunned that I didn't know he'd ever touched her. I feel my face begin to flush, bright with pain and embarrassment. I try to turn away, but my eyes are fixed on Molly's face.

"At first, Molly did not worry about her uncle touching her. She thought of it as only him loving and caring for her. In fact, she still is not certain how to think about what he was doing and is not certain it was ever wrong or 'sexual.'" Joanna makes the air quotes as she mentions the word sexual, then continues.

"In fact, Molly is still not sure what we mean when we say something is sexual. Ever since she's been confined to a wheelchair, sitting in her room, she has longed for more physical contact with people, especially with her uncle, whom she loves more than anyone, she says. The highlight of her days has been when he would come to get her, pick her up in his strong arms, carry her to his truck, and drive her to his house, where they could be alone for hours and hours. She loved being the center of his attention, especially after her mother started homeschooling her and she rarely saw any of her friends or teachers. She and Robert would watch TV together and played endless games of cards, which he taught her to play."

Joanna stops talking and quietly asks Molly if she should continue. Molly nods to her and gestures for her to go on.

I have turned my head to look out the window at Ruth's flower garden. I can no longer watch Molly's face. My heart is heavy in my chest and my breathing is shallow.

"When her uncle began taking Molly to his favorite spot, the hayloft in the barn, she was so pleased that he had taken her there. They both loved the smell of the hay and the sounds of the animals below them. She loved that he was strong enough to carry her into the loft, and that he had provided quilts for them to lie on when we were up there. They would talk for hours. Sometimes, they both fell asleep, and she remembers her dreams were so sweet with him lying next to her."

"Wait!" Molly suddenly erupts from her chair, sitting upright and leaning forward. I nearly jump out of my chair when she begins to narrate her own story.

"I need to tell you myself how much I love Robert, and

how much he loves me. I do not believe he was 'molesting' me. I would never call what he was doing 'molesting' when he touched my body so, so lightly. It almost tickled, it was so soft. I am so confused by everything, how nothing seems to be related, yet so much is related, and I don't know what has happened to me and to my body. I'm not talking just about the touching, I'm talking about my body changing in every way. This is hard. It is hard for me to talk about this to you, but I want to!"

Molly knows she's been talking too fast, so she takes a breath and looks around the room as though someone might say something or might question her. When no one says anything, but she sees all our nodding heads, she plunges on.

"Let me back up. When the neighbor would visit, bringing Mom the bulletins from church, you know, trying to get her, all of us, back to church, and she would do that *tsk, tsk*, kind of thing, you know, with her lips and say it was 'so sad' that I was such a big girl, just so sad that I was 'growing so fast,' when all I wanted to do was have my uncle come get me.

"That old lady made me feel bad about how much I was growing, how big I was getting, then I finally got it. She meant that I was, you know, getting 'womanly' things, like I had breasts and hair in my armpits, and hair other places, which she shouldn't have known about. But I knew she was talking about all that, and that I smelled. I smelled it myself, my sweat and other stuff was different, stronger, and I didn't get baths that often, because it was such a hassle for my mom, me not walking and her having to help me get everywhere, and the water heater not working because my dad was never home. It was difficult for her, but not for Robert, when I couldn't walk.

"I began to feel bad, too, about not walking, because I did that myself, you know." Molly stops and looks directly at me.

"Or maybe you don't know. Of course, Mom, you don't know. I stopped walking on my own. I did that!"

I try not to blink, to meet her eye and just listen, but I can't hold back the tears. I blink and blink. Molly pauses again, sensing the danger of the words she has decided to say.

"I stopped walking on my own. I just decided not to walk so Robert would come get me and carry me away. I knew he would have to carry me if I couldn't walk. I did that myself. I guess it kind of backfired, though, because after a while, I seriously couldn't walk and none of those doctors could tell us why. But I knew why, I just didn't tell anyone."

In my chair in the corner of the room, I have stopped breathing as I listen to my daughter talk about her decision *not to walk*. She does not seem happy to admit that she stopped walking on purpose, yet I hear pride when she announces, "*I did that*." Is this how she gained control over what was happening to her? Did she seize the only power she thought she had—to just stop walking? Was she trying to get my attention, and I was too dense to understand?

Molly does not look at me now. She looks, instead, at Joanna, and her voice changes as she talks more about being in the barn loft with Robert.

"In the loft, I did begin to wonder what we were doing. I loved it up there, but the touching changed. Uncle Robert was no longer just lightly touching my body, like he had done for years, he wanted me to touch his body, too. I never once thought about this being wrong, but I began to wonder what we were doing and why. We were definitely hiding, I got that, and we agreed not to tell my mother. That made me wonder even more. I realized we were not in the house where anyone could see us, and that seemed important. Uncle Robert began to talk about us sharing our secrets, telling each other what made us most happy."

Molly takes a deep breath and hesitates for the first time. She continues to speak directly to Joanna.

"Why do I need to share all of this with anybody? I forgot. How will this help you help me? I keep getting confused about all of it again."

Joanna quietly answers her.

"Molly, we need to know what happened to you and how you felt about it. We want you to understand that what your uncle was doing was wrong, but that you were pretty confused about what was happening with him. At your age, we do not for a minute think what you did was wrong. What Robert did was wrong and, unfortunately, you are the one who has to face the consequences of his actions—that is, *you* are the one who is pregnant at the age of ten.

"When you realize that what he did was wrong, not what *you* did, because you are a child, then you will be better able to face your pregnancy and make a decision about what to do. We know this is difficult, and we are asking you to process a lot of confusing stuff in a very short amount of time, but we have no choice. The law says you must make a decision quickly, and we are here to help you think about that decision in the healthiest possible ways for you. Does that make sense?"

Molly sits with this answer and seems to accept it. She takes a deep breath and begins speaking again, directly to Joanna.

"Okay. In the loft, I have to tell you, I was beginning to feel weird about it. I wanted someone to know. I wanted him to stop. I wanted someone to catch us so I could quit. I wanted my mom to figure it out."

Molly blows hard through her lips and makes a loud noise. She startles everyone with this, and we all laugh nervously, including her. Finally, she looks directly at me and finishes her story.

"One day, when we were in the loft, I thought I heard Mom calling for us, but then I must have fallen back asleep. The next thing I knew, she had me in her arms and was flying down the stairs, fast! She ran with me all the way home. She laid me down on our old sofa, and I pretended to still be asleep. I figured it was best if I just kept quiet for a while. She never once yelled at me or asked me what was going on. I guess she knew or had her own ideas about that, but she wanted to protect me. That's what I thought.

"I am used to my mom taking me to doctors, but I had no idea why she started taking me to these other clinics. I didn't know what getting my period actually meant, or what it meant if I didn't get my period. Well, I knew there was blood in my panties sometimes, but I didn't know what that meant, *exactly*. I didn't know anything about all that. I guess I missed the 'sex education' course at my school. Anyway, it was all a big surprise to me, you know, connecting my period to being pregnant. I just didn't know. I guess now it all makes more sense, and I can see what my uncle was doing was really wrong, because even at my age, at age nine, I could get pregnant. I didn't know that, but he should have. I'm only ten, now, you know, so I didn't know. Children don't know this stuff, really, we don't."

The silence in the room is deafening, and I am deeply ashamed. After holding my breath for what seems like an eternity, I slowly begin to breathe again. I want to defend myself, but I know I can never fix what I failed to do. I look at the floor and wait.

Joanna, Sandy, and Carol shift in their chairs and begin to move around a bit. None of them speaks. I think this is exactly where Joanna has wanted to bring Molly—to a place where she recognizes that what Robert did was wrong and that she did not ask for this pregnancy at all. Joanna wanted her to know that she could seek an abortion without feeling like she was betraying the love she felt, and still feels, for her uncle.

Molly is exhausted and says she doesn't want to talk any more. She begs the women in the room to tell her what to do. The voice she uses is no longer the voice of a child. She is maturing before our very eyes.

"Please," she begs. "Help me understand what I should do now."

Dr. Sandy is the first to speak.

"Molly, I, for one, want to tell you just how proud of you I am. You have been through a lot, and yet you have been able to share so much information with us that can really help. I totally get that you are just now beginning to understand some things for yourself, huge things, that you didn't understand before. Even though we are here to help you in any way we can, we cannot tell you what to do. We can give you our opinions, how we see things from our point of view and offer to help you do what you decide to do.

"I respect what you have told us about your uncle. You have been honest about your feelings for him, and it may take years for you to come to some deeper understanding of all that. As a medical doctor, I can tell you that your young girl body is not prepared for a pregnancy or childbirth. That's my opinion."

Carol seems anxious to add her point of view, too, and starts talking before Sandy has quite finished.

"Molly, she is right. What he did will be called molestation and rape in a court of law. You need to know that. A girl of nine or ten cannot legally consent to sex with an adult man. Because of your age and his, he is the responsible one here, and he has broken the law.

"But all of that does not change the fact that you are seven weeks pregnant. Unfortunately, you are still a child, and you must make some very adult decisions about your body and your pregnancy. Personally, and as a lawyer who works as a *guardian ad litem* with some young clients—which means I go to court to argue for the best interests of the child in cases that involve them—I can say I do not believe it is in your best interest to have a baby at this age, not only medically, as Sandy has pointed out, but in a lot of other ways, too. I think you have a much better chance at a good and normal life if you have time to be a child, get serious physical therapy and a good education, and much later have a family of your own, if that's what you want, when you are an adult and make that choice."

As they speak, I am silently thanking these strong, powerful women for what they are saying to my child in this moment. I try to smile at Molly, but she doesn't respond. She is waiting for the others to speak and give her directions. I decide to offer my own as well.

"Okay, Molly, as your mother, I'll tell you what I think. My opinion is that you and I should do everything possible to find a doctor and a clinic where you can get an abortion. I am not afraid to say that out loud. We're running out of time. Pregnancy is a difficult time for any woman, and I do not believe a young girl's body, or your mind, is prepared for the stress of a pregnancy and certainly not childbirth."

Joanna and Sandy, Ruth and Carol echo my words and offer some of their own. When no one seems to have anything new to add, Molly nods her head as though she's had enough. Abruptly, she turns her chair toward Ruth's master bathroom and asks me if I will help her draw a hot bath so she can sit in it. I quickly agree and rise from my chair.

But before we leave the room, Molly turns to the group of women gathered there and says in a clear voice.

"Can you all work on that for me? I'd like to go to Kansas as soon as we can—to a clinic that can help me. I want to find someone who can give me the two pills that will make me not pregnant anymore. I've had enough confusion. I'd like a 'do-over,' if that's possible. I do not want to be pregnant, and I do not want to live in this wheelchair. I want my legs back. I want to go to school and have friends. I want to live with my mother somewhere, but not at home, somewhere more like this town."

My heart flips in my chest. Molly and I are on the same page. We will work together on a "do-over" for her. She will get a second chance at a normal life. It may take a while, and it won't be easy, but she will get her chance. In this moment, I don't fear my own possible arrest and prosecution. Clearly, I will have to deal with the reality of that soon. Just not yet. I recognize there's a very real chance I will go to prison, but I think it will be well worth it to get Molly to the other side of this disaster. I owe her that.

After I get Molly to bed, I go back to the living room and

talk with Ruth and her friends for another hour. Everyone agrees to help Molly do what needs to be done, including me. I will be the one to take her to Kansas to the open clinic, but I'll need their help to get us there. Everyone agrees to do their part. Plans are made, and I am hopeful all will go well when I drive across state lines and break the law again. That thought gives me chills, but I know I have to carry on with these plans and keep Molly out of the Bootheel story as long as I can.

Before everyone goes home, Joanna wants to add one more thing to our conversation.

"Alice, and all of you as well, there is something that's really bothering me about Molly's story. With all the doctors Molly has seen, *someone* should have caught the red flags about Molly's behavior, things she has said and done for years, things that even a basic course in psychology should have alerted a professional to the signs of child abuse and molestation. Molly had severe mood swings, she wet the bed, she had nightmares, and she stopped walking! What the hell?

"I don't mean you, Alice, I'm afraid many mothers aren't really told to look for signs of abuse and molestation in our homes and communities, especially if they feel they have a pretty good idea of who the child is spending time with. And, I hate to admit it, but you had every right to trust your brother, and this is one of the saddest things in this whole story. Had someone, anyone, picked up on this earlier, this pregnancy might have been prevented.

"Sorry if I sound harsh, but as I heard Molly talk tonight, I felt so bad that she had to navigate all this by herself. She was really struggling with so much, and she dealt with it as best she could. Unfortunately, her deciding not to walk made everything that much worse. I don't think we have a very good grasp of the power children have to call attention to themselves. But, in the end, they are just hoping someone will notice and help. Okay. My sermon is done. Sorry if I got preachy."

Lots of heads are nodding around the room, and I want to

disappear. Joanna is so right. Everything she says makes me feel even more responsible for Molly's confusion and her lack of knowledge. I know, too, that I should have thought about Robert, who spent more time with her than anyone other than me. That's something I'll have to live with, the rest of my life. The fact that I did not once suspect him makes me guilty of so much more than stabbing him.

# Chapter 14

## Crossing into Kansas

Ruth's house is cool in the dark morning hour when I wake early, not able to lie in bed any longer. I am anxious, not knowing what today will bring. It's all set. This is the day. Molly and I are driving to Kansas. Others have made the arrangements so that we can go and come back as quickly as possible. The last two days have dragged by minute by minute, us waiting to know when we can leave.

I wrap myself tight in a spare robe of Ruth's and shuffle out into the soft light of the kitchen stove, where she sits waiting for a call from Brenda, telling us everything is set to go. She has a hot cup of coffee and motions to the pot, inviting me to join her. I welcome the warmth of the cup, wrapped with both hands, as we sit bunched up at the end of the table. I hope Molly is still sleeping, but I doubt she can forget even for a moment what today holds for her.

Briefly, we speak about the film we watched together last night after Molly had gone to bed. Joanna had cued up "48 Hours in a Kansas Abortion Clinic" on her phone as an example of what Molly and I might expect going to the Kansas clinic for her abortion. Only six minutes long, the film follows a mother who has crossed state lines from Oklahoma to get her daughter to a clinic in Kansas, where she has applied for an abortion. There is nothing graphic or alarming in the video, but we decide not to share it with Molly, only because the message of the film is about how Kansas has been overrun with requests for abortions, now that so many surrounding states have banned them. We agree we do not want Molly worried that the clinic might not be able to help her. She doesn't need to worry about one more place that could turn her down.

What I most appreciate about the film was the steady narration in the mother's voice. Although I am bothered that the mother feels the need to wear a mask and never show her face, the reason for her anonymity is clear. She is willing to drive her daughter anywhere to get the services she needs, even as new laws are being passed to prosecute anyone who helps another person cross a state line for an abortion. The mother is fearless, saying she'll cross that bridge when she gets to it. The most important thing, she says, is protecting and supporting her daughter, no matter what happens. Watching it, I felt her message was directed straight at me. It took my breath away, even as it fortified me for the days ahead. The dread and anticipation about Molly's pregnancy are almost over, but who knows what next week will bring? *One step at a time*, I remind myself, hearing my mother's voice in my head, but refusing to finish the thought with her favorite prayer, "*sweet Jesus*."

Ruth's phone vibrates on the table, interrupting our thoughts about the film. She talks briefly in low tones with Carol before she puts the phone on speaker and places it between us on the table. I strain to hear the lawyer's voice detailing what we must do. I hear the words "things we didn't anticipate being a problem," "molestation and rape," "disabled minor," "the stakes in taking her across state lines, and *consent*." It's hard for me to understand what Carol is talking about, until I clearly hear the words "the consent forms are on the Kansas clinic website, so you can easily print them off and get Wilson's consent as quickly as possible."

When I hear that last sentence, I panic. *I can't handle this, not right now! I need Wilson's consent? How am I going to get that?*

I bolt out of Ruth's house and fly into her backyard. I am so angry. *One more thing I'm supposed to do before we can leave. I need to be in my car driving west with Molly, right now! We have an appointment we need to make—today!* My brain is sparking little electrical charges that keep my eyes from focusing on Ruth's flowers.

Mixed with my frustration is the fact that Wilson is in jail, awaiting news about his own arraignment for trying to strangle Robert. There's no way for him to download anything, or sign any papers, or drive them to Columbia. None of that can happen. I want to laugh out loud. All of this is so ridiculous, but not funny at all. If I start laughing, or crying, now, I might not be able to stop. I close my eyes to stop the fireworks, but they are still there behind my closed lids.

What is Carol thinking? I certainly do not have time to drive back down to the Bootheel and get Wilson's signature on a consent form for Molly's abortion. What's wrong with this picture? I can't even count the ways this is ironic, not to mention the fact that the law requires parental consent for a minor child who is seeking an *illegal* procedure.

If I go home right now, I'm a sitting duck. I know the police are watching my house, waiting to arrest me for whatever crimes they think I have committed. For sure, they will be at the jail, if I go there to see Wilson. The police would like nothing better than to haul me into the same jail where my husband sits. No one knows yet how our crimes are related, but soon enough the media will get a whiff of our story, and they will pull it apart without understanding any of the facts or the reasons. Richard and Walter, the two policemen who came to my house, will be right there, ready to lock me up. They would relish the thought.

I force myself back into the house. As the sun comes up over the crest of the house next door, I talk quietly, telling Ruth more than I have up to this point about Wilson and Robert and the police in Sikeston. I tell my aunt that I stabbed my brother in the loft and left him there, not knowing if he was dead or alive. I tell her the police have the pitchfork I used, with my fingerprints on it. I tell her Wilson is in jail for trying to strangle Robert, after I told him about Molly's pregnancy. I try not to tell her too much, but it's all connected, and I keep talking. I want to protect Ruth, just as I did with Barb, by not telling her things she would have to lie about if ordered to testify in court, but now I've passed that point and we are in too deep. Can I protect myself and Molly? The fewer people who know what I did, the better, but I feel my story spooling out of my mouth, seeking the ears of those who have sworn to help us.

Ruth takes my story in her stride. She agrees that I simply cannot return to the Bootheel and risk facing the police just yet. I need to get Molly to Kansas, see that she gets her abortion, and bring her back to Columbia, before I can tackle the problem of facing what I've done. She pats my shoulder, then excuses herself to call Brenda again. They talk for a while, as I finish my coffee, trying to stay calm. Ruth returns and puts the phone on speaker. She tells me to speak directly to Carol, who is now with Brenda.

"Hi, Carol," I say in a tight voice, "this is Alice."

"Hi, Alice, I think, maybe, we might have a solution." Her words do not inspire confidence. "Maybe" and "might" are not reassuring, but I listen to her carefully, anyway.

"I'm trying to find out if your husband would sign a scan of the consent document for Molly's abortion. Do you think he would sign it, if someone took it to him in the Sikeston jail?"

I have to think about that for a minute. Then, remembering how angry Wilson had been when I told him what Robert had done to Molly, I decide he would cooperate, if he knew it was important for him to support his daughter now.

"I know the name of my father-in-law's lawyer in Sikeston. You could send him a link to the consent form online and ask him, lawyer to lawyer, to download and print out the form so someone can take it to Wilson to sign." I'm thinking fast about what could possibly work to get Wilson's signature as he sits in jail.

"It has to be today," I insist to Carol. "Stan's lawyer can make an official call to the jail, giving them a heads-up that someone from his office is bringing some legal papers for Wilson to sign. The lawyer could encourage Wilson to read the consent form carefully, and then sign it. Once he gets the form back to his office, he can scan it and send it to you via email."

Carol ponders the plan, noting how many people we will be contacting and what kinds of information will be evident in our conversations. The contact with the lawyer will be privileged, and Carol will ask for his total discretion. Against my better judgment, I have to trust Wilson to know what to do. I'm actually depending on him to conjure the unexpected fierce, protective father who emerged when he knew Molly had been molested. I'm hoping his anger has not dissipated during his long days in jail, and that he will realize the importance of signing the form.

While Carol takes care of the legalities of consent, Brenda double checks the details about our trip across the border, which will now be a day later. Phone calls are made in code. Emails are sent with secrets embedded in them. Particulars are left out, vague references inserted. In these communications, Molly and I are referred to as Claire and Rita Johnson, mother and daughter. A designated taxi is requested at a certain time the day after we arrive at the hotel in Olathe, and the driver has been alerted that "Miss Johnson" is in a wheelchair. They give the driver the address for where he will be taking us. Brenda assures us this driver has worked with them many times before and knows to be on time and not to talk to anyone about his riders. She is careful to ask if his taxi can accommodate Claire's wheelchair, and he assures her that should not be a problem.

The clinic, which is near Overland Park just across the state line, has been providing legal abortions, performed by a dedicated medical doctor, for nearly thirty years. They were one of the first in the region to offer the option of abortion pills to appropriate patients. They are experienced and professional, and all preparations have been made in advance. I am informed that our room at the nearby hotel has been reserved for two nights, and the desk clerk has received food vouchers for us while we stay there. I have to chuckle to myself, thinking Molly and I will get an "all-expenses paid trip to Olathe, Kansas. Wow!" My own attempt at humor fails me. This part of Kansas is not beautiful as the Shawnee word "Olathe" suggests and was established as a complex hub of railroad tracks built to accommodate the demands of moving humans and cattle to the plains of western America.

But thanks to the efficiency of modern technology, I am saved from making a trip to get Wilson's consent for Molly's abortion. By the next morning, I have both the consent form signed by Wilson, along with my own, in a file folder I will carry with me to Kansas. After all the planning, the discussions, the confessions, and the counseling, I expect the trip to Kansas to be fairly easy. Although I have never driven this far west, I am confident I can do it. I will drive on the same Interstate we traveled from St. Louis to Columbia, just this time in the opposite direction. I-70 crosses the exact center of Missouri, east to west, from St. Louis to Kansas City. Years ago, when the Cardinals were playing the Royals in the baseball playoffs, it was dubbed "the I-70 Series," and some people still joke about that. I figure one half of the Interstate probably looks pretty much like the other half, east to west.

Molly and I are both unusually quiet as we say goodbye to Ruth in the morning light. She hugs us both and reminds me to drive carefully. She looks Molly in the eye and tells her she can do this.

"You are a brave girl, and soon this will be over. You and your mother can always come here and stay with me."

I am glad to hear Ruth say this, although I am also aware that this may not be possible, given the fact that the cops are fast on my heels, ready to pounce if I stay in one place too long. I have all the instructions and the names of the people who will be waiting for us in Kansas written in some hidden notes on my phone and the address of the hotel written on the back of an envelope, one I will destroy when no longer needed. We have bottles of water and a few snacks to get us there. We have no luggage, only the few provisions Ruth and the others have supplied for us, stuffed into an old gym bag Ruth found in her closet. We each have soft, worn T-shirts for sleeping, toothbrushes, underwear, and a new outfit each of pants and shirts for the drive there and back. We regret not having the bags we had packed for our trip to Hand of Hope, but I'm thinking that was a small price to pay for our liberation.

In my eagerness to complete this chapter of our lives, I somehow forgot to factor in the mercurial summer weather in Missouri. I should have known such a momentous trip would come with another gauntlet to pass through. We leave Ruth's house in the pre-dawn stillness and drive straight into thunderstorms, torrential rain, and hail most of the way from Columbia to the Kansas border. My new confidence about driving on the Interstate wavers as the rain pummels my car, obscuring everything outside the windshield. Several times, I am forced to stop under an overpass to catch a breather from the ungodly claps of thunder and the rain lashing against the windows. The traffic is at a crawl. I know it is dangerous to pull over, but it is more dangerous to drive, when I cannot see the road or the cars in front of me.

To bolster my nerves and not cause more anxiety for Molly, I turn up the radio, loud. Through the pouring rain, we sing along with every Taylor Swift song that plays. I am surprised to hear that Molly knows all the lyrics to all the songs, while I have to merely fake it whenever she goes off on stanzas I've never heard before. After at least forty-five minutes of the lashing rain, I slowly navigate the car back into the emerging sunlight. Like most states, ours has a favorite saying, "If you don't like the weather in Missouri, wait a minute." I'm thinking today this has totally been true. I feel blessed to see the sunlight on the front of my car and watch the puddles of water evaporate in the warm air. I decide the rain is a blessing on this day and try to forget anything other than being with, and protecting, Molly.

After nearly four hours, when it should have taken two, or three at most, we cross the state line into Kansas. I didn't know Molly was awake, long after our marathon singing spree, but I am pleased to hear her clapping her hands, when we pass the "Welcome to Kansas" sign. The rain has finally stopped dripping, and the directions take us straight to the hotel in Olathe. I make a joke about the size of the hail we had encountered, making a circle with my thumb and forefinger larger than a quarter. Molly snickers in the back seat and claims it wasn't "nearly that big." We have a careful little laugh over this and agree the weather has been "a pain in the ass," although we had fun singing together. Molly loves it when I use words she is not allowed to say, so she grins at me when I unload her wheelchair and bring it around to her door.

"This chair is a pain in the ass," she says, looking to see if she can get away with saying that. I just agree with her and let it pass.

She wheels behind me to the front of the hotel but stops at the revolving doors. She waits until I go inside, look around, and point to where she can get through a different door. Once inside, we are greeted warmly by a large woman standing behind the reception desk. Her dress is bright blue with enormous red poppies spread across the top and the bottom. Her lipstick matches the color of the poppies on her dress, and her smile is a mile wide. Her voice booms like she's in a theatre.

back to me in the lounge, ready to talk with the counselor and the nurse, with me in the room. I am grateful none of them asks why I'm lying on the floor. We sit there for a while as the nurse explains what they have learned from Molly's exam and her ultrasound.

Molly is actually more than seven weeks pregnant now but still well within the legal guidelines in Kansas, they tell us. The doctor talks with Molly about the procedure with the pills she is suggesting for her and tells us she hopes to see us the next morning with Molly's decision. I call our trusty taxi, who comes as quickly as he can to pick us up and take us back to the hotel. After dinner, we each have an ice cream cone, compliments of Delores.

Later, in our room, we talk about the counseling sessions and the ultrasound photos Molly saw in the clinic. I can tell the photographs and the discussions have been unsettling for Molly, although this time there was no talk of God or how she and Robert had sinned. We slip into our soft T-shirts and lie on our backs in the dim light of the room. I do not miss the snarky, angry daughter I have come to expect, but I worry when she is soft-spoken, thoughtful, prepared to talk to me without the edge I have grown accustomed to hearing from her.

"It is weird, Mom, to actually see inside my body. I didn't know what an ultrasound would be like. It was cool. I thought it might hurt, but I didn't realize it is just a photograph of my belly."

She is quiet for a bit. I sense Molly is thinking about what she might feel comfortable saying next, how exactly to talk about what she has inside of her.

"I am so glad, the, the 'embryo'...?"

Molly makes air quotations in the dim light with her fingers, letting me know this is how the staff at the clinic have been talking with her about what is in her body.

"... is only about the size of a blackberry right now. It really is not a baby yet, and that makes me feel better, for some reason. I'm not sure why. How would you feel if it was in your tummy? Would you have an abortion?"

"Yes, I would," I tell my daughter, thinking this conversation should never, ever happen between a mother and her ten-year-old daughter. "If I wasn't able to care for another child, I would definitely have an abortion. Does that make you feel better?"

"I guess so. I'm not sure. All this is a lot, you know."

Molly sits up on the bed, staring down at me. She is not angry, just direct.

"You should have told me more when I first started my period, Mom. I know you were freaked out, but you should have told me. That's what you are supposed to do. Maybe I could have been smarter with Uncle Robert, if I had known more than I did."

I'm floored by Molly's words. I burst into tears and know instantly this is exactly the wrong thing to do. I try to breathe deeply and staunch the flow. I look her in the eye as best I can and beg for her forgiveness.

"You are right, Molly. I hope someday you can forgive me. I wish I could have been smarter and stronger. I do."

Before we both get too sleepy, I ask her how she is feeling about tomorrow, and if she knows what she will do. Molly's answer is far beyond her years. As I hear her talk, I believe my daughter is mentally ready to make her decision, and that she will be okay, in the end.

"I want to go back to the clinic in the morning and get this over with. I'm really tired of thinking about it all the time. I have learned a lot more than I ever thought I would learn. I don't think I'll ever be quite the same as the other kids in my classes, but I want to go back to school and catch up. And, Mom, most of all, I want to learn to walk again. That's first on my list, to walk into a classroom and be 'normal' again. You think I'll be able to do that?"

"Absolutely," I assure her, desperately hoping this is true.

"I want to go back to the doctor and take the first pill.

That's what I want to do. Then I want to go back to Aunt Ruth's and figure out what we're going to do next, after I take the second one."

After some time, I think Molly has finally drifted off to sleep, but suddenly she is sitting up again.

"And one more thing, I want to say," she announces as though she's nowhere near asleep.

"It is totally unfair that I am the one going to Kansas City to get an abortion, having to worry about what's in my body, nervous about the law, or whatever, and whether or not I want a baby. This is just like bleeding. Boys don't have to bleed, either. What the fuck?"

Molly flops back onto the bed and turns her face to the wall.

"Ah, you would be correct in that, my dear daughter," I whisper. "It is totally not fair. It's always been that way, and I don't see how that can ever really change. Good night, sweet girl. Welcome to the world of women."

The next day, when the mandatory wait time has passed, Molly and I return to the clinic. We had called the taxi last night and asked him to pick us up as early as possible the next morning. He tells us he will be at the hotel by 6:00 a.m. I hope that's early enough to avoid the protestors, who are likely to appear at the clinic at any time. We are relieved that no one is there when he pulls into the parking lot. Again, he takes out the wheelchair and sets it up for Molly, and I follow her through the doors into the foyer.

Once we are in the clinic, Phoebe, the counselor, asks Molly if she has thought about what she is doing, and if she is sure about her decision to have an abortion. Molly assures her that she has thought a lot about it and wants to do it. We are invited to wait in the small room to our left, and Phoebe stays with us. We all sit quietly for a few minutes, not speaking, until Dr. Constance comes to the door and asks Molly if she is ready. I am grateful to hear her ask if I can come, too.

"Can my mom come in with us?"

"Of course, as long as she can be quiet," Constance smiles at both of us and gestures toward her office door. As we follow Molly in her wheelchair, the doctor turns to me and smiles.

"It's going to be all right, Mom," she says. "Let's get this girl back on her feet."

I dare not leave Molly for the next two hours. She takes the first pill and nods off as she lies on the cot in the room. After an hour or so, she asks me what time it is. I tell her it is now past eight in the morning. We can both see the sun filtering through the curtains in her room. Cautiously, I ask how she's feeling.

"Okay," she says and tells me she'd like to use the bathroom. I move to get the wheelchair, but she asks if she can just lean on me to get to the toilet. I'm pleased to help her and hope this is part of her new plan to try and walk again on her own. Right now, her legs seem weak and wobbly, but we move together easily into the bathroom, and I help her sit on the toilet. I notice her feet don't touch the floor and am reminded for the millionth time how young my daughter is and how wrong this setting is for her. I vow to get her out as quickly as I can. When she wants to go back to her room, we hobble back, in step, but with all her weight on me, just as it should be. I welcome the chance to hold her up.

The second nurse suggests I walk Molly down the hall and back, to see if we can manage that. We do, with quite a bit of effort, and meet the doctor at the door of her room when we return. Dr. Constance takes Molly's other arm and helps me position her onto her wheelchair. She looks at her eyes and asks her how she's feeling. Molly admits she's still sleepy and hopes she can sleep in the car on the way back to Missouri. With that, she nods and hands Molly the envelope that contains the second pill she will take in two days back at Ruth's. Inside, she has also put her card with her phone number. She tells Molly she can call anytime if she has any questions.

"Goodbye to you both. I'm happy I got to meet you both, although I wish it was under different circumstances. Molly, there will be counseling available to you when you return to Columbia, please take advantage of it. You are a strong and brave girl, I can see that. Believe in yourself and things will be better soon, I promise. Goodbye to you both, and good luck."

Suddenly, the doctor surprises me. She becomes all business, her voice sharp with instructions.

"Alice!" she barks. "Call the taxi now and be totally ready for him when he arrives. It will not be good to have him wait outside for you, or for you to wait for him. Trust me. Get out of here as quickly as you can."

Not really understanding her urgency, I am quick to gather our few belongings and dial the taxi's number to come get us. When I see him turn into the driveway, I motion for Molly to follow me. I pull the front door open for her to wheel through, just in time for both us to see a mob of protestors gathered on the sidewalk, surely not far enough from the door to be legal. They begin shouting the minute the sliding door closes behind Molly's chair. The group of about nine people carry signs and push them aggressively toward us, not quite sure which one of us to target with their crude messages covered with fake blood dripping down in three-inch letters.

I see Molly's face turn a bright pink, then red, and tears begin to fall, as she reads the signs flashing before her on the sidewalk.

***SHAME ON YOU!***

***GOD WILL PUNISH YOU FOR KILLING YOUR BABY!!***

***WHY DID YOU KILL YOUR BABY?***

***YOU ARE GOING TO HELL!!!***

***BABIES HAVE RIGHTS, TOO!!!***

We stand mute next to the door, as the protestors march in a circle, pushing the line they are not supposed to cross. They scream. They yell. They spit. They shout at the taxi driver, when he pulls into the parking lot. I want to shout back at them. I want to scream, yell, and spit, too. Can't they see my child is in a wheelchair, unable to move away from their assault? My ears are ringing with the force of their shouts, my face twisted in anger as I help shuffle Molly from her chair into the back seat of the taxi. She sits as low as she can in the backseat and turns her head away from the window.

As we drive away, I watch the driver's face in the mirror and wonder how often he does the job of collecting girls and women from this clinic and hustling them to safety. He gives nothing away, until I hear him mutter, "Assholes," as he screeches the tires in retreat. I watch the protestors as they watch us leave. I think about Mary and the counselors at Hand of Hope. I want to think they aren't evil people, but people strong in their beliefs and not shy about sharing them. Today, that doesn't help me, though. I want to yell out the window. I wish I had a sign that read:

***Rape, Incest!!***

***Rape, Incest!!***

***She's a Child, Too!!***

***Back Off!!***

The words I have conjured stay with me long after we leave the parking lot. I have been rolling them around on my tongue for some time. They seem inseparable, yet they are not quite the same. Rape is not always incest, but incest is always rape. *That was it. Incest is always rape*. I keep hearing the line, "Sometimes, but not always, there are exceptions in the case of "rape or incest..." What if it's both? And is there a special dispensation for little girls raped by their uncles? There should be. There should be a dispensation for little girls betrayed by the men they love and depend on the most.

The silence once we leave the clinic parking lot is complete in its relief. The taxi ride is uneventful, the small hotel a welcome sight. Molly wants a hot bath, so I leave her to soak by herself. I order some comfort food for us both from the diner across the street, and a chocolate shake for Molly. Hopefully, tonight she can get some sleep. I still have some melatonin in my bag if she needs it.

As it happens, neither of us sleep very well, and the next morning Molly is anxious to get back to Columbia and Aunt Ruth's house. She feels safe there, surrounded by women who listen to her and are eager to help. I am hoping the cops are not waiting for me. Delores meets us at the counter when we go downstairs and offers us water and snacks she has packed for the road. We thank her for her kind help at the hotel, then get in the car to retrace our drive across Missouri's flat miles back to Columbia. I am relieved to see no storm clouds in the sky, only a gray haze that suggests the day will be warm, but the sun may not make an appearance. Somehow, I find this soothing as I turn the car east, where the fragments of our lives wait for us to return and pick up the pieces.

In the car, Molly and I talk about little things, about the cat that lives in the shed behind our house, about her strict grandmother, Gail, how she and Molly often butt heads. Molly asks me if I'm serious about moving away from where we live, and she reminds me of my plan to leave the Bootheel for good. I am happy to agree.

"Oh, yes," I tell her. "I definitely want to move away, too." Then, I spin a tale I hope can become reality, although the obstacles still in our path may make this very difficult. I try to measure my words with confidence but not pretend to know everything about our future.

"As quickly as we can, with your grandparents' help, and your dad's, we will sell the house in Sikeston. Maybe then, with Ruth's help, we will find a place to live in Columbia near her and the university campus. The first thing we need to do is get you into physical therapy for your legs. Eventually, you can return to school, and Ruth says there may be jobs available in town that I might be qualified to do. I might also be able to also take some courses at the university, she says. Right now, I can't imagine what those might be, but I have come to trust Ruth, and she is willing to explore my options with me. She will help us both, in fact."

We get back to Ruth's house before noon, and right away, Molly crawls into her bed, eager to lie down. I rest on the bed with her for an hour, and later, we sit and talk with Ruth about our trip. We tell her about the doctors and nurses at the clinic, and how kind they were to us. Molly tells her about the hotel and the flamboyant manager with the bright clothing and booming voice. We tell her about the taxi driver, Edwardo, who makes this trip often to drive other women and girls who need his help. By the time we finish our tale of crossing the border into Kansas, I realize that Ruth has heard similar stories many times before from other women and girls who had made the same journey.

Joanna comes over after dinner to sit privately with Molly and talk with her about the abortion and how she's feeling. I am thankful to see them disappear into Molly's room. I know this is exactly what Molly needs, and I am so relieved Joanna is there to talk with her.

In two days, Molly takes the second pill the doctor gave her. We are both glad to be with Ruth, while we wait to see how her body reacts to the medications. She had no cramping after the first pill, and I am relieved that she doesn't have any problems after the second one, either. A day or two later, she does have some bleeding, as the doctors told her to expect, but nothing serious. That day, Molly wants to stay in bed with the blinds pulled, so I treat her like a queen and bring her food on a tray. Carol comes over and spends an hour with us, encouraging Molly to talk about the trip to Kansas. That evening, Molly is happy to learn that Dr. Sandy will stop by to check her vitals and see how she's doing. We couldn't be in a better place.

After Molly goes to bed, I tell Ruth that I should return to the Bootheel and take care of some things there, before I can return and perhaps stay with her for a while. In the next breath, I also tell her I am afraid to return, because I do not know what might happen while I am there. I absolutely do not want to take Molly with me, but I also feel terrible leaving her so soon after our trip. I cannot decide what I should do, but Ruth has a thoughtful opinion.

"If you think you absolutely need to go down there, then you should go and sort things out. You're running out of time with whatever you're facing with the police. You did what you needed to do to help Molly, now you need to take care of your own legal stuff. You shouldn't feel bad about leaving Molly here. You know she's comfortable with me, and both Joanna and Sandy will be checking in with her as well."

Once again, I'm so grateful for this woman who has come into our lives. I know she's right. Molly will be fine with them, and I can make a quick trip, in and out in one day, to gather all the legal papers in the safe, our bank cards, Molly's birth certificate, the car title, and the house title. I also need to make certain Gail and Stan have all the papers needed to sell the house. I am assuming they will be willing to do this with Wilson's input. After all, he had told me he'd leave the house and furniture to me, when he called to tell me about Maureen. I'm hoping the idea of splitting it into equal shares will appeal to him. There are just a few things in the house that I'd like shipped to me in Columbia, once we get a place of our own. I will tell no one I plan to come home, not even Barb, although I certainly hope I can see her when I'm there.

In addition to the house and documents, I also need to check on Robert's condition and find out what the police have learned in their investigation. I have no idea how I might find out this information without alerting the police, but I need to know what's going on. I also need to visit Wilson in jail. We need to make some decisions together, so we can get on with our lives. But how I might pull that off is beyond me. There's no way I can appear at the police station and ask to speak to my husband. I'd never get out.

# Chapter 15

## Terrors in the Bootheel

Early the next morning, before I leave, I explain to Molly that I need to go back to our house in Sikeston to get some important papers and some things of hers and mine, so that we can stay in Columbia. My plan is to drive down, get what I need, and drive back to Columbia. I remind her that she's in good hands with Ruth and all her new friends. I leave her with tears in my eyes, even though she tells me she'll be fine, and I believe her. I promise her I'll come back quickly. I just hope I can keep that promise.

I get in my car and drive for three and a half hours. The day is clear, the road smooth. I've made this trip enough times lately to feel comfortable with the traffic, even on the beltways that loop around St. Louis. Fifty miles later, south I-55 narrows to two lanes in each direction, a welcome change. I find myself behind an enormous tractor pulling a cumbersome combine that waddles like a duck across both lanes. The farmer is encased in a glass cab rocking with his Bluetooth headphones on his head. I wonder what he's listening to as he drives slowly down the highway, oblivious to the cars and trucks anxious to pass him and be on their way. I don't mind slowing down. I'm not in any hurry to face whatever waits for me.

Later, I will laugh at how naïve I was. There was no way I was going to get away from the Bootheel without more drama. I cautiously drive down our street and glance over at Robert's barn, which must be empty now of the few animals he kept. I notice the lights are still on in my house, the porch light bright, even in daylight. There are no cars in my driveway, none parked on the street.

Once inside, I check the refrigerator. Two Buds, courtesy of my friend Barb, no doubt, two orange sodas, a half-bag of shriveled hot dogs, crusty American cheese, and exactly three slices of deli ham, curled on the edges. The bread on the counter has taken on a shade of pale green, and there are no crackers to speak of in the cabinets, but I'm starving. I roll the ham around the sliced cheese and eat it in three bites. I open a Bud and wash it down. It's hot and stuffy in the house, but I'm not taking the time to open all the windows today. I need to get in and get out.

Like a thief, I crawl on my knees to the safe Wilson keeps under the desk in the corner of the den. I know the combination is Molly's birthday, 03-30-13. I punch in the numbers and wait for the click. When it opens, I pull out all the documents and make a big pile of them on the carpet, not taking the time to sort them right now. I crawl out and shove them into a plastic bag with little handles from Walgreens. I put the bag on the kitchen table, while I head upstairs to sort and gather clothing and things Molly and I will need. I systematically move from one closet to another, throwing our belongings into several large trash bags I can easily carry out to the car. I find a box in Molly's room and put our more fragile things in it, hoping I can get back to Ruth's with everything unbroken. I throw in a few stuffed animals, a stack of books, and Molly's ballerina jewelry box, my shampoo and conditioner, my favorite bracelets.

I am dragging some of our bags of clothes down the stairs, when I hear a noise below me. I freeze. Footsteps, a cough, a man's voice. Cautiously, I lean my head around the end of the stairwell to see two men in uniform standing in my kitchen, next to the open back door. I jump back and stare at them before I yell.

"What are you doing here? How did you get in?" I lean over the railing and stare down into the younger man's face.

He smirks as he indicates with his sweeping arm that the door was wide open. The older man states their names, but I don't catch much more than "Richard" and "Walter." I had seen them before on my front porch, a time that feels like years ago, but impossibly has been little over a week. Besides, I know who they are. I went to school with Richard and everyone in town knows Walter. Richard starts talking as I come down the stairs and gather the black plastic bags around my feet.

"So, Mrs. Campbell, where have you been? We've been out here to your house several times in the past week, but you're never here. No one seems to know where you've been."

I say nothing. Richard has changed since he first came to ask me questions about my brother. That day he'd been solicitous, kind. Today, he's obviously frustrated, even angry.

"We've even visited your husband's parents, but they claim they don't know where you've been, either."

Richard is definitely trying to get me to say something, anything, but I resist. When I don't take the bait, he continues.

"Oh, and we went to visit your brother in the hospital and your husband at the jail, but they couldn't tell us anything either. How is that? Why doesn't anyone know where you've gone and what you're doing? Of course, your brother just woke up a couple of days ago, then got strangled, so he's not in great shape for talking, but how come nobody knows where you been?"

I work hard to stare down the intruder in my home without flinching. I am tired and hungry, but I'm also terrified. I do not want to talk to these men or tell them anything about where we've been. I figure it is none of their business, but they would disagree with that, I'm sure. I shrug once, but I offer nothing in response to Richard's mention of my husband and my brother. Even if he could talk, I'm pretty certain Robert won't want to talk to the police, at least not until he's given some serious thought to the story he's going to tell about his time in that hayloft. Seems Wilson isn't saying much, either, which is a great relief. I'd like to think they are protecting me, but I know deep down that isn't the case. I know the clinics would not reveal a thing about Molly or me, nor would Ruth. So, I wait to see if Richard will keep prying.

His next words send a chill up my spine.

"Well, since you won't tell us where you've been, let me tell you what we do know. We've been able to track your cell phone and your car. That's how we know the exact address of all the places you've been. You've been a busy lady, this number in Columbia, and that address in Kansas. We know your car crossed the Kansas state line and went over to Olathe and Overland Park. So, what's over there that you needed to check out? Was your daughter with you?"

I will my face to stay calm and try not to react to his provocations by looking out the window. I am tired of his ugly face and his insinuating questions. Through the fields, I watch a blue car on the blacktop heading our way. I don't realize it's Barb until she pulls into my driveway. I panic, thinking I should warn her to leave, but Richard's body looming behind me changes my mind. Maybe it's a good thing my friend is here. Barb's not afraid of anything, or anyone, for that matter. I could use her company in my kitchen, a witness to the two policemen questioning me without permission. I notice Richard doesn't slow down, even when she comes through the front door without knocking, lugging a large bag of what must be groceries. *How did she know I was home?* Richard continues to sneer at me.

"Well, as Robert's sister and all, you might be pleased to know that we've been working pretty hard on his stabbing case. I'm sure you've been really worried about your brother, seeing as how you're so close, you must be really concerned about him, all laid up in the hospital, no news yet about whether or not he's going to make it. Aren't you worried about your brother? You should be worried sick about him. Shouldn't you?"

My eyebrows jump a bit when I am forced to picture what I did to Robert. I can feel a blush creep up my face, and my eyes begin to burn. I fight the urge to yell at this man standing in my kitchen taunting me. I wonder why he's so angry, his manner doesn't seem all that professional. What have I done to personally anger him?

I nod, slightly acknowledging I'm thinking about my brother. I am, but not the way he's suggesting I might be. I cannot reveal one single thing or our whole sordid saga will begin to unravel. Our trip to Columbia and Kansas is tied up with what Robert has done to Molly. To reveal his actions toward her will only raise more suspicions about my involvement with the stabbing in the barn. That information, I know, will provide them with a solid motive for Robert's injuries, and that means involving Molly. My mind spins away from Richard's voice.

Pretending I'm not that bothered by the men in my house, I slowly walk to the refrigerator and pull out a cold beer and open it. I gesture with my can to ask Barb if she wants it, but she shakes her head no. She looks around the room, calmly taking in the fact that there are two policemen in my kitchen, one of them talking nonstop. I'm surprised, and relieved, when Barb speaks.

"I'm Barb," she says, matter-of-factly. "I'm Alice's friend. I brought her some food." She sets the bag on the counter and proceeds to put the food away in the cupboards and the refrigerator, like she lives here. The men watch her as though they've never seen anyone put groceries away before. Finished, she folds the bag, puts it under the sink, and pulls out a kitchen chair. She sits down on it, suggesting she's here to stay. I almost smile, so glad she's here.

Richard stops talking to watch me drink my beer for a few

moments, then turns to look at Barb, who is quietly waiting to see what's going on. Not bothered by her presence, Richard begins his tirade again.

"Well, since you're not going to help us, Mrs. Campbell, let me tell you what we have learned. We have the address where you went in Columbia, and we have the name and number of someone who lives there. We also know you went to a small hotel in Olathe, Kansas. We suspect you went from this hotel to an abortion clinic with Molly, because your daughter is, or *was*, pregnant. She got an abortion there, didn't she? And after, you drove back to the same address in Columbia.

"What do you say to all of that? How am I doin'? Huh? Do we have all of that about right? And why are you back here today, packin' up your stuff? Planning on leaving again so soon? You might have to rethink that plan, just sayin'."

I do not answer, and Barb has mastered a blank face that reveals nothing.

"Okay, let's try again. Was your daughter pregnant and have you been trying to get an abortion for her? *Did* you get an abortion for her? How old is she, anyway? You know abortions are illegal in Missouri, don't you? Of course you do! Did you know that you both can be prosecuted for crossing state lines to get her an abortion? Did you know that?"

I am breathless hearing all that Richard knows, or thinks he knows. I'm not certain I can stand much longer, but sitting down seems impossible. I swallow the beer and try not to look at him. He knows way too much. Yet, he knows none of the reasons, not really, and I get the sense he wouldn't care if he did know the why. So, they know where I have been, okay. So what? And all that nonsense about how we both can be prosecuted for crossing state lines, I am hoping this isn't true. I wish I had thought to click "record" on my phone, so I could share this with Carol and Ruth.

Richard finally pauses after throwing all his questions in my face. He looks pleased with himself and sits down in one of my chairs to gloat.

I only nod my head again, as though I am thinking about all that he has just said to me, but I tell him nothing. My heart is beating too fast, and my hands are clammy. I take another sip of my beer and look over at Barb. I shrug to say I have no idea why these men are here or what I can do about it. She shrugs back.

Suddenly, I am jolted back into the room, when the older cop steps toward me from behind the table, pulls something out of his back pocket, and slaps it down on the table with a thump. Barb jumps out of her chair.

"The sheriff told me to get your fingerprints. So, little lady, you put your index finger right here for me and press down hard."

I am so startled by what Walter has said that I extend my finger onto the ink pad without thinking. I see Barb shake her head that I shouldn't, but I don't react fast enough. He presses all my fingers down hard on the pad. When he closes the pad shut and puts it into his back pocket with a grin that isn't friendly, I know I have just screwed up, big time.

Richard stands abruptly and strides toward the front door, but before he opens it, he turns back to me with a few last words.

"We are on to you, Mrs. Campbell. We know more than you think we know. If you have gotten an abortion for Molly, we will make certain you will be prosecuted in Missouri for that, for helping someone get an abortion, crossing state lines to do it, and maybe for murder, murder of a helpless little baby."

Then, for good measure, Walter opens his mouth, for a final jab of his own.

"And that's just the beginning, *Mrs. Campbell*. Thanks for the fingerprint. We've got the pitchfork used to stab your brother at the lab, and we're pretty sure it's got your prints on it. What do you say to that? If your prints are on that fork, then we'll be back with a warrant for your arrest for possible murder, given that Robert may not make it. Assault with a deadly weapon, for sure, in either case. We just don't get it, stabbing your own brother. He helped you a lot, people around here say. What's wrong with you, anyway? Are you just a crazy, ungrateful woman?

"Why would you stab him and leave him up there in the loft to die? We're trying to piece it all together. Why did your husband come back and try to kill him, too, there in the hospital? What you folks got against your brother?"

I stand frozen in my kitchen. I can hear Carol's voice in my ear warning me to "say nothing!" So, I don't, hard as it is to keep quiet.

Finally, the two men leave, pulling the front door closed behind them. I am horrified to think that I just gave them my fingerprints. I turn to my friend and blurt out the first things that come to my mind.

"Oh, my god, Barb! It did not even occur to me to ask him why, or to wonder if he could just come out here and tell me he needed my fingerprints. And why, I wonder, why do they think I stabbed Robert? If folks around here say he really helped me, they must also know that Robert and I were really good friends and helped each other. Why would they suddenly suspect me? If they don't know about Molly or that she was there, that's a good thing, right? Then why would they think I stabbed him? How much trouble am I in?"

Suddenly, I know I've said more than I should have. Until this moment, Barb knew nothing about Molly being in that barn with Robert or that I possibly *had* stabbed my brother. Shaking all over, I turn to her and step into her arms. We stand there, heart to heart for a long time. She tries to reassure me that things aren't so bad, but I know that's not true.

"You know what I have to do, right? I have to leave, NOW! Can you help me get these bags into my car?"

I throw some extra clothes, and the plastic bag of papers I have collected, into a duffle I find in my husband's hall closet. We both carry out the black plastic bags and stack them in the backseat and the trunk. Barb collects water bottles and stuffs them into a paper bag with some fresh bread and ham she had just brought over. I gulp down the rest of my beer, throw away the can, and check to see that I have my wallet, money, credit cards, and my driver's license. I leave the house keys on the counter. I know Gail and Stan have a set and will be able to get in. I start to turn out all the lights in the house, but then decide I should leave it looking occupied. I lock the doors and start my car. Barb is already yelling goodbye and has gotten in her own car. I yell back that I'll call her tomorrow, even though I know this may not be wise or possible. She waves as she pulls out of the driveway, and I don't wait for the dust to settle.

I buckle myself in and wonder if I can call Ruth from the road. I can be at her house before midnight if I don't stop any longer than to pee and get gas. I need to go where Molly is and where I have a network of friends who know my story, or most of it, and who can help me navigate whatever is coming next. I cannot stay home for one more minute, and I know I can never return. My heart aches to think I might not see Barb again, ever, or at least for a long time.

When I merge the car onto North I-55 for the second time in less than a week, I realize I'm leaving my old life behind. I drive and drive, avoiding towns and gas stations. For the first time in my life, I wonder where CCTV cameras might be hiding. Somehow, the open road has become my friend, the safest place I can be in the dark.

Ruth's number is on speed dial, so I tap it and continue to drive as I wait for her to pick up. On the third ring, she answers, just as I knew she would. I tell her we cannot talk openly and hope she understands to be careful about what she says. She does not ask where I am. I tell her I will be "in her area" soon, maybe later tonight. We talk in code, not mentioning any specific locations. Neither of us mentions my coming to her house. Ruth tells me that Carol already has plans to come the next day to catch up on my case. I am relieved to hear this and tell her to please let Carol know that I may be needing her services *very soon* on another part of my case. Ruth understands and says she will relay the message. We hang up.

The next phone call I make is to my mother-in-law. I can't worry about anyone knowing about my calling Gail, either. I try not to frighten her, but I tell her that she must not tell anyone else that I have called her, or where I might be. Once Gail agrees not to tell anyone else about my call, I explain that I have left town again, and that I need her and Stan's help to sell our house. I know they have copies of all the sale info, deeds, the title, the inspections, etc., because Stan gave us the down payment money for the house. For this reason, I believe he should be able to help us sell it. With a confidence I don't really have, I explain that Wilson should get half of the sale of the house, and I should get the other half.

I tell Gail that Wilson is already living with another woman, and that they want to get married. I suspect Gail already knows all this, but I don't ask. I explain that Wilson is going to need cash to pay bail and for lawyer's fees to help him get off the rap of strangling my brother. When I get off the phone, I breathe a deep sigh of relief. I know I should never have come back home, but I was convinced I needed to get the papers and our belongings. Maybe I shouldn't have risked it. Now, I will have to do everything that needs to be done from a distance, or I will find myself in jail next to Wilson.

I'm driving the back roads, going from one small town to another. When I see a small gas station, I pull off and fill up. I can't afford to run out of gas, so I take a chance and stop. While the pump runs, I step inside the building to use the restroom and grab a hot cup of coffee. The grumpy woman behind the counter tells me they don't have a bathroom I can use, and I nearly cry. When she sees my face, she jerks her thumb toward the back door. I can't imagine what I will find back there in the dark, but I walk out and see a small shed a few yards from the station. With only a faint light from the windows of the main building, I push open the door and nearly gag from the stench. I stare into the dark toilet and pray I don't surprise a snake or a huge spider. I crouch over the stool and empty my bladder. I hadn't realized how much I needed to pee, and the relief was momentous. When I try to flush, the lever won't budge. I creep back to the station, knowing I've added to the mess in that shed. I take my cup of coffee from the counter and thank the attendant, who does not bother to raise her head or acknowledge my departure. I can't leave fast enough.

I walk quickly back to my car and open the door. On the side of the building, I can barely make out a dark sedan sitting in the shadows with its motor idling, its lights on low. I cannot see the faces of the two people in the car, but I wonder if it is Richard and Walter. I'm scared, now, and my shaking hand threatens to spill my coffee. As calmly as I can, I ease myself slowly into the front seat, put the cup in the holder and start the engine. I lock all the doors, but I know none of this can save me if these guys want to take me in or harass me. I drive off with the gas pump still in my car. I hear it bump as it falls out on the pavement.

I pull around the row of gas tanks and turn my brights into the dark car, but both figures turn their faces away before I can see them. The driver mocks me with a tip of his hat, just before they pull out and follow me down the access road to the Interstate. I decide the Interstate is safer than the back roads at this point, so I take the exit and pull onto the ramp. I drive the speed limit, knowing they could follow me all the way to Ruth's. I have no idea what to do. Why didn't they just arrest me there at the gas station? What game are they playing? There's nothing I can do but head north and continue my trip to Columbia. I set my cruise to exactly 65 and resign myself to a long, slow drive followed by two men who have decided I am worth following all night if need be. Where I might go in Columbia, rather than Ruth's place, I have no idea, but I need to think of something fast.

At Kingdom City, about twenty-five miles east of Columbia, I try to confuse the men behind me by quickly pulling around the back of a trucker motel. I hide my car behind a propane gas shed, run in a side door, and register for a room. The bored man behind the glass wall seems not at all surprised to see me there, a woman, alone, asking for a room, so I just go with it. He wants to know if I need an hour or all night. I tell him all night. He smirks and hands me a key card.

The room smells of urine and other things I cannot imagine, and the walls are paper thin, but I need somewhere to sit quietly and plan before I get back on the highway. I'd like to think I've lost the men in the dark car, but I'm guessing I've just frustrated them. If they saw me pull in here, they will have to stay in this shitty place tonight as well or sleep in their car. Serves them right. I sit for a long time in the plastic chair that hurts my butt, wondering what my options might be to reach someone in Columbia without calling them. I use my email account again and send a message to Ruth, hoping she might check her email tonight. Of course, she doesn't, and I can't think what else to do. After an hour of frustration, I lie down on the grungy bedspread and stretch out my legs. Then, I have it. Molly has the kids' messenger app on her phone, and I have access to it. I had gotten it for her on one of Wilson's old phones as a way to encourage her to talk to some of her school friends. She had only contacted a few of them, but I thought maybe that was better than nothing. I wonder if by any chance Molly might still be awake and have her phone on. I highly doubt it, but it's worth a try. I open the app and send her a feeler message:

"Hey, Molly, are you there? I need to talk to you and Ruth."

Nothing. My phone rings and rings, but I don't dare answer it. I send another message to Ruth's email, but no response. I can't remember ever feeling so alone in the world than I do right now in this godforsaken, seedy hotel, unable to talk to anyone I know or who could help me. I fight back the tears and wait for daylight.

At 6:30 in the morning, my phone pings. I leap to grab it and see that someone has answered my message to Molly.

"Ruth here. What's up?"

I'm so relieved to hear from her, I fight back the tears again.

"Cops are close by, tracking my phone, following my car. Where can I go in Columbia without getting caught?"

"Stay tuned," Ruth responds.

A long hour later, she writes again.

*"At 9:00 go to the gas station on Tenth and Walnut. Go in to front door and out the side door onto Walnut, cross the median to the public library, go upstairs to adult fiction. Use computers at back windows. Wait. Carol's asst will come. Be patient."* Now, I truly feel like a bandit on the run, but I get into my car and drive to Columbia, the dark car not far behind. I pull into the gas station at Tenth and Walnut as directed by Ruth. With my duffle bag strapped across my body, I take down the fuel gun and pretend to fill up my gas tank. I leave it hanging in the car for the second time in two days. I walk into the building and swiftly slide out the side door. With energy I didn't know I had, I leap across the median and walk into the library without a backward glance. I take the elevator to the second floor, find adult fiction, see computers on the back wall, and sit down in one of the chairs, my heart thumping in my chest. I pretend to be doing research on strawberry pie recipes while I keep my eye on the stairs and elevators on the far wall. I wait. I need to go to the bathroom again, but I don't dare move.

The other computer chairs fill up with other users, and I double-down on my recipe research. I print out several recipes and study them with care, making notes in the margins with the three-inch yellow pencil available on the table. I don't look anyone in the eye, and no one pays any attention to me. After about forty-five minutes, a slim, short-haired woman dressed like a lawyer sits in the booth next to me, throws me a slight smile and taps on the computer as though she knows what she's doing. She leaves a small stack of printed papers on her desk and mumbles that she needs to use the restroom. "I'll be back," she says to no one in particular.

Not at all sure I'm reading this woman correctly, I wait until she's near the restrooms and follow her. Cloak and dagger stuff, this is. What if it's not Carol's assistant? I have nothing to lose, I think. Well, I do, I remind myself, I have a lot to lose, but I make my way to the restrooms, anyway. When I enter, no one is there, but one stall is locked. I hear a toilet flush, and the lawyer-like woman emerges. As she washes her hands, she whispers that her car is a red SUV parked on the south side of the library. I should give her three or four minutes, take the elevator, follow her out, and get into her car as quickly as I can. She will have the motor running, waiting for me.

"I'll take you to Ruth and Molly," she says, then darts out the door, wiping her wet hands on her linen pants. If I had questions about who this woman is, I don't have them now.

I wash my hands and dry them, open the door, leave the restroom, take the elevator and head toward the back of the library, hoping this is the south door. I open it, see the red SUV waiting at the curb, run to get in, and off we go. I can't resist looking behind me to see if we are being followed, but I'm pretty certain the dark car won't be able to track me now. I make sure my phone is off.

"Hi, Alice," the woman says to me as I jump into her car.

"I'm Melanie, and I work with Carol. I'm happy to meet you. Ruth will call the station about your car, and they will have it delivered to an address she will provide for them.

"Hi," I am breathless. "Thank you so much for helping me—and Molly. You mentioned you'll take me to Molly."

"Yes, we did some fast thinking this morning after you messaged Ruth, and I'm taking you to someone else's house for the time being. Ruth and Molly will meet us there. I don't know how long we can hide you, but we felt it was important to reconnect you with Molly as quickly as possible. Carol has filled me in a bit about your situation, and I'm truly sorry for what you and Molly had to go through. Now, we're hoping we can get you both settled a bit, before you have to deal with your legal issues."

"Thank you, thank you." I'm gushing, but I don't care.

"I can't thank you enough. I've never felt so alone as I did last night. I had no idea they would follow me and track my phone, and my car! They know Ruth's address and the hotel where we stayed and—"

"Okay. Don't say anything more," Melanie cautions me. "The less I know, for now, the better. Just stay as calm as you can until you can be with everyone else. Okay?"

We drive for about twenty minutes outside of town, down a quiet country road to a house on a few acres. It's an older home, cared for, lush with flowers watered regularly, I can tell. When we arrive at the front door, I recognize two of the women we met at Ruth's house that first night, Stacy and Amber. They welcome us warmly and open the door wide to reveal Ruth, Molly, Joanna, and Carol, all eager to hear my crazy story.

I first go to Molly, relieved to get a big hug from her, although I can tell immediately that her spirits are low. The doctor had warned us she might be depressed for a while, or confused, or unable to talk about what happened in Kansas. I was prepared for this, but I am still concerned. I hope I can have some quiet time with her soon. I tell her I'm sorry I was gone overnight, but I don't tell her why.

Ruth wants to know what happened in the Bootheel, and I open my mouth to explain about the cops in my house, but I see Molly's eyes on me and stop mid-sentence. Carol cautions me to not say too much. She tells us the less people know, the less everyone will have to worry about what to say, to whom, and when. She also does not want to create a situation where anyone has to lie for us.

I nod at Carol and turn my attention to Joanna, who has

been meeting with Molly while I've been gone. She promises to come back tomorrow morning with some possible plans for her. Carol checks her calendar and tells us she will try to come at the same time, so that I can fill her in about my legal situation, all still very vague. She explains that Molly and I will stay at this country house for the next few days, hopefully a place no one knows about. Ruth will go back home, so that if anyone comes there looking for us, she will be able to say we are no longer staying with her. She will return at odd times to be with us, hoping to avoid anyone following her.

I can tell that Molly is confused by our awkward discussion, but perhaps she is remembering the policemen who were at our house before we drove to Columbia. I know I should try to explain more to her, but I also know I shouldn't. Mostly, I need some sleep. I am exhausted from the driving and the terror of my trip back here. Molly seems very tired, as well, and I need to find out how she's doing. We all say goodbye, but I take a moment to walk Ruth to her car and steal a few seconds to talk about Molly.

"She seemed glad to be back at my place," Ruth tells me. "But I can tell she isn't doing great. She seems both sad and angry at times. Her fuse is very short and, basically, she's not eating much. I'm just so glad you are back here to be with her. Maybe you and Joanna can set up a regular plan for her to spend time with Molly."

Ruth gives me a big hug and tells me she's so happy I am back in Columbia. She's not as happy as I am, I tell her. I fall asleep with Molly in a big fluffy bed in the back room of the country house and pray we're safe.

# Chapter 16

## A New Start for Molly

The next day, Joanna comes and spends time with Molly in our bedroom. Dr. Sandy, who was the first person who examined Molly in Columbia, has also driven out to check on her. After spending an hour of therapy time with Molly, Joanna talks with all of us, including Molly in our conversation. She asks Molly if she can share what she's thinking, and Molly agrees with a quiet nod of her head.

"Okay," Joanna begins. "In my professional opinion, Molly has been having a tough time since coming back from Kansas. Now that the abortion is over and her body is recovering physically, Molly isn't quite sure what comes next. She knows she may never see Robert again and that you and her, Alice, probably will not be living in your home again. All the confusion and mixed feelings she had about her uncle and being pregnant, going to Hand of Hope, then to Kansas has left her feeling 'empty,' she says. Do I have that right, Molly?"

Again, Molly just nods her head. She doesn't make eye contact with anyone except Joanna, who continues.

"We have talked about how all the emotions Molly is

feeling are absolutely normal, given what she has just gone through, all things that would be difficult for anyone. We've talked a lot about how Molly is still just a child and needs some extra care and attention to help her feel better. In my professional opinion, Molly needs to see a mental health therapist at least once a day and, at the same time, begin some consistent physical therapy for her legs. The sooner we can get Molly back to her new normal, the better. What do you all think?"

I am quick to agree with Joanna, but I have no idea how to make all this happen. My mind is still diverted with images of Richard and Walter, the fingerprints, and them standing in my house. Before I can respond, Ruth and Sandy chime in with their agreement, and I see Molly release some of the tension in her shoulders and look around at all our faces. This was what Joanna was waiting for, I can tell. She promptly moves on to a solid plan.

"I do have an idea," she tells us. "But I need a few minutes on the phone to nail it down."

She walks over to a chair in the corner of the living room and begins to make phone calls. We can hear only snippets of her conversations but enough to know she is trying to find a facility that can accommodate Molly as soon as possible. Hearing her talk on the phone, outlining her plan takes me back to the night with Mary when she also told me she had a plan and needed to make some phone calls. I shiver with the memory and hope this will not be a repeat of our last experience. I still feel vulnerable and shaky, cautious of the life Molly and I have stepped into, but I am also resolved to trust Ruth and her friends.

I needn't have worried. Half an hour later, Joanna returns to the kitchen, where we sit drinking Ruth's iced tea. She joins us at the table and explains that an excellent licensed therapist she knows and trusts works at a rehab center on the east side of Columbia and has agreed to take Molly. The clinic has a good reputation for their post-stroke care, as well as their physical and mental rehabilitation program. She assures us the staff is skilled in all aspects of women's health and recovery. She says the clinic pairs physical therapy and occupational therapy with mental health counseling provided by her friend, Rachel, and it might be the perfect fit for Molly right now.

Joanna's friend has indicated that she can get Molly into the rehab center as early as Monday the following week, but we will need to move quickly. Rachel wants us to come to the rehab center today for her to get some information about Molly, what she is going through, and what she needs in rehab. Luckily, Joanna can serve as Molly's liaison and fill in a lot of information needed, since she has been counseling her already. Although it breaks my heart to think of Molly's motivations when she stopped walking, I am thankful she could trust us enough to explain what she willed herself to do.

Her decision not to walk doubled as an attempt to get more attention from Robert, while also sounding an alert for me to understand what was happening to her, a sign I couldn't read. Now, over three years later, Molly's legs actually do not work, but I have to believe that knowing the motivation behind her disability will help the physical therapists decide how to get her back to walking on her own. Telling them what happened without upsetting Molly or making her feel betrayed will be the tricky part. When Joanna tells us the good news about the rehab center, I watch Molly's face to see if she thinks this is good news as well. She is not smiling, but her face is calm. I figure that's the best we can hope for right now.

Over the weekend, we have lots of down time together in the country house and on the covered porch facing the flowers in the backyard. Stacy and Amber fix light lunches and bring them outside, along with juice and tea. Mostly, they leave us on our own to talk about what will come next. I just hope I can keep everything else at bay until we get Molly settled in recovery.

On Monday, Molly seems both apprehensive and curious

about going to the center. Rachel has sent a wheelchair van to the country house to pick us up, and Molly seems to enjoy sitting in the chair, strapped down to the floor of the van, but her apprehension shows when she asks me not to leave her alone when we get there. I promise to stay with her as long as I can, but I remind her that rehab therapy needs to start as soon as possible, and this is something she needs to do on her own.

When we arrive, Rachel greets us in the office and asks two young physical therapists, Theo and Kristen, to guide Molly over to the equipment section, where they will do a physical assessment. Rachel and I watch them from the door of her office, and I wave to Molly in a show of support. The two PTs seem to know and like each other, and they make jokes that include Molly as they put her through her paces. I'm glad to see her laugh. They are also busy marking Molly's electronic chart on their cell phones. They show no concern when she cannot pull herself out of the wheelchair, cannot stand on her own, cannot take even a single step on her own feet. Instead, they brace her on each side and take her to an area where she can hang on to two horizontal poles and shuffle her way across a blue exercise pad. When Molly cannot do this, either, they simply join her on each side and guide her arms and hands to accomplish one successful "walk" from end to end. They call it a "group walk" and praise her often, giving her "high fives" throughout the session.

Soon, I notice that Molly has stopped looking over to the office where she can see me sitting with Rachel. Her face has changed to one of fixed determination, her lips tight between her teeth, a mirror of my own when stressed. At noon, Molly disappears into another room for lunch with the therapists, while Joanna joins us in the office to eat sandwiches delivered by someone in the kitchen. Joanna does all the talking, explaining to Rachel what she has learned about Molly thus far. I am relieved to hear her speak, so I can hear how she talks about Molly. When the rehab office manager asks if we have any insurance, I am relieved to be able to produce the insurance card that covers our family. Another of the perks of Wilson's job is our medical coverage. It will save Molly's life in more ways than one. I wonder how long we can use it, but I try not to think too much about what may happen in the very near future.

After I meet with the staff, it is up to me to explain to Molly that I want her to stay at the rehab center when I go back to Stacy and Amber's house. At first, her eyes fill with tears. Rachel can see her dismay, so she turns quickly to take us to see the room they have already prepared for her. Molly is impressed with the quiet room with plants in the window, a private shower, a television, a bookcase filled with books other patients have left there, and two beds with a curtain drawn between them. There is plenty of room for Molly's wheelchair to move around, even in the oversized shower.

"Lucky you," Joanna looks at Molly, who looks confused about why she should feel lucky.

"This is a double room, but for right now you won't have a roommate. I'm guessing this is fine with you?" She grins at Molly as though they share a secret.

"Molly, we want you to be happy and comfortable here. All of us think this is the very best possible place for you to get better. Just know you are never, ever alone here—there's always someone close by, day and night. I'll be here for sure in the morning when you wake up, and I'll take you to breakfast before you begin physical therapy, how does that sound? In time, you may want to eat your meals with the therapists and other patients. We'll see how it goes."

Rachel tells Molly that soon, she will introduce her to the night staff, who will be at the desk in the hallway during the late hours. She can talk to them anytime she wants, if she wakes up or can't sleep. They will fix her hot chocolate and make sure she's comfortable. Molly nods with a half-smile. I can see her assess the room. Her face suggests maybe this won't be so bad. Her own room and bathroom, her own television with a remote and no restrictions. No mother, either, for a while, just her and the therapists. It might even be fun. We remind her that she will get lots of time with Joanna, and the PTs will be working with her three times a day to get her back on her feet and walking. I wonder if she can decide to walk just like she had decided *not* to walk. I have no idea if this will be possible, but Molly seems ready to try.

"Mom, it's ok. I'll be fine. I know I need to do this. I'd like to try. Mostly, I'm tired, but I would really, really like to learn how to walk again. That's what I want the most."

That evening, Carol stops by to talk with me about my upcoming legal problems. I recount my unpleasant conversation with Richard and Walter, and we talk at length about what the police in the southern part of the state can do if I am living in Columbia. Carol isn't quite certain they will be able serve a warrant for the charge of taking my daughter over state lines to get an abortion. The new laws are just appearing on the books and haven't yet been tested. First, they would have to prove that Molly had, in fact, gotten an abortion where the procedure had taken place and what doctor was involved.

Carol tells me she will help me with my legal situation as it pertains to the abortion, but she is hesitant about agreeing to represent me in the case of stabbing my brother in the barn loft. She explains she is not the kind of criminal lawyer I am going to need but promises to find a lawyer for me in Columbia.

"For one thing, I have no idea how your motivation for the assault would, or would not, help you in court. Obviously, your behavior was a crime of passion. You believed, when you stabbed your brother, that you were saving your daughter from a predator and a rapist."

When, I say, impulsively, "I literally caught him in the act," Carol is startled, when I try to take it back.

"I'm sorry. I did not mean to say that."

I had just implied that Molly was there, but Carol ignores my outburst. My guess is she already knows I'm trying to keep Molly out of my story.

"Well, you did not, in fact 'catch him in the act,'" she points out, gently.

"Perhaps you found him with Molly, maybe asleep, mostly unclothed, in the barn loft, and that was enough to convince *you* that he had done terrible things to your daughter, that he had, in fact, impregnated her."

Carol continues as though she's in a courtroom.

"And, certainly, your only thought at that moment was that you needed to stop him and get your daughter out of there, immediately. I get that, but..."

Carol checks to make sure I understand what she is saying, and that I am ready to hear more.

"The fact that neither you, nor Molly, were in immediate mortal danger of Robert hurting either of you *in that moment* in that barn loft—you did say both he and Molly were sound asleep—might hurt your chances of getting off easily. While your suspicions and actions might be understandable, even honorable to some people quick to empathize with a mother's fury, I have no idea how this would play out in a court of law. The fact that Robert is still in the hospital, and it isn't clear if he will live or die, makes the charges even less predictable.

"Of course," Carol points out, "the entire case is complicated by the fact that your husband, Wilson, also tried to kill Robert for the same reason—for molesting and raping his young daughter. His, too, was a crime of passion, but was based on information you had given him. Certainly, lying in his bed in the hospital, Robert was not posing an immediate threat to Wilson either. What does the law say about parents defending their children from assault and rape? Or finding a child with a man in the loft without their clothes on? Is that the same as 'catching them in the act'? I really couldn't say, but I doubt it."

I'm certain Carol can see the confusion on my face and is quick to reassure me she will continue to find out the details of the law in Missouri.

For days, I drive back and forth from the country house

in a borrowed car to visit with Molly, often eating lunch or dinner with Rachel or Joanna in the common room. We settle into a kind of comfortable rhythm, and I can sense that Molly is feeling good about what she is accomplishing at the center. So far, no one has suggested how long Molly might need to be there, although her progress seems to be steady and encouraging. I begin to wonder where I can stay next. I know I cannot stay with Ruth's friends indefinitely. They need their privacy back, and I need to figure out what's next for Molly and me. I've bitten my bottom lip raw again wondering what can happen and when. A worried monologue begins in my brain, keeping me agitated and unable to sleep at night.

*Gail told me she talked to Wilson on the phone at the jail and says his checks have been suspended until he is released or charged. I cannot move out until I have the money from the sale of our house in Sikeston. Who knows when that might happen? I believe my in-laws are trying to sell it, and they tell me Wilson is cooperating with them, but who knows when or who might buy it?*

"Soon," she had said without any emotion, "money will be a problem for all of you."

*I imagine Robert in the hospital where they've put him back into an induced coma to increase his chances of surviving. I don't know what I want to see happen with him. He should die for what he did, that would be fitting justice. But I'd rather see him tried and convicted of grooming and raping Molly. I want him to suffer through a trial and spend the rest of his life in a prison where other prisoners attack him for molesting a child. I have read about prison justice for hurting children. That would be better. He should live in fear for his life. Dying is too good for him. That's a quick and easy exit from all the harm he has done. He has wrecked all our lives. Where do we go from here?*

I shake my head to get rid of the reel that keeps going in a loop in my brain, surprised at my need for vindication, for revenge. I need, once again, to focus on Molly, although that gets harder every day that I have to wait for news from the Bootheel.

On the evening of the sixth day back in Columbia, Joanna comes over to talk with Ruth and me about Molly's time in rehab.

"I think Molly is in a much better place than she was a week ago," Joanna reports.

"The counselors are not able to give me specific details about their sessions with her, but they tell me she is progressing nicely. Her mood is certainly better than it was when you drove back from Sikeston, and she has made a friend or two with some of the other residents. As for her walking, it is very slow going, and some days it seems that lack of progress is what depresses her the most. To my knowledge, she is not talking much about the abortion itself or about Robert. She did ask once if he is alive and what has happened to him. They have only told her he is still in the hospital. She apparently had no real reaction to this information. One thing they've all noticed is that she bites her lower lip, sometimes until it bleeds. Her lip is having a difficult time healing, because she just keeps ripping it open." I listen to Joanna carefully, soaking up every word I can about Molly. So many things hinge on her time in rehab. I realize I am biting my lip, too, a mirror of my daughter.

After we discuss Molly's progress, I ask Joanna about women's shelters in Columbia and whether or not we might qualify to stay in one, at least until our house sells. Ruth, who has been sitting quietly while we talk about Molly, erupts from her chair.

"Absolutely not! You are not going to a shelter, not on my watch! We're family, and family helps each other out. I have this house with three bedrooms and no one but me living here. That's obscene. If you need a place to stay, you're staying with me. I actually love having you in my home, and I'll be so happy to have Molly, too, when she is released from the center. There are great schools in my neighborhood, and we'll use my address to get her registered in September. I don't want to hear any more about that. You can start looking for a place to live later, when you have the money to rent or buy, some place for you and Molly. End of story."

I am so grateful when Ruth insists Molly and I stay with her, my eyes fill with tears and threaten to roll down my face. Tears of joy, this time, tears of relief.

# Chapter 17

## Arrested

After not seeing the dark sedan for some time, we all agree that it's time for me to go back to Ruth's house, and I'm happy to be with her. After about a month, I have begun to relax. We go shopping for groceries, cook dinners together, and talk long into the night about what our future might hold. I realize we mostly talk about Molly and me, and I wonder if Ruth would like to talk about her own life. I have no idea if she would welcome sharing any of that with me. Ruth is only 68, active, healthy, reads books, watches films, helps other women with her friends and colleagues, and occasionally teaches a course at the university.

"Ruth, we're always talking about me. Can I ask you about your life, and what it's been like since your husband passed away? If you don't want to talk about it, just tell me, and I'll drop it. But I'm amazed at the life you have built here in Columbia for yourself. How have you managed to do that?"

Ruth doesn't hesitate to smile at me, as she reaches over to pat my knee.

"That's fine, Alice, it's all good. I'm glad you asked. It's been three years,and I'm stronger and better able to talk about it, but losing Douglas was extremely painful for me, as you can imagine. I don't know how much of my story you know from family, but I gather not much, since you never really got to know any of us growing up. We should have tried harder to stay in touch.

"Also, I'd like to say, I am so sorry my sisters and I didn't reach out to your mother more than we did. Angie was a wonderful woman, and we loved her dearly, but we didn't really reach out the way we could have. I guess we were afraid to 'rock the boat,' so to speak. James was a quiet and serious man, not one to make friends easily, and was never really interested in us, our husbands, or our kids. We sensed it was his choice not to interact with family much, his more than Angie's. She would write to us sometimes. Her letters were always upbeat and happy, all about you kids and the chickens, or a coyote that got into the hen house and killed her favorite rooster. I always loved her handwriting. She had the most beautiful cursive I'd ever seen, and I know she was proud of it.

"Your mother never wrote anything very personal. I never got a note that suggested she was anything but happy and content out there on whatever farm James was trying to work. And phone calls were expensive back then, so we really didn't call each other, you know, unless someone died. Eventually, Angie was so deaf it made it almost impossible to talk on the phone anyway. I guess, too, I would have been reluctant to say anything, or ask anything, in a letter, worried that maybe James might read it. I knew she didn't drive, so I guess we should have gotten together and gone to see her. She must have been quite isolated. Today, I would ask different questions. I know so much more than I did then about how her life might have been really difficult, especially without anyone checking on her and making sure things were okay."

I had never heard anyone talk about my parents like that. To me, they had no interior lives that I would ever think about. They were just Mom and Dad, and Robert and I lived with them, avoided them when we could, and mostly thought about how to escape their lives and find our own.

"Wow, I didn't mean to go on and on." Ruth is embarrassed. "And that's not even what you asked me, was it?"

"Oh, don't apologize. I'm just so happy to listen to you talk about anything, but certainly talking with you about my mom is a real treat. You've made me think more about her, and whether or not she was happy. You're right, she was certainly not someone who would 'rock the boat' or say anything negative about our father. Maybe adoring our father made it easier to live with him."

"Well, then, I'll try again to talk a bit about myself," Ruth laughs.

"I had meant to say that I always wondered what my sisters and our extended families thought about me when I left my first husband. I'm pretty sure none of them liked what I did, or understood. My first husband, William, was a farm boy I met when we were all quite young, but I wasn't happy being with him. He was really smart, but also arrogant and hard, and he certainly didn't want me to go to school or work or do anything 'out of the ordinary.' Luckily, we only had the one child, David, who went to college in Iowa, eventually, and has made a good life for himself.

"After we divorced, which was unusual then, especially in our families, I went back to graduate school, where I met Douglas. He was already a professor, but we became friends, as I was older than most of the students there at the time. We got married, and eventually I became a professor myself. I was the only one in our family who did anything like that. I can just imagine the way some of the family might have talked about me during those years. And don't forget, I already had a son, who was only three or four at the time, which made it even worse, I'm sure, in their minds.

"So, to get back to your question. Douglas was the absolute opposite of my first husband. He was very smart, but also interested in people and human social behavior, how people interact and how they make meaning in their lives. He was a musician, too, which I loved. We were married for over thirty years, and all of those years were happy ones. David was in and out of our lives as much as he could be, and we had a great life together. It was wonderful."

Ruth stops talking and studies her hands in her lap, as though reading some message there. I know not to interrupt her thoughts.

"Being alone now," she finally continues, "has been the most difficult thing I've ever had to do in my life. I miss Douglas in ways I cannot even explain. There is an enormous hole where he, and everything he was and did and believed in, used to exist. I know he's still with me in spirit, but I've had to find ways to fill that absence. I know I'll never be able to fill it, so I have to build things around myself to protect me from the loneliness and the pain, to fill my days and my evenings, mostly the evenings. The work I do with my dear friends gives me purpose, because it is so important.

"Maybe this makes sense in terms of the ways I have intentionally embraced my relationships with other women, with some of my former students, and why you and Molly coming into my life makes so much sense to me and is so welcome.

"I am thrilled that you followed that thread of a memory to find me. You had to be quite the sleuth to do all that on a cell phone, tracking me down with only the name Ruth, who 'maybe taught English at the university in Columbia.' What were the chances of that working out?"

Suddenly, Ruth becomes very serious.

"I want you to know that no matter what happens, all of us will continue to work on your case as best we can. And, for me, this isn't about your and Molly's case, but it's about you being family."

I can tell she's trying to decide how to say something else.

"Okay, I'm just going to say this. If the worst happens, if

you actually go to jail or prison, or whatever happens, when Molly is released from rehab, she will come here and live with me. If necessary, I will become her legal guardian, enroll her in school, and make sure she has anything and everything she needs. I want you to trust that I will do this, no matter what. I know, too, that Carol will help you as much as she can with the legal stuff, and Joanna and Sandy will also do what they can do to help Molly. All of us will do that. I know it's been overused, but I still love the thought that 'it takes a village,' to raise a child, and that's what we are here for, women helping women."

Tears are sliding down my face, and I don't try to stop them. I need the release. Ruth talking about a possible future when I'll be in prison is terrifying. Not because of what I may have to endure, but to face the reality that I may not be here for Molly, that I may not be able to live with her, raise her, protect her as I should. I wait until the tears slow down, before I try to speak.

"When I think about going to prison, which seems to be a very real possibility, as much as it pains me to say it, I do not regret anything I've done that might put me there. I do not regret attacking Robert. He needed to be attacked for what he did. I believe I saved my daughter from a sick man, someone I had once loved so much. I *do* regret not seeing what was happening, but I do not regret punishing him. Even more than that, I do not regret finding help for Molly and taking her out of state so she could get a safe, legal abortion. I would do all of this over again to help my daughter. But I was out of my depth, you know, trying to protect her after the fact, and I'm afraid I'll have to pay for that by being forced to leave her. At least for right now, both Molly and I are safe and at peace, and I have you to thank for that."

I smile at Ruth.

"Molly and I both have our own demons to deal with, but we can do that together, surrounded by women who have sworn to stand by us. I can't think of anything better than me finding you."

* * *

My sense of peace is shattered two days later when "Officer Richard" calls my cell phone. He seems excited when I answer, eager to tell me that a warrant for my arrest will be delivered soon at Ruth's address by the Columbia police department. I cannot imagine why he is so breathless telling me this. Why would he even care? He sounds drunk, or giddy, with his belief that he has cornered me. Oddly, his rural speech is exaggerated, comical. I want to laugh at him, but I don't. Why would he revert to this hick way of speaking, just when he's finally gotten me in his grasp?

"Better get ready, girl, your time is nearly up. We're just waitin' for the warrants to come through. Better pack your bags. Maybe you thought you'd get away with all this crap, but not so, not so! Wanna know what these warrants are gonna say?"

Silence. I have no answer for this man. I wait, knowing he's about to tell me.

"One's gonna be fer 'attempted murder,' for stabbin' your brother with a pitchfork. 'Course if he dies, it will be 'murder with a deadly weapon.' Ha, ha. That's a good one. Ya hear that?"

Richard stops talking, thinking he can intimidate me through the phone. He's right.

"Didn't think that would happen, did ya? You think we're just a bunch of hillbillies down here. Well, we got ya dead to rights, didn't we?"

I still don't say anything.

"You still there? You'd better listen up. The other warrant will be for 'murder of an unborn human baby,' for assisting your daughter to cross state lines for an abortion. She was more than nine weeks pregnant [she wasn't], and you knew that was wrong, banned, against the law! That's why you took her to Kansas, that's 'murder' to the good folks who make the rules in this state. That *baby* had arms and legs and all that other stuff, a protected human life! Disgusting! How can you kill a little baby like that? Beats me. That baby could've had a life, you know, a good life, somebody would've taken it, took care of it. You playin' God? You knew it was wrong, didn't you, sneaking her off like that to some butcher up there who will go to hell, along with you.

"Anyway, there you have it. Didn't get a chance to say this to you before, and I probably won't have a chance to say it again, but you're a terrible person, a bad mother, a murderer, and you should not go free. You should spend your life behind bars for what you done. Then you'll have to meet God and pay again for your sins. He will send you straight to hell where you belong! You'd best be getting' ready, little lady, your time is nearly up!"

I am stunned as I listen to this officer of the law vomit his words into my ear. I can hear the rage in his voice and even though I cannot see him, I can imagine him red in the face, his features strained with emotion, his teeth bared, the spit flying onto my face. I listen to this man I know nothing about, and I have a revelation.

For the first time, I actually get it. Richard is not at all angry about me stabbing Robert, that's not really it. Maybe I had my reasons, he might think, or Robert had it coming. I wonder what he would think, if he knew what Robert had done to Molly? Would that have disgusted him, too? Would he defend Molly against her uncle's crime? But I know that isn't the issue here.

Richard's anger is righteous anger. For him, this is an indisputable moral issue. People assault each other all day, every day, and some of them kill each other, that's true. That's what people do, and he sees it all the time. What Richard objects to, with all his being, is the *abortion*. I had "assisted" in an *abortion*, as guilty as the man, or woman, with the "knife," although it wasn't a knife, in this case. In his mind, I had participated in the killing of an innocent *baby*. Nothing anyone might say about "a little seed," or "an embryo," or "an unformed fetus" can deter what he believes. He can picture that tiny *baby* in his mind. I can hear his angry breathing down the phone line, and I think of the tortured faces of the protesters at the clinic. I wonder if he marches outside Planned Parenthood in his free time, carrying one of those blood-soaked signs.

"See ya soon, killer."

When I hear the click of the phone, my body is shaking so hard I slide down to the floor and rest there, leaning my head against Ruth's kitchen wall. He, and millions of other people like him, will never waver in their *belief* that God-given life begins at the moment of conception, or even before. They might argue every egg in a woman's body is a *baby*. It boggles my mind—sacred and inviolable life summed up in the handy phrase, *a baby's right to life*.

I have heard all this before, of course, from the counselors at Hand of Hope, but they were never angry with Molly and me. They believe everything Richard does, yet they choose a tone more kind and understanding. Their God loved both of us and wanted Molly to "do the right thing," so He could forgive her. They promised a better life for the "baby" in Molly's tummy, if only Molly would carry that "baby" to term and give birth to it. They'd take it from there. They believed someone would want to take that child and raise it as their own. Their conviction was equal to Richard's, they just chose a different path to get there. As soon as Molly wavered, they were ready with fresh coffee and warm muffins, soft voices and loving hugs, anything to change her mind.

Yet, I wanted to argue to the air in front of me, to Richard, and Mary and her pro-life friends, to the protestors with their obscene signs, to anyone who would listen, that my daughter is an *already-born human being,* a child right here, right now, a ten-year-old girl with arms and legs and a good brain, *alive and deserving* of a better life than the one she has been given thus far. And there is a way to grant her that different life. I accept whatever blame is mine for Molly's sadness, her vulnerability, her inability to walk, her isolation, her molestation, and her pregnancy. My crime was not seeing the signs and being the best mother I could be. That was my crime, not noticing, and that will be my sentence for the rest of my life. For birthing Molly, I am forever responsible for her well-being, for the life that is already here, and who was, before Robert intervened, a thriving, healthy little girl.

Richard is right in that sense, I must accept my responsibilities, and that's what I'm doing. Once I realized what was going on, my job became clear. I knew I had to get Robert out of our lives, by whatever means necessary, remove Molly from the Bootheel, find a clinic that could help her, get her into rehab with professional help to deal with what has happened to her and learn to walk again. Most importantly, I knew that I must continue to protect her in every way possible. Richard's voice still echoes in my head, and I realize I may have come to the end of my ability to do this. I may be taken out of Molly's life soon. My ability to protect her is vanishing. My calmness comes with the understanding that my fate is out of my hands, and Molly's future is secure. Sitting on the kitchen floor as the light fades in the room, a new mantra begins to loop through my mind, not a hopeful mantra, but a truthful one that will help me face my future.

*—This is real. I will be charged for both crimes and sentenced by a court of law. This is my life now, and I may go to prison.*

*—This is real. I will be charged for both crimes and sentenced by a court of law. This is my life now, and I may go to prison.*

*—This is real. I will be charged for both crimes and sentenced by a court of law. This is my life now, and I may go to prison.*

I sit on the floor for a long time, before I move my stiff body and struggle to stand up. I decide to make some coffee and ask Carol if she can drop by some time soon, perhaps later this evening. I tell her I have heard from the police and need to talk to her. I am amazed by my sense of peace. I am devastated, yet I feel centered somehow. I cut vegetables for a salad to share with Ruth and steady my hand on the knife.

That evening, Ruth and Carol pour glasses of rich red wine, and Carol offers a toast.

"Here's to Molly's future."

We smile at each other and clink our glasses, pleased with what we could do to get Molly back on track. I wonder if this will be my last glass of wine with them, or maybe my last glass of wine, ever—the last sparkling glass with good friends in a lovely, comfortable room. I am full of dread thinking about my arrest, what it will be like, and where they will take me. I repeat my vow to protect Molly, both with the stabbing and the abortion, but I also realize my ability to protect Molly is quickly diminishing. Carol agrees. She cautions me that I need to protect myself. She tells me I will have to be very careful what I say to *anyone* from here on out, even more than before. Ruth turns on a light in the corner, and Carol talks with me about what I can expect in court.

"Okay, first, I don't think we have time to find you another lawyer right now. So, let's start with what Richard told you. Once the warrants are served, we will have limited access to you, depending on the rules and whims of the police department in Sikeston. At the arraignment in front of a judge, you will not be asked to speak, *except* for declaring your plea. We'll talk about that more, but that's all you need to think about for the arraignment. I will walk you through the kinds of things you can plead in this state.

"My guess is the first thing the Sikeston police department will do is extradite you back to the Bootheel for the court proceedings. That probably makes sense to them because the stabbing occurred in Sikeston. With the concurrent warrant about crossing state lines to assist in an abortion, that trial will likely be set later, maybe at the state capitol in Jefferson City, to be prosecuted by the Assistant State Prosecutor, if it ever happens. Given that you are living here with Ruth, and Molly is in rehab here, I'm thinking the first thing we should try to do is to argue that all proceedings should be scheduled in Jefferson City, since it's only thirty miles south of Columbia. That would keep you up here close to all of us and Molly. Of course, I don't know if this will work, but I think it makes sense to try to keep you up here for everything, if we can."

I nod in agreement, trying to process what she is saying. We talk for about an hour before she gathers her things, insisting that I contact her *immediately* when the warrants have been issued and delivered. She wants to read the language of the warrants carefully and determine what we need to do in response, and when. I walk her to the door, hug her tightly, and whisper a desperate *thank you* as she leaves.

By Monday, I am off balance. I can't concentrate on anything. I have heard nothing more, and no one has delivered anything to Ruth's house. I can't eat. I can't sleep. I try to be upbeat with Molly, when we go to visit her, but it is becoming more and more difficult not to panic. I try to put everything into perspective. Being with Molly helps. Thankfully, her progress at rehab lifts my spirits. The physical therapists are encouraged by her determination to walk, and the counselors say they believe Molly is coping well mentally, as well as physically, to the trauma she has experienced. Molly has been talking about the abortion, and she seems better able to process it. Before we get to the clinic, I pick up a pizza we can share with Rachel and Molly's therapists.

Once we're in the front door, Molly walks across the short hallway using a walker. She is tied to the walker with a wide therapy band, which is attached to a therapist, but the fact that she is out of the wheelchair and on her feet is beyond any of our wildest hopes. Her PT slowly walks beside her, trying not to assist, letting her do it herself. They both flash big smiles when we come in the door. I blink away my happy tears as we sit to eat the pizza, while Kristen, the physical therapist, and Molly chat about a TV series they've been watching. Girl stuff, silly stuff, normal stuff. No matter what happens next, I think, this moment is worth everything that has happened in the past few weeks.

The following Tuesday, the wait is over, but nothing's going to plan. When I answer the doorbell at Ruth's house at 12:30 p.m., Richard and Walter stand on the doorstep, both in their official uniforms. I am flustered to see them there. Without an invitation, Richard walks into Ruth's house and proceeds to put handcuffs on me, fastening them behind my back. He is enjoying this way too much.

"Alice Marie Campbell, I am arresting you for the aggravated assault with a deadly weapon and attempted murder of Robert Malone Holden, on the 9th of July 2022, in the city of Sikeston, in the county of New Madrid, in the state of Missouri. We have been authorized to take you immediately into custody for arraignment at the county courthouse in New Madrid. You will be taken into custody today and delivered to the Sikeston Police Station until your arraignment tomorrow, where you will hear the charges against you read before a judge in a court of law. You may retain a lawyer at this time, and the lawyer may be present at your arraignment. We must caution you that if you do not say anything in your own defense now, it may hurt your defense at a later time. Do you have any questions?"

I am speechless, until I realize I have to ask them for permission to call Ruth.

"Okay, okay, sorry, you surprised me. I didn't know I'd have to go now, like now, today, this minute. Can I call my Aunt Ruth so she knows I'm leaving, and let her know she'll have to be in charge of my daughter?"

Richard and Walter glance at each other. Walter responds.

"Well, I guess that's okay. You give me her number, and I'll call her, since you can't use your hands. But we got to get going 'cause we've got to drive all the way back to Sikeston, like now. Bitch of a thing, havin' to drive all the way up here, just to get this here gal done stabbed her brother, and leave again."

"And I'm hongry, you hongry, Richard?"

"Yep, I shore am, Walter, I'm definitely gittin' hongry, and I just might get 'hangry' if I don't get some food soon. Long drive back to Sikeston," Richard chuckles.

The policemen are having fun at my expense. They seem to be performing some ridiculous conversation for my benefit. I can't imagine why, perhaps to frighten me even more than I already am, who knows. I hate to admit it's working.

Walter takes out his cell phone and nods for me to give him Ruth's number. I call out the numbers and watch Walter tap them into his phone. When Ruth answers, Walter asks, "Who's this? Is this Aunt Ruth?" He's being silly.

"Who is this?" Ruth is wary, I can hear it in her voice.

"Why, this is Officer Walter Ulmer, police from Sikeston, come to take your niece to face the judge for what she done to her brother. She says you need to get home now, so you can take care of her daughter." Walter pauses and looks at me, addresses me instead of Ruth, who is still on the phone waiting for him to talk to her.

"Now, that can't be your daughter what you took to Kansas to get an abortion, can it? Now, where's she at these days? Where's that one what got the abortion?"

I look away from him, thinking I might be sick all over the floor and motion for him to talk to the phone, to Ruth.

"Hello? Alice?" I can hear Ruth's voice, totally confused. "I'm on my way. Please don't leave. I'll be there in a few minutes."

But Walter decides they don't need to wait for Ruth to come home. He talks into the phone.

"You just tell her, here, that you'll take care of her daughter. Can you do that?"

He holds the phone to my ear. I speak quickly to Ruth.

"Ruth, I'm so sorry. I had no idea they would come all this way to get me and take me back to Sikeston like this.

Please check on Molly when you can. And please call Carol, tell her what's going on. Thank you so much! I'll call you as soon as I can."

"Of course I will, honey. I'll take care of everything. You just take care of yourself. I'll check to see if we can come down there to see you and bring you clothes and other things. I'll also find out if Carol can be with you at the arraignment. We will talk soon. Be brave. I love you. Bye—"

"Okay, les' go," Walter pulls me toward the door.

"Can I at least get my purse and my phone charger? My glasses? I'll need those, please."

Richard asks where they are, and I nod toward my bag on the floor, my phone on the counter, the charger over by the toaster. He gathers them and carries the lot to the car, walking behind me and Walter. He straps me into the back seat and locks the door. I'm not sure why, since I certainly can't escape with handcuffs on. He walks to the driver's side of the car and gets in. Walter sits in the passenger seat and checks the GPS on his phone, reciting to Richard the streets to backtrack the way they came into Columbia. They continue to talk like the redneck cops they are, but exaggerated. Somehow, they are showing their power over me, both stressing that they are merely good 'ole country boys but men who can do me harm.

"I 'member seein' a Burger King on the way in, would that do fer you?"

Richard nods and drives away from Ruth's house. They do not ask me what I want to eat. In fact, they do not feed me all the way back to Sikeston. At one point, they make a big deal of releasing me from the handcuffs still awkward behind my back and offering me water from a bottle, then they walk me into the roadside bathrooms.

Richard shouts too loudly into the women's side with a smirk on his face.

"Everybody out of the Women's. Now! Police Officer with a handcuffed prisoner."

He waits.

"Anybody still in here? Man comin' in!"

He walks me into the bathroom, uncuffs me next to an open stall, backs away only a few feet and tells me to do my "bidness." After a few minutes, I know I cannot pee with him out there. I wait a few minutes, then I flush anyway and speak toward the open door.

"I'm done."

He cuffs me again and walks me to the car. I am thankful he does not make eye contact with me, nor does he mention my crimes again.

I spend the night in a holding cell at the Sikeston Police Station. I wonder where Wilson is, if he is close by or in a different building. I am cold and miserable, but I am afraid to lie down on the bench in the corner. I pull a small scratchy blanket over my shoulders and decide to sit upright all night. They take my purse away from me and refuse to let me have my phone. At 8:00 p.m., they let me make one phone call from the phone in the hallway of the jail. I don't know Carol's number without my phone, so I call the one number I know best. When Ruth answers, I speak quickly, not knowing how long I have.

"Ruth, just let me talk. I'm in a cell at the Sikeston police station. I'm fine, just scared and cold. Please call Carol and see what she can do from there. I'd hate to ask her to drive down here, but I don't know what else to do. I guess I don't need a lawyer for the arraignment in the morning, but I'd love to talk to her first, or find out if there's anyone down here she can call, just to help me out for a couple of days. I'm terrified, and these two guys are idiots. I don't feel safe with them. The more they act like deranged rednecks, the more I think they could actually hurt me."

Just then, Walter abruptly takes the phone from my hand and guides me back to my cell. He walks over to his desk in the center of the building, as I collapse onto the flat bench. I pull the blanket close around my ears and sob into its folds, wiping my nose on the wool, feeling the scratch of the wiry fibers. I do not wail the way I long to do, nor do I scream into the dank air of the smelly station. Instead, I let myself sag and give way to complete and total grief.

Later, in the dim light, I realize my bottom lip is bleeding onto the scratchy brown wool. The red disappears quickly into the brown coils, which makes me wonder how many other people have bled on this blanket, or worse, then decide I cannot worry about that right now. My lip had nearly healed during the time we had returned to Columbia after driving to Kansas. Had I forgotten all the other terrifying things that had made me shred my lip for weeks on end? Absolutely not, but somehow Ruth's home, and her friends, had lulled me into a kind of pleasant dissociative state of well-being. I had found some peace, had actually been eating and sleeping again for the first time in a long time. My mind had settled into a kind of magical stupor where things were not dire every moment, where my anxieties were not tearing me apart every day. Molly was safe and doing better. I had time to think and walk and breathe. Those days are definitely over.

"Hey, Lady!"

I sit bolt upright when Walter bangs on the bars of my cell and yells at me.

"Listen up! You alive in there? Just got word from the court clerk. The judge says he don't want no lawyers at your court thing tomorrow. He wants it short and sweet. In and out. So, you'd better be ready with your plea for the stabbing. And, he says, he's got a copy of the second warrant about assisting in an abortion, so your gonna have to have a plea for that as well. Just saying, be prepared."

I panic.

*Stuck in this stinking jail without access to my lawyer, how the fuck am I supposed to "be prepared?"* That's what I long to yell back at Walter.

I do not know what an arraignment is or what it's for, or what will happen there, and after—what will happen after? These yahoos in this horrible jail either don't know the answers to my questions, or they sure as hell aren't going to share that information with me. But instead of yelling at him, I speak to Walter in the most level voice I can muster. He is walking out the door.

"Can I talk to my lawyer on the phone early in the morning, before I am taken to court?" I do not add "please," but I know I should. Walter continues out the door—

"Please?"

Before Walter actually hears my question, I know he's left the office and is already talking to someone else. I can hear their voices just outside the door. I yell for them to come in and talk to me, but the door doesn't open. I do not hear any engines starting, so I think maybe they've not left the station. Where are they? Is there another room in the building where Walter sleeps? And Wilson, is he here? Without any answers, I spend the night sitting on the bench that is supposed to serve as a cot, leaning against the concrete wall and shivering through the long hours. At midnight, I break the silence with another question.

"Hello? Any chance I could get another blanket or a pillow?"

My words echo in the empty room. No one responds.

I let my head drop to my chest and close my burning eyes. I am terrified that I will be alone with whatever happens the next day. I shudder to think the judge might share Richard and Walter's beliefs about abortion and "throw the book at me," whatever that means. I try to talk myself off the ledge I've crawled onto.

*What's the worst that can happen? I seriously don't have a clue. Will I spend the rest of my life held prisoner in a place like this, sleeping on a wooden bench and treated like a mongrel dog? What kind of fantasy did I weave around myself in Columbia? What impossible dreams did I claim as my own? Wake up, sweetie, this is not a fairy tale you're living. This is real life shit! And I have a feeling it is only going to get worse.*

At 7:40 the next morning, Walter appears at my cell door, my phone in his hand.

"This your mother-in-law, what's her name? Gail? She's callin' to let you know that Robert woke up yesterday out of his coma, and he's talking. Thought you'd like to know."

"Oh, my God!" I am startled fully awake by this news. I have so many questions. *What does this mean? What will it mean for my arraignment? What is Robert saying and why is he talking to Gail?*

I feel the flush of blood rush into my face at this unexpected development and am startled when Walter thrusts the phone at me through the bars and grunts.

"Take it."

Before I put it to my ear, I can hear Gail's smoky voice already talking to me. She talks in a steady stream, not pausing for me to respond.

"Alice, that you? Heard they had you in jail. Don't know what any of this will mean for Wilson, or you, for that matter, but the hospital called to tell me that Robert was awake and asked maybe we might want to talk to him, seeing as how your parents are both dead. They didn't know who else would want to talk to him or go see him. Does he have any friends that you know of? Wonder if they'd take you over to see him. Hummm? But then again, guess you might not be too eager to do that, since they say it was you that stabbed him with that pitchfork. What was that all about, anyway? Well, I guess you had your reasons. Just strange that he's woke up and no one to tell it to, and no one to go see him. I already called and told Wilson the news. He's glad Robert woke up, because they can't slap a murder rap on him now, if he's alive. I guess he needs to get better, or whatever, then maybe Wilson can get let out, you think?"

I have a hard time absorbing what Gail is saying. That doesn't seem to matter to her, though, she just keeps talking. Walter gets impatient and puts his hand through the bars.

"Gimme the phone, you're all done with that."

I try to say goodbye as I release the phone, but Walter is already gone with it.

At exactly 8:30, Richard comes into the police station and talks in low tones to Walter, who has fallen asleep, his head on the desk at an odd angle. I hadn't heard him come back in, and I watch the two of them carefully. I wonder what they are talking about. They both look over at me, then Richard leaves the building. Walter makes his way, awkwardly it seems, back over to me.

"Well, don't know if all this will help your case or not—"

Walter is not exactly looking at me, but more at the floor.

"The judge has decided not to have your arraignment this morning, after all. They took him the news about Robert waking up, and how he might live, and I guess this is making him think twice about your case. Who knows? Maybe they'll have a grand jury now and ask 'ole Robert what he says about what happened. Guess it couldn't hurt, now, could it?"

While he's here with the phone, I ask him if I can call Ruth to check on my daughter. I also want to call my lawyer, I tell him. She should know what's going on. Walter hesitates, then abruptly walks out, talking over his shoulder—

"Don't know. Have to check." His words barely reach me before the door slams behind him.

I watch the door for what must be thirty minutes, but when Walter returns, he doesn't seem to be in any hurry to tell me about my phone privileges. He walks back to his desk to drink the thermos of coffee just delivered by the same woman in an apron who had brought food before. I watch her slide another plastic tray under my door, this one pink, with two biscuits, a slice of bacon, and some yellow stuff that must be reconstituted eggs. I am hungry, and the food smells delicious. I mumble a low, "Thank you" to the woman and salivate like a dog. I love breakfast food and wish I had butter and jam for the biscuits. My mother's voice slides through the jail bars and reminds me, *"Beggars can't be choosers."* I stuff a dry biscuit into my mouth and try to be thankful. As I chew, I remember another favorite of my mom's, "*People in hell want ice water*," and that one seems to fit the day even better. I am glad my mother cannot see me in jail, scarfing down prisoner food, or know that her daughter brutally stabbed her son. *What was she thinking*? my mother would wonder. I know exactly what I'd been thinking, but I don't want to dwell on that right now, so I eat my breakfast before anyone can take it away from me.

After breakfast, I hear my phone ring. Walter must have it on his cluttered desk, and maybe he even charged it. After all, their main source of information about me and Molly is that damn phone. But I am glad to hear it ring, hoping it is Ruth with news from Carol.

Walter answers my phone with a bored drawl.

"Hello, who's this?"

As he talks, Walter walks my phone across the open space to my cell and hands it to me through the bars, his fingers slick with bacon grease. It nearly slips to the floor when I grasp it in both hands, so eager to talk to Ruth. Walter grunts at me.

"Okay, they said this would be all right, but you got five minutes. You hear, five minutes and this phone call gets shut off. Got that?"

"Ruth, is that you Ruth? Hello?"

"Hi, Alice, this is Carol. Ruth is here, but I figured they wouldn't give you a lot of time, and I need to talk with you before that arraignment."

"Yes! Thank you. Thank you. I'm desperate to know what all this means. What is going to happen? What do I say? Wait, Carol, you should know and tell Ruth, Robert woke up yesterday, and he's talking."

"Okay. Well, that's a new twist, but one thing at a time. From what I understand, they want to arrest you for two crimes, for the stabbing and for crossing state lines to get an abortion for Molly. Right? Remember what I told you before you left, about the arraignment?"

"Yes."

"So, they want you to come without a lawyer, which isn't really fair, but there you have it. The judge will be the only person there, with you, the recorder, and the guard. Families of both the defendant and the perpetrator can usually come to the arraignment, but since they're both the same and they are both dead, there won't be anyone else in the room. The judge will read the first arrest warrant and ask you how you plead. Then, he'll read the second one and ask you how you plead.

"In most states, you have three choices to plead. You can plead 'Guilty,' which means no trial, and the judge will most likely announce your sentence in a few weeks or a month, who knows. If you plead 'Not Guilty,' there will be a trial, witnesses will be called, and you will be judged by a jury, with the jury and judge deciding on your sentence. Finally, in most states, you can plead 'No Contest,' which means you admit that you did commit the crime, but you believe there are extenuating circumstances that you want taken into consideration by the judge before sentencing. This may be entered as a 'Not Guilty' plea or a 'Guilty' plea depending upon the court and the judge, different states differ on this. Either way, you get to tell your side of the story to the judge.

"But in Missouri—are you listening? Sorry, I know I'm talking too fast, too much information all at once. Of course, it has to be different in Missouri. Here you can take something called an Alford Plea, which basically says you believe the evidence against you is good enough for a conviction, but you *still claim you are innocent* or something like that, something that means *you're not exactly guilty of a crime* because of the circumstances. I know this sounds confusing, because it is confusing! Lots of lawyers say this is not a good plea to take, because you really don't know where it will go from here, but it's up to you how you want to plead."

I have no idea what to say to all of this, so Carol keeps talking.

"I wish Missouri had the 'No Contest' plea, because it allows you to explain but also maintain your innocence, in a way, does that make sense? I don't want to tell you how to plead, but it seems to me the Alford Plea might be the best route for you to take, at least here. You admit having stabbed your brother, but you are able to tell the court you had good reasons for doing it. You were protecting your daughter. There's no real way now to say you didn't do it, if they have fingerprints on the pitchfork, for example, but you are surely innocent of trying to kill him. The fact that he woke up, of course, means no death incurred. On the other hand, he can certainly testify that you stabbed him with the pitchfork with malice, if he wakes up enough to talk.

"I really cannot say if it will sway the judge for you to explain what was going on and what you were thinking, for him to go easy on you or not. We've talked about the fine lines between what you saw and what you assumed you saw. I think you've got a fairly good case for leniency with a 'crime of passion' defense and, of course, it helps that Robert has woken up. So, it will likely be a charge of 'assault with a deadly weapon.' There is no malice or aforethought with this crime. You didn't think about it before you did it. You stabbed him in a moment of fear and rage for your daughter. Protecting your daughter against rape and assault of any kind is probably a defensible action, but where this falls within the law in Missouri is anyone's guess at this point. I wish I knew criminal law better than I do.

"Of course, this may also work for your husband, but he may get off easier because he trusted that you were correct when you told him Robert raped your daughter. He thought that was a given, and it was in response to you convincing him that your brother had raped his daughter that he went after Robert in the hospital. His crime, too, is likely to be assault in the moment, a 'crime of passion,' but I don't know how that will play out. I hate to tell you that in this case, Wilson will probably do better than you with the judge, because he's a father protecting his daughter from a rapist, and all that."

At this point, I really don't care what is going to happen

with Wilson. I just want Carol to tell me what is about to happen tomorrow at my arraignment, and what I should say in that courtroom.

"How about the 'assisting with an abortion' charge?"

"You know, that one is going to be really tricky, but I don't think we need to worry about it yet. Because this is so new and there is no precedent that I know of, I really cannot tell you how this will be presented by a prosecutor or how you should plead. Perhaps the same goes for this charge as well. You have not claimed that you did not do this—that is, take Molly from Missouri to Kansas for the sake of getting an abortion for her—so maybe the safest route might be something similar to 'No Contest', again, or an Alford Plea. Also, in this case, there are mitigating circumstances that could be shared with the court that might convince the court to be lenient with you under the circumstances, like Molly's age and the pregnancy being rape and incest, and that she is disabled. Obviously, the two crimes are connected to the rape and defense of your daughter from a predator who impregnated her, but that point is going to be sticky, too, because the fetal matter, the embryo, has been destroyed. We can't prove paternity for Molly's pregnancy. So, in essence, it will be your word against Robert's, and I suppose he will have a different story from the one you will tell. Not to say what you saw isn't true, don't get me wrong, it's just that he may have a story that refutes yours, and unfortunately, there's no way to prove it one way or another, especially without saying Molly was there."

Carol stops talking to let me absorb what she has just told me. My brain is spinning with far too much information, most of it I don't understand.

"I know it's a lot to process in such a short amount of time and over the phone. I wish I could be in Sikeston with you, but today that's simply not possible, so I'm doing the best I can to help you. And it seems, this case is going to move very quickly through the courts, at least so they can keep you locked up. I doubt the judge will let me be with you in any of the next hearings, especially if you plead something like 'No contest.' Then, it's pretty much up to him to call the shots and run the show. No doubt he will call Robert to testify, as the only witness to the stabbing and supposedly the perpetrator. I have known judges to go to the hospital to get a witness statement in cases as critical as this one. That certainly wouldn't be hard in Sikeston. I wonder if the judge is as inept as the two policemen you have been dealing with. I know this is unkind, but I also know the Bootheel is notorious for shady dealings and under-the-table negotiations, as well as hick rednecks who have little education and less good sense. Ouch. Now, I need to stop with the negative characterizations and just try to help you. Sorry about that."

Walter shoves his hand into the cell again and announces my time is done.

"Gimme the phone, lady."

I hesitate, then hand the phone back to him. I sit down to think about what I have just learned. Carol's advice seems pretty straightforward and sensible. I definitely do not relish the idea of denying any of what I have done, but I also want a chance to explain what happened, and why I had to do what I did.

*The judge would understand, right, about what I saw in the barn? I was protecting my daughter. In that moment, I knew Robert was guilty, and that's why I stabbed him and got my daughter out of there.*

I shake my head to stop my thoughts from derailing my focus. Right now, I have to think about the arraignment, and what I am going to say. If they ask Robert to testify, would that sink me? What would he say? Surely, there's no story he could tell that would let him off the hook, is there? Will Wilson be testifying, too? How would their cases be linked with mine?

There is so much I don't know, and I have no support system down here. No one who can help me. I'm so pissed. I had put my trust in two men, and they had both betrayed me.

*Fuck*. I feel my anger rising, bile in my throat. *What a crock!* I am tormented and exhausted. I haven't slept in the cell, and I am more depressed than the day before. I have stopped eating the food the apron lady brings, and I drink only water. Walter and Richard have all but disappeared. Someone has left me another blanket, but no pillow.

# Chapter 18

## Court

The fourth morning I spend in a cell, I wake up from a kind of exhausted half sleep that I slipped into while sitting on my cell floor. The sounds of voices, different voices, women's voices, ring in my ears.

Am I hallucinating? Dreaming?

I blink and look through the bars across the room. I can see Ruth and Carol dressed in power suits and sensible shoes, insisting Walter let them into my cell to help me clean up and put on fresh clothes for my court appearance. Walter seems overwhelmed by these two women standing in his jail and complies with their requests rather quickly. He allows me to go to the bathroom with Ruth, while he awkwardly stands guard in the hallway. Does he actually believe the women are going to try and break me out of jail?

When we come back into the station office, Carol takes charge of the conversation with Walter.

"As you know, Walter (she calls him by his first name, intentionally, to let him know she is in charge now, I suppose), Mrs. Campbell has an arraignment today at 11:30 at the courthouse. I believe it is customary for the police department to make certain their prisoners get to their court appearances on time. Do you have a vehicle for this purpose? Both Ruth and I will be accompanying Mrs. Campbell to the courthouse, even though we may not be able to go into the hearing. It is your job to get us there safely and on time."

Walter does not ask any questions, he simply gets his badge, gun and keys. He locks the office up and gestures for us to follow him out to the police van. I am astounded and relieved. This is exactly what I've been praying for, someone to take charge, someone who knows what they are doing.

Carol hands both Ruth and me bottles of water and sits up front with Walter for the drive to the courthouse. We hold hands in the second seat and hug each other twice. I feel as though I've been rescued by powerful warrior-women, here to take care of whatever is about to happen. The courthouse is exactly seven and a half minutes from the police station where they've been holding me. Walter gets out of the van first, then indicates we should follow him into the building. Whether he has forgotten to put me in handcuffs or not is a good question. He doesn't seem too worried about it, and no one mentions it. We arrive at Judge Garner's courtroom, which is clearly marked on the door, with "A. Campbell" listed for 11:30 on the list of scheduled arraignments. Walter points to a long bench next to the courtroom door, suggesting Ruth and Carol have a seat, while he takes me through the double doors. They make no sound when they close behind us.

After a few minutes, Walter reappears and gestures to Carol that she can follow him into the courtroom. She does, and we are surprised to learn from the clerk that the judge has given permission for her to stay, "since you are already here and all," he says. Carol thanks the clerk, then pushes her luck by asking if Mrs. Campbell's aunt, Ruth Gideon, may also enter the courtroom, as she is the defendant's only living relative, on her mother's side. This is a stretch, Carol knows, but who is going to check? Then, she adds that Ruth is also in the building, just outside the door.

The clerk seems confused, but he obediently trots over to the door of the judge's chambers and relays the request. Both Ruth and I are amused and relieved at how quickly Carol has taken over the scene in the courtroom. Soon, the clerk returns and indicates it is okay for Ruth to join us as well. Carol takes a seat next to me at the defendant's table, and Ruth sits behind us in the family benches. For the first time, I can see the Prosecuting Attorney and his assistant, sitting at the other table opposite the one we are seated at.

We do not have to wait long. I remember Walter's claim that the judge wants this to be quick, in and out, no time wasted. I am not sure if this is a good thing or not. The clerk orders everyone to rise with the traditional litany, "All rise. Hear ye, hear ye, the Honorable Judge Steven M. Garner, presiding." Dressed in his long official robes, the corpulent judge slides into the courtroom and sits behind the bench at the front of the room. His face is pudgy, his eyes black slits that assess the room in a glance that is not at all friendly. His bench is nearly on the same level as the rest of the seats, not looming over us, as I had expected. He settles himself in his seat with some effort and adjusts his back pillow, as the clerk mumbles to the mostly empty room.

"You may be seated."

The judge asks the defendant to rise, and I do. I can barely stand there in front of him, knowing just how important it is for me to do and say the right thing, not having a clue what that might be. I place a shaky hand on the edge of the table to steady myself. At least Carol is here to help me file my petition, my Alford Plea. They must have left Columbia in the dark before dawn.

The judge reads the first warrant, "charging Mrs. Alice Campbell, the defendant now in the room, with the intentional stabbing of Robert Holden, her adult brother, a felony charge of 'assault with a deadly weapon,' on the 2nd of June 2021, in the barn loft at the residence of the same, in Sikeston, Missouri, at 2:30, or thereabouts, in the afternoon."

The judge gets straight to the business at hand.

"Mrs. Campbell, on the charge of intentionally stabbing Robert Holden, your own brother, a charge of 'assault with a deadly weapon,' on the 2nd of June 2021, how do you plead?"

I try to speak, but my throat is so dry and clogged nothing comes out.

Carol steps up quickly and speaks for me.

"Your honor, Mrs. Campbell wishes to petition for an Alford plea in the case of stabbing her brother in the loft of his barn."

The judge is not particularly happy to hear Carol's introduction of my plea, but he can see that I am still clearing my throat, not able to speak yet. He looks directly at me and asks me to say in my own words why I want to take this plea. I clear my throat again and try to answer as clearly as I can.

"Sorry, your honor. I want to take this plea, because I have learned about the pleas I can take in most criminal cases—and actually none of them are exactly what I want to plead. I am petitioning for the Alford Plea, because I cannot, in good conscience, file a 'Guilty' plea or 'Not Guilty' plea. I am hoping my plea can be treated as a plea of 'No contest,' instead."

"Would you care to elaborate, Mrs. Campbell?"

I clear my throat again and take a quick drink of water, surprised to be asked to speak on the matter.

"Well, your honor, I must admit to you that based on the facts, there is enough evidence to say that I did stab my brother in the loft of his barn. But, I believe, sir, that if you hear why I did it, you might be understanding, perhaps, even lenient, with your sentencing of me for my actions."

"I'm intrigued, Mrs. Campbell. I'm afraid we do not have the time for you to explain today what these particulars might be, but I will honor your request for an Alford Plea, as long as you understand you cannot change that plea after today to 'Guilty' or 'Not guilty.' Do you understand?"

I do not understand at all, but I nod at him in the affirmative and then remember to say, "Yes, I understand."

The judge nods toward the table opposite ours and states, "Let the Court be informed that the Prosecuting Attorney has reviewed the application for an Alford Plea and has approved the arrangement for this plea."

The judge frowns as he studies the second warrant on his desk.

"Mrs. Campbell, it seems I have another warrant here, charging you with assisting a minor child, your own adolescent daughter, across the state line from Missouri into Kansas for the express purpose of getting an abortion for her in that state. To this second charge of assisting a minor in crossing state lines to get an abortion, how do you plead?"

Once again, Carol inserts herself into the proceedings.

"Your honor, Mrs. Campbell wishes to also file a petition for an Alford Plea in the case of assisting another person in getting an abortion by crossing state lines. As in the case with the stabbing charge, Mrs. Campbell does not dispute the fact that she did assist her minor daughter, a ten-year-old girl, across state lines for an abortion. Again, she believes if the court hears her testimony as to what the mitigating circumstances were for this action, the court will find leniency for Mrs. Campbell for her actions."

The judge looks at me and offers one comment.

"Well, it seems you have been a busy lady, Mrs. Campbell. I assume these actions are directly related. Do you plead as your lawyer has stated?"

"Yes, your honor, I do."

The rest of the afternoon is a blur. I try to hear what is going on around me, and what everyone is saying, but I simply cannot process anything. As we leave the building, Carol is happy to explain to Ruth and me that the judge has granted the petitions Carol submitted for Alford Pleas for both charges, and the court will let them know soon what is to follow.

She has also convinced the court that I am not a flight risk, that I have "ties to the community," and that I have never been charged with any crimes before. She petitioned the court to allow me to stay in a hotel with my Aunt Ruth in the meantime, until I am called back to court to testify for myself in the stabbing case. Carol says the judge himself is still not certain what will happen in the case of crossing state lines to assist someone seeking an abortion but suggests this may have to go to a state court in Jefferson City.

The judge will keep us informed. I will need to wear an electronic ankle bracelet for the duration of the court hearings and stay in a hotel with Ruth. Carol and Ruth sign the bail papers to get me released, while an officer accompanies me to a different room to attach the security band to my ankle. He instructs Ruth to go back to the jail with Walter and retrieve all of my belongings, including my phone, and Carol says she will text Ruth the address of the Best Western. I love the way Carol is at the top of her game and has taken charge.

I am faint with relief, and I am more than willing to comply with the judge's orders that I stay in the hotel with Ruth—the thought of a hot shower and a clean bed seem more than I could have dreamed for. I hug Carol and thank her over and over. She says she is pleased with the arraignment, but she warns me my battles have just begun. At least they won't be treating me like a town drunk or a common bum in that terrible cell anymore, at least not tonight.

"That's something," she says.

Carol places a call to the Best Western. She had seen it on the Miner exit as they drove past it coming into town. She reserves a double with two queen beds for Ruth and me, and a single room for herself next door. We sit silently in the taxi all the way to the motel, where Ruth arrives not long after with my stuff from the jail and some beer and chips. Carol starts talking as soon as we get in the door of our room, going over the arraignment and what might happen next. I am too exhausted to do anything more than listen.

After the hottest shower I can stand, I take a few minutes

to sit on the tiny balcony that overlooks the parking lot and the overpass for the I-55. The evening air is balmy, and I can smell the mimosa blossoms that line the back of the hotel. No matter how common, these fragrant flowers console me and remind me of my own backyard and of my mother's fencerow on the farm. Sitting there in the dusk, I think about what I can say to a judge to help my case. I truly do not want to go to prison, but I also know I want to tell the truth, at least a truth I can live with and that might lead to Robert being arrested and prosecuted for what he did to Molly. I reach into my jacket pocket for a pen and paper, thinking I might write down what I could say to the judge.

My pen, poised on the paper, does not move. Where would I have to start? How long would I have to talk? What would a judge want to hear? What might convince him to be lenient with me? I start with "talking points," something I'd heard someone say on television.

*—I am a married woman with one daughter, Molly, who is ten, but my husband is often away from home for long periods of time. In fact, he has recently told me that he has found a new woman to marry and is not likely to live with us again.*

*—I don't drink, not really, more than a beer or two, or do drugs, or party, or gamble.*

*—I have tried to be a good wife and mother.*

*—I had to quit my job to care for my daughter and home school her, because she is disabled and in a wheelchair, a chair that doesn't move. She lost the full use of her legs when she was turning seven, and I home school her now.*

*—I needed help with my daughter because my husband has basically abandoned us, and my brother has always helped me with her. ~~He was her babysitter~~.*

*~~Molly, my daughter, started her period when she was nine~~.*

*When Molly turned ten, I discovered she was pregnant.*

*I ~~came to believe I have reason to believe~~*

*I discovered my brother, her uncle, had been molesting her and is the father of her child.*

~~*I stabbed him with a pitchfork when I found them half naked together, asleep in the barn*~~

My pen crosses out the last item on my list. I stop writing and put my pen back in my pocket. My list isn't working out very well.

Drawing my breath deep into my lungs, I know this is the one thing I should never, ever say to anyone—that Molly was in that barn loft with Robert when I stabbed him. If I say that, the judge will want to talk to Molly, and then Molly will be involved in this case, and God knows what Molly would tell the judge about her and Robert, about all of it. I cringe as I remember what Molly told us at Ruth's house, that she had *liked what Robert was doing with her, that she loved Robert*. If she said those things to a judge, what would happen to her? Dare we trust the officials to understand why a little girl would say such things, not having a clue what was actually happening or what he was doing to her? No. I know the answer to all of this is a resounding NO. For all these reasons, I know Molly cannot be my witness for the scene in the barn. The judge must never know she was there.

I pull out the pen and try again.

*I stabbed him in the barn with the pitchfork, because I had reason to believe (too weak?) he had gotten my daughter pregnant.* ~~*I wanted him to pay (sounds like revenge) I had evidence*~~*. (too strong, did I?)*

My paper is a mess. What are the magic words?

*I was protecting my daughter from rape and incest. I was only protecting her.*

*This is also why I took her to Kansas for an abortion. She is only ten years old, and she cannot walk. I wanted to protect her from a ruined life. She is way too young to be a mother. She is just a child herself, and she needs to learn to walk again. She is in rehab now at a place where she is getting the physical therapy and counseling she needs to hopefully lead a normal life.*

If I don't mention that Molly was in that barn loft that day, surely Robert also will not mention this fact. It would never be in his best interest to say his young niece was up there with him, half dressed. Would it?

If this is all I tell the judge, what would happen to Robert? Likely nothing—and this pains me deeply. This is how men get off the hook. This is how rapists and abusers get away with their crimes by claiming innocence, and no one contradicts them. Is this the price I will have to pay for Molly's freedom to live her life?

It is very likely that Robert will deny everything and get away with it all. Would he do that? I try to imagine how he might frame it. At this point, he must know that his actions have been wrong, very, very wrong. He could say he was minding his own business in his barn loft, moving hay for the animals, when his crazed sister came up and stabbed him in the gut. He had no idea what set her off, he might say. He could feign total innocence and act as though he did not know why I was so angry.

I need to stop thinking about what Robert might say. It is getting dark out on the balcony and difficult to write any more. I hear Carol come back to our room and kindly suggest that I might want to go to bed. I hand my paper over to her and wait for her to read it.

"You know, driving down here from Columbia this afternoon, I pretty much had these same thoughts," she says.

"At first, I couldn't quite formulate what I was thinking or why, but as I unraveled it, I knew the important thing would be to keep Molly out of the account. She was there, but she was actually asleep. She may have seen you grab the pitchfork and stab Robert, but she may not have totally woken up. Apparently, she doesn't have much memory of you picking her up and carrying her back to your house, and I'm not certain she knows, even yet, why she was pregnant. And then, of course, she told us she stopped walking on purpose to have more time with Robert, and/or hoping you would notice something and somehow rescue her. This is all a bit complex for a girl of ten, and I understand exactly why you want to keep her out of this.

"Molly's testimony would no doubt confirm your guilt in stabbing your brother, which does you no good, but it might also suggest that her behavior with Robert was consensual and, as she told us, she 'wanted it and she enjoyed it'—that is, in her child's mind, she did. Although legally she is too young to consent to sex, this may complicate your case far more than you think or want. I have no idea how a judge would react."

Carol stops talking and looks at me. I don't know what she wants me to say. She waits, then tells me we can talk in the morning. She leaves our room with a last thought.

"One more thing. You can tell the judge a shortened story that provides your reasons for stabbing Robert and for assisting your daughter to get an abortion, or you can try to hang Robert."

I go to bed trying to figure out what to do with that. I don't think I slept at all, my brain going in circles I couldn't control.

The next time I go before the judge, I tell him the whole story, or as much of it as I can without exposing Molly. Carol and I have gone over the words I wrote out on paper and have agreed that I can still tell a story that is truthful, but not complete. I think Carol has her doubts about how this might influence the judge, but she keeps her fears to herself.

With her and Ruth as my support, I stand in the courtroom and tell the judge about my life, my children, my husband being gone, and how Robert has helped me with Molly. I admit I have always loved my brother and trusted him, but when I discovered that Molly was pregnant, I was frantic to figure out what man or boy had ever been alone with her. Eventually, the only person I could suspect was Robert. I realized it was my brother who had impregnated my daughter.

I start to explain that I went over to Robert's that day to find—

But then, I stop talking. The courtroom is silent, yet there is a roar in my ears, a mighty warning that I must stop talking, now! The judge waits for me to continue, but I cannot. My mind is spinning furiously—

*I cannot say that I was looking for them*
*I cannot say Molly's name*
*I cannot say that Molly was in that loft without her clothes*
*If I do, he will want to talk to Molly.*

I clear my throat and will myself not to cry or pass out. When I dare to speak again, I sputter as I tell the judge about the day I walked over to Robert's place. I know my story will sound lame and weak, but it's the best I can give him. I tell him I could not find Robert in the house or in the barn, so I walked up the stairs to the loft, remembering how much he had always loved the hay—

I stop again. Without the picture of Molly up there lying asleep with Robert, their clothes in disarray, I know my story falls apart. It was only *in that horrendous moment* that I even suspected my brother of his despicable crime. It never occurred to me to think of him as anything but a loving, kind, generous man, a great brother and uncle.

Faltering with my words, I modify my account right there in the courtroom, standing in front of a judge. I tell him I had begun to suspect my brother had been molesting my daughter and that he had likely gotten her pregnant. I tell him I had "evidence" that Robert had done it. By the time I got to the loft, I was raging with what I knew he had done, so I reached for the pitchfork, stabbed him, and ran back to my own house. Then, realizing what I had done, and that he might still be alive, I called the police.

The judge is watching me, waiting to see if there's more I want to say. The look on his face is one of suspicion, his brow furrowed, his eyes narrowed into their dark slits. I know very little of this makes any sense to him. The story I have told doesn't compute. I know it's full of holes, and he must wonder why I am lying, what I am leaving out.

"And that's why—"

I stumble forward with the last of a story that I know is crumbling into tiny pieces that fall to the courtroom floor.

"That's why I had to take Molly across the state line to Kansas to get her an abortion quickly, because she is only ten and the father of her baby was her uncle, which is both rape and incest. By the time I realized what he was doing, she was seven weeks pregnant. The clock was ticking."

The judge says nothing, only hits his gavel and abruptly leaves the room. Court is dismissed for the day, and I am released back into the protective custody of my lawyer and my aunt. We silently drive back to the hotel and wonder together at the effects of what I have done.

The next day, we learn the judge has sent the clerk to the hospital to ask Robert if he can remember what happened to him in the barn loft. According to the testimony brought back to the court, Robert does not claim amnesia, he merely tells the clerk he is tired and confused. In court, the clerk tells the judge that Robert looked like he might pass out or die any minute, so he was quick to talk to him while he was semi-alert.

The judge takes the recorder from the clerk and puts the machine on his desk, so we can all listen to the man's voice, a bit thin, but quite convincing in its simplicity. We hear what seems to be the voice of a common man, not very educated, a brother confused about why his sister stabbed him in the barn. I listen with horror as Robert tells his version of what happened that day. The recorded voice is weak, and I can imagine his eyes fluttering off and on as he talks to the clerk. His quiet words fill the courtroom. If they had not told us it was my brother talking, I wouldn't have recognized the voice.

"Mr. Holden, please, can you tell us what happened to you in your barn loft, in your own words."

At first, Robert must have tried to lean his head toward the microphone but gives up when it's obviously too difficult. The clerk offers to hold it closer to Robert's lips and he speaks again.

"Actually, I don't really know what happened to me. Well, that's not right, I do know, but I have no idea why my sister stormed into the loft and stabbed me with the pitchfork. I remember that moment pretty clearly, her standing over me, the rusted tongs of the fork raised over my head, her face red and angry. The God-awful pain when she stuck it into my belly. I just don't know why she did it."

At this point, there's a long pause, apparently so Robert can catch his breath.

"I had been asleep up there, so I'm sorry if I misremember. I love to go up to the loft to nap sometimes when it's warm, because I like the smells and the sounds of the animals below. I've loved it since I was a boy." The voice falters. He tries to clear his throat.

"You know, I love my sister, and I love my niece. I feel especially close to Molly, because I have been her babysitter since she was a baby. I never minded taking her to my house and entertaining her for hours at a time so my sister could go to work or get groceries. I like to help her. Molly and I have a special bond." Robert coughs and asks for a drink of water.

"You know, I wonder if my sister has gone a little mad. She's been lonely for a while now with her husband gone months at a time for his work, and her alone with her daughter, who is now a cripple. I know it's been hard on her, so I've tried to help where I can, doing stuff around her house, fixing things that need fixing, bringing her fresh vegetables. I never wanted anything in return for these things, but I sure enjoyed it when she offered me dinner or extra biscuits to take home. I sure like her biscuits, same recipe as our mother's."

I clench my hands in my lap as Robert lies through his teeth. He knows exactly why I stabbed him. He wasn't just "asleep" in that loft, he was asleep up there *with Molly*, with his underwear bunched around his feet. I could stab him again, right now, I am so angry.

Robert's voice is too faint to hear, until the clerk asks him to repeat what he's just said.

"I was saying," he continues, his voice faint, "I don't have many friends, never did, so mostly I just stayed close to Alice and Molly. I sort of adopted them, I guess. I live a simple life, mostly fixing old cars folks bring over, helping them run a little longer, stretching their dollars as far as they can. Maybe she just snapped, my sister. I could see how that could happen, what with her life, and all. I've always loved my sister," he says again, for emphasis.

With that, we hear the sheets rustle as the man must have shifted on the bed and the courtroom is totally quiet.

* * *

The next morning, the judge sends the uniforms to bring Wilson Campbell from the jail to the courthouse to provide his testimony for trying to kill Robert in his hospital bed. I can hardly look at Wilson sitting in the witness chair, looking as though he's been wronged by everybody, but especially by Robert and me.

"Okay, well," Wilson clears his throat and thinks a minute before answering the judge's question about why he strangled Robert.

"I admit that I strangled my brother-in-law in anger and desperation. I know I shouldn't have done that when the guy was flat on his back in the hospital, maybe even dying, but I wasn't really thinking, I was just so mad. I strangled him because my wife had just explained to me that my daughter, Molly, was pregnant, and that Robert, my wife's own brother, had raped her.

"I work hours away on farms in northern Missouri, but my mother called to tell me some strange things were going on with my wife and daughter and that I ought to come home and find out what was happening. When I got home, my wife was hysterical. She told me she had stabbed her brother because he raped Molly and begged me to 'do something,' because Robert wasn't dead yet. I was angry with them both—my wife, because she didn't watch over our daughter as she should have, and Robert, because he had dared to touch *my little girl*! He did that! He touched her while I was away, working, when

I wasn't there to watch over and protect her. It seemed like I had to go home and straighten out the mess Alice had made."

I nearly laugh when Wilson begins to loudly cry, as though in grief, his mouth open, tears falling down his face. I've never seen such a performance, and certainly not from my husband. There he was, in court, blaming me for everything, for not watching Molly, for not protecting her from my brother. I glance at the judge's face, but he doesn't show a thing. When he can compose himself, Wilson continues with his story.

"I admit I have not been at home much for the last year or two, but this is a good job, and I send all the money I make back to my wife and daughter. I had provided a good house, all the appliances Alice needed, money for clothes and shoes for Molly. I admit that working means I'm hours away from my family, and maybe my wife and I have drifted apart because of that, but I love my wife and daughter and did everything I could to take care of them.

"When my wife told me what Robert had done, I saw red, I really did! My own brother-in-law had raped my daughter, while I was away working. I was furious. I left my wife at the house and drove straight to the hospital where Robert was and tried to strangle him. I admit I did that, but I don't think I was actually trying to kill him, I just felt like I had to do something. I thought Robert should pay. I was so angry that he would betray my trust and molest my little girl. That was the extent of it, I was just so furious I couldn't help myself. I'm really glad Robert woke up, because I certainly don't need a murder rap, but I'm still angry if he really did get my daughter pregnant. She's just a child, after all. Robert should pay for what he done."

I can hardly breathe, sitting there on the bench next to Carol. My heart sinks, and my head begins a dull, throbbing ache that I suspect is here to stay. Whatever defense I had worked out with Carol probably isn't going to help me now. These two men I had trusted and loved had both betrayed me—in my life with Molly, and now by their treacherous words in this hollow courtroom.

My trial, such as it is, does not drag on too long. In response to my Alford Plea, the Prosecuting Attorney goes through the motions of presenting all the evidence against me, as though we were at trial, which is standard and, in many ways, supports the basis for my Alford Plea.

When we are ordered back to court the following day, the judge orders me to rise and face the bench. I have a pretty good idea what is about to happen, but by now, I am not afraid of anything he can say to me. I stand proud of what I have done to continue protecting Molly. At any turn, I could have made a blunder, said the wrong thing, and he would have insisted Molly testify. But I never even said her name. I erased my daughter from the story and continue to pray that she can get on with her life without further interruption. I know the judge's decision will seal my fate, and I will probably go to prison for a long time, but it will be worth it. I understand completely that without Molly's presence in my story about the hayloft, the judge feels he has no recourse but to find me guilty.

I look him in the eye and wait for whatever he has to say to me. He speaks as though I've been naughty, and he is shaming me.

"Mrs. Campbell, after listening to the testimony of you, your brother, and your husband, I think it is possible that you did snap. Of course, I am not a psychiatrist, but I have no reason to assume that anything you have said here is actually true. I must tell the court that I see you as a desperate, lonely woman, who became a very bad mother. You did not do what you needed to do to get help for your daughter after she stopped walking. You left her in her room with a chair that did not move and failed to watch over and protect her. I suspect there were other men or boys who visited with Molly over time who certainly could have molested her, but you would never have known, because you were not watching her closely enough. Maybe you weren't even home. Perhaps you did not check on your daughter enough.

"On the other hand, why would you leave your daughter alone for hours with an adult man, even if he was her uncle? Men have desires they cannot control, we all know that, and a single man alone for years left for hours with a pretty, helpless little girl may have succumbed to his natural instinct to touch her. You served up your daughter to him on a platter, that's what you did. Then, you were surprised and enraged when it backfired. You had a free babysitter for years so you could go out, see your friends, go shopping, whatever. You could leave your home and your child for hours at a time. Robert was a good, loving, helpful brother, who may have been guilty of something, but you have absolutely no proof of what.

"What is this 'evidence' you say you have that proves he is guilty? You and your lawyer have offered nothing for proof that he molested the girl, nothing at all. Furthermore, by getting a quick and illegal abortion for Molly, you have removed the only proof of paternity. Was that your intention to cover whatever you knew, so you could blame Robert? I suspect there's more to this story than you're telling us. Now, it's your word against his. There is no evidence; there is no proof of anything, in fact. You've made certain of that.

"I have heard the testimony of both Robert and your husband, and there is absolutely nothing and no one to corroborate your story. You have only one friend, you say, someone who really cannot speak to what you were thinking, or what you were doing, and has no idea what happened in that barn. That's pretty pathetic. The people around you know only what you chose to tell them.

"I don't actually know what the definition of a good mother is, but I would say you are a perfect example of *a bad mother*. I do not know what your strategy is in choosing the Alford Plea, but I concur there is enough evidence that you committed both these crimes. Perhaps you hoped to cover up your own failures as a mother, but I have heard nothing that suggests there are mitigating circumstances such that I would change anything about the charge against you for 'assault with a deadly weapon with the intent to kill.' You most certainly are guilty of stabbing your brother in his barn and leaving him there to die. Your fingerprints have been identified on the handle of that pitchfork, and that's good enough for me. Furthermore, I have heard nothing that suggests you might have had a defensible reason for your actions. I believe you are most fortunate that Robert Holden did not die, or you would be facing a charge of murder.

"In terms of your husband trying to strangle your brother, it seems his actions might be a good example of a 'crime of passion,' much more than your own, yet you are complicit in his actions as well. You convinced him that your brother had molested and impregnated your daughter. Any father might have done what he did, trying to defend the honor of his daughter. He, too, is fortunate the man did not die, so in that way you're both avoiding a murder charge. How the courts might have treated you then would be anyone's guess, but as it is, it is likely that your husband will get a citation and nothing more. That is to be determined. The fact of your husband's decision not to be with you over long periods of time may attest to the fact that you are, indeed, a difficult kind of woman and may not have been a good wife, either. I cannot speak to that, but it raises a concern. A case in point might be that upon returning home after over six months away, you incited your husband into a rage that sent him off to attempt to kill your brother.

"In two days, you will appear in my courtroom again to hear your sentence. It is my job to sentence you for the crime of stabbing your brother in a rage based on what you assumed he had done. I can only presume you intended to kill him. This does not erase the fact that you stabbed him in anger for assumptions you made about him molesting your daughter without any evidence of his actions. Since you have no witnesses to the contrary, I am required to find you guilty of this charge.

"As for the charge of helping your daughter cross state lines for an abortion, that will be handled in another court at a future time. That is all."

The judge pulls himself from his chair and shuffles out of the courtroom, as the clerk orders everyone to stand. As soon as I can, I collapse on the chair behind me and lean into Ruth's arms.

Two days later, Judge Garner sentences me to "thirty years' time" in the Women's Correctional Facility in Chillicothe, fifty miles north of Columbia, "with no chance of parole," the toughest sentence he can give me for "assault with a deadly weapon, with the intent to kill." Should Robert die, he informs me that my sentence will be revisited at that time. As I leave his courtroom for the last time, he reminds me again that this sentence does not reflect the charge of assisting someone in crossing state lines for an abortion. That charge will be dealt with later, probably in Jefferson City, the capitol, by the Assistant State Prosecutor.

"If you are found guilty of those charges as well—and I see no reason why you would not—your sentences will be commuted either as concurrent or consecutive to the sentence you have received here today. That is for the courts to decide."

After the judge leaves the room, the clerk tells us that the judge has signed several petitions that pertain to the welfare and custody of my child. He proceeds to read them to the court.

"The judge has agreed to the petition put forth by your maternal aunt, Ruth Gideon, of Columbia, Missouri, to be the legal guardian of Molly Elaine Campbell, subject to an agreement with Wilson Campbell, her father, who has indicated he will agree to this arrangement, as he will likely be living in different places and will not be in a position to care for his daughter properly. Ruth Gideon will make decisions about Molly's care with the advice and consent of her mother, Prisoner Alice Campbell, whenever possible. For the time being, Molly will remain in the residential rehabilitation center in Columbia, where she has been in therapy for both mental and physical difficulties she has endured over the past several years.

"Ruth Gideon, a retired university professor, living in Columbia, has sworn to pay all expenses related to Molly's rehabilitation and therapy and to regularly report her progress to her mother, Alice Campbell, while she is in prison. Dr. Gideon also has pledged to send Molly to any school she chooses for high school and college in the future and support her until such time she can support herself."

When the clerk has finished speaking, I can hardly bend my knees to sit down. The best thing I've heard is that Ruth is now the legal guardian of Molly. Whatever else the judge said today has drifted out the high windows of the courtroom. I will have years to think about the horrible things he has said about me. I can only hope that with time the echoes of his voice calling me a "terrible mother" will fade. I will have thirty years to convince myself that he is wrong. I look at Ruth and Carol standing beside me and try to smile as an officer puts handcuffs on my wrists. He guides me past the benches toward a door that will take me away, likely for the rest of my life.

In truth, I am relieved to hear the judge's final rulings on my case, only because they are *final*. No matter what my sentence is, I know I have kept Molly away from the courtroom and her name out of their mouths. It hasn't been easy. Every decision *not to tell the whole truth* was a strike against me. Even in my proudest moment, when I was forced to stand there and listen to that pompous ass of a judge explain to me, and to the court, that men had "natural instincts" they could not control when left alone with young girls. For not protecting my daughter from these basic tendencies in men, he had called me a "bad mother." My ears rang with his judgment, even as I knew it was a lie. As I am driven back to the police station, I know I am truly alone. I am in free-fall, exhausted from keeping it together long enough to protect Molly, not able to think beyond where I put my feet.

# Chapter 19

## Prison

Three days later, heading north in a prison van, dressed in a gray uniform two sizes too large, I am an empty shell of a person. I have been dragged and driven from one place to another, and I have lost every single thing that ever mattered to me, including my home, my own clothes and belongings, my daughter, and my freedom.

After my court appearances and the harsh condemnation of the judge, Ruth and Carol returned to Columbia, and I was not able to see Molly again before heading to Chillicothe, the oldest women's prison in the state. Whatever life I had before everything that happened to Molly and me is now over, never to be resumed. The emptiness I feel is absolute, everything sucked out of me and tossed aside, no longer relevant, no longer real, no longer needed.

With the husk gone, I am newly born, raw, but alive.

Staring straight ahead past the heads of the guards sitting in the front seat, I imagine two doors floating in the mist above the wet windshield. Behind the first, I picture myself a crazy woman glaring at my cellmates, daring them to come near me, so I can bite off their faces. Behind the other, I am covered in blood, my body slashed with a shiv someone provided, when I went looking for a way to die. I turn my head to look out the side window of the van at the trees that pass by in a blur of brown and wonder if I can possibly conjure another fate, one less dire. I know if I do not find a place for my desperation somewhere, I will be forced to endure a long and painful living death.

When the van carrying nine convicted women finally arrives in rural Chillicothe, a dark cloud hangs over the stark brick buildings of the oldest prison in the state. The once-red walls are black now from age and neglect, a testament to the state's disregard for its women prisoners. The thought of living behind these walls, away from Molly and Ruth and our new friends, makes me dizzy. Instead, I devise a plan taken from Molly's own playbook. I decide to disappear. If Molly can refuse to walk, then I can refuse to be present.

Before I get off the bus, I will myself to become an empty container without any mass or volume, a cylinder with a tight-fitting lid, a vacuum. I will feel nothing. I will say nothing. I will no longer be me. I owe the world nothing. I will not go crazy, and I will not choose death, but I will not choose this life, either. When the van doors open, I step outside myself and watch the person I used to be walk into her new life from a distance.

Prisoner #919 doesn't talk. She walks slowly and refuses to make eye contact with anyone. She walks barely upright, her body a spoon curved over her sculpted belly. No one approaches her. When required, she points and gestures. If touched, her skin tightens around her skinny bones, refusing sensation. Her brain shrinks inside her skull, a dry prune unwilling to engage. She fears nothing, because she doesn't look around or think. If she is pushed or shoved in the showers, she does not feel it or react. If someone takes her belongings, she shrugs and turns away. She asks for nothing and offers nothing. She is wilfully invisible.

When Ruth calls the prison and asks to speak to Alice

Campbell, Prisoner #919 refuses to take her call. She believes she must cut herself off from everything and everyone she knew before. Continuing to talk with Ruth or Carol or Sandy, or even Molly, will only cause her pain. She is unwilling to engage with pain, hope, despair, anger, frustration, longing, desire, loneliness, boredom. Everything has to go. To deny herself everything will be her protection. To choose "life" in prison means she must feel nothing at all. In order to do that, she must encase her body and her mind in a thick layer of impenetrable matter. When the warden relays the message that Ruth wants to visit and bring Molly to see her, #919 shakes her head "no." She does not want them to see her in this place, and she must not allow herself to think about seeing them. She must not anticipate such a thing. This is what she believes. She can never be vulnerable again, not ever.

*Every night*
*She sleeps*
*an unformed mass of cells,*
*her face touching the blanket under her head*
*her knees tucked into her chest*
*her arms tucked under*
*in child's pose.*
*She breathes in imaginary fresh air,*
*as her brain waves weave patterns*
*of her daughter's hair*
*her eyes*
*her hands*
*her feet*
*soothing images that swirl softly around her,*
*warm her breasts*
*her legs*
*her arms*
*her pubis*
*her feet*

*her back.*
*She weaves a cocoon*
*of remembered touch*
*and smell,*
*then slowly breathes them in.*
*She feels safe*
*warm*
*secure*
*loved*
*cared for.*
*Of course, she is none of these things, yet she pretends to sleep.*

In this prison full of women, #919 refuses to be one of them. Day after day, week after week, month after month, for one long year, she chooses to be nothing but a hollow outline. She imagines herself as existing only in the space underneath her skin, refusing to peer out through her eyelashes at anything beyond. She denies anything on the other side. Day and night, she wills her mind to stay in the past. She remembers, imagines, feels, tastes, touches ghost images of her beloved daughter. She remembers Molly's baby arms hugging her, her lips on her face, her fingers in her hair and ears, her body slippery in the tub. She floats in the warm water blowing bubbles with her. The bubbles float between them on the water and in the air. She sees her daughter's laughing face reflected in the soap bubbles. Her raven hair, her red lips, her brown eyes sparkle and share the light with her mother's own blue ones, which have lost all their color and offer nothing to those who might look inside.

*At night*
*every night*
*she becomes a tight bud,*
*she turns her back*
*to the world.*

The guards warn the prison doctor that Prisoner #919's sanity is precarious. The doctor doesn't buy it. She says, "She's just out for attention. She's depressed. I've seen this before. She's getting used to the place. She'll get over it."

During her solitary time, the mind of #919 wanders through her former life, her life with Wilson. She remembers feeling trapped in her life as a wife and mother. She remembers feeling frightened by Molly bleeding, by Molly *not* bleeding, by Wilson leaving, by Wilson's betrayal, by her loneliness, by her cold in-laws, by Robert's betrayal, by the idiotic cops, by the judge and the courtroom, by her act of brutality, by Molly's abortion. Every day she had felt trapped by the world that closed in against her.

One day, out of nowhere, she has the utterly surprising thought that she has been wrong all along. She was never trapped. She was as free as a bird. She could have flown anywhere, any time. In that other life, there were no cages, no bars, no guards. She had let herself *believe* she was trapped. She had accepted woven chains of family duty, of marriage, of motherhood, of womanhood, wrapped around her, always winding tighter and tighter, until they had strangled her. She was mummified, although she was not dead. She had convinced herself she was a prisoner, trapped in a life she had surely chosen with good intentions. She pondered this revelation for days, turning it over and over in her mind.

Then, weeks after, from somewhere even deeper inside her, comes a more powerful revelation. She realizes she wasn't *trapped,* she was *stuck*, and being stuck is not the same as being trapped. Believing she could not move, or leave, or refuse, or change course, had mired her feet in muck so deep it was impossible to pull them out. Like so many women, she stayed in one place thinking she couldn't, and shouldn't, move. After a while, like in a long-ago fairytale, the make-believe chains had become actual chains, the mud actual mud. Like Molly's legs. Molly decided not to walk, and in time, it became a reality. She believed she didn't have a choice. Big mistake.

In this moment, the separated parts of my/her self begin to merge. The old Alice comes back to embrace the prisoner that I am today. I realize these revelations are available to me now, because I am in a true prison. I am physically trapped in this building by locks on the windows and doors and by the armed guards who patrol the halls, the cafeteria, our sleeping quarters, our bathrooms, our showers, our time outdoors. I cannot go anywhere away from this place, possibly for the remainder of my natural life. Recognizing this truth puts the opposite in relief. We cannot recognize freedom until we encounter true imprisonment. There were no locks on the doors, no armed guards, no absolute rules that could not be broken in my other life. I lived in a world of constructed rules and regulations, designed and enforced by those who thought they could control me. But I wasn't trapped, I realized, I was stuck.

For days, I float through the spaces of the prison, deep in thought, prising apart the nuances of my discovery, wondering what I can do with my new-found knowledge.

One morning, I wake before the others and sit on my bed in the thin dawn light, watching the room change from dark gray to misty blue to rosy pink to golden, an emerging watercolor on the pocked concrete wall that comes in soft whispers and disappears with a promise. I recognize my quiet moment as an epiphany.

If nothing else, I am alive. And even if I am physically imprisoned, my mind cannot be trapped without my permission. My body can be constrained, my liberty taken away, but my mind cannot be imprisoned. My mind is who I am. My mind is my sanctuary. I spend my day in a daze, moving my body slowly, obeying commands without thinking about them.

Hours later, I am startled when the call for "lights out" comes, and it is time to find my bunk and resume my sleeping position. This time I do not try to block out the night, rather I seek a way to acknowledge and embrace it. My mind takes over my body.

I have decided there *are* three doors. I could kill myself, so I do not have to be imprisoned, but that seems a waste. I could go mad, which doesn't sound like much fun at all. Or I could emerge to face my life in a different key, with a new voice, new curiosity, and new talents. What do I have to lose? Well, years of my own precious life, *my only life,* that's what I have to lose. Years and years of whatever I can imagine, create, enjoy, savor, nurture, and love. I ask myself this question: is there anything at all in this godforsaken place that I could love, and, if so, how could I find it? The challenge is immense, but for some reason, I know the first place to look is the library. Tomorrow, I will sign up for dusting and shelving the stacks of books in the library and disappear again. But this time, I will escape into a world that just might save me. I have to believe there is something here, in me, worth saving.

The next morning, I stand up a little taller and nod to one or two people in the hallway. My neighbors give me lots of room to do my thing, curious why this morning is different. It's as though I've just arrived.

At breakfast, rather than shuffling my way through the line and pointing, I move my tray with intention, call out the food I want, move confidently to find the cups, and fill mine with hot coffee. I join a table, nodding slightly to those nearby, and enjoy the bland food as best I can. In the afternoon, after a morning of mindless chores, I find the prison gym and begin loosening up my body, learning how to move my hips again, how to hold my hands comfortably at my sides, walk with ease. I explore the way my neck holds up my head and move it around and sideways to get out the kinks. I pay attention to the smell of sweat, freshly oiled machines, greasy mats on the floor. When we are allowed outside, I feel the air on my skin and breathe in as deeply as I can.

For months, I have followed close on the broken-down heels of women walking in front of me, obeying orders but never engaging. I stopped when they stopped, walked when they walked, moved when they moved. Today, I look ahead, not down, and take note of everything I see, storing it away as the data of my new life. I stride across the grass and notice how soft it feels beneath my thin sneakers. I pick up my feet and run on the track, aware of the rough surface so unlike the grass. I push my weak legs, asking them to move my body once around the loops and down the home stretch. At the end, my mouth is open wide, gasping for air, my body heaving from the staggering effort of one lap. When I speak, which is rare, I do not recognize my own voice. I wonder if it is the same as it's always been, or if it, too, is new. I am conscious of the sound of it in my head and decide on the spot to cultivate a voice that is deep and full, never pinched or apologetic, not high pitched or accommodating, something assertive, but not aggressive. I welcome the challenges of this new morning.

Throughout the day, I have a private conversation with my shoulders. When I can feel them scrunched around my ears, I talk them down, tell them to back off, roll them slowly and remind them to relax, to not let fear or anxiety invade my body. I work to control my breath, never fast and hurried, but slow and steady. I am reinventing myself as a stand-alone person, something I've never been. I am relieved to be free of Wilson and Robert, of Gail and Stan, of my house that is no longer my home, my town that is no longer my town. Although I desperately miss Molly, I remind myself that she is in a place where people are trying to help her heal both her body and her mind. Without the demands of my former life, I wonder who I could become now. And how does one grow in this place of locked doors, constant orders, and confining rules?

I pass the weeks doing what is expected of me, no more, no less. I obey the rules, mostly, and sign up for library work, so I can be around the books and magazines we are allowed to read. I take every opportunity to be outside, to play softball, to run the track, to rake leaves, or plant spring flowers. The librarian and I are not friends, but we tolerate each other in passing. We only talk when she explains how to take care of the books, how to check them out to the inmates, how to put them back correctly on the shelves. She doesn't seem to mind that I sometimes sit down on the floor, my head bent over books when the late afternoon light creeps into the room and illuminates the spines of the books on travel, life in the oceans, the desert, and novels that promise escape. I don't share my choices with her, and she doesn't ask me any questions. I am not certain she knows my name. The worksheets we fill out require only our prisoner number, the time, the date. In my head, I call my co-worker "Snarky Library Lady."

"Did you get those books that came in yesterday afternoon checked in and put back on the shelves?" she barks.

I nod my head and move toward the back of the stacks, eager to dust and shelve, pour over the photographs, disappear. I wonder what her made-up name for me could be. I can't even imagine.

Life in prison is a dull, daily routine. I eat, sleep, walk, exercise, shower, read, watch TV, play softball on Sundays. One week, I got really sick with the flu and had to spend a week in the infirmary. That was worse. I had no books, didn't exercise, couldn't play softball. The fact that I had no one to talk to wasn't unusual, but the time I spent isolated and alone wore on me in a different way. I was relieved when I got back to my bunk and my regular routine. I reminded myself to notice the warm bodies that marked the perimeters of my day, my night. At least in routine there is some solace, a smooth pattern that buffers the day. If there is a disruption on the cell block, it never includes me. I hover on the edges, seeking the dull rhythm away from danger. I am not secure enough to engage, even with the allure of violence, the satisfaction that would surely come with hard blows on the skin, the testing of a muscle, the reminder that we are flesh and blood bodies aching for connection, powerless to find release. I dare myself to take on some angry woman in the cafeteria or punch a guard who stands and watches our naked bodies in the shower. I hunger for the exhilaration, the rush of adrenaline, the release of the powerlessness I hold so tight. It never comes.

I rarely sleep in the top bunk of my designated corner of the room where all the women in my block sleep. Sleep is something other women get to enjoy. Even though I try to guide my mind toward warm and gentle things, I am never quite able to escape fully into deep sleep. If I doze off, I wake abruptly to find the pitchfork in my hands. I can feel the weathered wood of the handle, the grooves from years of use. In my mind, I bring it over my head over and over again, stabbing Robert, feeling the rusted fork tines catch on his skin as they puncture his body. Blood spurts, and I see my brother coil in pain and open his eyes in horror.

I have fallen off the top bunk several times during my nightmares of stooping over Robert's bloody body and lifting Molly's form from the bed of hay. In my dreams, I make the leap onto the stairs leading out of the hayloft. My bunkmate is always startled when I come flying off the top bunk and land with a thud on the hard floor with no cushion for my fall. She is not generous or kind about my nightmares. Angry, her raspy voice breaks the quiet of the night with an angry, *What the Fuck?* She turns back over and covers her head, not bothering to see if I am injured. Finally, she stops the nonsense by taking the top bunk, a relief for both of us.

Before lights out, I read the books I have checked out or simply taken from the library. I slowly leaf through the books with color illustrations, photographs from foreign countries, Paris, the American West, the Tetons, the mountains of Washington State. If I hadn't been so stuck, I think, I could have gone to visit all those places. It wasn't that far, really, or so difficult. I could have done it. Years ago, Molly and

I could have gone together. But I didn't know I could, or didn't believe I could, or I doubted myself, or I forgot to imagine or dream a different life. Regrets are cheap in here. I try to avoid them, but I am not always successful.

The conversations in my head make me wonder if I could have handled Robert's molestation and rape of Molly differently. What if I had just taken Molly home that day, without stabbing Robert, and driven away. I could have taken money from the bank and headed out, getting more money as I drove west. We could be free now, Molly and me, together on the road, driving away from everything and everyone.

This alternative scenario plays out in my head, until I remind myself that Molly was already pregnant. It was too late to rely on myself to deal with a situation I could not control. I had to have help. I remember the lonely nights and days on the road, and the joy in finding Ruth. The very best thing that has happened to us was finding Ruth. She is our guiding spirit. She was there, at the door, welcoming us into her home, gathered with her friends and colleagues to embrace us and help us navigate what was happening. We needed Ruth's "village," just as she had. Now, in prison, I am no longer part of the village of care for Molly. I can do nothing at all for her now. I am locked away, unavailable, disappeared. *What good am I to her now?* I know I will have to find an answer for this question, but I must figure out what good I am to myself, first.

I plow through the holidays and try not to think about what Molly is doing on Thanksgiving, or Christmas, or New Year's, still not talking to anyone outside the prison. I am not ready.

In January of the new year, I stand in the hallway near the warden's office and read a large red and black flyer tacked on the bulletin board. The announcement is for a writing course that will be offered in the spring by a university professor who has agreed to come teach at the prison. I had heard rumors of such courses a few times from other inmates, but none had been mentioned in my time here. No other details are mentioned about the course, just a short, library pencil attached to a string meant for the sign-up sheet. I'm surprised this is a totally voluntary invitation, which doesn't seem possible. "Sign up if you want to join the class," the flyer reads, the first I've seen like this.

The course will begin in two weeks. Not knowing a thing about what this might be like, I stand still in the hallway thinking seriously about signing up. Both "Full Name and Prison Number" are requested on the sign-up sheet, which makes me even more curious. In here, nobody wants to know our names, only our numbers. I stare at the flyer, knowing I should keep moving down the hallway to wherever I'm supposed to be, but I cannot seem to move. It's almost like I am a real person reading something posted at the post office or at the public library in my former life. This is not an ordinary sign-up sheet. It's an open invitation. I am intrigued, but I decide my name will not be the first on that sheet. Instead, I slide on down the hall, thinking I might burst with something that feels a little like excitement.

I turn right into the cafeteria and try to imagine which of the women there might sign up for the course. I hesitate at the door and glance around the room at the women who live and eat in my block. I have learned almost no one's first name during my year here, so mainly I've come to know the other women by their number, sometimes their last name, their faces, their hair, their body, sometimes their smell. I know where some of them sleep, and I have encountered others at the softball games or running the track when I go outside, and of course I see them in the cafeteria three times a day. Knowing not to look too long or too hard, I let my eyes roam the women in line to receive food on their trays, noting which ones get iced tea or a piece of fruit, then I look around at the tables nearest to the one I always choose. I know nothing about the women at "my" table and never feel I can talk to any of them. Some of them look rough to me, angry, distant, protected by thick skin, and I wonder if that's what I look like to them. Others are harder to read, shy, withdrawn.

My glance settles for a moment on a younger woman standing near the end of the last table, a woman so thin she moves like a reed in the wind, her hair long and unbraided, her eyes vacant as she sits down. She takes tiny bites of the food on her tray. Her thin lips form a grimace like the food insults her. It probably does. *Was she once a good cook? Was she a gardener who only ate fresh vegetables and killed her own chickens? I wonder how this girl can sustain her body on so little food, and I imagine her slowly disappearing from the cafeteria altogether.* My curiosity about her surprises me.

With an imperceptible motion, I allow my eyes to move across the table from Thin Girl to rest on a bulky woman with broad shoulders and a large mouth covered in bold, red lipstick. Unlike Thin Girl, Red Lipstick shovels food into her mouth so fast I half expect her to choke. Every day, she eats everything on her tray, stands at the table gulping down a full glass of water, strides over to the disposal area, places her tray on the conveyer belt, and leaves as though she has a train to catch. She does not look around the room before she is gone. I wonder what Red Lipstick's story is. She intrigues me for the first time.

My covert assessment of the other women in the cafeteria continues for days. I have given them silly names, because I have no other way to remember them. In my head, I chart where certain women prefer to eat, which table with which other inmates. None of the women hold loud conversations, unless there's an argument. Big Dyke sits at a table with Red Lipstick most days, and Thin Girl seems to gravitate toward Gray Lady and Warrior One, who seem to like sitting near the windows. Shy Daisy always sits alone, and I usually sit across from Peter Pan and Wendy, two women who often come to eat at the same time but never even look at each other. Today, I'm pretty sure they are mumbling words toward their trays that are meant for each other. Only Annie

Oakley and Warrior Two seem to know each other fairly well, judging from their body language and the fact that they always sit at the end of the last table in the room on the far side. I do not feel drawn to anyone in particular, and I feel, if I am being honest, that I have nothing in common with anyone here.

Occasionally, my eyes will meet those of another woman in passing, maybe when she disposes of her tray, or grabs an orange juice in the mornings before the breakfast rush, but we both avert our eyes quickly, alert to the possibilities of sending a misunderstood signal or causing some kind of trouble. I am frustrated when there is a fight in the cafeteria, mostly because I am never able to figure out what has just happened. I only see the aftermath, a jostle or an arm punch, someone tripping someone else who falls into the back, or the front, of another woman, and a kind of chain reaction raises a ruckus loud enough for a guard to intervene. I want to know what interaction between the women has broken through our bland existence. Who broke a communication rule, and what are those rules? Who insulted someone? I just want to know that the prisoners *do interact* beyond what I see. Surely, there is something I am missing. Each of the women, including me, has assumed a blanket face of nonengagement that serves as a kind of protection.

Nothing in our world invites us to let our masks down and get to know one another, so, of course, we don't initiate social behavior bolder than a nod. I know I certainly haven't been privy to any situation where a more comfortable interaction might occur, or, God forbid, one in which we might become friends, or even enemies. Since I do not know how long any of the other women have been here, or how long their sentences are, I always assume I am the newcomer, the outsider. I convince myself it is just me who is out of the loop, out of step, not in the know about how things work in the prison. My first months in hibernation were absolutely necessary for me to survive, but I also know it put me behind in terms of my social skills and prison knowledge. Or did it? Does anybody else know this stuff?

When exactly do prisoners learn about the make-up of our community? I recall no orientation when I arrived, no opportunities to chat with other prisoners in a safe space, no information shared about who my companions are now, what they have done, who they were in their "other" life. I was thrown into this place with no compass, no tools for navigation. The rules are barked at us as negatives, and none of the rules provide an opportunity to learn anything else. For our crimes, we have been demoted to kindergarten. Signs throughout the prison bark the orders we hear in the hall all day:

**WALK IN A STRAIGHT LINE**

**DON'T TALK**

**KEEP YOUR HANDS TO YOURSELF**

**DO NOT MAKE EYE CONTACT**

**DON'T TALK**

**DO NOT CLUSTER IN GROUPS**

**KEEP WALKING**

***DO NOT GO NEAR THE FENCES***

***DO NOT CLUSTER***

***DO NOT TALK***

***DO NOT TALK***

***DO NOT TALK***

The guards only yell out last names in reprimand or prison numbers when that is easier and meant for specific women. Most often, we hear insulting references to those who test the guards' patience.

"Hey, Asshole, look lively, this ain't a funeral."

"Pick 'em up, Lazy Bitch, and get the fuck out in the yard."

"Hey, 919, pick up your smelly feet, we ain't got all day."

"Hey, Cunt, finish up and clean your tray, move it!"

The hallway is empty, when I find myself standing in front of the bulletin board for the fourth time in two weeks. This time, I actually take the yellow pencil hanging from a piece of red yarn and add my first name, last name, and my prisoner number to the list of women who want to participate in the literature and writing course. I recognize none of the names already on the list, but I am relieved to see them there, scribbled in pencil. The first meeting will be Thursday night just after dinner. I note the room number and walk away, not at all certain what this class might do for me, or for anybody else, for that matter. Just the anticipation of something new makes me want to skip down the hall. I don't.

Thursday evening, after a short stint scraping stuck food off trays in the cafeteria, I venture down the hallway to the room that has been designated for the first session of the course. The door is propped open. Other inmates are also filing into the room, after taking care of their chores and visiting the toilet. The chairs in the room are already set up in a circle, not actually touching, but in an arrangement that feels completely different from other informational meetings or the TV room, where all the chairs are always facing in one direction, eyes straight ahead, discouraging conversation.

I stand for a moment in the doorway, my eyes resting briefly on each of the women already seated. I recognize Snarky Librarian, reminding myself this is not a kind way to refer to my co-worker, but so far that's all I know about her. I have met her only on the occasions when I have managed to snag library duty. I am surprised to see Thin Girl from the cafeteria, and Red Lipstick, who scarfs down her food, then I register the older Peter Pan and her companion Wendy, who has put her thinning hair into braids with little pink plastic butterflies attached. I am moved by the small gesture toward vanity by a woman who must be nearly eighty, in prison no less. I briefly dare to look at her face, which is deeply wrinkled and darkened by some long-ago sun. For some reason, she looks directly at me standing there in the door frame, so I duck my head and aim for an empty chair on the other side of the room.

As I glance at Shy Daisy, who is also quite old, I realize for perhaps the first time that most of the women in the room are not young women. How many years have they been in here, I wonder. Twenty years? Thirty? Forty? Fifty? I agonize as the possible years of sentences march through my mind. Thin Girl seems to be one of the youngest, but I can see now she is not actually young. Stealing a glance to look more closely, I guess her age as closer to 60, tough to know, given every woman's identical drab uniform and worn face. That's why the one woman's butterflies and the other woman's red lipstick make me want to smile, or cry. Of course, I don't do either, but I already feel more comfortable in this room full of women. Why, I couldn't say.

I have the fleeting thought that I might even get to know some of these women, but then I remind myself that I have nothing in common with any of them. Feeling out of place, I recognize the nervousness that creeps up my neck. Yet, the room, the circle of chairs, the bodies of the other women, the lack of guards, works some kind of magic. As I sit quietly in my chair within that circle, I feel the tightness in my chest release just enough for me to take one deep breath, something I welcome like a long-forgotten friend.

Everything is different already, but I don't have the nerve to look around the room, even when I become aware of movement in the corner behind me. I cannot see the person who is shuffling around me, but I assume it must be the teacher.

Gradually, I can see her body as it turns toward the circle of chairs. A glance tells me she is dressed in an ordinary blue shirt and black pants, a worn, gray sweater, and comfortable boots. She is moving toward the door to quietly welcome the last women who enter the room. When no one else arrives, I hear her shut the door into the hallway. She does not lock it, but the very fact that she closes it firmly, in a way that implies our time in this room does not belong to the guards waiting outside, or to anyone else who is not here in this room, makes me feel almost giddy.

Once the door is closed, the stranger enters the circle and finds a chair. My heart melts as this lovely woman from another world smiles at everyone and welcomes us to her class. I feel ridiculously happy for the first time since I don't know when, but I try not to smile. I never know when smiles are appropriate in here. I try to feel if the energy in the room is friendly or not, wondering if everyone who came has a similar reason for being here. Then I think, why did I come? I couldn't say. It worries me that I have nothing in common with the other inmates, but not knowing what is about to happen gives me hope for at least *something different* to happen. Like obedient children, we sit quietly in our chairs, a few shuffle their feet, or wiggle in their chairs, rearrange their legs, someone coughs. *Whatever will they have to say to one another?* I wonder. Then I have a sobering thought that surprises me. *What if they and I are not that different?* Where did that come from? A different question arrives. *What will we have to say to one another?*

"Hello, hello, welcome," the woman who has come to sit with us keeps repeating, as she looks around the room. Most of the chairs are filled, and I can feel a little hum of anticipation that I have not experienced before—not anger, not tension, not fear, not dread, not boredom, but something else. When she speaks, we are all relieved, knowing we can turn our gaze to her with permission, instead of looking at each other, which is usually trouble, or staring at the floor, which is what we often do. The teacher is here to be looked at and listened to. *What a relief!* Everyone seems to relax a fraction when she sits in the circle with us. Not one of us, but also not a guard or the warden.

I dare to raise my eyes and gaze on the face of the stranger with big smiles for everyone. She is a pleasant-looking brown woman with curly hair, gray at the roots when she bends her head, not young, not old. She maybe has a bit of powder on her cheeks and some light lip gloss. Other than that, she wears no makeup and has large red glasses that highlight her brown eyes and accentuate her fairly large nose. She is dressed neatly in black jeans, a white button-down shirt, and a soft brown cardigan. She keeps a bottle of water near her chair and drinks from it, occasionally.

I hadn't realized I was thirsty, until I saw that water slide down her smooth throat, so when she reaches into a small red and white cooler and produces enough bottles of water to go around the room, her gesture surprises all of us. No one, but no one, has offered us a cold bottle of water since we arrived here. We try to hide our pleasure as we each pull off a bottle from the plastic holder.

I watch our visitor and think how comfortable she seems in a room full of prisoners. She smiles, knowing we are checking her out. To be fair, she must be checking us out as well. I have no idea what to expect next.

"Welcome everyone! I am Sheliah Williams, spelled with an "h" at the end, don't ask me why my mama thought that was a good idea. I'm a professor in the English Department at the University in Columbia, about an hour and a half south of here." Her voice is clear and unhurried. We listen respectfully as she tells us a few things about herself, and why she is interested in doing classes like this in the women's prison. She tells us she has done similar work at other prisons and has learned a great deal about women and their lives by doing this. She also believes deeply, she tells us, that the classes are useful for the women who participate in them. She does not elaborate on this point, and I wonder what might benefit the women in this room, including me, but I'm willing to find out.

Sheliah tells us more about herself, where she was born, where she grew up, a bit about her family, her siblings, that she has been married to the same man for thirty years, a good man, she notes, "for the record," and has two grown daughters and one granddaughter—and one on the way. She says she went to college in Mississippi but has been teaching at MU for over twenty years and considers Columbia her home. She tells us she is very pleased to live so close to the prison, so she can come regularly. It is one of her favorite places to teach. I can't imagine why.

"Does anyone have any questions for me?" Sheliah looks around the room, her eyebrows lifted, inviting anyone to ask her anything they want to know. No one admits to a question.

"Before we start, I do want to tell you that Warden Crowder wrote a grant to make this course possible. As you know, there aren't many opportunities for classes in prison, certainly not ones with an actual teacher from the university. So, we're kind of an experiment for the warden, and she's hoping this kind of thing can happen more often here at Chillicothe. I just thought you should know why I'm here, and I'm delighted the warden has taken the time and effort to make this happen. I sincerely hope you will find it useful and even fun to come here every week for the spring semester. And, I almost forgot, you'll get three hours of college credit for the completion of the course, which is extra nice.

"Okay. Let's go around the room, and you introduce yourselves to everyone else. And add a few things that you think might be of interest to this group. Let's start over here. Why don't you share your name, where you're from, and a bit about yourself."

She gestures to her left for the first woman to speak. There is no pressure to speak, she says, just a friendly invitation, something we have all forgotten how to do. The woman to her immediate left happens to be Snarky Librarian.

"Well, guess I'll go first." Snarky glances quickly around the circle and tells us her name. Seeing her here, I realize just how large a woman she is, not fat, just large. I had realized she was tall, but even sitting, she towers over most of us. She is a dark-skinned woman with a tight Afro, streaked with gray throughout. It would be difficult to guess her age, but I can see she is not young.

"I'm Dorothy Wilder. Guess you may have seen me if you ever come to the library. I like books, so I signed up to work there, also because I like the quiet, and it's easier than mopping floors."

I think we are all stunned to hear another inmate's voice talking about herself in this way. Some of the women chuckle at her comment, agreeing library work would be easier than some other jobs, like mopping floors. She pauses, not quite sure what else to say. But then, she speaks again.

"I grew up in Maine with a single mother, six siblings, you know the drill. We didn't have much, but our mom really tried. The problem was all the boyfriends she kept bringing home. That didn't work out so well, so I left home at fourteen and got hitched to a guy that was just passing through. We were on the road, him stealing stuff and getting high and drunk, while I got pregnant and had a couple of kids. I shot the son-of-a-bitch six years ago, and I reckon I'll die in here. He had it coming, I will say that for sure. Not so sure that's what I was trying to do, kill him, but it sure did the trick. I got 30 years with 'no chance.' You can call me Dot."

I notice that by the end of her speech, all of us are actually looking at her. It's like some tiny thread has been released into the air, lifting our faces like balloons toward Dot, an opening not available in our normal interactions.

Sheliah thanks Dot and nods toward the next woman in the circle. As each one woman speaks, I try to remember at least first names as I listen to their brief stories. I doubt I will retain all of them, but I try to link their names with their faces, or their bodies, or how they dress, anything to make the name stick in my mind and take the place of the pretend names I've already given them. Greta, a very pale white woman, wears braids all over her head. Pat, who acts like a dyke, but might not be, it's hard to tell, wears red lipstick. Frances is a black woman with a lisp. Jessica, a shy Hispanic woman, actually smiles for a second. Betty, who is dumpy and looks like a nun I once knew, has tight curls on her head that must have been red at one time. Sophie, who acts like a scared rabbit, is Asian and squeaks out only a few sentences, mostly with her eyes closed. Stef, who wears a lot of eye makeup, has dyed her hair raven black and sneezes several times while she talks. I wonder if she has a nervous tic. Kelly, who has a frilly blouse under her standard-issue uniform shirt and a pink bow on her ponytail, could have been a cheerleader at one time. In turn, we each add our abbreviated story to the mix.

I am paying so much attention to the other women's names and trying to remember who is who, I almost miss the fact that every single woman in the room, in this circle, has killed someone. I have to repeat that to myself. *Every single woman in this circle is a murderer or an almost murderer, including me. What the hell?* And dear Sheliah hasn't batted an eye. She nods and thanks each woman in turn for speaking, for sharing her name and information with the group, without once noting the elephant in the room. *You are all killers.*

Ashamed of my thought, I amend it. *We are all killers (or tried to be).* I had not expected this at all. Women in prison, going about our daily lives, our routines, do not sit around and share information about ourselves. We rarely talk about what we did or the sentence we got. I've barely heard anyone say how long she'd been in prison or when she hoped to get out. Yet here in this room, sitting in this circle, with the door shut and a woman asking us to talk about ourselves, we are all doing just that. When my turn comes, I do the same.

"Um, I'm Alice, Alice Campbell. I was born and raised in Missouri, down in the Bootheel, which is a hard place to live, as some of you might know, was married, maybe I still am, not sure, have one daughter, and I tried to kill my brother because he hurt my daughter, Molly. Almost succeeded. Got 30 years with 'no chance.'" I decide not to make it more complicated by adding any details at this point. I nod at the next woman to speak.

After all of us have spoken, given our names willingly, and shared our crimes with the group, Sheliah looks at each of us, one after the other, and nods her head.

"So, how many of you knew this much about each other before tonight?" She waits to see a show of hands, raising her own to suggest we raise ours, if we knew any of what we have just learned about each other. Not one woman raises her hand. None of us knew even this much about each other. Yet, we live together, eat together, work together, play softball together, sleep together, shower together, wash our clothes together. But before this session, we knew not one vital thing about each other, not even our full names.

Sheliah continues to talk, smiling at us broadly.

"I find this to be true almost everywhere I go to teach classes in prisons, or in women's shelters. We guard ourselves very carefully, even when we live in close quarters, don't we? Now, I have a confession to make. I knew something about all of you before you even knew it about each other. I'm guessing that some of you do not realize that parts of the prison are segregated. Not by race or nationality or sexuality, but by crime. I already knew that all of you have been assigned this particular block because of the crime for which you were convicted. That is, all of you were convicted of murder, or attempted murder."

So, she did know! Sheliah laughs freely at our confused faces.

"Not fair, right? But it's the truth, and tonight's little session illustrates this is the case. The reason I also use this as a way to segregate the classes is that I want you all to know from the beginning that you all share some very basic facts and experiences with each other. However, even with this very brief introduction, we really don't know much of anything else about each other, do we? I hope to change that in the next few weeks." My heart does a little flip.

"My point tonight is that each of you has a narrative, or a story, that you tell yourself—about yourself—one you also use to tell others about you. We all do that. Some of our narratives are accurate, some are not. But the important thing is that this first narrative you tell about yourself is very, very important to you. It's like a handy-dandy condensed version of a very complicated and interesting person. But it's only the tip of the iceberg, right?

"So, let's think about what your narrative was tonight. Of course, I gave you some directions, and I modeled my own story for you, but this is how you summarized your entire life story to share just now: You have a first name and last name, and sometimes the name you want others to use. You were born and grew up somewhere. You had parents, were married, or not, had kids, or not. You tried to kill someone, or you did kill someone. You got a severe sentence. Thirty years seems to be a favorite and in Missouri, you all know, 30 years 'with no chance' *means* thirty years with no chance of parole. You also know 'Life, with no chance' is life with no chance of parole. Now, you are in prison, serving your time. Some of you added a few details, but mostly, that's the standard, condensed version of who you are. It has been my experience that women who kill are different from a lot of other women, both in prison and out of prison. Usually, women only kill once, or try to, and in most cases they have a damn good reason for their actions. Would I be right?"

We all nod our heads in agreement.

"If women are bank robbers or thieves of other kinds, they generally are serial thieves, and they steal a wide variety of things. The same might be true of those who commit fraud or cheat on their income taxes or cheat in other ways, but women who kill are unique. In these classes we are going to hold over several weeks, I'm hoping we can discover together what makes you unique, but also what makes you similar to the other women on this prison block. I believe exploring these questions will create an environment where we can all learn about ourselves and each other, enriching our lives and creating a new space for living, for creating, for sharing, and for growth. We will do this by writing our stories and talking about them. How does that sound? Even in a prison with locked doors, I believe this kind of creativity can happen."

I want to stand up and yell *Hallelujah!* This is exactly what I need and want. A way to go forward, a different path, a new journey, and a guide. Of course, I sit quietly and do not yell anything. I glance around the circle and see that several of the faces that were so serious, or angry, or sad at the beginning of the class have softened, imperceptibly perhaps, but I know it's true. I know this, because I am feeling it, too.

Sheliah looks around the room and asks if anyone can name every other woman in the circle? She says she does this in her classes as a kind of ice breaker.

"Often, there are one or two people in the group who have almost perfect recall, others have almost none. It doesn't really matter, but it might be fun to try."

"Anyone?"

I am shocked to see Snarky Librarian, oops, Dot, volunteer to give it a try. The exercise is brilliant, because in order to name the other women, Dot has to look at them, each one in turn, sometimes for more than a split second. Remarkably, Dot has a near photographic memory and successfully names every person in the circle, except for Shy Daisy, whose name is actually Rose. When she is done, the other women laugh softly and clap for her success. She tucks her chin and waves her hands about like she doesn't want this kind of attention, but I can see she is pleased with herself and appreciates our quiet applause.

Sheliah smiles at Dot and thanks her. She invites other women to also try to name everyone in the circle. A few can do it. I don't have the nerve to try, but with each round of naming, I learn more names and try to attach them to the faces in the circle. Again, brilliant. By the end of the exercise, most of us are laughing. With the laughter, I feel the air in the room shift. My body feels warm and included for the first time since I arrived.

"This is very interesting," Sheliah notes. "A few minutes ago, we all knew only a few sentences about Dot after we heard her narrative. Now, we know something else about her, something that is not at all related to where she comes from or what crime she has committed. We now know that Dot has a really good mind that is sharp enough to remember about thirteen names of women she has just met tonight. My point is this. All of you are more than the narrative you just shared. You are more than where you were born and raised, and what you did to wind up here.

"Your narrative, Dot, has already expanded. We are not defined by those first things we say in our narrative. We are much, much more, and it's important to remember that, because we are all complicated human beings, and I know that gets erased in a place like this. It is my conviction that learning more about each other, and about ourselves, can only enhance our lives, no matter where we live them. And please notice that by saying, 'we,' I am including myself. I am not a prisoner, but if I participate in these sessions, my life will be changed as well. I am part of this circle.

"Thank you for participating. I am well aware how little you are free to talk to each other or learn about each other in here. So, I thank you for signing up, for coming, and for speaking. I recognize all of this took courage on your part. We need to finish for the evening soon, but I want you all to come back next week on Thursday evening, same time, same place, and we will continue to explore our stories together. I am your guide. Because I've been working with this idea for some time, I have learned a lot about how to proceed and what might work best for the group. I only ask that you come, participate, and trust me. Now, before you go, I have one more thing. A little gift."

Sheliah reaches under her chair and pulls out a large stack of new notebooks, all in different bold colors, and a handful of felt tip pens. She makes a joke about the pens, saying the warden would only approve the felt tip ones, because any other pens would have a sharp point, a danger to themselves and others. She couldn't give us spiral notebooks, either, because the wires would be dangerous. She makes a silly grimace, and we all chuckle. How absurd to believe that because we killed our spouse, our partner, our brother, we might try to stab another inmate, or a guard, with a pen or a wire. The irony is not lost on us.

She hands out the notebooks and the pens, asking us to pass them around until everyone has one. I am ridiculously pleased to receive this little gift and flip through the empty pages with my thumb. We all take a minute to put our names and numbers on the front cover of our notebook, then attach the pen to the cover, so we won't lose it.

"One last thing," Sheliah says. "I have an assignment for you."

We groan like we are in sixth grade again, and Sheliah laughs at us.

"Ah, come on. It's not that bad. Maybe you'll even enjoy this. Over the next week, I want you to write a few paragraphs about yourself. In this class, I want you to write your own narrative. You told us all what you did that landed you in prison, but I'd like for you to think about the fact that you are much more than that narrative that has come to define you. You are much more than that narrative. I want you to think about what that other narrative might be.

"If it's easiest to start at the beginning, then just write your earliest memories from when you were a child. Try to describe where you lived and maybe something about your parents or siblings. Just try. As you write, you will probably begin to remember more, which is a good thing. Just write whatever you can and don't worry about spelling or punctuation or anything at all. Just write."

Sheliah stands up and moves her chair away from the circle and stacks it against the far wall, suggesting we do the same with ours. We follow her lead and finish quickly. I move slowly, hoping for some reason to be the last to leave the room. I stand awkwardly as the other women leave, thinking Sheliah needs to know that I am actually different from most of the other prisoners. I say nothing, and Sheliah just smiles and thanks me for coming. "I hope you like the class, Alice. So glad you came. See you next week." I peek back to see her gathering her stuff and grabbing her coat. I have to stifle the smile that threatens to cover my face. The guards are impatient and urge me down the hallway saying it's getting late. I hardly notice.

That week in the TV room, in the dorm, sometimes sitting on a bench or a stump outside, I notice some of the women from class writing in their notebooks. I try to remember their names when I see them in the hallway or in the cafeteria, rather than the ones I have made up. Once in a while, our eyes meet, and this week we might hold the gaze just a tiny bit longer, now having a reason to connect. Maybe it's only a blink of the eye or a nod of the head to acknowledge that we recognize the other person, have something in common. I walk around thinking, *I am part of a group. We are a group.* The feeling leaves me breathless.

I also reach for my new notebook whenever I can. At first, I write about why I believe I am different from the other women in the prison, but when I try to write it down, I wonder if that's really true. I scratch out the first few sentences and try again. I try to write about growing up in the Bootheel, being good friends with my brother, how my parents were not at all social, how I met Wilson, on and on. Sometimes I get frustrated and cross out the pages and start over. My words seem empty. I try to be more honest, but it's hard.

On Thursday, a week later, the same group of women files

into the designated room. We each carry our notebooks and our felt tip pens. I notice everyone sits in the same seat as before, already feeling safer in that particular plastic chair. After we've settled, Sheliah asks if anyone would like to volunteer to read what she has written over the week. We all sit quietly, staring at the floor. No one has the guts to read what she's written. Sheliah doesn't seem to be concerned, she just waits with a small smile on her face.

After a long few minutes, Dot surprises us by saying, "Well, what the hell. I'll read some of what I wrote. Just a warning, it ain't pretty."

She pauses, looking at her notebook.

"Me, I was number one, the oldest. That sure didn't make me special. It meant I got to take care of all the babies that were still being born, one after another. It also meant I spent a lot of my time dodging the attentions of Mama's boyfriends. There were several of them over the years. One would come, and it seemed like he might stick around, but not too long he'd be gone, just like the others. Mama was pretty, but her luck in men was shit. One after the other would promise to get a job and help out, but none of them ever did. I remember one guy, he was real nice, didn't chase me around the house or make nasty jokes about my face or my boobs. I wanted him to stay, but he left, too. I was sad when I woke up one day and he was just gone."

Dot stops reading.

"Well, I guess that's all I want to read today. Hope that's okay."

Sheliah has a broad smile on her face. She looks like Dot just brought her a big slice of chocolate cake. She looks around the room before she speaks.

"Thank you so much, Dot. That was great. Can you all see how this narrative about Dot helps us to understand her so much more than the narrative she told last week? Already we can get a glimpse of the story of Dot's life, long before she did whatever she did to bring her here to this prison.

"Would anyone like to make a comment about what Dot has written and read to us?"

It's quiet for a minute or two, but then we all seem to have something to say. Greta points out that Dot's childhood was pretty tough. Red Lipstick talks about how rough it must have been to be the oldest and have to take care of the others. Several of the other women comment on Dot's mother being pretty, but choosing "loser" guys. When no one else has anything to say, Sheliah picks up the threads of their comments, saying how we already see the things in Dot's life that would eventually make her the woman she is today.

Somebody asks "where is this going?"

Sheliah nods. "Good question. Even in prison, you might ask yourself, are there ways to figure out who you really are and what your story is? Right now, you might not believe it, but you have a story to tell and it's worth writing down and it's worth sharing. We can always learn from each other."

I share a blank face with everyone else in the circle. How can we figure out our story and who we are in prison? I'm clueless.

"One thing you might keep in mind as more of you share your stories is where and when another person's story sounds like your own story. I think maybe we all share more of our life stories than we might think.

"Who's next?"

It takes a little more prodding on Sheliah's part to get another woman to share her story. I am curious when the woman I thought of as a dumpy nun speaks clearly and frankly about how everyone in her family thought she was "slow," even mildly retarded, and how she has come to believe that about herself. Her story is painful to hear, although she is clear and articulate when she speaks. Shy Rabbit doesn't fit her anymore. I realize I put that name onto this small woman and made assumptions about her without a shred of evidence.

The meeting goes past the hour when it was supposed to end, but none of us seem to notice, or care. Several more of us share our stories, and I, for one, can see lots of similarities between their stories and mine. Basically, we've all been treated like shit and expected to put up with it. We get put down, shamed, and beat for no good reason. When we fight back, we get more of the same by the judges and the courts. Shocker. What else is new?

Even though it's late and Sheliah might have been nervous about her drive home in the dark, she does not say a word or seem anxious to leave. She doesn't seem bothered to know the guards are waiting, either. By the time we quit for the night, most of us have shared at least something about the story we believe about ourselves. We have talked about husbands and mothers and brothers and children and how they have shaped our narratives. By the end of the session, or so it seems to me, we all sit up a bit straighter in our chairs, or casually cross our legs, or more easily make eye contact, maybe find a way to lean in to hear each other speak. For my part, I would have sat there all night if that had been possible. I drink in everyone's words and long to hear more. Sheliah waits until the last woman has spoken and tells us she is so pleased and proud of us for being willing to share our stories.

Finally, we rise from our chairs and begin to push them back as we reach for our notebooks and check for our pens. The noise is welcome to me: a bit of shuffling, scraping of metal on the floor, someone pulling on a slick jacket, stacking the chairs. Then, I hear something else. A new noise, a muffled word here and there, a chuckle from Dot, a question from Sheliah that is actually answered by one of the women in the class. Then I hear another voice, like an unexpected echo. It is *almost* a conversation.

As we trail out the now open door into the hallway, the guards must be startled to see us quietly chatting, asking a question, nodding a goodbye, until we make our way down the hallway toward our cell block. I want to stay as long as I can. I linger while I take a deep breath that feels exactly like hope. Before I leave the room, I make my way over to Sheliah and touch her hand. It is a light, fleeing touch. No one saw it, I made certain of that. I thank her for the class and leave the room, excited that I will see her next week, and the week after that. I haven't voluntarily touched another human being in over a year. I just wanted to see what it felt like.

All week, in the cafeteria, in the dorms, outside, the stories I heard in group filter through my brain. I had listened to the other women's words as though my life depended on it, which I think in some ways might be true. If I'm going to agree to have a life in this place, these women and their stories must be the foundation. We are members of a weird family now, as crazy as that might seem, not a biological family, certainly not a chosen family, but surely a mis-matched collective of humans who live, and eat, and sleep together, brought here because the courts decided we were unfit to live in society.

The women locked up in this prison have been sentenced to occupy the same spaces through all the hours of each of our days, weeks, months, and years, possibly for the rest of our lives. I shake my head to release that devastating thought. It makes me a little crazy, yet today I feel different, almost embraced by something I can't describe. To add talking, and listening to each other, to know each other's stories, adds a dimension that prison does not normally provide, and the safe circle Sheliah has created allows that to happen. As I move through the regimented days, my body has a new currency, the air around me feels less oppressive. I can see the floating air waves of the other women in the hallway as we move, as though something connects us across the space. The hollowed-out shell I brought with me to Chillicothe has filled out with new substance, fragments of stories, and my renewed relationships with the women in my family.

I notice little things, like the women from my group talking to each other once in a while, or choosing to sit at the same table, or even sharing a slight smile, a nod of recognition. Nothing overt, but it is there, an invisible thread. Women who did not choose the class keep to themselves, but

I know they can see the changes as well. New conversations pop up where before no one would dare speak. One day, in the cafeteria line, I hear Dot in front of me say discretely to Greta, behind her, "Tell me more about Memphis, I've always wanted to go there." The next morning at breakfast, Daisy, behind me, tells me she had lived in Sikeston once and basically really hated it. "Did you hate it, too?" she asks. I tell her, "I absolutely hate the place." Saying that felt good, for so many reasons. We follow each other to the end of a long table and sit down.

The women in the class are rarely warm and fuzzy, more often we are blunt and opinionated. We don't mince words. Prison has leeched us of the social skills we were taught about being nice just to get along with others, especially as women. I find the honesty in the room refreshing, thoughtful, even generous. When it is time for me to share, I am nervous as I relate my story and the many negative beliefs I have about myself. Like the others, I'll have to learn to develop a thick skin and am grateful for the wry, deadpan sense of humor that cushions their blunt opinions. When I share that I can't do anything, ever, without fucking it up, Pat nails me for believing that.

"Sorry, but I call bullshit. Who the fuck told you that? Your husband? I'll bet it was your old man, right? That dickhead told you over and over you fucked everything up. You know that's bullshit, don't you, Alice? That's just bullshit, and you need to let that one go. Think about it, Alice, think about it."

What I'm thinking is that Pat is about to get all up in my face, but she doesn't. She just sits there shaking her head and looking around for confirmation that she's right. The other women are nodding in agreement, some also calling "bullshit!"

At that moment, someone giggles and someone else starts laughing. Soon, we are all laughing hysterically, including Sheliah.

It feels so good to laugh. I have never laughed enough.

What was there to laugh about? Who had time to laugh with all the shit going on? But here we are, laughing our butts off, *in prison*.

When the weather becomes too cold and icy for me to go outside or run on the track, I begin to write long letters to my daughter. Some of them I send, others I tuck away in the back of my notebook. Maybe I will give them to Molly at a future date, I'm not sure.

In one of our classes with Sheliah, we talk seriously about our relationships with our family members, especially our children, now that we are in prison. Our discussions help me imagine a time when I could let Molly visit me. Maybe I could learn how to talk with her again. I haven't suggested this yet, but Molly has been answering some of my letters, which brings me an amazing flood of joy.

In class, Sheliah is quick to point out good writing, a catchy phrase someone uses, a miracle of a gorgeous sentence, or how someone captures an emotion on paper. The upshot of all this is that we carry our notebooks around whenever we can and steal a few minutes here and there to develop a sentence, a paragraph, a page that we can be proud of. I'm pretty sure this is a new experience for all of us. For me, my time to write becomes the highlight of my days, and my nights.

Toward the end of spring, Sheliah warns us the classes will end soon. The disappointment in the room is thick. We have come to rely on these sessions for our sanity. The anticipation of the class every week gives each week a new purpose, a goal—just make it through the week, the reward is going to class. But it's more than this. The class helps us think about the life we are living right now, not our past life or whatever our future life might be, but the life we have today, even though we are living behind bars. In class, we try to explain to Sheliah how much we will miss the class and ask her if there's any way for it to continue. With her help and encouragement, we develop a report for the warden that outlines why we believe the classes with her have helped us and why they should continue. Sheliah promises to type it up and give it to the warden herself.

In the late spring, when the class is set to end, I notice the warden standing at the door of our classroom when I walk down the hall. I pause and walk more slowly toward the door of our classroom. Are we in trouble, I wonder. Did our report piss her off for some reason? Had Sheliah been wrong to encourage us to spend our time on this and argue for more classes? Was the warden going to tell us they had to stop?

Finally, I couldn't stay out in the hall any longer and had to step around the warden to get to my place in the circle. I search for Sheliah, hoping for a clue about what is about to happen, but she is busy gathering some papers and making sure everyone has a fresh bottle of water. She seems perfectly happy and calm, as usual, but the faces of the other women in the room are as confused as my own. We raise our eyebrows and shrug in a collective worry.

Warden Crowder does not sit down in one of the plastic chairs—we didn't think she would—rather, she stands next to Sheliah's chair and begins to clap her hands. We are even more confused.

"I wanted to come down and thank you all myself, because I am totally impressed with what you have managed to do in only a few short months. Of course, I must thank Sheliah for coming to the prison and leading these sessions with you, encouraging you to write your own stories, for teaching you how to do all that. I also want to thank each of you for accepting the invitation to sign up for the class and take a chance." She looks around the room at each of us in turn and actually smiles.

She looks at Sheliah and claps again. Slowly, we all start clapping for her, too, and Sheliah's skin takes on a pink hue, her eyes are watering. She is embarrassed but seems delighted with our acknowledgement of what she has done. She shakes her head and waves her hands for us to stop.

"Okay, enough! Thanks, everybody, but I've loved every minute of this class, truly. I've never had such a great group of women so willing to write their stories and talk about them. It has been a total joy. What you are writing now will help you on your own personal journeys, and when we share your stories with other women, you will also be helping them on theirs."

When I look around the circle, I see several faces smiling broadly, and I add my own, just because I can. I think Sheliah is a saint to come here and work with us every single week, no matter how bad the weather or what else she might have on her plate at work, or at home. We are still clapping for her. The warden promises to let us know if the grant comes through to continue the class.

Not long after, I wake up one cold, shivery morning and decide before breakfast that I desperately need to see Ruth and Molly. It doesn't make any sense to me, but the fact that I have other women in my life now—Dot and Greta, Sylvia and Theresa, Rose and Gertrude, only makes me hungry for closer relationships beyond the prison walls. I recognize how much I need Ruth and Molly, Sandy and Carol, in my life. Keeping them at a distance does me no good, nor them, I'm guessing. Molly needs to know her mother, even if I am a prisoner. Certainly, working with Sheliah and the other women in our class has helped me understand that I am more than just a prisoner. Even in here, I am a person, and I have a life. It's not an ideal life, by any means, but I am alive, and I am living "a life." How I shape that life is yet to be seen, but I lose everything if I squander the possibilities. Reaching out for my family and friends is the first step to expand those possibilities, and, surprisingly, I have the power to do that.

The next morning, during my first phone call with Ruth, I finally suggest that she bring Molly to visit me in the prison. She is delighted to hear this and agrees to bring her as soon as she can. She also says maybe it might also be a good idea for Joanna to bring Molly for a visit. She has diligently continued to work with Molly, guiding her through her rehab and discussing her life now that she's back in school and living with Ruth.

I am delighted to hear all these plans and realize just how

much richness their presence here would mean for me. The past year of working through and writing so much of my own story, as well as listening to the other women in our class, has convinced me there has to be a cautious path forward, one that includes anyone who wants to come visit me here and be part of my life now.

Ruth tells me that Molly has become more and more focused on the fact that I am in prison. She consistently asks to come to visit me and wonders if there are ways to appeal my sentence. This worries me, because I really do not see any way that I might ever get out of prison, and I hate for her to get her hopes up for something different. Ruth and I agree that we will discuss all this with Molly as she begins to regularly visit with me. I just want to work on building our relationship back to the closeness we once had.

Finally, Molly's visit is approved, and I am notified when Ruth has a date to bring her. As the day grows closer, I am nervous, happy, anxious, worried, and fearful, in turn. I feel like I'm going on a first date, getting married, expecting a child, giving birth, and eating a great meal all at once. When they arrive, we hug for as long as the guards will allow, which is not nearly long enough. Together, we all move to a table in the corner of the visiting room, and I try not to stare at my daughter. I am stunned to see her walk into the room on her own and realize how much she has grown. Her voice is different, and she is as tall as I am. Her clothes are stylish and comfortable, not flashy. I am embarrassed that she and Ruth have to see me in my prison uniform, but I try to just let it go.

Our first visit is filled with awkward moments. Molly seems shy about our surroundings, the hovering guards, her mother just one of several women who all look pretty much the same. I am glad I thought to wash my hair and pull it up into a ponytail. I carefully cleaned my nails, applied some lip balm, and put on a smile, just for them, but I know it's not enough to remind her of who I used to be. I ask questions about her school and her new friends, about her grandmother, even her father, but apparently she hasn't seen either of them. I do not dare ask about Robert. I know from Ruth that when he got out of the hospital, he packed up the family house, put everything in storage and disappeared from town. No one could say where he'd gone, and I didn't care, as long as he is out of our lives for good. Ruth assures me that he has never tried to find Molly, which gives me great relief.

Molly, Ruth and I sit in the far corner of the visiting room. After a bit, Ruth goes to find a bathroom, then sits at a different table with her phone and book to give Molly and me time alone. We are having trouble making conversation without her, so we are soon begging her to come back and sit with us. We both recognize how important Ruth is to our little family now. Together, they tell me some of the things they like to do, places they've gone for fun, the books they have both been reading, and the classes Molly likes best in school.

Several months later, Carol drives up to the prison to share some disturbing news with me. I try to take it in stride, but what she tells me is depressing. As my lawyer of record, she has been notified that the Assistant Attorney General in Jefferson City will be filing another warrant for my arrest. How would that work, if I was already in prison, I ask her? She isn't certain how that might actually happen, but she'll find out.

To me, it seemed like such a long time ago that I had taken Molly across state lines to get an abortion in Kansas, but apparently the law churns along at its own slow pace and the trigger laws are still quite new. The official letter informed Carol that some time had elapsed, because the state was only now developing both the language and the court procedures that would accompany an arrest for this crime. It seems the state offices are crowded with cases of assistance across state lines for abortions. Seems like such a waste of time for everyone, going after mothers, family members, and the "navigators," who continue to facilitate the much-needed journeys.

Carol tells me there also has been talk of arresting Molly, but she assures me this threat "has no legs." Even the most conservative rulings rarely seek prosecution for the person seeking abortion, only those who took them across state lines for the procedure. Carol would be notified, they told her, if and when a warrant for my arrest would be issued by the Assistant Attorney General's office. He was clear in the letter that the office "would pursue the law to the letter and would sentence Alice Campbell to the longest prison sentence allowed for her actions regarding her minor daughter's abortion." He would keep Carol informed.

We talk for as long as we are allowed to about the ramifications of this letter. In some ways, I am not fearful about this new development, which I have expected all along, but the fact that this prosecutor is definitely out to punish me brings new questions to my mind. Carol promises to find out everything she can in the next few weeks. I tuck away this new information and ask Carol not to share it with Ruth and Molly, at least not yet. She agrees, and I leave the visiting room sobered. I hadn't thought the charge would just disappear, but now that it is in the air, it bothers me.

* * *

After several months of Ruth and Molly visiting regularly, Molly tells me that she has written a letter to the judge who presided over my case, requesting that my case be reopened. In the process, the court informed her that Judge Garner had retired and that a new judge had taken the jurisdiction of his court. She learned the name of the new judge, a bit about her background and politics, and forwarded her revised request to the new judge's court.

Molly says she wrote the letter herself with Carol and Ruth giving her advice about how to make it stronger. Ruth adds that Molly's plan is to send her letter first to the judge, then the Attorney General of the state, then the Governor, all in the hopes that someone will reopen my case. If that doesn't work to get the attention we need, Carol has told them that she's located a human rights criminal attorney who is willing to take my case *pro bono* all the way to the state Supreme Court if necessary. Next time Molly comes to visit, she brings me a copy of her letter. She is so proud when she hands it to me across the table in the visiting room. Apparently, she typed it herself.

"Mom, this is the letter I sent to the new judge. I wanted you to have a copy of it, but I didn't want to ask for your permission to send it. In fact, I've already put it in the mail," she tells me, smiling as she puts the copy in my hands.

"Joanna and I have been talking a lot in our sessions together about how much I remember from the day in the barn loft and about how you have always tried to protect me from being interviewed by the police or a judge. But I'm ready now to talk publicly about what happened with Robert and what I saw in the barn that day. Joanna thinks it will really help me move on from all of this, if I am willing to state openly what happened and why. I think she is right, and I want to do it, because we think the truth might help you get you out of prison. I know this won't be fast and lots of things have to happen first, but we wanted you to know how hard we are all working to get your case opened again."

After they leave, I try not to think too much about what their joint efforts might mean for me, but anything that might let me tell the whole story of what Robert did, and why I should not be the one in prison would be a true gift. As long as Molly is safe from any accusation, and those looking at my files understand she was only an innocent child and had no idea what was happening to her, I'm okay with them trying. In fact, I'm more than okay. Even the hope of having a life outside these prison walls, to live with Ruth and Molly and our extended chosen family would be more than I could ever imagine. I reread Molly's letter until the paper is creased and worn thin. I treasure it for so many reasons, and I carry it in my pocket everywhere I go, all day every day. At night, I slip it under my pillow and pray for better dreams.

# Coda

I hear a crash in the hallway, the automatic lights flash on, and the door opens when someone pushes hard against it. I freeze and fold, melting over my feet. My thumb knows to shut off on my pen and slide the notebook under my mattress. There are rules, after all. I am still in prison, and the night guards can be harsh. I am locked in here, but I am not stuck. I am learning who I am, and Molly is finding herself, and learning who she can be in the world. I changed Molly's story, with the help of the women who stepped in at exactly the right time. I think it's fitting that Molly is trying to change my story, with the help of the same women who assisted me in changing hers.

In the meantime, I'm trying to write our story, here in the dark in the prison where I live. Our story is not unique—girls and young women, mothers and daughters all over the state, and in many other states and countries as well, are panicked, looking for answers, hoping for a clinic and a doctor to help them with unwanted pregnancies. Our stories are the invisible reality hidden behind all the rhetoric, the politics, the rules, the laws, the slogans, the beliefs, and the hatred. The world needs to hear our stories and consider our pain as worthy of consideration and compassion. As soon as the guards leave for the night, I'll slide into my corner again, pull out my little pen, and tell everyone why I'm in prison, and why they should care.

# Acknowledgments

The idea for this book emerged just after the US Supreme Court rescinded Roe vs. Wade and denied federal protection for legal abortion services to all women and girls throughout the United States in June 2022. Fears about losing our constitutional right to abortion had begun already during the pandemic and proliferated as rumors spread that the SC was poised to abolish all abortion care in the US. As soon as the ban went into effect, stories began to circulate about the difficulties women and girls were having trying to locate open reproductive centers willing to offer abortion services. Several states passed referendums that allowed for abortions in their state, yet the rules changed from day to day and state to state. One story in particular, about an Ohio mother taking her pregnant daughter across state lines for an abortion, caught the eye of the media and was told and retold over the next several months, joining hundreds of other stories that never made it to the national news. *Only Girls Bleed* is not based on any one of the stories that were circulating during this time, rather I wanted to write a novel that would illustrate how the changes in the law would affect ordinary women and girls, as soon as all the clinics closed down and the trigger laws went into effect.

During this time, I was in the process of moving from my long-time home in central Missouri to the woods of North

Carolina, where I had decided to write fiction full time. The first book I wanted to write would be about a young Missouri mother and her pregnant ten-year-old pregnant daughter, who cannot find any clinics or doctors who will help the girl with an abortion. My first beta readers were women friends I knew in Missouri who agreed to read the manuscript via email and give me feedback. That first version of *Only Girls Bleed* was truly a mess, but these wonderful friends persisted and helped me write a better second, and third, and fourth, draft over the next two years. In this regard, I want to thank Betty Acree, Kim Ryan, Margie Sable, Marilyn Coleman, Jean Ispa, Kathleen Cain, Jean Zwonitzer, and Colette Schaef. From a distance, and also through email, I want to thank my long-time colleague, Margaret Mills, who lives on an isolated island in the Pacific Northwest but took the time to read my first novel.

Moving to North Carolina during the pandemic proved to be an adventure in loneliness. People were huddled in their homes, afraid even to chat with other people along the trails while walking their dogs. It has taken more than five years to establish new friends here, but those I've made have been well worth the wait. Not only are we book lovers together, but several of these new friends read the manuscript for *Only Girls Bleed* and have helped me make it a better book, especially Sheliah Logan (who read it twice in different versions and always reminds me to laugh whenever possible), Lu DeLoach, and Gail Chesson.

I want to thank my daughter, Kate Bloem, for reading my book and taking the time to talk with me about why she believes this story is important. Certainly, having two daughters was one of the reasons I was so devastated by the Supreme Court decision. It meant a lot to me that Kate read the book and continues to be invested in its success.

As always, I thank Sandy Rikoon, my beloved spouse and partner in life, for his continued support for my work, no matter what I'm doing at the time. While I was writing this novel, he talked with me for hours about the book and the characters I was creating, as though they were our next-door neighbors, not just figments of my imagination. He's a great reader and editor and always catches the stuff I hate to spend time thinking about, like dates and times and why one thing has to follow after another. He's in it for the details, and I always benefit from his keen mind, his companionship, and his kindness.

Of course, having all these people in my corner encouraging me would not have gotten my book published. Like so many other debut fiction writers, I knew nothing about the "publishing industry," when I started writing *Only Girls Bleed*. I had published ten non-fiction, academic books, with University Presses, but I'd never written anything for commercial publishing. I had a lot to learn in a short amount of time.

Once I had a completed manuscript, I spent over a year sending queries to literary agents who were looking for women's literary fiction, books on women's rights, and strong women characters. Many agents did not bother to respond to my query, but those who did seemed to be saying the same thing, something along the lines of, "We really liked your submission, and you write beautifully, but we don't think our publishers would be interested in a book on this topic." After receiving way too many responses like this to ignore, I began to submit my manuscript directly to publishers that did not require an agent. Most of these were independent presses with a specific mission, and I came to appreciate working directly with the presses rather than having to pay a gatekeeper to champion my book for me.

At Legend Times Group, UK, my book found its home. I want to thank Lauren Woolf-Jones, Commissioning Editor, who read my initial submission, asked for the full manuscript, and offered me a contract in June 2025. I also want to thank Tom Chalmers, the Managing Director, Fiona Wilkinson, Hannah Cronin, Sophie Goodfellow, and Liza Paderes for their unflagging support for and generous attention to my book. I especially want to thank my editor Cari Rosen, who not only did a fabulous job clarifying what needed to be done in order to make my book better, but was also willing to engage with me when our opinions differed. Thanks, too, to Sarah Cooke and Christian Müller, whose keen eyes caught all the little mistakes before the book went to print. I think it says a great deal that this UK press is more than willing to take on such a controversial and political book, while the US publishers were not. The powerful cover for *Only Girls Bleed* attests to the strength of Legend and its mission to support important stories that need to be heard.